HURRICANE
LOVE

HURRICANE

LOVE

Miami, Florida Hurricane Season, 1985

EVELYN COLE

authorHOUSE®

AuthorHouse™
1663 Liberty Drive
Bloomington, IN 47403
www.authorhouse.com
Phone: 1-800-839-8640

Published by AuthorHouse   02/20/2012

ISBN: 978-1-4685-5393-2 (sc)
ISBN: 978-1-4685-5392-5 (e)

Library of Congress Control Number: 2012903007

"He who does not accept and respect those who want to reject life does not truly accept and respect life itself."

Thomas Szasz

CHAPTER ONE

Judge Daniel Lawrence was known as the hanging judge in Buffalo, New York throughout the seventies, but never sentenced anyone to death. He believed that any governing body, which he represented, had no right to take a life, but it could demand life imprisonment for someone who did.

His mother asked him several times to kill her when she was sick and tired of living. He had neither the courage, he told her, nor the heart, to do so. Now, 1985 in Florida, he faced the strangest trial of his judicial career. He was on trial for murder.

"Monroe, do you remember that old movie, *They Shoot Horses, Don't They?*" Dan asked. "In it Jane Fonda asks her dance partner to shoot her, and he did." He and Monroe, his young defense attorney, leaned on the veranda railing of Dan's ninth story condo, peering seaward for hints of Hurricane Irene.

"Sure, Dan, but you can't expect me to throw that at the jury in your case," Monroe said.

"No, of course not. It just came to mind that Bev repeated that movie title so many times in the last five years of her life that sometimes I wanted to shoot her, which brings me to a strangely comforting conclusion." He gazed at his bird-of-paradise plants on the veranda swaying in the wind. "I don't pretend to understand string theory—you know the one that unites quantum mechanics, particle physics and gravity—but I'm beginning to think that we are connected to everything in the Universe, including each other. It's all energy. Our perceptions lead us to believe in separateness. So, if the jury finds me guilty, I am still part of the energy flow, open to whatever follows."

"And if the jury finds you not guilty, will you accept that verdict?" Monroe turned to face him. Wind ruffled his red hair. His perfectly shaped head reminded Dan of his long dead son's teddy bear. That image, popping up now, surprised him.

"Certainly," Dan answered with a grin. "You know, Monroe, I'm not as worried as I should be. In fact, I'm discovering contentment. The judgment is no longer mine to make and Bev is where she's wanted to be for five years. There's real freedom being an ex-judge."

"Speaking of where Bev is," Monroe said, "my biggest problem for your defense is where you buried her."

"Yes, that is a bit hard to explain. I'll do some thinking about that in the next couple of weeks." A strong wind sent them inside. Dan shuttered and locked the doors to the veranda. "You'd better get out of here, Monroe. I think Irene might hit downtown Miami tonight."

Dan shook Monroe's hand and closed the front door before his affection for the young lawyer overflowed. Monroe had little trial experience, but his excellent mind understood the vagaries of human behavior as well as the power of ethics. And, he could articulate several levels of abstraction in the search for justice.

Dan laughed. *How pedantic can I get?*

He lifted his boom box off a shelf and turned it on, enjoying the irony of His Honor succumbing to the latest in teen-aged entertainment while reflecting on string theory. Yet, maybe physics instead of chemistry could explain his marriage to Bev, as well as the bonds he still had after all these years with Lucille and Ralph.

He switched to a local AM radio station to listen to hurricane warnings and learn when the wind would bend his birds-of-paradise in half. The 1939 hurricane that tore up New England filled his vision now. He barely heard current forecasters describing Hurricane Irene, for once again he was rowing that twenty-foot sailboat off Pemaquid, Maine. He felt the muscles in his arms as if he were seventeen again, innocent and in charge of Bev, Lucille, and Ralph. He had led them from tree-crashing winds on St. Georges Island back to the sailboat. Then the wind died so he had to row. He'd felt relief until he had trouble breathing. When he couldn't get enough air he'd realized that they were sitting ducks in the eye of a hurricane.

The phone rang jarring him like a blast of wind.

"Hello?" he asked. His voice lacked air.

"Dan, is it you? This is Lucille."

"Well, Lucille. I was just thinking about you. These winds down here today brought me right back to Pemaquid." He could almost smell the acrid scent of his fear and feel the cold waves thrashing him.

"I heard the forecast for Miami. Are you careful?"

"Sure. Say, are you familiar with string theory? Monroe, my lawyer, was here today. Just before you called, I was laughing at myself for my pompous statements to him about concepts that I don't really comprehend, and then turning on my boom box as if I were a kid."

He heard her familiar laugh.

"You would," she said. "And yes, I've heard of the theory and don't understand it either."

"Where are you?" he asked.

"New York. New exhibit of my work. When does your trial start?" Her voice carried a light shrill of worry. "I'm coming down for it."

"A new exhibit? That's great, Lucille. Don't worry about my trial. Stay there and enjoy your admirers."

"I'm coming. So's Ralph—without his awful wife. So, nice guy, when does it begin?"

"October 4th. You know it's not necessary for either of you to come. Have you talked to Ralph? Rosalie won't want him to leave Nassau this time of year."

"Dan, you're on trial for murder, dammit. For once Ralph won't accommodate Rosalie's social schedule and we'll both be there. We can't be anywhere else."

"Thanks, Lucille," Dan said, feeling heat spread throughout his body. "Okay, Tall and Lovely One—I'll be glad to see you."

He said goodbye and hung up. It's a funny thing about hurricanes, he thought. They bind you for life with the folks you're with at the time. A deeper connectivity, like that of Heisenberg's uncertainty principle that space can never truly be empty.

Fascinating, but beyond my ken. I'm in the middle of uncertainty, anyway.

Feeling hungry, Dan headed for the kitchen. He stopped in the dining room realizing that he hadn't entertained any guests since they'd moved to Florida. Now, in this new condo, he could have Ralph, Lucille and Monroe over for dinner. He pulled a bowl of pudding out of his refrigerator and smiled, picturing Lucille when she'd lopped a spoonful of whipped cream into that prized antique spittoon when he first met her, when he was seventeen and in charge of the Port Clyde Inn at Pemaquid for the wildest week of his life.

*   *   *

He had been both scared and proud to be in charge of the Inn the few days the owners would be away. By Wednesday of that week, the wind had picked up. He secured loose shutters, rolled boulders against the banging gates and doors of the outbuildings, and tied down all the awnings. Every hour he went into the dining room to listen to the weather forecast from a carved oak radio console that crackled out hurricane warnings.

Each time a guest opened the front door, the wind tore at the curtains in the lobby. He pried loose a brick from the walkway and set it on the opened guest register to hold the pages down just as a middle-aged couple with a tall, redheaded girl blew in. She was taller than Dan, near six feet, and skinny. He saw a flash of white teeth when she smiled that seemed to fit her handsome, angular face. Dan straightened his bow tie, raised himself slightly on his toes, and slicked back his hair. That was when he'd decided to grow a mustache.

The couple signed the register. Dan assumed they were the girl's parents by the practiced quality of the way they ignored her. Their name, Grimm, fit their demeanor. Both the short, round mother and tall, pot-bellied father wore gray gabardine suits and highly polished shoes. Their daughter wore a yellow cotton shift and grass-stained sneakers. She tripped on a throw rug. Dan liked her immediately, and despite her unfashionable height, thought she was beautiful. He scanned the register and found her name: Lucille. The mere sound of it was soothing. Lu-cille.

After dinner the wind subsided. While Dan built a fire in the cavernous fireplace in the dining room, he watched the Grimm family at dessert and decided that Lucille was not clumsy after all. In fact, as she ate and talked, she seemed quite graceful. Perhaps, he thought, her natural grace accentuated those brief moments of clumsiness. He worked his way closer to eavesdrop.

"If only you would try, Lucille," he heard Mrs. Grimm say. "You're actually very pretty, and if you would just dress better, you'd have so many beaus."

Dan had his back to them. He wished he could have seen Lucille's face when she said, "Will a long dress shorten my legs?"

"Now, Lucille," Dan heard Mr. Grimm say, "You have to work with what you've got." The man sipped his coffee then replaced the cup on its saucer with a loud clink. "I give you charge accounts in the best stores and you go around looking like an Irish waif."

"All children are waifs," Lucille said in a low voice. Dan imagined her smiling.

Dan turned sideways so he could see them.

"Now stop that. Damn it, Esther," he said, turning to his wife, "she's quoting Gus again. I knew that Gus would be a bad influence on her someday. I told you that when we first hired him. But you didn't agree because he looked so much like an old world butler. Scalawag, that's what he is."

"Leave it, Charles, please," begged Mrs. Grimm.

Dan moved to the opposite corner of the fireplace in time to see Lucille spoon the whipped cream off her pudding and flip it into the antique brass spittoon behind her—a perfect shot.

*   *   *

A burst of sound from a loudspeaker interrupted the scene. Dan pulled himself back to the present, opened his front door, and stood, stroking his mustache.

"Turn on—radios," the building supervisor broadcast through the building's intercom. "We may need to—." The voice cut off, but the man didn't sound frantic.

Dan returned to his easy chair and memories of young Lucille during that fateful hurricane that tied him to Bev for the rest of her short, miserable life. Only Ralph understood why he'd thrown Bev's body into the bay at Pemaquid. How could he explain that to a jury

CHAPTER TWO

In a West Miami townhouse, Joanna Archer, a trial reporter for the Miami courthouse, applied polish to her recently acquired acrylic fingernails. The winds of Hurricane Irene increased their intensity as she stroked glistening red onto each nail.

A flash of lightning lit up the room like a giant strobe. She held her breath and released it. Why should she be nervous? She'd lived with violent storms all her life.

"You know, Beaumont," she said," sometimes a hurricane can be a blessing." Rain machine-gunned the sliding glass door to her left. She leaned right, lifting her narrow shoulders. "A good old gale blows out all the dead stuff in town."

The rain ceased its ferocious barrage. She chanced a cautious look up at her husband from her position on a hemp mat in front of their TV.

Beaumont stood bare-chested in his cut-off jeans thumbing through bills at the Formica bar. A new blast of wind rattled the shutters. She saw him tense his muscles beneath the layer of hair that spread up from his chest over his thick shoulders. She knew he hated hurricanes—ever since he nearly gagged to death when Hurricane Dorothy blew him into an open cesspool back in '79. With each increasing decibel of sound, his muscles twitched. He thrust his chin toward the south wall as if daring the storm to come closer.

"What d'you mean, blow out dead stuff?" He swiveled to face her. "What're you talkin' 'bout, silly girl?"

"Nothing." Joanna lowered her face. "I was thinking about the wind your mother says has to be really ill to blow nobody good." She watched him through the filter of her hair and wished she could just leave him. Get a divorce, even.

"Well, I don't much care for hurricanes, but they're damn good for business. Sure do tear the roofs off nice and neat."

Another blast shook the sliding glass door. Joanna studied him. The cords on his neck stood out—lariat thick. She'd admired his six-foot build and hairy body when she was a bride at nineteen. His eyes, so deep a brown that they held no light, once thrilled her. Now, from beneath a blue cap advertising Winchester Rifles, those eyes staring out the window rarely looked at her. Stubble darkened his jaw.

He *does* look like a man who shoots snakes, she thought, remembering her Aunt Martha's whispered remark that hot muggy August day when she married Beaumont. Fourteen tense years ago. While some women were burning their bras, Joanna had willingly entered a private prison, thinking it was her escape. And here she was today, still a parrot in a bamboo cage, the same cage she'd lived in all her life.

"Shit!" Beaumont said to Joanna. "Did you use our Visa card for groceries?" He pulled a dog-eared cigarette out of his pocket. "You're supposed to use the cash I give you."

"No, I didn't use the card." Joanna spread her left hand across an opened Time Magazine and applied a second coat of polish to her false fingernails. She didn't like the pink the nail-lady had applied. Peeking, she watched Beaumont compress his lips, tightening them against his teeth like the snare on a drum.

She felt a grin tugging at her own lips and wondered if she actually could just leave him—walk out and disappear. And not fall for another guy just like her father. She shivered at that thought and botched the polish on her left thumbnail.

"Here's another article on Alzheimer's," she said. The opened page on the magazine drew her attention. "There's a picture here of a white haired man—a judge, no less—who murdered his wife because she had it so bad. Good looking guy, too. They called it an assisted suicide, a mercy killing. Hmmm. I don't remember ever working in his court."

"I don't remember charging anything at Krogers," Beaumont said.

"Her body was found in Maine, but he's going to trial in Miami. Strange." She glanced up at her Aunt Martha's oil painting of a lighthouse that she'd hung over their fake fireplace. "I'd like to go to Maine sometime—in the winter."

"Are you sure you didn't charge nineteen dollars and thirty-two cents?"

"I'm sure. This judge's trial will be interesting. He loved her so much he risked his own freedom to free her." Her voice trailed off. She tried to imagine a love so strong that self-sacrifice would be a given. To help a loved one die for his own sake boggled her mind. *Could I do that and still feel like a whole human being?* She returned to the magazine, to a sidebar of an interview with the judge. She started to read aloud and then realized that Beaumont wasn't the least bit interested. Instead, she read in a low voice to herself. "Judge Lawrence says, 'Justice can encompass several opposing outcomes and still be just." She memorized the quote as the wind shifted direction, shaking the kitchen windows.

"Jesus, stop babbling. I'm trying to concentrate."

Ah, he whispers sweet nothings. She tugged at her hair and continued reading, now silent. Wow, she thought, this is really something. *'Justice demands balance between contextual circumstance and abstract law, between independence and dependence. It calls for balance similar to that needed to cross the Grand Canyon on a tightrope.'* Man, I wonder which court—I might be scheduled to work his trial.

She skipped to other examples of Alzheimer sufferers. Glancing up, she said, "And here's a woman—a college professor who can't teach anymore and she's only fifty-two. Jeez, I wonder what it's like to have your brain cells corrode and die. It must be awful."

"What the fuck are you mouthing on about now?."

Outside the storm grew louder. An abrupt gust whipped the shutters, tearing a corner loose from its hinges. Startled, she quickly pressed her elbow on the TV remote to get a weather report. A bespectacled weatherman flickered on.

"Hurricane Irene hit Guantanamo this afternoon, veered west of the Bahamas, and is now heading toward Miami," the weatherman said. "Wind speeds are up to ninety-five miles an hour."

Joanna knew hurricanes. She didn't have to move yet. She inspected her nails as she listened to the news. She wanted Beaumont to see how well she treated this new extravagance, these false nails, these useless, meaningless symbols of—of what? Not sexual allure, certainly. An inch of freedom, maybe. A fingernail's worth of free choice to waste money on vanity, or anything else she wanted.

When she finished her right hand, she spread her fingers across her knee and let them droop toward the mat. They reminded her now of blood clots. They'd been lovely pink fuchsias just yesterday.

"Good, old Irene's coming right to us." Beaumont said as he flipped through his checkbook and then closed it with a slap. "She'll give me a load of roofs to fix." A commercial came on. He stretched, and then stepped forward to glance down at the magazine." You say a guy killed his wife just because she went senile?"

"Alzheimer's isn't the same as senile. It's much worse." Joanna began to repair the botched thumbnail, slowly pulling the brush along the cuticle and stopping it with flair at the tip of the nail. "It says he's a Superior Court judge from Rochester, New York. I guess he thought it was better for her to die quickly. And, she asked him to help her do it. That must've taken some courage."

"What makes you go on? Man, you sit around talking shit when you know nothing about nothing. The guy had no right to kill his wife. He oughtta be fried." Shutters began slamming against the brick wall of their townhouse, punctuating his remarks. The TV crackled from a surge of electricity.

"Turn that damn thing off," he said.

She glanced at him and then at the television. The newscaster announced that President Reagan would be on in five minutes to explain his trickle-down theory. She pushed the power off with her elbow, and then unplugged the set.

"You're right, Beaumont," she said, hoping to appease him. "I don't understand economics, physics, politics, or—or advertising. Not yet, anyway. I don't know much—except what I read or hear in court, but it does seem that someone with shrinking brain cells might long to die but can't figure out how to do it." She returned to the mat and blew on her nails. "It must be pure hell, too, for the people who live with them."

She winced at the sound of his cracking knuckles, a habit he'd developed lately. He said it was his way of thumbing his nose at her high and mighty courthouse manners. She remembered when his anger used to be quick flares that subsided into ashes of apologies and lopsided grins. Now he wore his anger daily like his familiar, cracked leather jacket.

"Hey, don't worry about me," he said, spitting out the words. "If you come down with that old Kraut's disease, I'll drag you to a nuthouse, not kill you like that judge did his wife." He barked a macho, two-note laugh.

She lowered her head.

He took off his cap and peered at her, rubbing the red welt the visor had left across his forehead.

"So, Jo. What's with the phony nails all of a sudden? You usually go on at the mouth for days before making such a big decision." He rubbed his round belly. "What is it, twenty-five bucks a shot? Hell, woman, if you'd scratch my back—bring up blood with those fancy red nails—I'd pay for them myself."

She used to scratch his back. With short nails. With passion. How handsome he was. How kind. How different from her father, so different she'd run straight into his arms expecting deliverance only to discover her father in younger skin.

Beaumont's voice sounded more like her father's now, too. Before she was old enough to know to hide her eyes, her father had come home. She watched him stagger into their mobile home in Tampa. When he noticed her, he slapped her face.

"Don't look at me like that," he said. "I can read your mind and I don't like what it's saying."

Later she realized he'd misread her fear as contempt. She began to understand then why people masked their eyes. She let her hair grow to function as a veil. She fingered the edge of it now against her lower lip.

The wind roared. Beaumont jumped when a branch whipped against the window. His eyes flashed back and forth.

She lifted her chin. Her hair lightly brushed her shoulders as it fell back. She gazed at him, seeing him now as a sheep in bully's clothing. Lifting her hand, she pointed at him, rotating her red-tipped forefinger slowly at first, then faster and faster, reliving her childhood passion for the lasso. She'd never roped anything but a fence post, but she knew if she had a rope on her arm now, she could ring his neck.

Beaumont dropped his pen on the counter.

She rested her hand across her thigh and tipped her head. Once again, her hair curtained her face.

"Honestly, Beaumont, I don't think it's really any business of yours whether or not I get my nails done. Silly extravagance, of course, but I like it. It makes me feel a little wicked. Free."

"Well fucking-A! If it's none of my business, then you're none of my business." He slammed his palm against his forehead then picked up his pen and made a slicing motion. "It looks like we got an attitude problem here. Those stupid claws don't belong in a courtroom anyway. People'll think you're trying to upstage the judge. Besides, how can you hit the keys on your recorder? Daggers like that'll screw up your transcript."

"No way. I'm careful. As a matter of fact, I like the looks of them flashing over the keys." The sound of heavy rain beating against the side of the house drowned out her voice. She raised it. "Listen to that. Maybe we shouldn't stay here tonight."

"Sure we should. Hey, what's the matter with you?" He flipped off the kitchen light and shoved his checkbook into his hip pocket. Then, at once, the wild sounds from the storm subsided. He stared at Joanna. "A guy at work told me about an article that said court reporters have a real high stress job—almost as bad as air traffic controllers. The job must be getting to you. I never should've let you take it in the first place." He peered at her. "You've been acting mighty weird for the last few months. You'd better quit that job before you come down with Alzheimer's. Shit, your brain cells must be shrinking right now just from hanging around with those tight-ass lawyers." He laughed.

"No way, Beaumont. No way." She tossed back her hair. Her job was the best thing that had ever happened to her, the courthouse the only reasonable, courteous world she knew.

Beau's thick eyebrows formed a capital V, what she'd recently heard a lawyer call a Mephistophelean frown.

"Remember when you worked for that escrow company?" he asked. "Remember how nervous you got? I told you to quit then, too." His voice carried a load of condescension. "And remember how happy you were when you did quit and stayed home, where anyone with any sense would be grateful to just loaf around?" He paced the floor. "Shit, y' hand someone a easy living and they slap it away."

Outside the streetlights flashed, and then went out, leaving the dull glow from the pole lamp. She stared at him in the semi-dark and felt his eyes on her.

"I'm sorry," she whispered, "but I've changed. I am changing." She exhaled. "I'm going to make my own decisions now." Courage, she thought. It's past time to tell him the truth.

Beaumont's bulk took shape in the dark. He stood motionless, breathing audibly.

"You're just like my dad," she blurted, shooting the words at him. "Bullying me—telling me what to think, what to wear, even what to eat." She closed her lips, ashamed of the childish whine in her voice. She spread her hands flat across the magazine and blew on her nails. Controlling her voice, she said, "The job's not getting to me, Beaumont. You are." Her stomach tightened.

"Is that so?" he asked. He stepped away from the counter and planted his feet like a bull ready to charge. "Is that fucking so?" Head bent, shoulders bunched, he moved toward her.

Familiar dread enveloped her like viscous oil. She stretched forward from the waist, hands extended beyond the mat onto the linoleum as if she were bowing to him. She figured he wouldn't really hurt her in this position—just threaten until he was satisfied with her humiliation. She waited.

"I guess you need an attitude adjustment," he drawled as the city's electricity went out, killing all remaining light. "Who's your Daddy?" Who takes care of you?" His voice rose perilously. "I reckon those bloody red nails that say 'Fuck You, Beaumont' just have to go. He stepped lightly on her left hand.

She flinched. *What will he do now?* Then, as if she'd left her body to float near the ceiling, idly watching the scene below, she noticed that the sole of his shoe touched her wedding ring. He didn't press hard—just enough to pin her.

Wind whipped the palm trees along the boulevard with a deafening roar, ripping off fronds, scattering trash all over Miami. It tore the shutters off their windows and tossed them like dice onto the street. It dried the polish on her nails just as Beaumont reached down and tore off, from her middle finger, a long, well-varnished, acrylic nail. It was so tightly glued to her real nail that it, too, came off, releasing a scent of blood. The pain, sudden, intense, sent a piercing fire up from her finger through her hand, arm and shoulder. The wind muffled her scream.

CHAPTER THREE

Beaumont drove off to survey roof damage and pass out his flyers in the stillness of the wind-dead morning after Irene blew out to sea. She left fast, as some hurricanes do, with not a whole lot of damage in her wake.

Joanna packed her favorite novels, her court recorder, clothes, spider plant, and the Christmas tree ornaments she'd made out of dried fruit and sequins. Her hand throbbed bur didn't stop her. She moved into her aunt's condo on Brickell Avenue without leaving a note or telling anyone. Aunt Martha had given her the key just last week so Joanna could check on the place for the next four months while her aunt traveled Europe. Now Joanna understood why she hadn't mentioned this fact to Beaumont.

The balcony of the ninth floor apartment overlooked a yacht-dotted bay that filled from the teal waters of the Keys. And, it was located near the Miami courthouse so Joanna could walk to work. She looked forward to daily strolls along the river as she floated through the spacious rooms. The very air smelled of freedom this high up. Blessed solitude. No one following her from room to room, shooting verbal pellets at her. No one harping about the books she reads or the fucked-up criminal justice system. No one playing Iron Butterfly tapes over and over. Blessed, peaceful silence.

Beau wouldn't find her here, she was sure. He hadn't seen Aunt Martha since their wedding fourteen years ago. Joanna decided not to tell her mother or anyone else about this hiding place. It's time, she thought, to find a whole new set of friends—even a new family.

Beau might come to the courthouse looking for her. That thought gave her the willies. He wouldn't dare pull her out of court. Or would he? He'd torn off her fingernail. What else would he do? Drag her home by the hair like a caveman? Beat her up on the courthouse steps? He didn't used to be physically cruel, just verbally oppressive. She wondered if spousal violence grew from tongue-lashings to rib-breaking and nail pulling, to beatings then murder—like a progressive disease.

The sun set, sending shards of its rosy light through the balcony railing and tall oval windows. She jumped when the phone rang. Should she answer it? She picked up the receiver after seven rings. It was her Aunt Martha. Joanna collapsed to the floor and exhaled her greeting in a gush of air.

"I just talked to your mother," Martha said, "and she told me you'd left Beaumont. I thought I might reach you here. Actually, I'm glad you left him."

"Is it okay with you if I stay here?" Joanna twisted a lock of her hair. *How could my mother know so soon?*

"Of course, Honey."

"Did you tell Mom you gave me the key to your apartment?" Joanna held her breath.

"No. Should I have?"

"Please don't. She'll tell Beau where I am. "Joanna raised herself to the kitchen sink and leaned against the counter. A slight breeze from the balcony cooled her.

"You're right. I won't tell her, but she needs to know you're okay. Call her from the courthouse."

"I will. Tomorrow."

"That sister of mine always was a wimp."

Joanna laughed after she hung up. A wimp. So am I. So *was* I but no more.

*   *   *

Joanna lived in peace for two weeks. She indulged in dreams of getting a degree in political science or sociology and then becoming a lawyer. Her finger looked corroded, but it had stopped hurting, except when she hit the keys of the court recorder too hard.

Then, on the heels of Irene, Hurricane Julio hit Miami, threatening to blow it off the map.

"Here we go again," she said, peering at the black sky from her aunt's balcony. Hot wind blew from the East carrying a distinct scent of the ocean. She couldn't believe that two hurricanes in a row followed the same path. The building began to sway as if shoved by a bullying god. She turned on her aunt's old thirteen-inch Zenith. The screen flickered on and showed scenes of Julio scattering yachts across Biscayne Bay. "Helter Skelter," she said, and thought of Beaumont. Then she grinned. *I'm on my own.* Dust eddies danced on the balcony. She danced two steps and twirled. *Truly on my own, and I'm staying right here. Go ahead, Julio, blow me away.*

She sensed that her bravado lacked heart as well as brains and checked window casings. She then stripped off her jeans and tank top and took the fastest shower of her life. In vain, she searched for clean clothes, cursing the fact she hadn't done her laundry. She gave up and donned her old brushed cotton nightgown. At least it was clean. Although it was barely past eight p.m., the lace-necked nightgown flecked with red rose petals seemed suitable for watching sheets of water move sideways across the kitchen window—perfect for a night spent deliciously alone in a hurricane.

*   *   *

In the apartment across the hall, Judge Daniel Briggs Lawrence calmly waited for Julio, pondering the strange weather patterns that would bring two hurricanes on the same path within a month.

He watched the rain speed laterally across his window, glad that he'd moved his bird-of-paradise plants in from the verandah. He'd felt an unwarranted sorrow at the thought of them being torn loose by the wind. He thought he should offer a prayer to a power that could turn rain sideways and send people scurrying to schools and churches for a night on hard cots. Yet, he didn't know which god to approach. He supposed that a man should choose a religion by the time he reached his sixties, but decided he could ponder the makings of the universe just as well through science. All the religions he'd explored at his mother's urgings seemed too narrow.

His gaudy birds-of-paradise, stems slightly bent, looked poised for flight. He stood, leaned forward, and peered at the bright blue and orange creatures. That's the ticket, he thought, be brilliant in life and die fast.

A siren's wail over the noise of the wind startled him. He hurried out to the hall. The building's intercom blasted out two more beats of the siren followed by a human voice that crackled, "Everyone must–" The voice cut off. The intercom crackled again, "Every . . . must . . . vacate . . . premis . . . mediate—" The storm noise cut off a few more random syllables. Smiling, he turned back into his parlor, pocketed his nitroglycerin tablets just in case, and headed out again. *It's time. Hurry up, please. It's time,* he sang to himself, quoting Eliot. Then, adding his own words to Eliot's, *Opening time, closing time. Courthouse time. Fine that juror for every minute she's late. There's a time to live and time to die. Time told by a faceless clock.*

He closed his door and stopped dead before a vision. His new neighbor, directly in front of him, stood in her doorway, arms pressed against the door jambs, hazel eyes opened wide framed by long, straight, dark brown hair. She seemed quite young although laugh lines etched the edges of her eyes and the top of her attractive cheeks. Her light olive skin reminded him of his mother's favorite cameo. She was dressed in a blue floral-print nightgown with lace at the neck. Her high round breasts were heaving like those in novels that Bev used to read to him when he was trying to sleep.

"Good evening," he said, bowing slightly. "I'm Dan Lawrence." He nodded toward his door. "Your neighbor. We have to leave the building now. Are you coming?"

"Yes. I mean no. I'm staying here. Not dressed." She dipped back into her apartment and started to close the door. Dan caught it before it shut all the way.

"Miss? Ma'am? Will you please come with me? Let's get to the elevator while it's still functioning. I don't relish descending nine flights by stair." He raised his voice. "And I don't like leaving anyone alone up here. The whole building is swaying too much." He listened. No human sound. "Pardon? Miss—uh—" He waited for her name.

He pulled open the door and saw her with her hands grasping at a table cluttered with dishes, books, and unopened mail. He entered.

"What's your name?" he asked.

"Joanna. Joanna Archer. Forgive this mess." She looked down at the table, which, to Dan, looked relatively neat compared to the rest of the room. Cardboard boxes still tied in strings sat against a couch covered with what looked like dirty laundry and a toppling stack of hard and soft-cover books. A large spider plant sat on one end table, and though it was still September, home-made Christmas ornaments encircled the plant.

"Better hurry and get dressed, Joanna. I'll wait for you."

"It's kind of you, but I've decided to stay." She backed away. "I'm really quite capable of taking care of myself." She lifted her chin. Her hair fall away revealing high cheekbones and large hazel eyes with full dark lashes. Rain gunned against her kitchen window; the voice on the intercom crackled again.

Dan could feel the giddy movement of the building. He pondered for a moment.

"No, Joanna," he said, feeling an old sense of absolute authority, "come on. There's no time to do anything." He grabbed her hand and headed for the elevator.

"Wait." She hung onto the doorknob. "You don't understand. I've never before had the chance to take care of myself. This is it."

"Joanna," he said, enjoying the sound of her name despite the urgency of the moment, "there will be many more times in your life—far more than you want—to prove yourself." Dan let go of her and rubbed the top of his head. He studied her wistful expression and felt a strange tenderness. "Not against hurricanes. Save your courage for battles you can win." He leaned closer and looked into her eyes. "Or do you want to die?"

She lowered her chin. Her hair fell half way across her face.

"If that's what you want," he said remembering all those fights with Bev, "I sure as hell won't stop you."

"No, I don't—of course not." Her small shoulders drooped. She made a sweeping gesture toward her apartment. "It's just that I thought I could clean up here—oh, well, I guess I'd better go with you. Wait a sec while I find my raincoat. It's here somewhere."

"There's no time." The building shook violently. Dan pulled her into the hall, shut the door behind them and led her to the elevator. "It's still running," he said, aware of his pounding heart as they entered the elevator.

He watched the electronic numbers decrease as the elevator creaked downward. Suddenly the lights went out and the elevator shuddered like a wounded elephant. He felt her clutch his arm.

"We're going to crash," she cried out, "hang on."

"We're okay, Joanna. Elevators don't crash." He put his free arm around her.

After one small shudder, the elevator continued its normal descent, but in the dark. She released Dan's arm. He wrapped one arm around her shoulders and she sank into him. He detected a slight scent of face cream. His paternal feelings morphed into erotic.

"Head outside when we land," he said to her. "There'll be transport there taking people to shelters." The elevator landed with a soft thud and he released her.

She turned and looked at him before she headed for the revolving door that led outside—right into the noisy, wild storm. Outside, she stopped to wait for him. People were rushing in all directions, screaming at each other over the wail of sirens and roar of wind. A National Guardsman appeared from somewhere on the crowded street and guided them and seven other refugees onto the high bed of a canvas-topped army transport. Sheets of water soaked them in the short dash to the truck. Joanna's rose-petal nightgown clung to her body revealing its curves. She plucked at it like a cat tugging its skin for fleas, entrancing Dan.

Amazingly sexy, he thought. He wanted to sing. Joanna huddled against him when they boarded, and then the truck lurched away.

"Thanks for making me come with you," she said.

"You're welcome," Dan replied. "There's an old English proverb, you know. 'Death always comes either too early or too late.'" He wanted to touch her chin. "So you see, there's really not much use worrying."

"I never thought of that. Would it come too late or too early for you?" She exhaled audibly.

"Depends on what I'm doing at the time." He grinned.

"What did you say your name was?" She peered at him.

"Daniel Lawrence." He smiled. "Call me Dan."

"And I'm Joanna Archer, wearing a soaking wet nightgown."

"Well, Joan of Arc, don't worry. Soon it will be bedtime in some Red Cross shelter. I'd give you my jacket, but it's just as wet. I guess we'll have to drip dry." He knew his words were ordinary—fatherly—but his mind ripped off her wet nightgown and tore it to shreds. They spray dogs to stop them from rutting, he thought. Apparently, it doesn't work on men.

*   *   *

Dan tried to peer out of the truck for downed power lines, knowing he could trust the driver, but not quite able to. The driver took the sodden group on a jagged route to Coral Gables and left them in front of a large stone cathedral built near the Ponce de Leon Memorial.

Alighting, he took Joanna's elbow and ducked his head into the wet wind. He felt his football playing years in his body replay the scrimmage charge. Joanna charged with him, head down.

They entered the church with a nave the size of a tennis court and a huge statue of Christ bleeding on a cross behind the altar. Dan surveyed the cots set lengthwise from the side aisles, parallel with the altar. At the front, a double row had been set up perpendicular to the altar. The din of barking dogs ran counterpoint to the hum of subdued voices.

"There they are," Dan said, pointing toward Red Cross workers by the choir stall, "serving coffee, doughnuts and good humor to allay our fears. Let's find a couple of cots first. Besides being wet, are you hungry?"

She smiled, nodded, and lowered her face. Her hair draped forward again. He couldn't read her eyes.

He found two empty cots facing the altar near the main entrance of the cathedral. Gesturing toward one against the wall for Joanna, he sat on one parallel to it and let out a one-note laugh.

"Did you notice the statue of Ponce de Leon out there?" he asked, pointing toward the cot next to a wall. "Some of us could use a drink from that fountain right now."

"I think freedom is more valuable than youth." Joanna sat on the edge of the cot facing him and hugged her knees. "But freedom takes courage." She pushed her hair back from her face.

"Everything worthwhile takes courage," Dan said, impressed by her comment.

Two elderly men leaned against a stone pillar nearby. Dan noticed them during a lull in sounds from the moving crowd. He couldn't help hearing them.

"You shoulda seen the hurricane of '38 up there in Massachusetts." one said. "I saw a dog, big one, too, fly right by my window and I was on the second floor."

"Well, this one here's pretty damn bad," the other one said. "I just hope it misses my trailer. I don't own much, but it's mine free and clear."

A third man approached carrying a cup of coffee. Steam rose from it and fogged his glasses.

"Have you guys seen any TV folks?" he asked. "Usually Channel Four comes out here to interview. They were hovering over Hurricane Irene shelters, but I missed them." He sipped his coffee. "Heck, right in this here cathedral I got to talk on television a good two minutes during Hurricane Evelyn in '67. It replayed all over the country."

"Eavesdropping," Dan whispered to Joanna. "One of the perks of bad weather."

A Red Cross lady offered Joanna a quilt. She accepted and stretched out on the cot wrapped in it. The quilt had teddy bears embroidered on each square.

"Well, look at those little bears," Dan said.

"This quilt's quirky, but cute," she said, smoothing it with her hands. "It's not as embarrassing as sitting here in a wet nightgown."

"Good. I'm glad you have it," Dan said, thinking she looked like a child, unaware of his erotic interest in her. He lay back and stared at the Gothic ceiling. "You know, hours seem to stretch in a place like this. Time has no limit. Like death, I suppose." He felt an inexplicable sense of peace.

"What do you mean?" Joanna leaned on one elbow, looking directly at him.

Dan rolled toward her and noticed a bandage on the tip of her middle finger. The other nails were cut to the quick.

"I was just thinking," he said, "how death ends our usual sense of time. It ends both heroic and evil things and all that's mundane, trivial and banal, too." *Here I go again, ranting about Bev's complaints.* Abruptly he changed the subject. "Do you bite your fingernails?"

"No, never. Why do you ask? Do my nails look that bad?"

"Not at all." Dan swung his legs to the floor and struggled a little with his stiff back. "Your nails are fine. Pardon me for not minding my own business. I'm off to get some apple juice and doughnuts. Want some?"

"I used to wear long acrylic nails—bright red ones," he heard her say as he walked away.

Dan hit his forehead. *What am I doing? I'm old enough to be her father and about to go to jail for life.*

CHAPTER FOUR

Joanna dozed and then opened her eyes to the same murmuring tableau and whimpering dogs. She peered up at the darkness of the nave and listened for sounds of the wild winds. She pulled the teddy bear quilt up to her nose, wondering why her new neighbor hadn't come back with the apple juice. The screech of a poorly adjusted address system jolted her. She covered her ears until the sound stopped.

"Listen up, y'all." A man cleared his throat into the loudspeaker and then said, "It looks like Julio has gone out to sea without leaving a whole lot of structural damage. The winds have run down, but it won't be safe to go home until daybreak. Power lines are down everywhere from here through Miama. So y'all just make yourselves as comfy as possible—like the lady over there in her teddy bear blanket—and we'll all get through this here night."

Joanna felt the blood rush to her face. She wanted to kick the announcer in his "possible". Then she saw Dan returning and relaxed.

"Sorry to be gone so long," he said. "I ran into some acquaintances." He handed her a paper cup of apple cider and a gray doughnut. The cot creaked when he sat on it.

"Thanks. Nice of you. You know, you don't have to keep me company. I can take care of myself." She avoided his eyes and felt her eyelid twitch. *He looks familiar. Where have I seen him?* The air in the nave felt so thick a person could drown in it.

"But it's my pleasure, Joanna, not your need," he said. He drank his cider in one swallow and then belched. "Excuse me," he said, covering his mouth. "Guess I can't handle my cider any more. Time was I could knock down two or three shots with one gulp."

Joanna laughed. The air lightened and she mentioned a cousin with a nervous stomach whose burps would echo. She meandered now from one subject to another, feeling comfortable with him. Soon the sound of group snoring surrounded them like a stage curtain. The lingering smell of wet clothes covered the earlier acrid scents of fear.

22

Dan told her he had moved into the Brickell building a month before Hurricane Irene.

"I have some legal business to take care of," he explained, "so I'm in Miami temporarily. Of course, everything at my age is temporary."

"You keep talking that way. You look pretty young and hearty to me." *And damn good*, she thought. His name sounded familiar, but she was distracted by his lips. The lower lip was thick enough to kiss on its own, and his upper lip looked pale and moist under a thick, white mustache.

"It's not age itself." He smiled, sideways. "I just turned sixty-one and except for one heart scare, I'm healthy. It's a different challenge every decade I guess. Some people just give up the ghost while others can't seem to."

Candlelight along the wall behind her allowed her to examine his face. The soft look in his eyes contradicted his tight jaw. His shoulders reminded her of strong yokes that could pull a cartload of coal and his arms, lightly freckled, matched them. His hands, though comparatively small, could caress the moon. She felt face blushing at that thought.

"I used to think no one had the right to take another life," he said. "Now I'm not so sure. Ever drown a cat?"

"Course not," she replied, startled. She put her empty cup on the floor and lay down, dismayed with the turn of the conversation. Dan had reminded her of men she'd only dreamed of and never met. Kind. Good looking *and* kind. Until he asked that.

"Ah, forgive me, Joanna. Sometimes I say—" He turned his head to the left as if something significant had grabbed his attention, then he turned back to her. "Your turn. Tell me how you happened to move in across the hall from me."

Joanna longed to trust him. The cathedral filled with the sounds of early sleep, before snores. Light from a three-quarter moon beamed through a stained glass window on her left bringing in colors. She sat up, relieved to hear the warmth in his voice again.

"Well, I'm on my own now for the very first time in my life," she said in a low voice. "I finally got the courage to leave my husband after fourteen years. If I'd known it would be this easy—" She shook her head. "That's my aunt's condo across the hall from you. Golly, I hope the building is still standing."

"I'm sure it is," Dan said. "They're built to withstand strong winds." He touched her hand lightly.

"Good," she said, speaking quickly. "Anyway, my parents are freaking out. I won't tell them where I'm staying. And my old friends keep hassling me to go back to Beaumont—that's my husband—so I avoid them. I guess I'm between lives, so to speak."

"Do you have any children?"

"No. Beaumont didn't want any. I sorta wanted to have a baby, but you know, Dan, I wasn't sure I had what it takes."

"How old are, if you don't mind me asking?"

"Thirty-four come December." Joanna smiled as she felt blood rush to her face again and glad that it didn't show on her skin.

"Well, you have time if you change your mind. And change husbands. I wish we'd had a daughter." He rubbed his leg and then jumped up and paced around his cot. "Goddamn charley-horse," he said, grimacing. She heard him mutter as he paced, "Regrets—useless tear jerks."

"Is there anything I can do?"

"No. No thanks, it'll go away in a minute. Just one of nature's sentences for living too long." He massaged his calf and headed for the rest room.

"Hey, Lady, wanna get away from the old farts and have some fun?" A big teenager in red shorts muscled his way toward her. "I found a closet and got some weed to share with the right—"

"No thanks."

"Suit yourself," the boy said, and swaggered away. A German shepherd two cots down growled.

Joanna sat up and looked for Dan, but hearing a wolf whistle from the dark side of the nave, she hid under the teddy bears again, ashamed at being such a wimp.

Dan returned. She watched him place his glasses in his shoe and realized she hadn't noticed him wearing glasses. How come? Because he was so good looking either way?

He stretched out on the cot without speaking as if he assumed she'd fallen asleep. Shyness kept her from breaking the silence. She heard his breathing grow deeper and let herself relax into the visual limbo that precedes sleep: a flow of images that included radiant flowers, a man stroking the stem of a gladiola as if to help it grow, pink light fading to gray, floating into black.

*   *   *

Dan dreamed of his wife scolding him when she was young and fretfully pregnant. Joanna's gasp awakened him; he sat up fast. A figure knelt as if praying over her. A big guy in red shorts had his bare arm across Joanna. He grabbed the guy's shoulder and whispered, "What the hell are you doing?"

"Go back to sleep, old man. I'm going to entertain the lady." The young man laughed.

"Go away," Joanna said, her voice thick with sleep.

"Stand up young man," Dan bellowed, jumping up. At least his voice was still strong. "Get up and face me." All snoring in the cathedral ceased. A dog barked. Someone turned on a flashlight.

The boy stood. He was well over six feet. Dan moved in close and glared at him.

"Be a man, now, and leave like one," he commanded. They stared at each other in intense silence.

"What's your name?" Dan pushed his face in closer. "Your mother would be real proud of you right now." He felt his anger load the gun of authority at this jerk.

The guy seemed spellbound. Then he shrugged his massive shoulders and backed away.

"Fuck you," he whispered. It was almost a whimper.

"What's going on here?" A Red Cross official asked, drawing close. Dan told him. The officer took over and shoved the big teen toward the altar.

"Thank you." Joanna said and clasped Dan's hand.

She held it a little too long for his comfort before she released it. He sat on the edge of his cot facing her and let his hands drop between his knees, realizing how much he wanted to hold her in his arms. Light snoring resumed nearby.

"You know, it's too bad you don't have any kids," she whispered after a couple of minutes. "You're a natural. Are you still married? Tell me about your wife."

"She's dead." Dan listened to the breathing of those nearby, felt assured that no one could hear them. He wondered how much to tell her. Blunt facts can distort the truth. "We were married thirty-eight years and lived the last five down here."

"Did you want children?"

"In a way I had one for years . . . no, strike that. Yes, we wanted children. Actually, we had a son for a short while, but he drowned." It still hurt to say that out loud, as if uttering the words scraped his vocal chords.

"How sad." Joanna said, facing him for a minute before lowering her head.

"That was many years ago. We heal, slowly." He watched the moonlight play across her face. "Bev couldn't have any more children and for some reason we decided to forego adoption. I can't remember why. I have two very close friends who, I suppose, take the place of grown children."

"When did your wife die?" Joanna asked, "if you don't mind my asking."

"Almost two years ago. You know, she seemed content without kids, but I was obtuse. I discovered years later that she'd never been content about anything. Not that contentment is a given." He stood and stretched. This conversation called for more privacy. "Let's take a little stroll to the entryway, see if the stars are out in the moonlight."

She stood, wrapped the quilt around her like a bathrobe. They moved out of range of the sleepers to the vestibule.

"What do you do for a living?" she asked.

"Seems ironic now," he said with a laugh, "but I worked the justice world—a superior court judge. Twenty years, actually. Satisfied my need for children, I guess." He peered at Joanna, fascinated by her beautiful hazel eyes that shifted from light to dark as her feelings changed.

"So you're a judge." Her fingers fluttered as her lips opened in a smile that could stop a felon in his tracks. "What a coincidence," she said. "I'm a court reporter."

"That is interesting. How did you happen to choose that profession?"

"Well, I'd been married to Beaumont for ten years," she said, moving ahead of him, speaking fast "And I had no babies to take care of and not much to do all day. Beaumont's a roofer, you see, and makes enough money to suit him. I needed something to grab me—use me. All I have is a junior college degree. I love reading, but it's all intake." She stopped at the double doors that led outside. "Then I had this neighbor who had just retired from the court reporting business and had her own machine. She taught me the rudiments. With her encouragement I went to school and got certified."

"Do you like it?"

"It'll do. Careers come by accident for women, you know."

"They do for men, too, oh lovely one." He felt his whole face grin. "A friend of mine became a judge the same time I did. His father was a doctor in the army. He fell into law because that's all he could do with an English major from an army post in Texas. Finally he was appointed judge. That day he said to me, 'Now I'm every bit as God-like as the old man.' Different coincidences, different careers."

"And you?" she asked, pushing open the heavy door.

"I chose law as a profession. It suited my temperament. Then I fell into the judging business and discovered that it, too, suited me." He held the door for her. A warm breeze, like a toddler's breath, floated in.

"The air's so gentle after a hurricane," she said.

He nodded and stared at the stars. He almost took her in his arms, but she had turned away from him. Pure pleasure flowed in his veins. He felt desire again. Alive.

"So you just fell onto the bench," she said, looking sideways at him. "I fall into smaller places but I've been thinking I'd like to get a law degree, now that I'm on my own."

"You're such a delight. I know you'll do fine." He bowed, took her hand. "I am your new friend to help you along the way, not that you'll need any. And I am delighted to have another hurricane friend."

"Another? You have more?" She left her hand in his. He caressed it.

"Yes. Did I tell you about Lucille and Ralph?" He let go of her hand. "I mentioned my two close friends who sub for children, but not by name." He followed her back to their cots without speaking. Watching her lightly rolling gait, he wanted to put his hands on her hips and start a snake dance through the cathedral. He wanted to take her home to bed. He wanted to share her cot and knew in his gut the motive of the guy in red shorts. But, wanting something from another did not mean you could take it.

"Okay, tell me about these hurricane friends," she said when she'd reached her cot and sat on it. She looked up at him with her large hazel eyes, now quite light in color.

"Hurricane friendships are different somehow." He sat knee to knee with her and tried to collect his thoughts. "Ralph, Bev, who became my wife, Lucille and I were kids when we first met and got caught in a hurricane in Pemaquid. That's in Maine, by the way.

"I know."

Dan could see dirt under his thumbnail from the light of a nearby lantern. He took out his pocket knife and cleaned it. Images of the dead sailboat, the sucked dry air, and the sudden crash of gigantic waves tossing him over and under flashed across his mental screen.

"Go on," she said.

"Ah, yes. Well, Ralph eventually married Rosalie and Lucille married Arthur—neither of them—the spouses, that is, mean much to me, but Lucille and Ralph remain to this day as close to me as if that hurricane were yesterday." He pocketed his knife. "Funny, they didn't name hurricanes then. You were still hovering in Shirley Temple's baby heaven."

"Where were you when Hurricane Irene hit?" Joanna asked and lay back on her cot.

"In Miami. We didn't get hit bad enough to evacuate." He realized that his voice was barely audible. He raised it to ask, "And where were you?"

"Home. Where I used to live with Beaumont in West Miami. You were lucky. I guess I got a hurricane enemy."

"What happened?"

She stared at the high ceiling. It's a long story."

"We have plenty of time. Tell me." He stretched out on his back and wondered if he'd get a hard on listening to her.

Slowly, she told him about fourteen years of threats—minimal abuse, but still abuse—and about Beaumont tearing off her fingernail during Hurricane Irene when she finally realized that she didn't want to live with him ever again.

"It was the fingernail that did it," she said, "the final straw, as they say."

"It must have been a terrible marriage." Dan said, loving her. "I'm glad you're out of it. You may need a restraining order." He studied her bandaged finger and saw Bev reaching for the drink that killed her. "Still, things can be a whole lot worse than a torn off fingernail."

Joanna turned away, hiding her face. Dan regretted his remark. He heard people on nearby cots beginning to stir. A black Labrador nearby wagged its tail. Daylight filtered through the stained glass windows giving the vestibule and Joanna a honeyed glow.

"Smell that coffee, will you?" he said. "Not much time left here." He leaned close to her. "There are too many things I'll never know or understand. All my life I wanted to be right. Turned out I was only righteous."

She turned to face him again. He saw tears in her eyes and felt them gathering in his.

"I used to think I wanted someone to care for me and take care of me," she said. "Now I just want to make it on my own—learn how to be a feminist so I can eventually become a whole, uh, person." Joanna tossed back her hair and smiled.

"I can understand your need to prove yourself." Dan said, edging away. "Recently, though, I came to the conclusion that people really should need each other—openly, I mean. We have to walk a tightrope between dependence and independence. Correction, I have to." He made his fingers wobble on an imaginary tightrope between their cots. "True strength comes from being willing to need sometimes and admitting it." He realized now that he didn't recognize a need for Bev other than her need of him.

"I need too much—"

"Nothing wrong with needing others as long as we don't get swallowed up by them. Sounds to me Beaumont had you chained." Had he chained Bev? He stood and stretched. "Ah, my poor bones sound like a haunted house. Tell me Joanna, as we walk up the aisle to the altar—for coffee—what was the most important thing you ever did in your life?'

"I quit smoking."

"Yes. Yes. You'll make it just fine on your own."

"Well, this quilt doesn't embarrass me anymore." Joanna folded the teddy bear quilt and draped it over her arm. "Let's go."

They wended their way among the yawning and stretching people. Joanna handed the quilt to the Red Cross woman and then turned to Dan.

"Are you still working as a judge?"

"No, I retired."

"That's funny. I'm sure I've seen your picture somewhere." She fiddled with her now dry nightgown as if brushing off crumbs. The rose petals jumped. Dan saw them as fish mating.

"You may have," he said, focusing on her face. "What case are you working on now?"

"I just finished one and will begin a new one that's just coming to trial this week. Mercy killing case. Should be interesting. I forget the names." She handed him a cup of coffee.

"Then you'll be on the case for Judge Ogasaki in court twelve."

"Yes, I will. How did you—?" She came to a dead stop and stared at him. "Oh my God, you're the judge in Time Magazine! You killed your wife!"

CHAPTER FIVE

A red tour bus drove the "evacs" back to Miami. Joanna stared out the window but saw nothing. She didn't dare look at Dan nor did she know what to say. She knew she had to stay neutral or she could cause a mistrial and get fired. Remaining neutral in court would be impossible if she did not keep him completely out of her life.

"Speak to me, Joanna," Dan said touching her shoulder. "I want you to know I did not kill my wife, but I did help her commit suicide."

"I realize that, Dan," she said without looking at him. "I read about your case in Time magazine. It's just the fact that I'll be recording your trial." She turned to face him. "It was real nice meeting you, but I'm afraid we can't be hurricane friends until it's over. Sorry." Her voice cracked.

"I understand. I, too, am very sorry."

Tears stung her eyes. They rode in silence up to the ninth floor of their still-standing building. She rushed into her apartment and shut the door.

She rocked herself on her aunt's futon with her knees hugged to her chest. She had never known such warm affection from a man. "Kind" was the dumb word that kept coming to mind as she thought of Dan, and she thought of him constantly. Warm and kind. His voice had a gentle resonance that surprised her, not like any she'd heard before.

"What am I doing?" she asked herself. "He's old enough to be my father. He killed, well, helped kill, his wife. I have to record his trial—impartially. I could lose my job. I've got to stay away from him!"

She felt the need to talk to someone about Dan—how Dan would've made a wonderful friend—one who didn't need to control her or her opinions. She realized, with a sudden whole body ache, that she didn't have anyone to talk to except Dan.

She ceased rocking and felt a warmth just thinking about him, as if her insides were blending with hot molasses. Why did she keep picturing him? Because she trusted him? Because he wasn't anything like the men she'd known all her life? She stood and stared at her spider plant.

"Well, forget that!" she said aloud.

She took to peeking out her door and running down a flight of stairs rather than wait for the elevator on their floor. In the courtroom, she avoided his eyes, afraid of making errors recording or transcribing.

The days of jury selection dragged on. Monroe Cort, Dan's albino-like redheaded lawyer, gave each potential juror who appeared to be younger than fifty a preemptory challenge. Undoubtedly, he expected people with aged parents to be sympathetic. Joanna struggled for neutrality and detachment, hoping all the while that Mr. Cort's strategy would work. She nodded whenever Dan caught her eye and then looked down at her keys. It took all her concentration to record the words and not hear them enough to feel reaction to them.

Each evening after Joanna finished transcribing the day's proceeding she went to the employee lounge before walking home. Here she often encountered another court reporter, who, for reasons Joanna couldn't fathom, made an amazing transformation in her appearance from bland reporter by day to punk rock diva by night.

One day Joanna lingered to watch. The tall blonde didn't simply change clothes, she changed her total character. She emerged from a benign pastel look—silky straight hair, blue linen suit—to an exaggerated Madonna. She tossed onto the counter the items that transformed her: spiked purple wig, brass hoop earrings that looked heavy enough to stretch her earlobes down to her shoulders, black fingernail polish, sequined boots, and a very short black leather skirt.

Joanna felt both lonely and intrigued. She arranged trips to the lounge to coincide with those of her strange colleague. She had determined since her escape from Beaumont to live alone for at least one year and see if she could survive with her psyche intact. Now she realized she needed a friend. Dan had said that true strength comes from being willing to need others at times, like now. He was right. A casual friend would do and the blonde looked interesting—certainly unconventional.

*   *   *

Sherri Ann Taylor loved the clickety clack of her high heels on the marble floor that led away from boredom and to the employee lounge and fun. She flung open the door and grinned. There was the mousy chick again sitting with her back to the mirror.

"Hi, kid."

"Hi." The chick stood and held out her hand. "I'm Joanna Archer. I'm working in court twelve."

"I'm in nine. Hey, wanna try on my bracelets?" Sherri shook the hot, dry hand and felt a sudden compassion for her fellow court slave.

"No. No thanks, I mean, they're pretty, though," Joanna mumbled.

"Pretty? Shit, I didn't have pretty in mind. Say, are you single?"

"Yes . . . sort of. I'm separated." Joanna backed toward the exit.

"Great—I mean I hope it's great for you. Well, nice to meet you, Joanna. If you're looking for some fun let me know. I have an excuse for a car, but it runs, and the Sportatorium has great concerts on Fridays. English Dog next week." She adjusted her wig. "I'm not sure my eye-shadow goes with this—oh well."

"I might like to go to a concert sometime," Joanna said with a quick thrust of her head that tossed her hair out of her face. "English Dog? Let's meet for lunch first, okay?"

Sherri turned to answer, but the chick had disappeared. It will be a challenge to corrupt that lass, she thought. Give her the balls she wasn't born with. She laughed at her sexist thought.

*   *   *

Joanna ran out of the courthouse straightening her shoulders. Lunch was about all she wanted with Sherri, she decided, and slowed her pace when she reached the river. The sun had just set but the damp air had not cooled. She watched a quarter moon edge above a palm tree. A frog croaking for his mistress competed with the bee-like drone of the evening traffic. A young couple turned onto the river walk in front of her. They strolled with their arms around each other and their hands in each other's hip pockets. Joanna felt a sharp pain pierce the dull ache of her loneliness.

She first realized she was hungry when she rode the building elevator to her current home. She had forgotten to buy groceries. Here was one more proof that she couldn't take care of herself. Echoes of her mother's voice laughing, "Oh dear Head-in-the-cloud Joanna. I hope you marry Mr. Feet-on-the-Ground."

Recriminating tears burned. She saw Dan in the hallway when the elevator door opened. He turned first one way and then another and seemed so uncertain that Joanna didn't recognize him at first.

"Hello Mr. Lawrence," she said because she couldn't avoid him.

"Joanna, what a pleasant surprise." He pivoted toward her. "I haven't seen you outside court since Hurricane Julio left town. I've missed you. How are you?"

"I'm fine," she lied, curling her trembling fingers. "And you?"

"Fine, fine. How about forgetting court for an hour and join me for a glass of Asti Spumonte and some caviar on rye toast. Do you like caviar? It's only lumpfish, but it's good."

The temptation to accept made her knees weak. She leaned against her door. How she wanted to collapse in his arms!

"Thanks, Mr. Lawrence, but I have a date tonight," she lied.

"The name's Dan," he said. "Maybe some other time."

Inside, she flung the newspapers and clothes off the couch and herself onto it. Hot salty tears flowed down into her mouth. Soon the sobs hurt her chest so much she quit crying, splashed her face with cold water and sneaked out to a coffee shop where she ate a dry omelet. It had taken all her resolve to refuse Dan's invitation. With each tasteless bite, she came closer to the irony that she'd longed for a man like Dan for years, yet now she must reject him because she had to be impartial in court. She felt terrible and yet stronger than she had ever felt before. That she could say no to someone when she really wanted to say yes meant she had passed a major test.

A lengthy transcription of the preliminary hearing kept Joanna working much later than usual the next day. She missed Sherri's evening transformation. The sun had set by the time she left and the buzzards that hover over the Miami courthouse had gone wherever buzzards go to sleep. Strolling home near the river, she thought that she heard Sherri's cynical laugh. Joanna sidled toward the river's edge and stopped. Sure enough, it was Sherri. A young man, hair spiked into a Mohawk, had her by the arm.

"C'mon," he barked. "We'll be late."

"Hey," Sherri said, her voice exploding like a cherry bomb, "I told you I'm not going."

"Look, Babe, they're expecting us." His tone carried a threat. Joanna shivered.

Sherri spun away from him, shaking off her purple wig. Her thin blonde hair seemed to float as she shoved the wig into her purse. He grabbed her shoulder but again she shrugged him off and held her ground, glaring at him.

"Fuck off, Dude." she hissed and turned toward the river's edge. The guy flipped her off and then swaggered off in the opposite direction.

Joanna wondered what Sherri would do to Beaumont. Admiring such cocky strength, she decided to follow Sherri—learn something. Sherri left the river, and went around the corner of a building. Joanna followed and backed up against a damp wall. Ten feet away Sherri stood in the arms of a tall, slim man wearing a cream silk suit. Joanna ached to be right where Sherri now stood. She felt like a slinky toy as she sneaked away, hugging herself.

The next day Joanna saw Sherri flouncing toward the lower courthouse exit at noon and hurried to catch up with her.

"Hi Sherri. Going for lunch?' she asked.

"Hi, kid. Sure, come on." Together, like old friends, they ran across the street to a cafeteria. Sherri complained about the hours they worked. Joanna barely listened, feeling lucky to have company, She tuned in as Sherri said, "Shit, you and I put in fifty hours a week and here we are stuck in a cafeteria line, taking only a half hour for lunch so we can transcribe the morning's action." She mimed speed eating with her left hand. "Yet the judges, juries, lawyers, bailiffs, prosecutors, defendants and all those courthouse groupies take a three hour, three martini, raw oyster and conch salad lunch. With fresh baby arugula yet."

"I never thought of that," Johanna said, wondering what arugula was. Sherri's complaints amused her. She wanted to ask about the guy in the silk suit but Sherri would know she'd been spying.

They found a table in the shade and ate their spinach salads. Joanna learned that Sherri was divorced, child-free, and barely thirty. She kept up a running criticism of everyone who walked by.

"Gad, look at the guy in tight pants. Looks like he's trying to play Mercutio without a codpiece. And over there." She nodded toward three plump women. "Why do fat women wear T-shirts that advertise amusement parks when the only thing you can see is their spare tires?"

Joanna enjoyed Sherri's insults as long as they didn't include her. They started out to the courthouse and Sherri nudged her, pointing with her nose toward a plump couple devouring banana splits.

"Folks eat when they give up sex," she said. "By the way, which is your pleasure, food or fucking?"

Feeling her face flush, Joanna lowered it. She didn't agree with Sherri, but she hadn't managed to enjoy either lately.

"I used to like to do both," she said.

"Come out with me some night." Sherri draped her arm across Joanna's shoulders. "You gotta have some fun once in a while. Why else record all this daily drivel?"

"How long you been reporting?"

"About a year. I'm in it for the money." She pulled Joanna's hair back into a pony tail. "There. Now I can see your face. Yup. I've been saving five hundred a month. Gonna get me a night club in Houston, or L.A. Out of Miami. Somewhere young."

"That's some goal," Joanna said, admiring Sherri for having one in the first place. "Hey, I thought I saw you last night with a good looking guy in a cream colored suit. Did I?"

"Maybe you did. Maybe you didn't." Sherri grinned.

*   *   *

Joanna spent a lonely weekend avoiding Dan and wondering what Sherri was doing.

"Is your invite to the English Dog concert still open?" she asked when she encountered Sherri again on Monday in the employee lounge. "I'll go if I don't have to dress weird."

"Sure it's open." Sherri frowned at her. "But dressing up is half the fun. Here, try these on." She handed Joanna a pair of red and black checkered tights. "I bet you wear a high-necked cotton nightgown to bed."

"So what if I do?" Laughing, Joanna pulled the tights on over her panty hose. "What do you wear to bed?"

"Best looking guy I can find."

Joanna turned away so Sherri couldn't see her face redden. "Where do you find them?" she asked, stifling her embarrassment.

"Which, the tights or the men?" Sherri smirked and brushed her fine blonde hair, stroke after stroke like a heroine in a vintage movie. Then, as if she'd shifted roles in the film, she donned a new wig—pink and black. "I meet them at concerts," she answered, "bars, health clubs, bridge parlors—anywhere. Except you have to avoid the marinas. Those rich old duffers have been flying the cocktail flag so long they can't get it up anymore."

"Did you say bridge parlors? What are they?"

"That's where I first met Ricardo—the guy in the silk suit." Sherri leaned her back against the jewelry-splashed sink and looked straight at Joanna. She laughed bitterly and then continued, "Miami's full of all kinds of bridge players—mostly single—old, young, men, women, and in between, if you catch my drift. They meet in city parlors to play bridge, as well as to eye their partners for possible horizontal partying later." She turned and began to layer on the bracelets. "It's funny, but you can tell a whole hell of a lot about a person by the way he bids. Once I made the mistake of going to bed with a guy who consistently bid game. Usually didn't make his bid. Naturally he was a preemie"

"A what?"

"A premature ejaculator, silly." Sherri giggled releasing tight little balloons of sound. "All them transplanted New York analysts could learn a lot about people just watching 'em play bridge."

"Can you just go to play the game? I like bridge. I mean if I went to one of these parlors would it mean I had to go to bed with someone?"

"Depends on how you bid." Sherri cackled. "I'm just kidding. Since you like to play, let's go, just for the game."

"Okay. Say, are you going with Ricardo now?"

"Off and on. Sometimes he's a real dick."

"Well he's sure good looking."

"In a way he is." Sherri tilted her head to the right and closed her eyes. "He has such a long nose and super serious face—rarely smiles. Keeps a tight rein on his lips as if he's saving his brilliant flash of teeth for—who knows what." She paused and looked at Joanna's reflection in the mirror. "I think I've seen him smile twice. Both times he was triumphant at bridge."

"How long have you been playing bridge?'

"Forever." While Sherri blackened her nails with a particularly strong smelling polish, she began a monologue that broke only when she shifted hands. The nailbrush followed the rhythm of her speech. "I was weaned on bridge . . . in a New York apartment—Park Avenue no less. Fucking monopoly game address. My father's a retired Wall Street lawyer and my mother's a volunteer Republican with amazing power."

"Did they send you away to college?" Joanna wished her parents were half as interesting.

"Ha. Finishing school. Finished me off. I dropped acid and dropped out. Turned punk for laughs—shock value—even though I know I'm too old for it." Sherri drew a line down her nose with a mascara brush. "Just a split personality."

Finishing school. Joanna imagined a small women's college in Georgia, southern accents, harp lessons, poetry readings. She stared at Sherri's split face in the mirror. Her poor parents.

"How old are your folks now?" Joanna asked and then covered her mouth for being so inquisitive.

"In their seventies. They had me late—menopause brat—spoiled me rotten, they say. I don't know from spoiled, but I do know I rarely touch the edge of their lives, except for bridge. That's fun. And there's no other reason to be alive except to have fun."

Joanna wasn't sure she agreed with that but she liked the possibility of meeting men in a safe place. Rock concerts and bars were too scary. She backed up to the mirror and admired her checkered butt in the reflection.

"These tights are kinda cute," she said, "but what can you wear with them?"

"Anything." Sherri waved her arms to dry her nails. "The greater the clash the better the bash." She pasted the palms of her hands on her hips and wiggled her fingers. "Or nothing. They look great topless."

Joanna's eyes widened, but she smiled and tossed back her curtain of hair ready to consider some action now that she was finally free.

The following morning at seven Joanna walked to work wearing a pink cashmere cardigan to ward off the new morning chill. The seaweed smells green at this hour, she thought. Not green. What's the word for that smell—begins with an F. She took a deep breath. Fecundity, that's it. The river smells fecund, fertile. What a fine line separates fecund from foul, right from wrong.

Suddenly she remembered she hadn't taken her birth control pill with breakfast. At the curve where she could peer across the bay, she stopped, opened her purse and pulled out the plastic compact. She carefully removed today's pill and swallowed it dry. It backed up in her throat for a second, burning it. She had continued taking them post Beaumont even though, as she'd told Sherri, she had "absolutely no intentions of screwing anyone."

"Atta girl," Sherri had said, "Keep taking 'em. You should always be ready for spectacular opportunities—but check him for disease first.

"You mean AIDS?"

"Sheesh, girl," Sherri said, shaking her head in wonder, "only homos, heroin addicts and hemophiliacs get AIDS. I'm talking about the more mundane diseases like herpes."

Joanna couldn't imagine how she would check for mundane diseases, but having no immediate prospect in mind, she hadn't asked. She knew she would never have to check Dan.

That thought embarrassed her. She felt ashamed of thinking of him that way and shook her head hard.

She decided now, pacing faster, that the pill helped her keep clean—not foul and certainly not fecund. Pleased with the order developing in her solitary life, she turned away from the river and headed toward court. There she saw Sherri leaning against a column smiling up at Ricardo. Joanna stared at him, entranced. Something about him pulled at her. She decided he had the animal magnetism of Beaumont but twice as much class.

According to Sherri, he was half-Italian and half-Puerto Rican, but with blonde hair. There must have been a Viking in the woodpile, Joanna thought, and approached slowly.

"Hi, Jo." Sherri had seen her and beckoned. "This is Ricardo Alioto," she said, turning to him. "And this is my fellow court slave, Joanna Archer."

"Here's your chance." Joanna heard her say to him under her breath.

She wondered what Sherri meant by that. Ricardo was gazing so intently into her eyes she had to lower her eyelids or faint. At least that's what she thought.

"I'm happy to meet you—finally," he said. He surveyed her. "I've heard interesting things about you. Of course, Sherri neglected to tell me how very lovely you are." He took Joanna's hand, turned it over and kissed her palm.

Joanna felt the kiss traverse her body like a high-speed train.

"I guess I hadn't noticed how pretty she is." Sherri laughed.

"Oh yes you did," he said with the look of a conspirator. He turned to Joanna. "So you're a reporter, too. Do you like it?"

"It's interesting most of the time," she answered, aware of the mouse in her voice.

"Man, I'd hate it." He studied her face, caressing it with his eyes. "I prefer direct experience. Hell, court reporters just get to record what people like me get to live." He took Joanna's hand again. "Forgive me. I don't mean to put you down."

Joanna felt a rush of shame. He was right, of course. She'd lived under her father's thumb until she made her big move—over to Beaumont's thumb. Now, finally, she was free to live—to have direct experiences on her own—and yet?

"Hey, Ricardo," Sherri said, "the curtain's going up on this old courthouse. See you later, Jo."

Joanna moved away from them, backwards.

"If you want to experience life first hand, Joanna," Ricardo called to her, "let me know." He flashed a smile and turned around. Triumphant?

She watched him dip Sherri back over his arm and kiss her. Joanna's lips quivered. Later, while waiting in court, she wondered if she had the guts to go out with a man like that.

Joanna went to her bank in a nearby shopping mall during the lunch recess. As she stood in line, she looked down at a lower level where patrons of a Japanese restaurant lined up for sushi. A tall blond man in a cream silk suit stood at the bar with his back to Joanna. His arms rested on the shoulders of two women, one blonde, and one brunette. Joanna felt a jealous twinge in her stomach. The man turned the women around and glided with them to a table. The women looked like fashion models. The man held the chairs of each in turn. It was Ricardo.

He glanced up. Recognizing Joanna, he winked at her. She felt her skin tingle. Pretending she hadn't seen him, she turned away, furious with him, ashamed of herself. She spent the rest of the day trying to forget him, but his image persisted, competing with Dan's.

CHAPTER SIX

Early Thursday the morning sunlight danced across two large puddles in front of the courthouse. Joanna stopped to watch. A taxi forded the puddles with a delicate splash. A tall, thin woman emerged from the taxi. Slightly stooped, she appeared to be almost six feet tall. She wore her fading red hair in a bun. Thin wisps strayed from it and blew about her face. An equally tall and portly old man arose from his seat on the marble steps to meet her. His face was large and square with deep set brown eyes. He sported a navy yachting cap. They both moved as if they knew exactly where they belonged. Joanna admired their strolling approach to one another. She guessed they were in their late fifties or early sixties.

"Christ, Lucille," she heard the man say as she approached them, "I just don't know what to do. While trying to help Dan we may damage his case, and for some strange reason he doesn't want us to mention Pemaquid to the press . . . never did understand why he took her body there."

"Now Ralph, you do too understand," the lady replied in a clear voice redolent of class. "You know how that scene haunted him."

Joanna blinked. *What scene?* They had to be Lucille and Ralph, Dan's hurricane friends, his only family. She slowed her pace to remain behind them, smiling behind her hair. Dan had said they weren't married to each other, yet they acted as if they'd been together for years.

"Well, you're right. I guess I do understand. And he does have strong arms—for a judge," Ralph said. "I oughtta know."

They climbed to the top of the stairs and leaned against a column. Joanna hovered, pretending to read a book. *What did he mean, strong arms?*

"Look at those buzzards up there," Ralph said, pointing to the Mesopotamian looking cap on the building where several buzzards perched. "Funny, aren't they?"

"Courthouse groupies," Lucille said glancing up. "Tell me, Ralph, how's your sweet wife?"

"Ha. You never did like Rosalie. Why the sudden concern?"

"That's true, I don't particularly like her. But people do learn to tolerate one another, you know."

"You never liked anything I did." Ralph shifted his massive body and lowered his head. "Y'gave me a helluva what-for about going into dentistry. Remember? Always looked down your nose at dentists."

"Now Ralph, that's not true—never has been. Besides, I like the way you take care of my teeth." She smiled at him and touched his hand. Her teeth were long and youthfully white. "I just don't admire the way you live—million dollar house on the beach next door to stars whose names you drop. All fame and no character. Those are the people Rosalie likes. Oil slicks, good for nothing but shining up the seaweed."

"Ha! Your picture is plastered in art mags around the world. You're the famous one." He put his arm on her shoulder. "At least in your field."

"Does Rosalie invite dinner guests who even know there is such a field?"

"You got me there." Ralph laughed a deep belly laugh.

"You're not a famous dentist." Lucille's blue eyes registered mirth. "Few are, come to think of it." Sobering, she continued, "Dan's not famous, and I'm only half-famous, and in a dubious branch of the arts. Fame goes with the exotic people more often than with the thorough ones." She paused, brushed away wisps of hair that drifted across her forehead. "I'll give my movie stars a dash of panache, but I want my doctor and dentist to read the research regularly, and I want my judge to be eminently reasonable and fair—even against my wishes."

They climbed up all the steps while she spoke. Joanna moved up a few steps behind. *Wow, what a mouthful!*

"C'mon, old girl, let's figure out what we can do for our buddy." Ralph put his left arm around Lucille's waist.

They entered the courthouse. Joanna followed them, hungry for anything they might say about Dan. They all fascinated her, this hurricane group that had included Dan's wife. They were so different from people she'd always hung out with. They acted as if they had a right to be wherever they were at all times. She envied them for that and wanted to discover how they got that kind of confidence.

She stayed back in the hall after they entered the courtroom wondering why she was so torn about not seeing Dan, why she wanted anything to do with any man, why she needed a man so badly.

"Hi, Babe," cut through her thoughts.

Her neck bristled. She berated herself for relaxing her guard, for not realizing he would eventually come looking for her.

"Hell, Joanna, ain't you gonna say hello?"

Feeling his presence, a hovering storm cloud, she took two deliberate steps forward before turning to look at him. Her knees felt weak. As unobtrusively as possible, she leaned against a column.

"Hello Beaumont," she said. She thought she saw the buzzards inching lower—toward them.

He closed in on her, tilted his head to the side and flashed a boyish grin.

"I miss you, kiddo," he said. "When you coming home?" His black eyes seemed to drink in her body—part of his old line.

Never.

"I have to go to work now," she said stiffly.

"I know. Just wanted to see you for a minute—make sure you're okay and still beautiful." He jumped down two steps below her and looked up at her with the supplication of an altar boy. "I'm really sorry about the fingernail. Didn't know it was glued to yours." He reached up and grabbed her hand. "You've given up the phony nails, I see. I didn't mean for you to. Don't know what got into me that night. Hurricane or something." He paused, staring up at her. "Can you forgive me?"

"Shit, shit," she whispered to herself as she moved toward the courtroom. Her heart pounded and her mouth went completely dry. She turned and faced him. "No," she said.

"No?" The word barely contained his angry scream. "No?" he repeated, whispering. "I can understand, I guess. Jesus, it's not like I knock you around regularly. Never hurt you before. Shit, that Joe Pietro bangs the bejeesus out of Cathy every week and she worships the bastard."

"No."

"Maybe I shoulda—no, I guess not. Still, I don't want to hurt you. The fingernail—that was the first time."

"Not the first time." She forced herself to exhale.

"When did I ever hurt you before?" He sighed and sat down.

"Fourth of July, 1982." The words rushed out without inflection.

"Christ, what a memory," he said. "Where were we?"

"Daytona Beach." She paced three steps from the column then back. "Your family picnic."

"Hey, all I did was pull you by the arm."

"Broke my ribs."

"Jesus, one fucking mistake and you remember." Beaumont stood. "I bet you don't remember the time you wrecked my new motorcycle."

"I wrecked it. Ha."

"Yeah. You did. Chasing after me in it."

"Well, I got mighty tired of you slamming out the door saying you're gonna get laid." Joanna tossed back her hair and glared at him.

"Just words." He smiled. "You know that." Then he took her hand and said, "I'm really sorry, Jo. I miss you." Tears filled his eyes.

"Never mind, Beaumont." Joanna felt herself slipping into his web again. "I'll forget, eventually."

He rushed toward her, arms outstretched. She backed away.

"I have to go to work now," she said and this time turned her back on him.

"Sure, Babe. Where're you staying? I'll pick you up for dinner. Classy restaurant, my treat."

"No."

"What do you mean? You seeing someone else?"

"No. I'm not seeing anyone and I still say no. It's over, Beaumont." As she said it, she didn't quite believe it.

He grabbed her hand again, tight. She feared he'd crush the bones.

"Okay, girl," he said, relaxing his grip slightly. "I know you need some space. I'll grant you that. Just like to see you now and then—have a roll in the hay—like you want it—and a home cooked meal. You know, one of your casseroles. Beans and hot dogs get mighty old." He grinned. "Where're you staying?"

She pulled her hand free and reached for the door.

"So don't tell me. Your fucking mother will tell me, you know. She's on my side." He caught up with Joanna and clutched her shoulders.

"Beau—we're in the courthouse."

"So what?" His voice echoed down the corridor.

Joanna wanted to dissolve into the walls. Even as she stood in abject fear of him, she realized her deep embarrassment for the first time—that her choice of husband reflected on her—that she had had a choice after all—that she still did have a choice.

"Beaumont go away and leave me alone. You don't need me."

"Baby, I know I don't need you." He squeezed her shoulders till they almost touched her ears. "I'm obligated. You're my wife, dammit, and you're gonna give me your address so I don't have to tail you like a fucking dick. Got it?"

Joanna glanced around the empty corridor. Where was everyone? Ralph and Lucille had disappeared. Where? The judge would be in chambers, but where were the bailiff, lawyers, jury? Beaumont could deck her right here and walk out the doors scot-free. Fear careened the length of her spine.

The sound of approaching footsteps made her try to wrench away. She saw Dan coming toward them.

"Good morning, Joanna," he said in his calm, strong voice. "I presume this is your husband." To Beaumont he said, "I suggest you let her go."

"Stay out of this, old man." Beaumont said, but he released his grip.

"Go on now, Joanna. You need to be in court." Dan moved between Joanna and Beaumont, facing Beaumont.

Joanna backed away, heading doe the next entrance to the courtroom, but stepped behind a column to watch Dan close in on Beaumont. She remembered how he had squared off against the kid in the cathedral.

"It would be a good idea if you left now," Dan said to Beaumont.

"That's my wife," Beaumont growled.

Joanna's skin crawled. She realized that Beaumont didn't want her, just the idea of her. His wife—in a short nightgown.

"You don't own her," Dan said. "Let her go."

She watched Beaumont clench and unclench his fists. He rolled on the balls of his feet. "Who the hell are you?" he asked Dan. "What are you to her?"

"Just a neighbor and friend."

How I wish, Joanna thought. How I wish he could be my friend.

"How good a friend?" Beaumont nodded and grinned with his lips only. "You keeping her? And where do you live? West Miami? Coral Gables?"

"Let her go," Dan said.

Joanna wanted to throw her arms around Dan. She glanced at Beaumont and wondered what she'd ever seen in him. Handsome is as handsome does, Aunt Martha used to say. No wonder Dan's so handsome.

"Answer my question, old man." Beaumont slammed his fist into his open palm. "Where do you live?"

Steadfast, silent, Dan stared at him. Joanna watched, awestruck.

"C'mon, Man, out with it. What's your fucking address?"

"I might remind you, Mr. Archer, that you are standing in a court of law." Dan adjusted his tie and put his hands in his pants' pockets.

Beaumont glanced around uneasily, shrugged his shoulders and walked away

"I've got work to do, mister," he said over his shoulder, "but I'll be back, y'hear? And you'd better get out of my way."

Dan followed him to the door. Beaumont seemed to shrink in size.

"You still here?" Dan seemed surprised to see Joanna.

"Sorry," she said smiling broadly. "I didn't obey you." Sobering, she asked, "You didn't tell him where I live, did you?"

"Why would I do that?" he said, proffering his arm.

"I'd sell my soul for your kind of strength." Rather than take his arm with hers, she touched it with awe and stared at him in silence. His presence, she suddenly realized, had thoroughly erased stray thoughts of Ricardo. Laughing, she said, "but then I'd just be selling my soul for a soul. Guess I'll have to develop my own."

He nodded. His full white mustache smiled. The bailiff called Dan's name.

Joanna opened the door to the courtroom and entered. Looking back, she saw Dan watching her. She wished she understood the look in his eyes—or the mysteries of her own heart, for that matter. Would she be able to resist?

CHAPTER SEVEN

That evening Dan wandered through his apartment while waiting for Ralph and Lucille to pick him up for dinner. He thought his place needed some décor. He'd given away most of the stuff from their house in Coral Gables, but he still had the paintings and a few of Lucille's photos. He thought he should hang them now that he'd given up urgent control of his life.

He imagined Ralph commenting on his kitchen.

"Empty, isn't it?" Ralph would say. "Seems awfully bare. No food processors, blenders, espresso machine—just an old drip coffee maker and one pot holder. Jeez, I could do a root canal in this kitchen."

Dan guessed his cupboard *was* bare. Maria had been Bev's maid in Coral Gables and did all the chopping by hand the last two years of Bev's life. Dan hadn't wanted a maid. It didn't feel right, but Bev had a fit whenever he even entered her kitchen and then another when she tried to cook. Now, he smiled, remembering that Ralph had a household staff and no need for kitchen appliances either. It's called manual labor

He poured a glass of California Cabernet, took it out to the veranda and sat beside his thriving birds-of-paradise. They looked so inviting of conversation he put down his magazine. He missed Joanna with a strange longing even though he barely knew her. Her image, bent over the recorder in the courtroom, thick hair falling forward over her beautiful eyes and high cheekbones, haunted him. His shook his head now to dispel it and relax into the pleasure of being with Ralph and Lucille again. He'd always loved Lucille, but he had once hated the best male friend of his life.

Either we question our perceptions he thought, or we're imprisoned by them. No wonder Buddha is laughing in so many of his statues. When we give up our assumptions as he did, give up our convictions, our definitions of reality, we're never bored and are eager to see what happens next. Curiosity as salvation?

He stood, shivered with excitement at the thought. *I can look forward to my trial, like watching a good movie where you can't predict the end. Ralph, can I convince you?* He sat down, closed his eyes and relived the day he met Ralph just before the hurricane in Pemaquid, Maine that kept them going back there year after year. It was better than anything on TV right now.

*   *   *

The cook came into the lounge of the Port Clyde Inn and beckoned Dan to the kitchen. "Young gentlemen out here to see you. Wants a job."

Dan opened the door to the back porch and looked up at a large young man with deep-set brown eyes that shifted back and forth. *Suspicion or fear?*

"I'm sorry," Dan said, "we don't need any help now."

"My name's Ralph Conscetti," he said, extending his hand toward Dan. "I'm a good handyman—can fix anything, and I'll work for food."

Dan shook his hand and noticed Ralph's fingers were small for such a large man, though his grip was strong. A little too strong for comfort. He guessed Ralph's age at about twenty.

"What the heck," Dan said without looking at him, "c'mon in. I don't have any work, but I'll give you some leftovers when I finish with the guests."

"I'm going off duty now," the cook said to Dan. "My folks are expecting me tonight. Maybe this here gentleman can clean up."

"Sure. Go," Dan said. "We'll manage. Here, Conscetti, sit at this table. I'll be back after a while. Make sure you stay right here."

"Thanks. I'll be right here." Ralph sat at the end of the long rectangular table.

Dan returned to the dining room with misgivings. The guy was too big to mess with. Still, he couldn't just kick him out for being hungry. *Dad, what would you do with him?* As soon as he asked he knew his father would tell him to just hold his ground.

Dan returned to the kitchen after he'd served the last round of brandy and banked the fire, Ralph's height made him look as if he were standing, yet he sat where Dan had suggested, flipping through an old issue of Life Magazine. Dan strode over to the stove, piled a plate with leftover mashed potatoes, succotash and chicken fricassee, and set it before him. Ralph nodded his thanks and began to eat, chewing each mouthful several times before swallowing.

Dan sat at the opposite end of the table and watched, fascinated, wary. The guy was no bum, obviously; he'd had some training in etiquette. Also, he had a ruddy complexion that looked Scottish. Only the deep brown eyes matched his Italian name. Dan sat at the end of the ten-foot rectangular table and studied Ralph in the glare of a naked light bulb that swayed from a cord overhead.

"How did you get this job? Ain't you kinda young for it?" Ralph asked, watching Dan in return.

"Used to come here every summer with the folks, so I know the owners."

"Oh." He resumed eating. "I guess the state of Maine isn't exactly known for its opportunities."

"Why're you way up here?" Dan popped his knuckles. "Sounds like a Jersey accent. Where're you from?"

"I'd rather not say."

Dan stretched, but his jaw felt tight. Guy could be one of those wacky murderers that hide out in the woods. He wanted to move, but held his ground and stared at Ralph.

"Hey, are you on the lam?" Dan asked.

"Naw." Ralph chewed his last mouthful ten times before he swallowed.

"Trouble with a girl?" Dan didn't believe him, but it seemed safer to keep the conversation light.

Suddenly the kitchen door banged open. Dan thought the wind had come up again, but it was Lucille Grimm stumbling in—a flash of red hair rippling above the clownish image of long skinny limbs going in several directions without quite causing a collapse.

"Sorry to intrude," she said. "I was just looking around."

Bored with adults, Dan figured. He stood as tall as he could and welcomed her to their table, admiring her. He'd never seen such a tall girl, or such a beautiful head of curly red hair. Her breasts, though set low on her chest, were perfectly rounded.

"You're Lucille Grimm, right? I'm Daniel Lawrence and this here's Ralph Conscetti."

"How do you do?" Ralph said, tilting his head slightly to the right. He stood with his napkin tucked into his shirt collar and lightened the room with his smile. His teeth, though large and bright white, had little jagged edges.

"Care to join us?" Dan asked, pointing to a third cane-backed chair. He noticed an urgency about her that piqued his curiosity.

"Oh no," Lucille said, "I mustn't—don't mean to interfere."

"Stay," Ralph interrupted harshly as if irritated with her.

"Yes, please stay," Dan said, "and have some cake. He held the chair for her and kept his eye on Ralph.

Lucille smiled, softening the angles of her face. "Well, if you insist, I will have a small piece of cake.

"After all," Dan said, "you sent your dessert to the spittoon earlier."

She lowered her eyes. Dan watched two lovely pink carnations emerge at the tops of her cheeks.

She nearly missed the chair as she sat, but quickly righted herself. She clutched a large black camera in her left hand that could easily keep her off balance.

Ralph asked, "How old are you?"

"Almost sixteen."

"G'wan," he said. "When did you turn fifteen, last week?"

She ignored the question. Dan glared at Ralph. *Just wasn't polite to ask a lady's age. What's with this guy?* Dan placed a clean saucer in front of Lucille and pushed the cake toward her.

"Cut what you want from the center," he said. "The edges are dry."

Lucille positioned the camera dead center on her lap and reached for the knife. It dropped with a clatter on her plate then bounced off her camera onto the floor. With a quick thrust, she retrieved it and re-centered the camera.

"What's that, a camera?" Ralph asked.

"Yes," she said, patting it. "I'm going to be a famous photographer."

"Why?" Dan asked, bouncing a piece of the angel food cake onto her plate, "Why would you want to be someone who has to arrange a bunch of school kids for class pictures?"

"I'm not talking about that," she replied seriously. "I'm going to be a photographic artist, *and* make a living. It's a brand new art. Ever hear of Steiglitz? Someday I'll be in museums, too. Listen." She pulled a dog-eared pamphlet out of her pocket and began reading aloud about aperture and zone systems.

Ralph rolled his eyes and barely suppressed a burp. She read on and on, almost putting them to sleep. Dan held back the kind of laughter that builds up in church. He didn't dare look at Ralph.

"Well, if that ain't spiffy-durant," Ralph said. He turned to Dan, smiling. "Imagine, a girl making her own living from snapshots."

"Women have been making their livings for centuries—maybe not in her social class," Dan said. He got up to open the window over the sink. Conscetti made him nervous; fresh salt air might cut the tension. "Looks like we won't get that hurricane after all. It's calm as a baby's breath out there, and just as sweet." He sat down again. These two strangers in his kitchen were adversaries over nothing. What happened to Ralph's manners?

"Here," Dan said to Lucille, "try the cake."

She lifted the fork to her mouth then replaced it without taking a bite. With a sudden jerk of her left arm, she clasped Dan's shoulder so hard he felt a stabbing pain. Her pale blue eyes darkened.

"I need help," she whispered.

"Be glad to help," Ralph said, stretching all six foot three upward. He stopped chewing and flexed his muscles, casting a huge shadow on the far wall that moved with the swaying light. Dan stared at it.

"Promise you won't tell?" Lucille asked, looking at each in turn.

Ralph crossed his heart. Dan nodded.

She leaned forward. "My parents are up here looking for Gus. He's our butler—or was—ever since I can remember. Actually, he's my Yorick.

"Your what?" Dan asked.

"Yorick was Hamlet's servant," Ralph said to him. "A skull in the play."

"Anyway," Lucille continued, ignoring the interruption, "a few months ago he told me he was going to run away and become a communist. He said something about eating at a green table and traveling with other fellows." She bowed her head; tears flowed at angles over her cheekbones. "He was my friend." She hugged the camera. "Now they think he stole my mother's emerald necklace. I know he didn't because I saw the new maid take it."

Ralph sat down and resumed chewing. Dan wondered about him and thought Lucille shouldn't be so trusting of him.

"Didn't you tell your parents?" asked Ralph.

"Sure, but they don't believe me. They have it in for Gus—say he's a bad influence on me." She turned toward Dan. "He's my friend. I don't care about politics—I don't really know what a communist is."

Dan felt himself beginning to love her.

"I have a snapshot," she said to Ralph, "of the maid in my mother's room the day of the theft, but it's too fuzzy to make out. The light wasn't good enough in the hall. I hid behind a door and took her picture, but it looks like it could have been anyone. I suppose I should've said something at the time, but I wanted hard evidence." She looked at Dan. "Someday they'll invent a way to take pictures in bad light without a flash. Maybe I will." She rubbed the sides of her camera as if to imbue it with magic light.

Ralph rolled his eyes. Dan suppressed a smile. This long legged kid sure was fascinating.

"Anyway," Lucille said, swiping at her cheeks with a napkin, "my folks don't believe me and they're going after Gus."

"I'm not sure how we can help." Dan pulled a pencil out of his pocket and began doodling on cashier's slip. He wished he could draw better and capture the beauty of her jaw line. "The problem seems to be proving to your folks that Gus is innocent. Right?"

"That's impossible. I need you to help me warn Gus," Lucille said and blew her nose into a lace edged handkerchief. "See, he doesn't know about the necklace so naturally doesn't think anyone's looking for him. My father says he's around here someplace, but doesn't know where. I do."

"Do what?" Ralph asked.

"I know where he is."

"And where's that?" Dan asked, warming to the subject.

"St. Georges Island, just south of here, Lucille whispered. "He's staying with some fellow there. Guess they'll travel when they get back to the mainland."

"Well let's go." Ralph stood, casting his huge shadow again. "We'll put a kybosh to your father's plan. How do we get a boat?"

"Wait a minute, Ralph," Dan said. "Let's think this through. We need a plan and then a boat. I know where to borrow a boat. I think we can leave mid morning if the hurricane has gone to sea and the water's calm enough. You're sure he's on St. Georges Island?"

Lucille nodded.

"Okay, let's plan."

The cane chair creaked as Ralph sat down heavily.

Dan stood up to get a clean piece of paper and brought it to the table. He felt excitement crawling up his back. He'd never met a communist before. Leaning his head close to theirs, he slapped the table.

"This is history in the making," he announced. "At least our history," he added, feeling slightly foolish.

*   *   *

Of course, that all happened before the hurricane swept them overboard, before Dan attacked Ralph and bit his hand. Now he looked forward to re-connecting with his old friends and grinned when the doorbell rang.

CHAPTER EIGHT

The next day Ralph and Lucille arrived at the courthouse just as a chilly gust swept through the outer corridor of the courthouse, ferrying in dry leaves, and gum wrappers. Dan shivered and donned his suit coat, creased from being bundled over his arm since breakfast.

"Is that Monroe—your so-called counsel for the defense?" Ralph asked. He frowned at Dan and then peered into the courtroom "Jesus, Dan where'd you find the innocent?"

Monroe turned toward them and waved, blue eyes glinting behind rimless glasses, red mustache dominating his narrow face.

"Our innocent here is, or soon will be, the best defense lawyer in town," Dan said. "Grant you, he doesn't look the part."

"I'll say! He looks wet behind the ears," Lucille said. "How'd you come by this high opinion of him?" She shifted the strap of her big black purse to her left shoulder.

"Well, it's like this." Dan squeezed her hand. "I've been arbitrating cases here for New York acquaintances for the past couple of years and I've gotten to know the folk who work the courthouse. Of all the barristers around, Monroe has the most incisive mind. He's taciturn and calm. Makes the rest of us look garrulous in comparison." He smiled. "Yes, he's a good defense man—not because he gets acquittals—but because, well, because he's honest." Dan realized how vapid he must sound. *What is it about Monroe?*

"Honest," Ralph said. "I should have known. And that makes a good defense lawyer?"

"Conch-shell Conscetti, you go to hell." Dan laughed and socked Ralph's shoulder.

Ralph returned with a cuff to Dan's right shoulder.

White man's high five, Dan thought.

Lucille grabbed their arms. "Dammit, Man tell us why you hired Monroe. You need the best lawyer in town."

"Okay," Dan said, sobering. "I'll try. Monroe and I lunched together regularly—had some pretty good talks." Dan let his thoughts wander to Bev. He saw and felt Bev's fiery anger, contrasting with

Monroe's, eager, intense, yet calm presence. He smiled at Lucille. "Monroe's the kind of passionate man who can temper his passion with reason without killing the fire. When I try to be rational, I tend to lose all passion. You'll agree when you get to know him."

He saw Monroe beckoning, kissed Lucille, shook Ralph's hand, and slowly made his way to that unfamiliar seat facing the bench.

Courtroom 12 seemed smaller than the others. The press took up most of the seats. The prevailing scent of wet wood came from years of Florida humidity working on the oak railings. The bailiff ordered everyone to rise for the judge. Dan almost said, "Please be seated," forgetting he was not the presiding magistrate. Instead, Judge Ogasaki, a petite, ageless woman with sleek black hair, uttered the simple phrase that Dan felt reverberating through years of faith in jurisprudence.

She nodded at Dan. He returned the greeting, feeling strangely at ease. He had no idea how this would turn out, yet he couldn't deny feeling a little smug about his choice of defense counsel. Dan was sure that Monroe, in his mild, inimitable way, could pull the truth out of everyone, including the prosecutor, Jerome Ansletter, who hovered over all, shoulders rounding down his height of five or six inches over six feet.

Dan had the impression, watching Ansletter, of a eucalyptus tree with peeling bark. Dan adjusted his bifocals and squinted through the top, discovering to his amusement that the peeling bark was actually a suit coat with brown and tan stripes in an abstract design.

Judge Ogasaki knocked once lightly with her gavel. "This court is now in session—the State versus Daniel Briggs Lawrence, who is charged with the first degree murder of his wife, Beverly Duvoir Lawrence, on April 5, 1983. Is the State ready?"

"Yes, Your Honor." Ansletter stretched the vowels as if singing the opening line of an operatic aria.

"The defense?"

"Yes, Your Honor," Monroe replied in a monotone.

"The defense claims no murder was committed," Ogasaki said, looking at the jury,

"that it was an acceleration of natural death, an assist to suicide, to comply with the wish of the deceased." She paused and looked at the prosecutor. "The state hopes to prove its case that the defendant should be found guilty of murder in the first degree—perpetrated from a premeditated design. The burden of proof, of course, is upon the state which must show, beyond a reasonable doubt, those facts that prove all the elements of an offense against it." She took a sip of water. "The estimated length of this case is one week—four court days. You may now make your opening statement, Mr. Ansletter."

Ansletter approached the jury slowly. He leaned forward from the waist. The cowlicks sprouting in his dark brown hair added a comic contrast to his deep, stage-trained voice.

"Her honor has briefly described the issue here," he said. "I intend to prove beyond a reasonable doubt, that the defendant's actions subsequent to the murder taint his defense and that his offense is clearly against the state—premeditated murder."

Dan surveyed the jury. Monroe had fought long and hard to select a jury of people old enough to have ailing or dying parents and thus have some empathy. And, of course, no Catholics. But, you can only go so far. In the second row, a gray-haired man with deep brown eyes whose mother suffered from multiple sclerosis seemed particularly understanding. In front of him sat a tiny, prune faced woman with tight white curls who sat poised for taking notes. Her stated opposition to the women's movement had no direct bearing on Dan's case, yet it worried him some. Why would a woman object to women's freedom? But the tall, thin woman to her left, with an intelligent, softly lined face, offset her. This woman was a columnist for a weekly newspaper who focused on the problems of aging. He suspected she was not limited to so literal a mind as the curly headed one beside her.

He glanced at Joanna huddled over her recorder. He couldn't catch her eye. He smiled inwardly at her idea of selling a soul for a soul. She reminded him of a sturdy geranium in an orchid garden, a small red geranium peeking out from a bower of delicate cymbidiums. One day he'd tell her that fear was only an inch thick. One day he'd let himself need her. That thought surprised him.

"Premeditated murder, ladies and gentlemen," Ansletter said, "is first degree murder, a crime against the state, against mankind, and against God." He returned to his table in a flurry of papers.

Dan felt annoyed with himself for letting his mind wander so long. What had Ansletter said before that final statement? Concentration, he knew, was the key to winning anything.

"My client has pleaded not guilty," Monroe said as he ambled over to the jury with his hands in his pants pockets, "to any and all possible offenses against the state. The testimony will show that he committed an act of mercy at his wife's request. She was terminally ill, suffering the slow degeneration of Alzheimer's disease. She had no hope of recovery. He committed no crime—only the ultimate act of mercy." He smiled at the jury. "Forgive me for reminding you of what the bard said through Portia in The Merchant of Venice, 'The quality of mercy is not strain'd, it droppeth as the gentle rain from heaven upon the place beneath: it is twice blest; it blesseth him that gives and him that takes'" He lowered his eyes. "It behooves us all to be twice blessed."

Dan glanced back at Ralph and Lucille. He knew they'd have to smile since they were always quoting Shakespeare They'd wanted a more aggressive lawyer for his defense, but they'd soon see that soft-spoken, literate Monroe was at the same time cunning and tough. Ansletter was no more than bombast in comparison. Even now, calling the coroner as his first witness with broad gestures and booming voice, Ansletter's theatrics would be laughable if the trial were not so very real and personal.

The bailiff swore in a ramrod of a tall man, the coroner from Maine. pHe recounted the sequence of events of April 6, 1983 with the taciturnity of a long-term resident of Maine. A fisherman had hauled in the body of Beverly Duvoir Lawrence on that day, two miles south of Pemaquid. The coroner discovered her name from an inscription on her wedding ring, informed authorities, and performed an autopsy.

"And you determined the time of her death to be when?" Ansletter asked.

"Early to mid morning on April 5th."

"And cause of death, drowning?"

"No. Barbiturates combined with alcohol."

"Thank you. No further questions." The coroner stepped down and Ansletter called the pilot to the stand.

The pilot—Dan had met the young man only once before, on that day when everything was bathed in bright light and time had no rhythm. Today he looked ordinary, smaller, less heroic with skin pebbled from acne. He spoke with a tight voice as he answered Ansletter's questions.

"Yes sir. It was about nine in the morning when Judge Lawrence had me paged," the pilot said. "I was hanging around the airport trying to decide what to do. I wanted to fly—antsy, you know, but couldn't because I was dead broke from making a payment on my Cessna." He glanced quickly at Dan and rubbed his palms on his thighs.

"Go on."

"So anyways, I get on the horn and the judge here asks me if I'll fly him and his wife—who was too sick to fly commercially—to Maine right away."

"And—for the record—what day was that?" Ansletter hovered near Joanna.

"April 5, 1983." The pilot paused; the prosecutor nodded for him to continue. "So he asks me what I charge. I tell him seven fifty and without a moment's hesitation, he says okay. A stroke of luck, you know."

"Didn't this hasty charter make you suspicious?" Ansletter stepped back as if to get a total view of the man.

"No sir." The pilot's face flushed. "I just thought my luck was changing. Besides, he called himself a judge."

Dan caught a flicker of Judge Ogasaki's brief smile.

"Describe to the court what happened next," Ansletter said, projecting his voice toward the rear of the small courtroom.

"Well, we agree to meet at the airfield. I tell him where my Cessna is, and pretty soon they drive up in this black Lincoln. He pulls a wheelchair outa the trunk, shakes my hand, and proceeds to lift his wife into the wheelchair." The pilot glanced at Dan briefly and then continued. "She slumps forward."

"You didn't know she was dead?" asked Ansletter with his bushy eyebrows raised to inverted V's."

"No. You see lots of folks asleep in wheelchairs down here." He paused again and tugged at his shirt collar. "Anyway, he said he didn't need any help getting her on the plane so I went inside to get flight clearance. By the time I got back, he was sitting there beside her and holding her hand. Gives me the creeps now, but at the time I thought they made a handsome couple even with the wife in a wheelchair so young."

"A dead body's hard to ignore and even harder to lift." Ansletter faced the jury, eyebrows still raised in mock surprise, as if stuck there. "Didn't you see him struggle to get her onto the plane?"

"No, I didn't."

"And where did you land?"

"Brunswick, Maine."

"When?" Ansletter peered at the white haired woman in the jury.

"A quarter to three in the afternoon." The pilot started to slouch and then sat up straight. Dan felt sweat gliding down his back. He didn't dare look at Ralph and Lucille. Would they understand?

"What did the defendant do when you landed?" Ansletter asked the pilot.

"He said again that he didn't want any help. We climbed out of the plane and he paid me in twenties. While I was counting the bills, he lifted her off. Last time I saw them he was wheeling her toward the taxi stand."

"And you didn't think paying you in cash was suspicious?"

"Like I said, he was a judge—even looked like one."

"No further questions," Monroe said and the pilot stood down. Dan felt again the muscle strain lifting her onto and off that airplane, carrying her to the rocks at Pemaquid where they landed in that hurricane the year they all met, where they'd returned to every year since, where Buddy drowned.

Monroe nudged him. The prosecutor was calling the Lawrence's maid to the stand.

"Ah—Maria." Dan whispered. He hadn't seen the short, plump maid since he'd sold the Coral Gables house. "Will she help?"

"Yes," Monroe answered. "You'll see."

Ansletter asked her to describe for the court what she had witnessed on April 5, 1983.

"It was my day off," she said in a gravel voice. She avoided Dan's eyes by looking directly at the jury. "I couldn't find the tickets to the dog races. My boyfriend would kill me—sorry, just a figure of speech—so I had to find them. I thought they'd spilled out of my purse on the kitchen counter and—"

"Objection," Monroe stood and spoke as if he were commenting on the weather. "Witness should answer questions and avoid narration."

"Objection sustained," Judge Osaki said, "Please direct your questions, Mr. Ansletter."

Monroe sat down. Ansletter cleared his throat. Maria looked down at her lap. Dan felt a flutter of fear and reminded himself to think like Buddha, to anticipate with interest whatever happens next in this enduring mystery called life.

"What made you think the tickets were there?" Ansletter asked. "What kind of purse was it and did you see it spill?"

"Oh it's an ordinary red purse with three sections—"

"Objection," Monroe said, standing. "Relevance."

"I can prove relevance," Ansletter boomed, glaring at Monroe.

"Objection sustained," Ogasaki said. "Counsel proceed with the witness. Forget the purse."

"Yes ma'am," Ansletter said and then whirled toward the jury. "Maria, did you see the Lawrences?" he asked.

"Not right away."

"When did you see them?"

"After I searched the kitchen." She paused, glanced at Dan, and then continued. "I din't want to disturb the Lawrences so I din't tell them I was there."

"And what did you see?"

"I saw Judge Lawrence in the dining room pour from a bottle of vodka into a glass and hand it to Mrs. Lawrence" She rubbed her eyes, smearing her mascara.

"Vodka," Ansletter hissed. Then he turned to the jury and repeated, "Vodka." Raising his arms like a Russian soldier, he yelled, "Did he make a toast to her death?"

"No sir."

"What size glass?"

"A tumbler, water glass?" Maria made it a question. Her eyes looked like they'd pop out of her head.

"Did he fill it?"

"Yes."

Ansletter waved toward the jury. "No further questions."

Yeah, sure, Buddha, Dan thought, *I can look forward to my trial, like watching a good movie where you can't predict the ending. This one I can predict.*

"My God, this is awful," Dan whispered to Monroe. "How the hell can she help?"

"Don't worry," Monroe said. "it's not as bad as you think. The jury has to know what you did. Later they'll know why. We can use Maria to prove that your motive came out of a sense of duty. She'll be our last witness."

Ansletter returned to his seat. The judge looked at Monroe.

"No questions, your honor," Monroe said.

Judge Ogasaki then excused the witness and adjourned the session for the day in a voice so soft it startled Dan. He glanced around the courtroom and saw Joanna rolling her tapes and packing up her machine. Their eyes met briefly. He wondered what she thought of him now. *And the movie rolls on.*

He left to join Monroe, Lucille and Ralph at an inconspicuous Cuban restaurant near the courthouse, wishing he could dine alone with Joanna.

*   *   *

"Black beans and rice—good stuff." Ralph pored over the menu, rubbing his palms. "I don't dare eat it when Rosalie's around. She thinks it's—"

Lucille touched the back of Ralph's hand, quieting him.

"Please explain this trial to me, Dan," she said. "I'm quite befuddled, and damn worried."

Dan wondered if she meant shocked. Surprised he actually helped Bev commit suicide?

"Why the hell did you take her to Pemaquid?" Ralph asked.

"Right." said Lucille. "That's the part Ansletter will use—"

"I don't think I can explain," Dan said. He felt a sheer curtain or veil floating around his head. 'Shoot, Ralph, I just had to."

Monroe closed his menu. Ralph sat still, his breathing audible. Dan took a deep breath and exhaled as if he still smoked.

"Where to begin." Dan rubbed his forehead. "Look, I knew when I gave Bev that vodka I broke the law—that I might be tried for murder in the first degree—"

"Define that, please," Lucille said.

"In Florida, it's the unlawful killing of a human being when perpetrated from a premeditated design."

"And second degree?" Ralph asked.

"Second degree's the unlawful killing of a human being with malice aforethought but without premeditated design," Monroe said.

Ralph looked blank.

Dan felt a wash of love flow through him for all three with him at the table.

"In other words," Monroe continued, "our task is to convince the jury that although there was a premeditated design, it was Bev's design and Dan's intent was merciful and just." He leaned toward Ralph. "We know it's not going to be easy. We're going to take a risk and put Dan on the stand."

Dan heard a gasp and felt the pall of sorrow in their breathing, saw the deepened hue of their eyes. *If you love, you suffer.*

The waiter appeared with a carafe of house red and filled their glasses.

"To death," Dan toasted, "and its opposite." He addressed the question in Ralph's eyes. "Ralph, I want this trial to establish a precedent for mercy. There have been and always will be extenuating circumstances that affect verdicts. I hope my trial will force the courts to reassess variations in individual circumstances versus the abstraction of law." Still, he doubted. "Of course, that's just a secondary hope."

An image of Joanna's back hunched over her recorder floated through Dan's consciousness, followed by one of Bev when she was only fourteen and still sweet, still French—before he and the process of Americanization turned her to bittersweet then bitter. "You set a course of action," Dan said, feeling new strength in his voice, "and by God you follow through whether or not the course you set was wise. I believed mine was—after years' worth of agonizing. We'll soon find out."

Ralph asked, "What's the prosecutor's game plan?"

"That jerk," Lucille blurted.

"No," Monroe said, "Ansletter's okay, actually. He comes off as an amateur method actor, but I don't think he'll pull anything on you."

"Maybe," Dan said. "I'm lucky to have a prosecutor without political ambition. I suspect his theatrics come from basic stage fright. I don't agree with the man philosophically, but he's okay, I guess." He laughed. "Don't root for him, though."

"His game plan?" Ralph repeated.

"Check me on this, Monroe," Dan said, "but I think Ansletter will use every witness he can to show a motive other than the one I had. He believes I helped kill Bev because I couldn't stand living with her anymore, and will present evidence to support that belief."

"Too true." Monroe placed his hand on Dan's arm briefly. "Also, he might use the fact you were a judge against you. If you were some poor, illiterate, passionate slob of any other color, you'd have a better chance. But a WASP judge carrying a dead body onto a plane?"

"Most prosecutors would play that angle." Dan pictured the public outcry in Miami if he were acquitted. "I do think he'll use it, but not as his major strategy—"

A strong scent of peppery steamed chicken heralded the waiter with their dinners. Dan wished Joanna were with them. He wondered where she went every night after work and decided to invite her for dinner even though he knew she would refuse.

*　　*　　*

When the trial adjourned for the day, Joanna rushed off to her computer to enter the proceedings. Her fingers trembled over the keys. He is kind, she thought, kind enough to kill, or assist in killing. Most people wouldn't have the courage. On the other hand, Beaumont could kill—but never out of kindness. Recalling his grip on her shoulders, she shuddered.

She made so many little mistakes transcribing that it was almost six o'clock when she came to the point where the maid said she saw Dan give his wife a tumbler of vodka. Alone now, she allowed herself to react—first with horror then with compassion for Dan. The delayed feelings had twice as much impact.

But why, oh why, did he take her body to Maine? He'd mentioned Pemaquid that night in the cathedral. He'd talked about hurricane friends—where he'd met Lucille and Ralph. And Bev, too. Dan's son—drowned. Pemaquid? She felt a lump in her throat.

First she struggled to remember everything Dan had told her, then abruptly gave up to finish her task. Five minutes later, she hurried to the ladies room hoping to find Sherri, but no one was there. She stood in front of the mirror and pulled at her hair, spiking it. Without gel, it soon fell limply into place. Tears rolled down her cheeks.

"He's just a silly old man," she said to her fuzzy reflection in the mirror, "and none of my business. Why the hell should I care what he does with his life?"

Sherri blew in, a hurricane of words, and began her ritual unpacking.

"Man, what a day. Right in the middle of a long deposition my recorder broke—" Suddenly she stopped talking.

Joanna turned to see why and found herself under Sherri's scrutiny. She attempted a smile.

"What the fuck happened to you? You look beached. Never mind" Sherri said. "I don't wanna know. Let's party tonight, okay?"

"Sure—why not?"

"Wash your face. Go home and change your clothes—if you have anything indecent to wear—and meet me at the river around eight. We can crash the 'Discharge' concert—or somehow find some action. Screw this job and the goddamn courts."

Tension from the day's work collapsed. She felt her shoulders drop and imagined she heard a flamingo calling.

CHAPTER NINE

Dan rolled over in bed. A worm of a thought crawled through his mind but stayed hidden. *The prosecutor wants to make his case. I thought he was okay. What's wrong here?* He drifted off to sleep and woke up to a hurricane nightmare, the first hurricane of his life, outshouting the wind in the lounge of the Port Clyde Inn that one week when he was seventeen and had responsibility for the Inn and all its guests.

* * *

Dan ran from room to room, urging people downstairs. The Duvoirs, a French mother, father and daughter from Montreal, stood in their garret room watching the birches on the back slope bend to the ground.

"Madame, Monsieur," Dan said, "Come—allons—c'est tres dangereuse ici." He saw a smile play across the lips of the daughter, a brunette of 12 or 13 who already showed feminine promise in her sloping hips and large brown eyes. But he didn't have time to contemplate her.

"Allons," Dan said. "Toute suite." He took the mother by one hand and the girl by the other and led them downstairs. Mrs. Duvoir thanked him in half French, half English. She explained that she and her husband were quite ill—nothing contagious—and asked Dan if he would keep an eye on Beverly for a couple of days. After the hurricane, of course.

"Ma petite fille est . . . how you say . . . shy."

"It will be a pleasure," he said, admitting to himself that he felt hypnotized by the girl's eyes.

Dan watched over his flock for the next three hours, soothing and feeding them. Ralph helped serve while Lucille took pictures. The wind and rain raged all about, but inside the stone cave of the Inn, Dan knew they were safe.

Then, as if a conductor in the sky lowered his baton, the wind stopped. The sun came out flooding the room with light and hope.

"It's over," Dan shouted. "Let's go out and see what's happened." He took Beverly's hand and opened the lobby door. Ralph and Lucille followed.

Aside from some uprooted trees and broken shutters, the damage was amazingly minor. "Looks like we can still go find Gus," Lucille said.

"Only a few missing bricks," Dan said as he checked the boathouse. "The boats are fine. I guess we'll go after all." He surveyed the bay. "The sea's calm, but the air sure feels heavy. Is this how hurricanes end?" He jumped off the boathouse and headed toward the Inn. "Give me a few minutes to make sure everything's under control, and we'll set sail."

Dan and Ralph outfitted a rowboat with a rudder, mast and old canvas sail. More talkative now than he'd been in the kitchen, Ralph admitted that he was only seventeen years old and had run away from home. His father had died in the flu epidemic. His mother and he then moved in with her brother who helped raise Ralph. This uncle, a Methodist minister in Asbury Park, New Jersey, expected him to go to college and become, if not a minister, at least a doctor or member of a helping profession. Ralph didn't want to go to college as a pauper. He said he'd rather stay ignorant than sit in classes with well-dressed brats that he had to serve in some cafeteria or drugstore in order to pay tuition.

"So, one day we got into another argument about it," Ralph said, "and I ran away. Hell, I want to work with my hands. I've got good fingers. They can fix anything."

"Why not be a dentist?" Dan asked, beginning to trust him.

"That's dumb. Sounds as bad as Lucille wanting to be a camera artist. "What about you. What're you gonna be?"

"I don't know. Either an historian or a lawyer." Dan put two more life preservers in the boat.

"Lawyers are parasites."

"Huh, maybe, but aren't ministers too?"

"Yeah." Ralph stowed the oars then changed the subject back to Lucille, complaining about her long skinny legs and low set tits.

Dan changed the subject to the weather and launched the boat. Perhaps he shouldn't trust Ralph after all.

"Monsieur, can I go with you?" Beverly Duvoir asked in a voice half child, half throaty French woman. "My mother said oui."

"Go get a note from her and you can come." Dan laughed.

As Bev ran off, Lucille arrived wearing a white tennis outfit and carrying a racket—her subterfuge for the day. Her short skirt caught on a splinter as she climbed onto the boat. It ripped a large, three-cornered tear, which she ignored. Dan wondered if she knew about it and just avoided the embarrassment, or if she really was oblivious. His mother had fits about three-cornered tears.

Bev returned wearing a full skirted white dress with a V-neck that cut to her budding breasts. She had a note that did indeed say, "Oui." Dan helped her onto the boat. She sat at the stern hugging her knees, her large brown eyes full of wonder.

The morning sun gave crystal edges to the small, choppy waves, but no wind filled the sail to push them toward St. Georges Island. Dan figured they'd find Gus by noon and make it back to the Inn by three even if they had to row both ways. He flexed his muscles in anticipation and wished they had a racing scull.

"Seems like we're just going on a picnic. Did anyone bring food?" Ralph asked.

"I packed some peanut butter sandwiches and cold tea," Dan said. "It's all I dared filch from the pantry." He glanced at Bev. She sat immobile, a lovely white statue.

Lucille chewed on a red curl, darkening it with her saliva. Ralph rested one large forearm along the gunwale, letting his small, square hand dangle over the edge.

"It's mighty nice of you to bring sandwiches," he said to Dan.

Dan nodded in response, feeling yanked about by Ralph. *Just what kind of man is he?*

"I should've brought my camera after all." Lucille said and stood up. "This is so beautiful."

"Sit down," Dan said, wrestling with the oars as the boat tilted back and forth. "This ain't no yacht."

Ralph grabbed Lucille's arm and guided her down, shaking his head. The boat settled; they rowed a while in silence. Waves lapped the sides with a rapid drum rhythm Dan felt in his groin. Lucille leaned over and stared into the water. Dan could see, through the three cornered tear, a patch of unfreckled, creamy white skin on her inner thigh. He noticed Ralph looking at the same spot and shot him a warning glance. Ralph grinned. Beverly stared at them, her expression inscrutable.

"Look, isn't that smoke?" Lucille pointed toward the island. "I bet that's Gus's camp. It's a wonder the hurricane didn't blow them out to sea."

Dan pulled in the oars and jumped into the water when they neared the shore. He felt strong and confident tugging the boat toward shore.

"Okay, let's go find old Gus," he said, helping Lucille on shore.

"How about eating first?" Ralph patted his stomach.

"I couldn't eat a thing," Lucille said. "I'm just too excited."

"*Je n'ai pas faim*—pardon. I too have not hunger," Bev said as Dan helped her out of the boat.

"Fine. I can wait." Ralph tied the rope to a tree; Dan headed off into the woods with the others following close behind.

Black clouds appeared without warning and obscured the sun. Foliage stole what light there was. Dan stopped to listen. Lucille bumped into him. He could feel her breasts slide down his back as she fell.

Ralph helped her to her feet as a gale cracked a nearby tree.

"Back to the boat, quick," Ralph shouted, towing Lucille by the hand toward the shore.

"We have to find Gus," she yelled.

A tall spruce crashed across their path.

"Stop. Watch out!" Dan shouted. He peered ahead. The younger trees to the left swayed without breaking. "This way." He ran toward them, pulling Beverly after him. They made it to the boat just as another tree cracked in two, barely missing Ralph who had shoved Lucille ahead of him.

Dad, help. What do I do? Dan saw his father's face and knew to row away hard. He couldn't seem to get enough air. He felt his skin ripple up his backbone. Then he knew. He dropped one oar and hit his forehead.

"My God, we've been in the eye all along," he whispered. Then he shouted, "We're in the eye of the hurricane. Grab a life preserver." He dropped the other oar and handed Lucille the white ring when the wind hit—one hard, insulting slap from a giant's palm. The boat twirled.

Dan put a life preserver first on Bev then Lucille. Ralph clasped his arms around the bow. The boat flew out of the water then bounced off it again and again, skimming across the choppy waves, a mere pebble. Lucille's screams sounded no louder than a sleeping child's whimpers. Dan reached for her hand, but the unraveled sail wrapped around him, lifting both him and the mast out of the boat. He felt like a javelin hurled by a mysterious knight. A glimpse of a lighthouse registered just before he hit the waves.

* * *

Dan got out of bed, wiped the sweat off his face with a T-shirt and went out to his veranda. A sky full of stars and his birds-of-paradise greeted him. "That hurricane still haunts me," he whispered to the stars. "Sure, Dad, I'll do my best once again." He rubbed his eyes dry and went inside.

Ansletter might not be harmless after all. Why did I toss Bev's body into the sea? How can I explain the pull of that particular sea?

CHAPTER TEN

Joanna felt like the queen of spades wearing black tights, a white thigh-length tunic, and a black velvet cape. Sherri surprised her by showing up at the riverbank dressed conventionally in jeans and a faded T-shirt advertising the "In and out Burger." A bruise discolored the crook of her right arm.

"The concert's been cancelled," Sherri said. "Too much flack from the old line. So I didn't bring my car. Let's take the bus to a bridge parlor—make a couple of bucks."

"Bucks? What do you mean, money or men?"

"Hey, you're catching on." Sherri giggled. "I mean both. Men and a half-penny a point at bridge."

"I don't know, Sherri. I'm not good enough at the game to gamble, and I can't go dressed like this."

"Why not? You look great. I bet you give me a run for the money tonight. I spilled nail polish on my favorite wig so I said fuck it, and put on my jeans." She nodded her head toward the bus stop. "C'mon, let's go."

Fearful, Joanna tagged along, then, flinging back her hair, shook the wimp off her spirit. "Where did you get that bruise?" she asked Sherri.

Sherri glanced at her arm. "I gave blood the other day. Red Cross truck was in the neighborhood—I have type AB—hard to get." She rubbed the bruise. "Damn nurse kept missing my vein."

"My veins roll, too, so I avoid the blood drives," Joana said, feeling a new respect for Sherri.

"Here comes the bus." Sherri grabbed Joanna's hand. "Let's go take some chances on both money and men."

"What about Ricardo?"

"What about him?" Sherri asked. "If we're lucky, we won't run into him."

"What do you mean by that?" Joanna pulled her hand away.

"Nothing. Just kidding. Get on the bus."

Sherri chatted as they rode the bus to the stadium, entered a nearby bridge parlor, and signed up for partners. Two young men sauntered in within ten minutes and perused the names on the half-penny board. One was tall and lanky. His tight-jeaned legs reminded Joanna of pick-up sticks. The other was shorter, muscular. Brown eyes peered out from under the ledge of his forehead and moved with a quick intelligence. Professionally coiffed salt and pepper hair curled just under his ears. His handsome square jaw reminded her of Dan.

She shook off that comparison. Wasn't she here to live a little? To forget Dan? She turned to face this potential bridge partner and let herself feel an attraction for him. She knew that Sherri, taller than Joanna by two inches, abhorred looking down at men, so wasn't surprised when Sherri picked the tall one by standing and asking him if he smoked.

"Not anymore," he said.

"I'll play with you then; your head's clear. What's your name?"

"Moe Albright." He grinned at Sherri, revealing extra long eyeteeth and crinkly eyes. "What's yours?"

Joanna watched, as wary of herself as much as she was of them. The shorter one smiled at her. His teeth were small, but his eyes, though darting, seemed gentle enough.

"This your first time here?" he asked, reaching for her hand. His touch made her tremble with fear or longing, she couldn't tell which.

They wandered through the lighted rooms with Sherri leading the way, searching for an empty table. Joanna noticed the scent of nervous sweat from each cubicle. People of all ages and manner of dress—Caucasians only—shuffled, arranged their hands and studied their cards.

Sherri found an empty table with two decks of "Miami, City of Bridge" cards sitting in the center of it. By then, Joanna had learned that her partner was a high school computer education coordinator in Coral Gables who played golf almost every day after school and bridge most evenings.

"You'll never guess his nickname," Moe said with a high-pitched laugh. "It's Computer-lay, Comp for short, after a computer program he devised for the communication of relevant statistics in the mating game."

Joanna smiled. Her hands and feet tingled as if awakening from limited blood circulation. She hoped Comp was not too exacting a bridge partner.

Sherri pointed Moe to the seat opposite hers and slapped the palms of his hands. "Let's kill 'em, Moe. I'll keep score." She pulled a four of hearts from the deck and pushed the deck toward Comp. He drew a jack, Joanna a king, and Moe a ten. "Well, Moe, we're still partners," she said in her deepest voice. Turning to Joanna she lightened it. "Your deal, Kiddo. Give me a good hand."

"Does she really give a good hand?" Moe asked, winking at Comp.

"I see we've got two games going tonight," Sherri said.

The others laughed; Joanna faked one. Her stomach knotted. What in heaven's name was she doing here?

They began playing a few warm-up hands and peppered their conversations with sexual references. Joanna's dry lips curled upward at each one. Her hands perspired when it came to Joanna's turn to deal. A sudden silence at the table unnerved her. Comp counted his points—not audibly, but with his lips. Joanna couldn't quite read the number.

"Do you guys play Blackwood?" Sherri asked.

The men nodded. Joanna panicked. *What was Blackwood?* She bid one club.

"Hey Beautiful, are you playing the club convention?" Comp asked.

"She's too conventional for that." Sherri said with a long face.

"Four hearts." Comp bid and laughed one low syllable only.

Joanna tried to breathe and made it through several rounds. *This is fun*, she thought. *No it's not. I like Comp okay. He's funny and good looking and isn't mean like Beaumont. It is fun. Don't be such a wimp.*

The game came to a close when Comp made a four-heart bid. He grinned at Joanna.

"Shouldn't leave winners," he said, "but let's quit now and go to the Coucouri for some oysters. We'll treat."

*   *   *

En route to the restaurant in a cab, Joanna told herself she was having fun. She had barely thought of Dan's trial, and even enjoyed Comp's arm around her shoulders. Male arms, covered with soft brown hair, she thought, are quite kissable.

"Thank God the game's over," she said to Sherri as they slid into a Puritan style wooden booth while their partners went to the oyster bar. "I was a nervous wreck."

"You played fine." Sherri patted Joanna's hand then looked toward the bar. "Here comes the next game. Hope you come out on top, if that's your favorite position."

The men approached with a platter of raw oysters, a jug of house wine, and some crackers. Following Sherri's lead, Joanna slurped oysters, discussed the finer points of the bridge game, and drank the wine, snuggling against her partner. Comp refilled Joanna's glass to the brim. She giggled and sipped, thinking she should go easy on the wine. As Sherri entertained them with courthouse tales, Joanna continued sipping and Comp kept on pouring. Joanna decided she was having too much fun to care.

When the jug was empty Sherri and Moe said goodbye and left, wiggling and giggling.

Comp asked Joanna to go home with him.

"No, no. Not tonight," she said, feeling blood rush to her cheeks, adding to the flush she felt from the wine. "I need more time. I don't even know you."

"C'mon, girl, How much better can you know me after that game tonight? Bridge reveals character, you know."

She pondered this, and disagreed.

"Maybe next time, Comp. After I get to know you better. Okay?"

"Sure, Kid. You're timid, but true," he whispered into her ear. "I admire your integrity."

"Thank you," she said, fortified by his compliment. She glowed. Never before had she thought she might have integrity. Joanna the champion chameleon?

"I'll hail a cab," he said. "What's your address?"

In the cab she drowsed, feeling relaxed in Comp's arms and barely aware of his hand accidentally brushing her breast. Pretending Comp was the gentle and kind young man of her dreams, she didn't notice where they were until the cab stopped and they emerged from the cab into a barely lit trailer park.

"Hey, I thought you were taking me home," she said, startled.

"I am." He waved the cabbie on. "Let's have a nightcap first—a decent drink."

"No, Comp. I don't need anything more to—"

"It's okay, Jo. It's still early and I want you to know me better. You said you don't know me well enough." He cocked his head to the side. "Please?"

Not knowing what else to do she agreed, supposing she should at least thank him for dinner and call another cab.

He unlocked the door of a small trailer. A sour smell of unwashed dishes hit her like a slap in the face, dramatically clearing her head.

"This is it," he said. "Not real luxurious, but I wasn't expecting company tonight."

Comp lightly spanked her into the trailer. She didn't know whether to giggle or fight. She turned to study his face, but he bent over and pulled a bottle of Jack Daniel's out from under the bed.

"I'll find us some clean glasses," he said. "Don't worry."

"I'm not worried," she said in a voice so high-pitched it advertised her lie.

"I like that outfit you're wearing," he said as he poured the whiskey and added water from a tap that farted and gushed. "Real unusual. Let me take off the cape so I can see the rest."

He left the drinks on the counter, removed her cape, and then wrapped his arms around her. She stood rigid, expecting a kiss on her dry lips, but he didn't kiss her. To her great surprise, he dropped his pants and pinched her butt, hard. She struggled free of him. He grabbed her left arm and twisted it; she screamed. She thrashed her arms and gagged.

"So, Miss Underbidding Prick-tease, let me show you how to keep quiet when you bid game." He tore open her shirt and gave one hard tug to the front of her bra. It cut into her back.

She jumped toward the door; he pulled her back by the hem of her tunic.

"C'mon, Babe, you'll like it," he said, smiling. "I know you're no virgin."

"No, Comp. I told you I'm not ready for you."

"It's been five minutes," he said in a threatening tone. "How long does it take you to get ready?"

She exhaled, fighting for time, for clarity. Would rape be safer than fighting it? Once he'd come, he'd fall asleep and leave her alone just as Beaumont used to.

"Now, that's more like it," she heard him whisper,

The sobering smell of the place made her pray for escape. She couldn't match his strength. All she had was wit and not much of that. Should she seduce him? Should she weep? Suddenly she remembered Sherri's advice.

"Do you have herpes?" she asked

"Not that I know of." He stopped mid strip of his jockey shorts. "I think I'm immune. Why?"

"Well . . . you'd better wear a condom because I have some sort of disease down there. It's not herpes. Do you have any rubb—?"

"Sure I got rubbers. All kinds." His voice barked but his penis shrank like a punctured balloon. He sat on the edge of the bed, his pants crumpled at his ankles. "How do you know, anyway?"

"Blood test last week. I'm sorry, Comp. I didn't think we'd get his far. It's a mutant strand of syphilis." She lowered her head, grateful for the hair that fell forward hiding what surely must be a foolish expression.

"Mutant? That's bullshit." Comp stared at her. "Who ever heard of a mutant strand of syphilis?" He laughed, reached for his glass and took a large swig.

Joanna backed toward the door. Her cape lay at her feet; she didn't dare reach for it.

"What the hell, it's getting late anyway," he said, looking at her uncertainty. "I start teaching at eight in the morning, so I guess you'd better go." He pushed the door open with his foot. "See you around the game some time."

Joanna mumbled a goodbye, then tripped on the threshold and fell, landing hard on the asphalt, bruising her right hip. She felt the soft plop of her cape landing on her and heard the trailer door close. The tears burning her eyes felt like acid.

Limping, she found the river by luck. She sneaked into the elevator at her aunt's building twenty minutes later and clutched the cape over her torn blouse. Luckily, she was alone. *I'd better hide out for a while,* she thought. *Bastard believed me. Didn't even help me up after I fell on that awful driveway.*

Her face in the elevator's mirror mocked her. When she'd almost reached the ninth floor, she spoke to her disheveled reflection. "I guess I'm no damn judge of character—not my own—not even Dan's. He's the murderer, so they're saying, and this guy's a high school teacher—the nice guy. Or is Dan the nice one and Comp the murderer? Why do I need a damn man? Why am I attracted to men like Beaumont when I so much want men like Dan?" Then, picturing the soft, warm look in Dan's blue eyes, her tears flowed freely. This time they didn't burn.

CHAPTER ELEVEN

Dan sat on his veranda at dawn October 5th, the day he would take the stand. He admired the beak of one of his birds of paradise and watched the sun slide up over the blue-penciled horizon. It rose as if coming on stage for a performance. The bloated moon hovered in the low western sky, unwilling to give up center stage.

He straightened his shoulders. Today he, too, would perform. What should he remember to tell the court? That the sun rises at Pemaquid the same way—the same time? That the sea at Pemaquid is grey, not blue, and the horizon line is rumpled or obscured by low-lying clouds?

Your Honor, the sun penetrates these clouds, sending its rays in columns reminiscent of bad religious paintings, or stage lighting—bright circles of light on that black rock that slides forever into the treacherous sea that stole my son.

* * *

October 5th, 1952, he and Beverly celebrated Buddy's 4th birthday with a picnic lunch at Pemaquid. Bev and Buddy scrambled down the granite and basalt peninsula to feed bread crumbs to the seagulls. Bev, just twenty-eight then, came back to him where he'd sat leaning against a sun-warmed pine tree, reading. He had just put down his book on the practice of capital punishment in the 20th Century and picked up Finnegan's Wake again.

"Someday," he said to her, "I'll read enough of this novel to know why I struggled with it in the first place."

"I could say the same thing about our marriage," she said in a tight voice, frowning as she squatted on the rocks in front of him. "You're going to get pitch all over your shirt and I'll never get it out." Though the sun spilled over her in summer profusion highlighting auburn streaks in her dark hair, her small face held venom.

Dan braced himself against the tree. Here we go again, he thought, noticing again that she'd lost all traces of the French accent that used to charm him.

"Where's Buddy?" he asked.

"Gone off in the woods to hunt for goblins." She pointed north.

Dan heard the snarl in her voice and readied himself for the onslaught of recriminations that flowed from her as regularly as her period, yet not related to her menstrual cycle as far as he could tell. It just seemed it took her about a month to fill the bin of her resentments to overflowing.

She stared at him. He waited, knowing he was helpless in the face of each attack, knowing he'd respond badly and make it worse, and hoping she would finish it in one day this time. When she did finally empty her bitter cup, she came to him with increased affection, even passion.

"You don't love me as much as I love you," she said, her brown eyes riveting him to the tree.

"How can you quantify love?" As soon as he said it he knew he'd succumbed once again. He shook his head to be free of her gaze. Marital arguments, he thought, follow rigid rules of their own making. Lucille had described how she and her husband regularly fought about her passion for photography. And Ralph was perpetually jealous, which Rosalie fanned by flirting, and Bev and he got caught on love. Amounts of it.

He saw Buddy running toward him with his red plaid shirt flapping and his arms outstretched, holding a large seashell in both hands.

"Daddy, Daddy, look what I found."

"Slow down, son," Dan said, too late. The boy tripped, fell down, and sent the shell sliding down the rock into the breakers. Dan picked him up and held him, letting him sob on his shoulder. His breath smelled of milk. A wave of love swept over Dan for this fragile and beautiful miniature of Bev.

"Let me see if he's hurt," Bev said. "He shouldn't be crying if he isn't hurt." She tried to pull the boy away, but he clung to Dan's neck.

"Easy, Bev. He'll be okay in a minute. Won't you Bud?" The boy nodded and looked into Dan's eyes.

Dan returned the gaze. The depth in his son's brown eyes was a continual reminder of mysteries in the universe that he knew he could never discover by rational means, and that he could no longer deny. Slowly he let the boy down.

"I'll go get some goblins to find me another shell, Daddy. Okay?"

"Swell, Bud. You do that. But be careful this time and don't go too far into the woods."

The boy ran a few steps, stopped to grin at them briefly, and then pranced slowly away, placing one foot exactly in front of the other.

Dan chuckled, watching him.

"You've got him all to yourself, don't you," Bev said. She stood with her legs apart and her hands on her hips. Her print dress, too large as usual, billowed about her.

"C'mon, Bev. Let's not fight here of all places." Dan reached out for Bev's hand. "Besides, we're on vacation and it's Buddy's birthday."

"Huh. He wouldn't know what day it was if you didn't make such a big fuss over it." She ignored his hand. "Goes to his head. And you're not happy unless the others are here."

"And just how do you measure my happiness?" He felt trapped in his own defenses.

"Oh, get off your high horse." She glared at him, accenting the anger in her voice. "I can tell by the way you look. When Ralph and Lucille, and their so very insignificant mates, are here, your eyes light up. Now they're just a dull, washed out blue."

He smiled. "I've been reading James Joyce for half an hour. I guess it absorbed the color in my eyes." He hoped she'd smile in spite of herself, but her face grew more pinched.

"Daniel Laurence, quit mocking me." She punched his shoulder with her small fist.

"Sit down, Bev. Please tell me what's bothering you."

"You make it sound as if it's my problem," She backed up and glared at him. "Some feminine whim—that nothing's wrong with you."

"I admit to that line of thought," he said, scratching the skin under his mustache. It always itched when Bev attacked. "What do you want from me?"

"How many times do I have to tell you?" She sighed.

The ensuing silence rang in Dan's ears. He wondered how to ease her pain. Telling her he loved her, he knew from past experience, only inflamed her rage. A hug at this moment wouldn't work either.

"See what I mean?" she asked. "You're a goddamn mute. Sacré bleu. Well, for starters, you're turning Buddy against me."

"That's stupid!" he yelled, and then consciously softened his voice. "How do I do that?"

"Oh sure. I'm stupid. You make me do all the tending and disciplining while you sop up all the love." She widened her stance and put her hands on her hips.

"Sorry." He turned toward the woods. "Never mind. I was just going to look for him, but you go after him if you prefer."

"Go find him yourself."

"I'm damned if I do, damned if I don't," Dan said, exasperated.

"You're absolutely right." In her cowboy stance she looked like she was ready to shoot him. "That's what you get for being so damn logical all the time." She marched down toward the sea.

Dan wondered if he should look for Buddy or let her. He waited a couple of minutes, listening, but heard no voices. Was she looking for him?

"Buddy? Bud, where are you?" he called and then headed toward the woods wondering if her criticism fit. He was logical—didn't know how not to be. Actually prided himself on it. It was true that Bev did have the day-to-day responsibility. When he came home from work each night Buddy flew to him.

"Buddy," he called louder. *Where had he gone? Just like him to look for goblins.*

He searched the woods, crunching pine needles under foot. Beverly had a point, he admitted to himself. He did love Buddy so much it could seem that his love for their son took some away from her. Of course you can't pour love into a measuring cup and divide it up among people. *Half a cup for you, a third for you.* But he didn't know how to reassure her, to tell her that aside from these periodic battles he was among the happiest of men, and counted his blessings often.

It didn't take long for him to traverse the small grove and realize that Buddy must have gone off elsewhere. He hoped Bev had found him, and imagined Buddy hugging her, giving her the love she wouldn't take from Dan each time the strange, black moods claimed her.

Just in case Buddy had gone up to the lighthouse, he headed toward it. At least up there he could get a better view of the whole peninsula, this eighty-foot lava tongue perpetually tasting the sea. The sound of a breaking stick stopped him. "Buddy? You little devil, quit hiding." He turned back to the grove ready to play hide-and-seek. Again, there was no sign of the boy in the grove so he headed back to the lighthouse.

From the base of the lighthouse he saw Beverly lying on her back, knees up, arm across her eyes, her typical unhappy position. Disappointed that she hadn't found him, hadn't even looked for him, he called for Buddy again. Bev didn't move.

Anxiety pricked his skin. He scanned the horizon. A cool wind chafed him. He thought he saw something red bobbing in the surf, and ran to the edge, hoping it wasn't Buddy's shirt. Seaweed, he thought, peering. *No, too red. A tattered flag from a boat?* He crawled down closer and howled. It was Buddy's shirt.

With a roar of anguish he dove into the sea. The icy water cramped him. Pain exploded throughout his body. He fought it and the strong rip tide with the miraculous strength of his purpose. The red shirt bobbed and disappeared as he swam toward it. Then it reappeared and sank again. Finally he reached the boy, dove down, grabbed his shirt, and pulled him to the surface. He cradled the small body in his neck as the waves crashed and receded over them.

Seven waves before it's calm enough to get out, Dan thought, counting. When the calm came, he lunged onto the rock right where the waves had tossed him back in the hurricane of '38. He crawled out of the waves' reach and placed Buddy across his knees. Slowly he pushed on the boy's back, inhaling and exhaling himself, willing the boy to breathe in imitation, to take Dan's breath.

Clear water flowed from Buddy's mouth across Dan's sea-darkened corduroy trousers. The water seemed purified by the sweet lungs that held it.

"Let it beat," he begged God as he felt Buddy's pulse. "Let it beat." It did not. He turned the boy over and touched his soft cheek. Buddy's opened eyes had lost their mystery, and Dan knew the ultimate loss.

As if through a tunnel, he heard Bev screaming, a hollow sound, the most hollow, horrible sound of his life.

"You killed him," she cried. "It's all your fault." Then she hissed, "You brought us here every year."

*   *   *

His tears watered the bird-of-paradise. He stood, marveling again at the power of memory. How could he relate that tale in court?

Each year on Buddy's birthday she said he'd started their quarrel that day, that Buddy's death was his fault. And he took the blame. After all, he was the one with the Pemaquid pull. And he did take them there every year. Until today, he'd ignored the fact that she bore some of the responsibility, too. She had started the fight, and neglected Buddy because of it.

"Am I truly not guilty of murder in the first degree?" he asked, stretching his arms high.

He stared at the fading large-pizza moon and realized that their marriage from that day on was no more than a plastic imitation of one, like a window display at a Japanese restaurant. They lived afterwards in the memory of love, and made love once a week to keep that memory alive—when she wasn't sick. Then, when the real sickness hit, Alzheimer's defined by doctors, he believed he loved her, felt his obligation to her, and buried any of his own lingering needs.

"Did I want to punish her for robbing me of my son?" he asked in an audible whisper. "Did I refuse to kill her those five years of her begging to punish her for that deadly quarrel? Did I finally help her die to free me?"

The questions, he knew, were the answer. How could he defend himself now?

CHAPTER TWELVE

Joanna took everything washable in the apartment down to the laundry room following her bridge playing fiasco with Comp. She lugged her last basket of warm laundry onto the elevator at five in the afternoon. A long, slender hand reached through the doors as they began to close.

"Wait. Hold the door, please," said a tall woman in a green silk dress.

Joanna pushed the 'Open' button, and the woman entered, followed by the big man in strangely mismatched clothes who usually accompanied her. Joanna recognized them from court, Dan's friends, Lucille and Ralph. She was glad they didn't acknowledge her, yet she longed to know them. There was something about these people, she thought that she wanted badly. Confidence? Un-selfconscious charm?

Ralph reached around her to push the button for the ninth floor. He turned to Joanna and smiled when he saw it was lit.

"I guess we have the same destination." His bulk and smile seemed to fill the elevator.

They ascended three floors in silence. Joanna decided to imitate their confidence even if she didn't feel it.

"You're Dan's hurricane friends, aren't you?" Joanna asked. "I'm one, too—his friend, that is. Though a different hurricane. We're neighbors and had to spend the night in a cathedral during Hurricane Julio."

"Well, my, my. How interesting." Lucille peered down at her through the top half of her bifocals. "You're a lovely young lady." She extended her right hand. A camera case hung on her left arm. "I never thought of that term before, but we definitely are hurricane friends. I'm Lucille Grimm MacIntosh and this is Ralph Conscetti."

Joanna shook the woman's delicate hand and felt unusual strength in it—comforting strength—so unlike her mother's tiny, soft one.

"Hi. I'm Joanna Archer." She turned to Ralph. "Pleased to meet you."

"You're the court reporter on Dan's trial, aren't you? And his friend, too? Small world." Ralph beamed at her.

"The hurricane was earlier—we met before the trial started," Joanna said. She felt his smile flow down her body like a warm shower. The elevator stopped at the fifth floor. Her stomach flipped. The doors opened, but no one appeared.

"We're on our way to Dan's apartment for dinner." Lucille poked the close button. "Why don't you join us? I'm sure he'd be delighted."

"Oh, I couldn't." Joanna looked to Ralph for agreement.

"Why not?" He filled the elevator with his smile again. "Besides, I want to hear about your hurricane."

Then it's settled," Lucille said with a nod of her head.

"Mrs. MacIntosh," Joanna said, "I can't see Dan. Don't you understand, I'm working his trial. I mustn't *know* him."

"I don't expect you to know him," Lucille said through a sly, closed-lipped smile. "Even the most ardent hurricane friendships can be chaste."

"Hunh?" Joanna lowered her head to hide the blush. She clutched her laundry basket. "That's not what I mean," she said, feeling more intrigued than teased. The elevator came to a stop.

Lucille held the door open. Leaning over, she studied Joanna.

"Forgive me for teasing with the Biblical sense of the word. You knew him in the ordinary sense, *a priori*. Knowing him more now can't matter a whit." She laughed with a slight rasp and nudged Ralph's expansive belly. "So, Joanna, if you're inclined, *do* join us for dinner."

"I am inclined. I really am. I just don't think it's legal or ethical—"

"Oh, posh," Lucille said. "There are very few who understand ethics. I certainly don't, though heaven knows I've tried." She shifted her camera case to her right shoulder and asked Ralph, "Is it illegal?

"Let's ask Dan. Here, Joanna, let me help you with that laundry." He put her overflowing laundry basket in the hall. "Where's your door?"

"Right across from Dan—Mr. Lawrence's," Joanna replied. "I'm worried. What do you think his chances are?"

"It's hard to tell," Lucille said. "The outcome of this case will depend on emotion only—the jurors' hearts. The facts are clear." She frowned. "But Dan has a good reputation—among judges anyway. They used to call him the only hanging judge who wouldn't hang."

"What's that mean?" Joanna asked.

"I guess it means he was tough on murderers but didn't believe in capital punishment." Lucille smiled at Ralph. "Don't you remember the arguments you two had about that every other year?"

"Sure do." Ralph beamed. "Dan would say the state doesn't have the right to play God, and I'd shoot back, 'You don't believe in God,' and he'd say, 'that's irrelevant.'"

"Then you'd ask Dan," Lucille broke in, "how he'd feel if some burglar killed Bev—"

"And he'd say, 'I'm talking abstractions, Mister. Justice is an abstraction. What's right is always right.'" Ralph laughed. "Dumb bastard always wanted to do what's right, even as a kid when we first met him. Righteous. No wonder it took him so long to let Bev go, I mean help her go." He paused, lowered his head. "I wonder what I'd do in the same situation."

"There's a divinity that shapes our ends," Lucille said, taking Ralph's arm, "rough-hew them how we will,' and old Lear said, 'As flies to wanton boys, are we to the gods, they kill us for their sport.' Wasn't that Lear?"

"No, Gloucester," he answered.

"Oh, right." She flashed a broad smile at him and let it fade slowly, thin red lip descending over long white teeth. "Dan still believes in free will, the poor, sweet man."

Joanna wanted to take a class in Shakespeare so she could quote like that.

"Well, here we are," Ralph said. "No more arguments about dinner, young lady, just a straight 'Yes' will suffice. Besides, I'm doing all the cooking."

"And that means we'll have far too much delicious food," Lucille said.

"Okay, okay." Ralph's dazzling smile told Joanna that some parts of the world were actually trustworthy. "I'll come over as soon as I put away these clothes—uh, thanks. But please don't tell anyone.

I could lose my job." She hurried inside to clean up for an evening with the weirdest speaking but nicest people she'd ever met.

*　　*　　*

Dan sat straight-shouldered on a footstool out on his veranda, enjoying the slanted light of late afternoon. He watched the sun's rays cast bird-like shadows from his plants on the white stucco wall while Lucille fussed around him shooting pictures and tossing out words. He concentrated on keeping his mouth very still, foiling her attempt to get just his mustache and mouth to show feeling.

"Pemaquid '83," Lucille shouted, then squeezed the shutter on her camera which was aimed precariously close to Dan's face. "Pemaquid '38." He stifled a smile. He knew she wanted his mustache to show feeling, but he wouldn't let her have it.

Click. "Bev." Click. "Beverly Duvoir Lawrence." Click. "Ralph's Rosalie." Click. "Prosecutor's suit coats." Again, he contained a smile. Click. "Capital punishment." Click. "Coral gladiolas." Click. "Freedom." Click. "Joanna . . . aha."

Joanna?

"Perfect, Danny boy." Click, click, click. Lucille straightened to her full height. "Your mustache will soon be immortal."

"Well, it's nice to know some part of me will." He stood and stretched. "You little devil, you tricked me this time. How do you know Joanna?"

"Met her on the elevator." Lucille removed the film and packed her camera into its bag. "Talked her into coming over here for dinner—though she said it's unethical to see you socially and made us promise not to tell." She laughed. "She'll be here any minute. You don't mind, do you? I didn't think you would."

"Course not," he said, and hurried inside. "What are we having for dinner?" he asked over his shoulder. "Where's Ralph? I don't think we have any decent wine left. One of us should go get some."

"Easy, Dan," Ralph called from the kitchen. You've got plenty of good—" The doorbell interrupted.

*　　*　　*

Joanna watched Ralph set a huge platter of Gorgonzola linguine in the middle of Dan's round dining table. Wisps of steam rose from it. A fresh spinach salad and a loaf of crusty French bread sat on either side of it. She and Lucille applauded; Ralph beamed.

Dan held Joanna's chair for her. Unused to such courtesies, she bent her knees to sit and pulled the chair forward, surprised to discover he was helping her move it in close to the table. She watched Lucille fold her long body into her seat like a velvet drape drifting softly into place as Ralph held her chair. Joanna let go and released her breath. She heard Dan pull in his chair, but didn't watch.

"To a great chef, one who creates miracles out of meagerness," Dan said raising his glass in toast.

"Amen," Lucille said, lifting her glass. Joanna followed suit.

"Thank you, thank you, folks." Ralph served a large portion of the creamy pasta onto each plate. "A French writer once said that there's only one way to prepare for death: to be sated to the brim in heart, soul, spirit, and flesh. Shall we practice?"

"Ralph's been reading *Readers' Digest* again." Lucille laughed, this time in bell tones.

"Here's to heart, soul, and spirit as well." Dan lifted his glass and clinked it against Joanna's. "Welcome. May you come here often with or without Ralph's cuisine." He resumed eating.

Joanna followed his move and let the creamy gorgonzola pasta awaken her senses as it flowed down her throat. She relaxed into the taste and feel of it and watched the interplay around her. Lucille leaned toward Ralph when she took a bite of the pasta, as did Dan, moving in concert with her as if choreographed. Then Ralph would lean back and take a drink of his wine. Dan and Lucille would then take a drink. *I want to dance with Dan, too . . . No, what am I thinking?*

"You know I can't come here often," she said, "not yet."

"I understand your worry," Dan said, putting down his fork. "Currently, here, it's neither illegal nor unethical to see me outside of court, but I understand your reservations." He grinned. "However, I think it would be most unethical to avoid me. Seriously, I'm rather fatalistic about the outcome—"

"You fatalistic?" Lucille asked. "Dan, you shouldn't be. You have to fight. Do you want to be convicted?"

Joanna felt her throat tighten as she waited for Dan's answer.

"Up until yesterday," he said, "I thought not. In fact, I wanted more than anything the public recognition that I'd done the right thing." He rubbed his forehead and looked at each of them. "I wanted to die not only sated, as Ralph suggests, but I wanted to go to my grave with the belief I was a good man, for the most part, and that my major decisions were right ones. I thought so then, anyway." Dan stared out toward the veranda where his strange plants swayed in the breeze.

"And now?" Joanna asked, suddenly conscious she'd been holding her breath.

"Now?" Dan turned to her. "I'm not sure if my motives were pure."

"Now Lawrence, cut that out." Ralph grabbed Dan's upper arm. Slowly he released his fingers and leaned back. "For Christ's sakes, you haven't defended yourself yet and your lawyer's practically mute. Let me talk to him."

"Easy does it, Ralph," Dan said softly. "Monroe's doing just fine. Probably has timing in mind. But go ahead, phone him whenever you want. By the way, did you call Rosalie again today?"

"Okay, I'll change the subject." Ralph broke off a hunk of bread and layered on the soft butter. "Yeah, I called her this morning. She misses me."

Lucille turned to Joanna. "Rosalie is Ralph's wife. They live on a ranch in Nassau."

"A ranch? There?" Joanna felt like a little kid.

"Yup," Dan said, "a regular breadfruit plantation."

"They're just teasing me, Joanna," Ralph said. "Though I generally prize my hands and what they can do, I have to admit I have a brown thumb. Can't raise anything except breadfruit on an island whose soil reaches up and clutches at seeds flying by."

"He has Nigel, a wondrous gardener," Lucille interjected.

"Did you raise children on your ranch?" Joanna asked, regretting the question immediately. She noticed quick glances around the table.

"Funny," Lucille said. She dabbed her lips with her napkin and leaned back from the table. "We didn't actually make a pact to be childless when we were kids in that hurricane at Pemaquid, but it turned out that way—not one of us has any children, though Bev and Dan did once." She glanced at Dan. "I guess, except to meet on Independence Day every two or three years, our Pemaquid vows were mainly . . ." Her voice trailed off. She turned to Ralph.

He lowered his eyes and reached for the wine.

"Did all four of you meet in that hurricane?" Joanna tossed her hair back, clearing her face.

"Yes, we did." Dan's blue eyes seemed to darken as he looked at her. She felt relieved when he turned and said, "Go on, Lucille, explain us if you can."

"Let me try first," Ralph said. "I want Joanna to get an unbiased view of Dan."

Laughing, Lucille and Dan gestured for him to begin. Ralph stood behind his chair and used it as a lectern.

"Daniel Briggs Lawrence," he began, "earned his keep as handyman and assistant host for the Inn at Port Clyde, Maine. His parents, the well received Lawrences of Boston, espoused honesty, proper manners, regular habits, and good health derived from the daily ingestions of each food group and one or two ounces of spirits." He pointed at each of the serving dishes and the wine as he spoke.

For the next ten minutes he described Dan's rise through childhood summers at the Inn to manager just before his freshman year at Yale when all four first met and when Dan would not let Ralph make a pass at Lucille.

"What gave you that idea?" Dan asked with a laugh.

"I was there, Charlie. You told me to lay off."

Lucille peered at Ralph through her glasses, and then removed them as if to see him more clearly.

"I didn't know that," she said. "I thought both of you were more interested in little Bev."

Joanna listened intently, realizing suddenly that basic doubts live forever, generation after generation.

"Did you and Ralph ever have a romance?" she asked Lucille.

"I was only fifteen." Lucille ignored the question with an enigmatic smile. "We went our separate ways, then met every few years thereafter, and sometimes in between. When we were in our twenties, Ralph found Rosalie and I married Arthur MacIntosh." She rested her chin on her hands. Her eyes seemed to retreat briefly. "Then

I chose to remain childless for the sake of photography—art—if you will. Arthur divorced me twice for that. I wish he were alive to divorce and re-marry me one more time." She laughed. "Such is destiny. And Bev, Dan's wife, had a child, but he drowned and she couldn't have any more, as far as I know, and didn't want to adopt."

"I know." Joanna peeked over her wine glass at Dan, who met her glance with those light-charged eyes, and held it. She felt her heart pounding. She wanted to know everything about Dan, and yet knew she shouldn't even let herself be tempted.

"Ralph's Rosalie," Lucille continued, "was the oldest of nine children in a home beset with genteel poverty. She vowed to be rich and child-free in revenge, a social powerhouse. Right, Ralph? Can't say I blame her. She's Ralph's favorite child."

Dan exploded with laughter which he quickly stifled.

"Now, Lucille," Ralph said,

She cut him off with the 'stop' gesture of a traffic cop.

"I tolerate, Dear. I tolerate." She let her hand drop to her lap. "Anyway, Joanna, do you have children?"

"No, too scared. Too much of a kid myself to raise one, I guess."

"Well, you're about the right age to be our daughter," Lucille said. "May we adopt you?"

"I'd love it," Joanna said and then tilted her head forward to curtain her face. She felt wonderfully embraced.

"You're still young enough to have children," Ralph said. "I recommend it before it's too late. Of course, you should have a husband first."

"What for?" Lucille asked. "Lots of single women now are having children, some by artificial insemination, and rearing them alone."

"Oh, I'd never do that," Joanna said. "I'd like to have a baby, though. Maybe when I discover a true sense of independence." She heard her voice gradually disappear.

"Yes," Dan said as he twirled his last forkful of linguine, "when one gives in to need as well."

"Listen to the Man, here, espousing dependence. Who's he kidding?" Ralph guffawed.

"Himself," Lucille stood and patted her camera. "But these mustache shots will show. C'mon, Ralph, let's leave the clean-up to them. I'm getting tired, you need to phone Rosalie, and I want to print at dawn tomorrow and then go to the trial to cheer when Dan takes the stand.

"I'll be waiting for your routine, Lucille," Dan said. "And needing it."

Joanna jumped up. As much as she wanted to hear Dan's Pemaquid story, she knew she had to leave with Lucille and Ralph.

"Sorry, Dan, I can't stay to help. You must understand. I shouldn't be here in the first place. Maybe after the trial—"

"I do understand, Joanna." He held her hand and led her to the door.

She wanted to stay, to ask, *Dan, why, oh why, did you throw your wife's body into the ocean?* Instead, she slipped away fast.

CHAPTER THIRTEEN

"I don't get your defense, Dan," Ralph whispered as they entered the courtroom. "We're stuck with parameters so broad Ansletter could drive a semi through them pedal to the metal. And he will."

"Don't worry." Dan smiled at him. "Monroe knows what he's doing." He waved back-handed and headed for his seat directly across from the one he knew so well for so many years.

"All rise," the clerk called out and Judge Okasaki entered. Once seated, she opened the session.

"The State calls Dr. David Rosenberg to the stand," Ansletter sang out as he smoothed the hair on the back of his head,

Dan wanted to tell the prosecutor that this was a courtroom, not the Met. He turned to watch the bailiff swear in a tall, balding, narrow shouldered man wearing a dark brown suit and matching necktie.

Ansletter established the doctor's credentials: neurologist, expert on Alzheimer's disease. "In your opinion, Dr. Rosenberg," Ansletter asked in a normal tone of voice, "could someone who had suffered from Alzheimer's for several years make a specific request for mercy killing?"

"No." Rosenberg shook his head. "People who have this disease don't make rational requests. They tend to hallucinate most of the time—talk to non-existent people and see strange creatures. Also they have an exaggerated sense or no sense of the passing of time." He nodded decisively. "They don't concern themselves with the concept of death, and certainly not the time of death."

"In your practice, what kind of care do you recommend for victims of Alzheimer's?" Ansletter rocked slightly on his heels.

"I usually recommend nursing hospitals or home nursing as the disease progresses. Caring for Alzheimer sufferers is far too emotionally and physically draining for family members to sustain for any length of time." Dr. Rosenberg crossed his legs, revealing an inch of white skin on one ankle above his black socks.

"No further questions, Doctor." Ansletter covered his mouth by fingering the smile lines on his cheeks, and returned to his seat.

Dan knew Monroe wouldn't let the doctor leave such a false impression of Beverly, and waited with heightened anticipation as Monroe slowly stood, adjusted his glasses, and approached the stand with his thumbs in the edge of his pants' pockets.

"Dr. Rosenberg, in your extensive practice have you ever seen an exception, someone who had Alzheimer's disease yet did not behave, as you just outlined, all of the time? In other words, could someone in the throes of this disease behave normally on occasion?"

"Alzheimer's Disease," the doctor said after uncrossing his legs, "in layman's terms is a generic name for a great variety of mental disorders among the elderly. Nevertheless, what you may call normal behavior is rare."

"I didn't ask if normal or rational behavior is rare, I asked if it were possible." Monroe's voice, though low and soft, seemed to reverberate in the stillness of the courtroom. His tan suitcoat hung decisively from his straight, well balanced if not broad shoulders.

"Uh . . . yes," the doctor replied. "It's possible." He glanced at the jury.

"Do you consider age fifty as elderly?"

"No—"

"Mrs. Lawrence was diagnosed as a victim of Alzheimer's at age forty-six. Since she wasn't yet among the elderly, could she possibly have moments of rational thought?"

"Yes, she could but she wouldn't request her own death." The doctor sat up straight and glared at Monroe.

"Can you categorically state, Monroe said without raising his voice, "that this woman whom you have not met, nor examined, could at no time request her own death?"

Dan thought the freckles on Monroe's white face popped out, the extent of his show of emotion.

"No, not categorically. I'm speaking from a—"

"No further questions, Your Honor."

"The witness may step down." Judge Ogasaki said. She leaned forward as if she were admiring Monroe's shoes.

Dan wondered if Bev had been sick since Buddy's birth. Those periodic bouts of anger. Her demands for equal amounts of love. Her attack the day Buddy drowned. Appalled that it had never occurred to him before now, he felt a painful regret. She must have been sick all along and he'd done nothing. He heard Ansletter calling him to the stand and focused on the man's errant hairs re-sprouting like sturdy weeds, obstinate like the man himself. Then, for relief, Dan turned his eyes and thoughts to Joanna.

She sat with her back to him, hunched over her recorder. He couldn't figure out why he felt so much affection for this elusive girl who seemed more waif-like every day. He could see the vertebrae in her back bone rippling beneath her yellow cotton dress. As if she felt his eyes on her, she straightened.

Dan entered the witness stand and placed his hand on the Bible, that thick-grained cover soaked by the sweat of countless witnesses swearing to tell the truth. He was pleased they still used a Bible here for swearing in even though he knew its words were written by men, and precisely for that reason.

But how could anyone live up to an oath to tell the truth? This morning, reliving the day of Buddy's death, he realized he'd never really known truth, though he'd assumed he did when he was the judge so much in control in Buffalo. Truth's too elusive, he thought, too subjective. It slips in a court of law like a Dali watch over the edge.

"I do," he said to the bailiff. A sudden image of the trees at Pemaquid bent over in the wind surprised him. He shook it away to concentrate.

"On the morning of April 5, 1983 in Fort Lauderdale, Florida," Ansletter bellowed, as if in a windstorm, "you willfully and in your right mind carried out your plan to kill Beverly Duvoir Laurence, age fifty-six. Is this true?"

"To help her die, yes."

"And, in the late afternoon of April 5, 1983, in the town of Pemaquid, Maine, you delivered her body to the sea."

"Yes."

"The defendant admits to the premeditated assisted death of his wife, yet pleads not guilty." Ansletter paused and slowly surveyed the jury. "How can this be?" He turned back to Dan. "Were you in love with your wife at the time of her death?"

Dan glanced at Monroe, wondering why he didn't object to this strange question. Monroe looked sleepy, a sign he was planning strategy. Dan knew to answer the question.

"I loved her. I was not 'in love' with her."

"Please, a simple yes or no." Ansletter drawled, a hint of boredom in his tone.

"No," Dan resisted the urge to snap at Ansletter.

"Did you say that you gave her that lethal glass of vodka to release her?" The prosecutor's face flushed.

"Yes."

"Also to release you?" He stressed *you.*

"No, sir."

"Did you choose the date of her death?" Ansletter strolled away from Dan, turned around and cocked his head like a Terrier listening for his master's voice.

"No. She did. It was her mother's birthday." Dan lifted his glasses and rubbed his eyes, annoyed as usual by the fluorescent lighting in Florida courtrooms. Why not have windows, natural light?

"She chose her mother's birthday for her death?" Ansletter asked, closing in on the witness stand . . .

"Yes."

"According to the medical testimony we've just heard, she'd be too confused to ask you to kill her, specifically, on her mother's birthday."

"According to the medical testimony we've just heard, such lucidity is possible now and then," Dan said, resisting the urge to sigh.

Ansletter paced a few steps away again, patting the back of his head.

"All right then," he said, "given this possibility, when did she ask you to, as you say, release her?" He faced the jury.

"She first brought it up in 1975. April of that year. Then many times later. I refused." Dan spoke flatly to Ansletter's back.

"Is it true you personally took care of her all those years instead of placing her in a nursing home?" Ansletter still face the jury.

"Yes."

"This kept you in control—"

"No," Dan said. He wanted to shout but felt a familiar rawness in his throat and softened his tone. "She dreaded going into an institution more than anything. She'd spent many years visiting her mother in the best nursing home in Buffalo." He cleared his throat. "Bev—Mrs. Lawrence—said it didn't matter how good a place it was, that ending up in any institution was the worst possible outcome for anyone."

"In the years of her disease, did she ever attempt suicide?" Ansletter turned back to Dan. His face reflected skepticism.

"No." Dan reached for the water pitcher, poured himself a glass and drank half of it. He wanted to explain somehow why she never attempted suicide. "Bev never could do anything all by herself. I wanted her to travel, or at least risk meeting new and interesting people on her own. The ritual battle of our marriage revolved around her inability to enjoy herself away from me."

"Nice narration." Ansletter's baritone rose. "However, we've been led to assume that this was a rational deed of mercy, yet you yourself testified that you threw your wife's unsanctified body into the sea. Was that an act of mercy?"

"Irrelevant," Monroe objected.

"Objection overruled."

"Repeat the question, please." Dan said.

"You and other witnesses have testified that you took your wife's body all the way to Maine and then threw it against the rocks, into those icy waters? True?"

"Yes. I don't know why I did that," he said. He heard Lucille and Ralph gasp in unison and wanted to embrace them—tell them that this was far too personal to make any kind of sense.

"We have here a former judge, mind you," Ansletter said, grinning, "who claims he had no malice aforethought, yet he hired a pilot to fly her body to Maine, then dropped her like so much excess cargo into the sea. You call that mercy? Ha." He turned toward the jury. "The quality of mercy is a bit strained here, I'd say."

Dan's heart pounded.

"May we approach the bench, Your Honor?" Monroe asked as he stood, steady and clear-eyed.

The judge nodded, held a brief whispered conference with Ansletter and Monroe. Dan strained to hear their legal arguments, but Ansletter's large body blocked their voices. Soon Ogasaki called for recess until the following day.

Dan felt a sudden need for Joanna. Why? To help her in her quest for a soul, to see her toss the hair from her face and smile with confidence? To recognize his own needs? To laugh again with someone young?

Joanna slipped out from behind the bench. Dan let his dream go and returned to his seat as the courtroom slowly emptied.

What if I have a stroke instead of a heart attack. Who will kill me?

The jurors filed out, stifling yawns of released tension, Dan thought, stifling a yawn himself.

He closed his eyes and deliberately relived flying to Pemaquid that strange white day.

*   *   *

The most significant thing was the bright light everywhere. Her white pleated dress, the white of her pillow, the whiteness of the sky on that long flight. Taxi ride to Pemaquid, those neatly stacked cords of wood beside each farm house, depleted now by the long winter, illumined as if by lightning. The cold moist air on his face. Never had a day seemed so bright. He had to squint as he wheeled her up to the white lighthouse. Even the ocean looked white in the fog. Melville's chapter on the whiteness of the whale came to mind. *Virtue?*

He checked the grip of his Nikes on the wet part of the rock. They held. He cradled Bev in his arms. Such a light body. Slowly he kissed her goodbye, braced his legs and held her to the sky. Every muscle in his body moved in harmony giving him a muscular thrill that he imagined great dancers must experience. He felt a rightness he had never known before. Finally, he could experience the scene with Ralph holding Bev that branded his memory. Finally, it would stop haunting him.

When his arms began to give way under the weight, he lowered her to his waist and carried her down the sloping rock peninsula into the sea. He pushed her out from the rock and waited as the water soaked up her billowing white dress and the tide pulled her out to sea. She floated briefly, and then sank beyond the strangely gentle breakers coming from St. Georges Island. He climbed up in the deep stillness to the lighthouse in his white, wet shoes and surveyed this rock peninsula for the last time. Slowly, painfully, he trod back through the goblin inhabited spruce forest to Pemaquid. The light—

"C'mon. Court's adjourned." Monroe said, nudging him.

CHAPTER FOURTEEN

Joanna slowly stirred the sugar in her coffee and stared out the kitchen window at thunderclouds filling the sky—white as Dan's mustache on the edges, dark gray as her mood within. She knew there was more to the Pemaquid story than she would hear in court. She hoped that Dan would someday tell her all of it.

"I shouldn't see him," she said to the clouds. "I really shouldn't see him."

She thought about writing a note to him. But how?

Dear Dan, Thank you for a lovely evening. Much as I'd like an encore, we can't see each other again. I'm sorry.

Why? Oh shit, why? She asked herself. Professional ethics is out. He won't buy that. He said he understood. I don't understand anymore. Beaumont might—might what? Dan can handle Beaumont no sweat. Besides, Dan's not a lover. What exactly is he? A father? Twice my age. Why does he seem so young?

Try again. *Dan, I'm falling in love with you, and you'll leave—perhaps for prison.*

I can't say that. *Dear Dan, I need to make it on my own before I deserve the smallest attention from a man like you.*

Surprised at that thought, she leaned against the kitchen table. Deserve. How can I deserve . . . what must I be? Dan is so sure of himself, so clear.

She twisted a strand of her hair and felt her mouth ready to chew it before she noticed the old habit and tucked it behind her ear. She hated being a wimp like her mother.

How does a person go about building a backbone? Stock answer: know thyself. Lucille would probably say, "To thine own self be true." How the hell do you do that? Know what you want? And what you don't want, like Beaumont and Comp?

And Ricardo? She remembered the sushi bar, her reaction to seeing him with those two women. Well, she'd succeeded in ridding her mind of Ricardo by seeing Dan. Maybe now she should reverse the process.

The phone rang. Startled, Joanna jumped and hit her forehead on an opened cupboard door. Pain coursed through her body and returned to throb in its original spot. Dazed, she reached for the wall phone.

"Hello?"

"Hi, partner in crime." Sherri said. "How are you? How did you make out with Comp?"

"Let's get together so I can tell you just how badly I made out with that jerk." Joanna pulled an ice cube from the freezer and rubbed it across her forehead. Despite the pain and the subject of Comp, she was glad to hear from Sherri. Somehow Sherri made a buffer for Dan.

"Struck out, Huh? So did I—that night." Sherri paused, briefly, and then spoke in a rush. "Remember the Viking, Ricardo Alioto? I'm pretty sure he blew you away. Anyway, he's back—still rich, sexy, and so much fun. Reckless. How about seeing him tonight?"

"Yeah, I remember him." Joanna had an image of a train coming at her and felt the excitement of riding the rails where no cars can go plus the fear of that huge engine roaring in. "Why do you want me to see him?"

"With me, too, that is." Sherri coughed and cleared her throat. "I just thought it would be fun to deal you in."

"Well, I was just thinking about him." Joanna studied the thunderheads. "Actually, Dan helped me stop thinking of Ricardo. Now I want to forget about Dan."

"Who the hell is Dan?"

"I thought I'd told you. He's my neighbor. I met him just before I met you, during Hurricane Julio." Joanna paused, and then said softly. "He's Judge Lawrence, the defendant on my current trial."

"Shee-it, girl. No wonder you didn't tell me. Have you slept with him?"

"Don't be silly." Joanna shook her head in disbelief, and then laughed.

"You know, Sherri, I've always been so damn needy, I'm afraid I'll fall in love with the first intelligent, decent man I meet no matter how young, old, rich, or poor." She tossed the ice cube into the sink for the pain on her forehead had calmed. "How did you get to be so free?"

"I just don't give a damn anymore." Sherri giggled and then said, "Freedom's a fucking paradox, you know. So's self-sufficiency, but I pretend. What do you say to having dinner with Ricardo and me tonight? He's hot to see you, too."

"Hey, not so fast. A paradox means two opposing ideas are also true, right?"

"Yup. That's what I mean," Sherri said.

"Then how is freedom a paradox?" Joanna rested the phone on her shoulder and rubbed the bump on her forehead.

"Now she wants an essay. Philosophy 101."

Joanna imagined the college in Georgia, Sherri sitting by a fireplace on a white occasional chair among nine other young ladies nicely draped around the room, listening to an old professor.

"Okay, here goes." Sherri cleared her throat. "In order to know what freedom is we have to know boundaries, right? True freedom has no boundaries and is, necessarily, an illusion. Follow me?"

"Yeah. Sort of."

"I like to believe I'm free of my parents, but I'm not." Sherri paused, and then said, "Also, every time I put forth the effort to make a good choice—freedom means choice—I discover I make the same kinds of mistakes without any effort by just jumping in feet first."

"Example?" she asked. Sherri didn't sound like the same person. Joanna was all the more intrigued, discovering another facet to Sherri's personality

"Shit, I don't know. Okay, I choose to play around. It's fun—challenging. I mean, I can't go to the moon, but I can moon over Miami."

Joanna pictured Sherri atop the courthouse mooning Miami and laughed out loud.

"I don't get that as an example of anything," Joanna said, "but I like it."

"Okay, seriously," Sherri said. "Here's one. If I try to get all the facts before an election and make a rational decision, I end up voting against Reagan simply because my parents think the jerk walks on water. So I don't vote. And Bush—my God. Don't you think dullards should be outlawed? Wouldn't it be fun if it were against the law to be dull?"

"Yeah, but who's gonna decide what's dull? Tom Robbins says that one man's ennui is another man's coronary." Joanna stretched the phone cord into the living room and perched on the arm of a chair. "Did you ever want any kids?"

"Joanna, you're too much. Come out with a great quote followed by a cliché. Besides, I already had a kid. She'll be four next month."

Joanna felt the receiver slip from her fingers. The cord retracted, pulling the receiver into the kitchen. She slid to the floor and caught it.

"Sorry about that," she said. "I hope it didn't hurt your ears. Where's your baby now?"

"I don't know. Gave her up for adoption."

"How come you never told me this before?" Shocked, Joanna again revised her concept of Sherri.

"I dunno. I guess the subject never came up—like Dan. Enough of this, let's play. Ricardo really wants to see you again and so do I."

"I'm not up for a date, Sherri. Sorry." Something didn't feel right.

"Hey, he's my date. We just want a threesome to ease the pressure. C'mon, honey, practice some independence, discover new boundaries, live it up while you can." She waited a moment and then said, "He's really loaded—rains hundred dollar bills everywhere he goes. He wants to take both of us to that fancy Hilton by the airport for a stone crab and blackened fish dinner. Not too shabby, huh?"

"You said, ease the pressure." Joanna's fear subsided, dampened by Sherri's outrageous greed. "What pressure?"

"Did I say that? Well, I'm not really sure. Don't worry, though. You'll be safe, and you can dress any way you want."

"Punk? Or what you call my sweetie pie look?"

"Either one. We'll pick you up at eight tonight."

With a leftover sense of foreboding, Joanna agreed, and replaced the receiver.

"The only way to find out what I truly want," she said to herself, "is to experience again and again what I'm not sure I want. Sherri likes me. I guess that's worth the risk." . . . Feeling virginal, she decided to buy and wear the white lace-trimmed dress she saw in a boutique window, despite the price.

*   *   *

Sherri arrived at the condo at eight on the dot wearing a black jersey dress and her own blonde hair. Ricardo escorted her. He wore a black silk suit, white dress shirt, black and white necktie, and cream colored shoes. He kissed Joanna's fingertips.

"I'm delighted to see you again," he said, lowering the lids over his light blue eyes.

She was prepared to smirk, but he didn't seem to be mocking anyone.

"White becomes you," he said. "Accents that lovely pelt of dark hair."

A few minutes later, en route to the Hilton in his custom built black Ferrari, Ricardo turned periodically to smile at Joanna seated in back. Strange, she thought, Sherri had said he didn't smile much.

Sherri made fun of other drivers; Ricardo asked Joanna if she'd noticed the "rosy fingers" of Miami dawns. Joanna still felt anxious despite their casual conversation. His questions took a deeper turn on the outskirts of Miami.

"What was the most significant decision you ever made?" he asked.

"To leave my husband after fourteen years." She took a deep breath and held it a few seconds, surprised at her open response.

"That takes real guts," he said, looking straight ahead, but glancing at Joanna in the rear view mirror now and then. "Now, I'm definitely in favor of couples working at making the marriage go, but if you can't, then get the fuck out. Pardon my French."

"Hey, no need to apologize for your language," Sherri said. "We speak the same one, and it ain't French, Puerto Rican, Spanish, or Italian."

"Touché, Mademoiselle." He patted Sherri's thigh as he stopped at a red light. "I was raised by a great aunt down on the Keys. She made it hard for me to recognize equality in language so I slip now and then." He turned back to face Joanna. "So, what's your greatest ambition?"

Joanna pondered that for a few seconds. They would laugh at her dream of getting into law school after reading Shakespeare. Instead she conjured animals: giraffes, polar bears, dolphins, gazelles, Arabian stallions.

"I'd like to stop being a chameleon," she said in order to ease the tension creeping up her neck like a lecher's fingers.

"You don't have to answer his questions, you know," Sherri said with a one-note laugh.

Ricardo laughed along with her. When the light turned green he accelerated the Ferrari to eighty in a few seconds.

Joanna marveled at the crystal chandeliers as they entered the Hilton dining room. The headwaiter greeted Ricardo by name and led them to his "regular" table. She wondered if Ricardo's closed-lip smile was one of self-satisfaction or simple anticipation. Soon, though, she felt like purring—pampered by the soft sounds and colors of the room and the weight of the thick tablecloth against her knees.

"I feel mucho lucky dining with two beautiful women, a study in contrasts, black and white." Ricardo said and then sampled the Oysters Rockefeller that mysteriously appeared. He moaned with pleasure and leaned toward Sherri. "For example, Sherri is the blonde angel in black devil clothes and Joanna is the dark lady in a pearl white angel dress. One, I know, the other is still a mystery. What more could a man want?"

"What's angelic about this?" Joanna tugged at her white sleeve.

"The high collar." Sherri whispered. "But so what? Ricardo's paying you a compliment."

"You're a love present waiting to be opened." He grinned at Joanna. "Besides, nothing could hide those great, er, that gorgeous figure anyway."

Joanna felt the blood rush to her skin as she warmed to this strange, generous man. She ate one of the oysters and relaxed as it slipped down her throat. *Such luxury.*

What do you mean by dark lady?" Joanna asked Ricardo after the waiter retreated with their oyster dishes.

"Maybe you're like the dark lady of Shakespeare's sonnets." He reached over and lightly touched her hair. "Actually it's your deep brown hair, majestic cheekbones, and olive skin that give you an air of mystery—as if you have a secret you haven't disclosed to anyone, not even to yourself."

"Wow, man, can you ever lay it on." Sherri tipped over her glass, but caught it before any wine spilled

Joanna felt like kicking her under the table, but Ricardo's light laughter and quick, simultaneous embrace of both of them restored her good feelings.

"Remember when you introduced me to Joanna?" he asked Sherri. "I knew at that moment she had potential."

Joanna remembered that he'd said court reporters only transcribe life without living it. Well, she'd show him.

"Get me a couple of bottles of your best Cote de Rhone, William," Ricardo said to the waiter who materialized before them. "I'll let you choose the vineyard, but make sure they're hearty and full bodied."

"What do you do for a living, Ricardo?" Joanna asked, impressed by his savoir faire,

"I'm a charity racketeer."

"A what?" Joanna heard him, but didn't understand him.

Sherri tossed back her head and let out a robust chuckle.

"I'm a charity salesman—Goodwill, United Fund, Shriners, you name it. I run several of the larger charities in Miami—solicit enough money to keep them going and siphon off the rest. My commission so to speak."

"You're kidding," Joanna said. *A charity racketeer? He can't be serious. He'd get caught if he kept saying things like that and they were true.*

Once again, he looked as if he were trying to contain a smile. The waiter arrived with their pasta course. Joanna decided he was teasing her and changed the subject by commenting on the scent of the porcini mushrooms before her.

"Have you ever been married?" Joanna asked as the wine gave her fresh courage.

"No. I don't believe in serial polygamy."

"What's that," Sherri asked. She put down her fork and turned toward Ricardo. "Cheerios married to Fruit Loops and Shredded Wheat at the same time?"

"No," Ricardo laughed. "It's Bran Chex married first to Weatbix, then later on to Frosty Flakes." He turned to Joanna. "Let's ignore this smartass." He patted his lips with his napkin. "Seriously, most men want more than one woman, and I suspect many women want more than one man in a lifetime. Why pretend we don't, then get divorced and remarried every seven years?"

"I lasted fourteen," Joanna said, suddenly losing her appetite despite the superb wild taste of the mushrooms.

"Ah, double seven. Without fucking another man?" Ricardo asked.

"Sure. It didn't occur to me to cheat."

"It occurred to me," Sherri said, "every time a hunk got in the shade of my wig," Sherri tilted her head sideways and grinned.

"It occurs to most of us," Ricardo said smiling at Sherri. "We're animals, really, and, with a few notable exceptions, not of the monogamous species." He fingered the lapel of his black suit coat and winked at Sherri before turning his blue eyes on Joanna. "For instance, I know I want to make love to both of you. Why should I marry Sherri, divorce her to marry you, then go back to Sherri when I really want to love you both at once?"

Startled, Joanna glanced at Sherri.

"S'okay," Sherri whispered to her.

The dinner lasted for three hours: oysters, stone crabs, blackened scrod, baby carrots, broccoli flowerets, rack of lamb, two bottles of dark, rich wine, pears dipped in melted Gorgonzola followed by Sambucca.

"Here, Love, try this Sambucca," Ricardo said gazing still at Joanna. He poured the clear liquid into a liqueur glass.

"Thank you." Joanna twitched at the thought of his making love to both of them. Yet, she couldn't remember ever feeling so desirable, so womanly. When she sipped the licorice flavored liqueur, it sent fingers of heat throughout her body.

"A man can be truly gentle with women," he said and ran his little finger down her forearm. "If he doesn't delude himself about what he wants."

"You're right," Joanna said. She tried to meet Sherri's eyes, but they were glazed as if she were somewhere else.

Is she drunk? Joanna wondered. *Am I? What's going on? Are they just teasing me or planning something weird?*

CHAPTER FIFTEEN

Ricardo and Sherri strolled around the hotel gardens in the light of a full moon while Ricardo smoked a small cigar. Joanna stumbled along beside them, feeling awkward and courageous at the same time. Then he drove them to his home for a "visual feast." Joanna leaned back against the plush seat and watched lighted street lamps whiz by. "Hey, you guys," she said, "this is so much fun."

Sherri turned and grinned at her. "It's about time, kid. You're overdue in the fun department."

Ricardo turned onto a circular driveway and leered at her as the garage door opened on cue from his remote.

God, he's cute, Joanna thought. *I wouldn't mind being alone with him right now*. She followed him and Sherri through a large kitchen and down three steps to a living room with an acacia tree in the middle that reached almost to the top of the vaulted ceiling. A floor to ceiling, glass wall separated the house from the adjacent country club greens on its southern exposure. Ricardo said the glass was golf-ball proof. Moonbeams highlighted the white carpet and ebony furniture.

"Now I'm going to show you the pièce de résistance," Ricardo said to Joanna, "a room fit for two queens, my bedroom. But don't get the wrong idea, Joanna. You won't have to meet the dark side of life . . . unless you want to." He winked at Sherri.

The wink annoyed Joanna. *I'll show you. I can meet any dark side you have to offer, buddy*. Straightening her shoulders, she followed him into the bedroom. Almost as large as the living room, it had the same vaulted ceiling, except this one was tiled in foot-square mirrors. The glass wall on one side of the room looked out on a rose garden and a huge, A-shaped pool. Six feet above the apex of the A, a round Jacuzzi overflowed into the pool with the gentle sound of running water. Joanna wished she'd brought her bathing suit.

Ricardo led them by hand toward his over-sized bed. It was covered in black satin. Several white pillows of assorted sizes were propped against the ebony headboard. With a gesture of welcome he urged them onto the bed. Then he crawled between them, lay on his back, and pressed a button on his remote. The electric bed groaned and moved, slowly becoming a king-sized lounge chair, propping their back and knees for comfortable viewing. They faced an expanse of black velvet drapes.

"Is this the visual treat you promised us?" Joanna asked.

Sherri wiggled into her seat and Ricardo pushed another button on his remote. The drapes opened revealing an electronic wall.

"Voilà," he said. "Here it is."

The television screen, which he called a "high resolution monitor," looked to be the size used in bars for football games. Ricardo pushed another button and on came the opening of Verdi's Otello performed in the outdoor theater of Verona and captured on disc, giving it a clarity far beyond Joanna's experience. Four small "state of the art" speakers placed in each corner of the room provided quadraphonic sound.

Ricardo explained the story as the opera progressed. Joanna decided the man really had class.

With an elaborate remote, he fast forwarded to the willow song in Act IV. At the end of it he slid off the bed and produced a bottle of cognac from an ebony sideboard nearby, three small crystal glasses, a black enamel tray bearing six lines of cocaine and three ivory straws.

"Hey, guys, aren't you afraid of getting busted?" Joanna shivered. *Dear Sweet Jesus*. Ricardo just shook his head and patted her hand. "Enough opera," he said, changing discs. "Next we'll watch Bojangles tap dance in a scene from a 1933 movie. Black and white—my favorite colors incidentally. Wait till you see him bedazzle Fats Waller. Meantime, a little refreshment?" He took off his suit coat and necktie and tossed them on a white upholstered chair. When he loosened his collar Joanna could see a tangle of blonde chest hair. She wanted to touch it, smooth it.

"Merci," Joanna said when Ricardo handed her a glass of cognac. She accepted the glass but stared at the coke, wondering what to do. She knew it was awfully expensive, but her only knowledge of it came from that Woody Allen movie when he sneezed and sent the costly stuff flying.

"Want a toot?" Ricardo asked.

"No thanks. What does it do?"

"It's sort of like Novocain," Sherri said, grinning. "The only difference is in the reaction. Novocain deadens your pain. Cocaine wakes up your pleasure. Try some. If you don't like it, leave it for us." Her voice was gentle and loving.

Joanna relished Sherri's affection for her, and then felt a rush of gratitude. Other than Aunt Martha, no woman had really cared much about her. Now she wanted to reciprocate—give back to Sherri by being cool. "This is like Momma and the ice cream man." She giggled.

"What ice cream man?" Sherri asked.

"Never mind." Joanna felt her cheeks redden. Why did she bring that up? She didn't know for sure that her mother had an affair with the ice cream man. "Look," she said and pointed at Ricardo.

He placed an ivory straw at the end of one line, leaned over and inhaled it through his right nostril. "This is how you do it, Joanna. Clean stuff here—won't hurt us. Want to try?"

"I hope I don't sneeze," Joanna said.

Sherri handed Joanna a straw and helped her place it on a line. "So what if you do, Ricardo always has more. Now, just suck it in like a juicy dick."

"My God, Sherri," Joanna said in mock horror, backed by Ricardo's guttural laugh. She returned to the task and carefully inhaled only a speck of the white powder without spilling any. Relieved, she giggled. Otherwise she felt nothing. "Well, I did it," she said. "I'm no longer a coke virgin. What am I supposed to do now?"

"Nothing you don't want to do, sweet baby," Ricardo said after he'd let out a deep guffaw, "and anything you want to do. Here's your chance to live, kiddo. Let somebody else transcribe it." He leaned over and sucked up another line. Each nostril now bore a residue of white, like frost on a porthole. With a flair, he brushed away the powder with his handkerchief.

"Here goes a serial whiff," Sherri said, "left nostril for Fruit Loops." She inhaled the line so quickly it seemed magical to Joanna. "And right one for the cheery, cheery Cheerios." She inhaled again, brushed off her nose with the back of her hand and grinned. "Last line's for you, partner. Sniff her up."

Though she still couldn't see why the stuff was so highly rated and expensive, she pretended to take her turn, scolding herself for being such a wimp. Sherri and Ricardo applauded then settled back in their electric bed positions to watch tap dancing. Joanna joined them, feeling mellow from the cognac, but no more than that.

Ricardo pressed the remote, and on came a very black Bojangles singing, "With a snap in your fingers, and a rhythm in your walk . . ."

"I've never seen anything like this," Joanna said leaning back. She felt her arm touch Ricardo's, and let it stay there.

When the tap dance ended, Ricardo got up and switched the video to Ginger Rogers and Fred Astaire in "Swing Time." He pulled Sherri off the bed and took her in his arms, imitating the dance on screen. Joanna recalled the scene in "Pennies from Heaven" when Steve Martin danced with Bernadette Peters. They had shrunk to tiny figures imitating the screen-sized Fred and Ginger.

Sherri threw her high energy into the act. Joanna thought they looked like professional dancers. She felt a pang of jealously and scolded herself once again for feeling it.

Suddenly Sherri grabbed Joanna's feet and Ricardo held her wrists. They swung her over the bed like a hammock, then dropped her and fell on top of her, laughing hysterically. Joanna laughed with them, enjoying the physical contact. She really wanted to be cuddled, but roughhousing was almost as good.

Soon their laughter subsided. Ricardo pushed one button that returned the bed to its original flat state and another that clicked off the video. The sudden silence was a fourth presence that embraced them. Ricardo had said Joanna could do anything she wanted. What did she want now?

All three lay on their backs, Joanna on the left, Ricardo in the middle and Sherri on the right. Slowly Ricardo stroked their thighs. Joanna relaxed into the pleasure of his touch. Sherri stroked his right thigh and gestured to Joanna to accompany her on the left. She did. Occasionally they ran into each other's hands, lifted their heads and grinned at each other across Ricardo's chest. The moon gave them just enough light.

Suddenly she felt sober. *What am I doing?*

Ricardo sat up. "Okay, Sweethearts, it's strip toss time—an old game where we take turns littering the room with our stuff. My necktie and coat have started. Sherri, go for it."

Sherri took off her earrings and threw them onto the floor by the window. Joanna felt wrenched from her doubts. I'm here, she thought. I've come this far to find out what I want, and I do want him. "So here goes," she said aloud, and tossed her watch under the bed.

Ricardo took off his shoes and threw one toward the door and the other under the bed. Then he ripped off his shirt and tossed it up toward the ceiling. It ballooned down, landing softly beside Joanna. Sherri tossed her bra in the air.

Moving very slowly, Ricardo caught it. He reminded Joanna of an old-fashioned clock needing a wind-up. Then, as if suddenly wound, he came back to life. "All right, my lovelies," he said, pulling a hundred dollar bill out of his pants pocket, "it's time for another whiff." He rolled the bill into a straw, handed it to Joanna, and pulled out another black tray bearing six lines of "pure snow."

Joanna held the rolled bill lightly against her left nostril and inhaled the line as if she'd lived among bluebloods for years. With that one move she flew right out of Beaumont's class into an airy one where men watched opera, disdained monogamy, and did recreational, rather than desperational drugs. "This ain't at all bad," she drawled, "but am I supposed to feel something?"

"Just our luck," Ricardo said to Sherri. "Our ex-virgin here is the one in a hundred not affected by good stuff."

Sherri grabbed the hundred dollar straw, inhaled two lines in a flash, and handed the bill to Ricardo.

"Lie down, silly ex-virgin," Sherri said, "and we'll make sure you feel something." She tickled Joanna's armpits and belly. "C'mon, take off some clothes."

Ricardo, now completely naked, sat cross legged on one corner of the bed, blue eyes widening as he watched. His erection pointed at them. Joanna stared at it, frozen.

Sherri crawled over to Ricardo and closed her mouth over it. Ricardo leaned backwards and groaned. Slowly Sherri moved her head up and down.

Almost hypnotized for a few seconds, Joanna came to and jumped off the bed.

Abruptly, Sherri rolled over onto her back. "Your turn, virgin."

"Wait a minute, Sweeties," Ricardo said, "I get to play the piano, too. Joanna? You're still dressed."

Sherri sat up. "Let him play with us, Joanna. It's okay. I love you and this is the only way I can show it."

I love you. Joanna had never heard a woman say those words to her. Father, brute that he was, often said them. Mother never. Beaumont said them every other day like a parrot. Women? Never. Could she herself say them? Tears filled her eyes. "Sorry, Sherri. I can't . . . I need to go home. You stay."

She grabbed her purse and ran, leaving her watch under the bed.

*   *   *

The soft, round tones of distant church bells blending from all directions lifted Joanna out of her dazed slumber. Bright sunlight illumined the dust particles on the alarm clock beside her. It was eleven a.m., Sunday. She touched the clock to see if it was real, and then ran her fingers up her thighs and arms to discover true flesh, a sense of wholeness.

As if she were a tongue, worrying a cavity in a tooth, she re-constructed the hours with Sherri and Ricardo—line by line, wincing at those moments when she had laughed and felt the internal expansion of . . . of what? Not love.

The church bells seemed to be mocking her. She wanted to cry, but couldn't produce one tear, not even the kind that burned.

She wanted to crawl to Dan, confess, find absolution. But for what? Her greatest crime had been breaking some law about drugs. No. She had broken a deeper law, a law not yet on the books, a law about banality, superficial pleasure to kill the pain of needing someone. Is pleasure Sherri's defense?

For hours she roamed through the apartment or lay still, first reflecting, and then dozing. By late afternoon she finally let a natural hunger for food arouse her. She put a potato in the microwave and took her vitamins. From habit she pulled out her birth control pills and then felt a strange new revulsion to modern technology.

"Let me be ripe again, fertile like the river," she said, and threw her pills into the trash. "Let me be chaste too, at least until it's right." She knelt beside the overflowing wastebasket and wept.

"Let me? Who the hell am I praying to? I will be chaste—foul smelling each month. So be it. Hungry too. Lonely. At least I'll grow a backbone."

CHAPTER SIXTEEN

Dan returned to the witness stand when court reconvened on Monday. He wanted very much to know and tell "the whole truth." But he saw truth as beautiful and elusive—a star, pulsating with shooting rays so delicately connected to their source he couldn't see how the parts related to the whole.

Each day awaiting the trial he'd grown less sure of his case. His recent recall of the day Buddy died almost convinced him he was guilty as charged. Nevertheless, he raised his hand and swore to tell the truth, the whole truth, and nothing but the truth even if it felt like a charade.

"We've established," Ansletter said, "that you gave your wife a full glass of vodka knowing full well that she'd taken barbiturates, enough to kill her with the vodka. You gave it to her on the morning of April 5, 1983, and then hired a pilot to fly you and her body to Maine. I suggest that both actions negate your defense. What was your motive?"

"Why I gave her the vodka?"

"Yes." Ansletter rolled his eyes. Dan fought the urge to mimic him.

"Objection," Monroe said. "Your honor, the instrument of death does not fall within established parameters."

Judge Ogasaki looked at Dan for a long, silent moment.

"Objection overruled," she said. "The subject does have bearing on the case and falls within parameters regarding the defendant's subsequent actions on April 5th."

Ansletter patted his hair and leaned uncomfortably close to Dan's face. Dan could smell mint on his breath.

"You gave your wife vodka," Ansletter said "knowing full well what barbiturates she had taken that morning—knowing full well she would drink it all—knowing full well she would die. And you say that's not premeditated?"

"This was her choice, decided years ago when she first began to badger me about it."

"Badger?" Ansletter boomed. "She badgered you? Sounds as if you found her pretty hard to live with."

Dan felt rage spreading through his neck. He controlled his voice.

"In many ways she was very difficult. She had Alzheimer's. Do you know what that means?" Dan saw Joanna turn and look directly at him for the first time in court. Her hazel eyes shone with concern, buoying him.

"Is it true," Ansletter asked, his back to Dan now to face the audience, "that because your wife suffered from Alzheimer's she exhibited such erratic and irrational behavior anyone would want release—"

"Objection," Monroe interrupted. "The question is argumentative and assumes facts not in evidence."

"Objection sustained."

Ansletter swiveled abruptly and faced Dan. "Let me rephrase. Your wife, Beverly Duvoir Lawrence, badgered you to kill her. You claim she was lucid enough to make that decision?"

"Yes."

"And what was her lucid rationale?"

"She wanted me to suffer her death, too—with her."

"The logic escapes me." Ansletter turned toward the jury. "Yet you complied with her wish."

"It was the least . . ." The logic escaped Dan now, too. He had suffered her death intensely even though he wasn't sure when she died and what exactly killed her. His own death, he hoped, would be mercifully fast. When a heart stops beating, it's all over.

"To recap," Ansletter said stroking his long chin. "We've established that you helped kill your wife and then flew her body to—to where in Maine?"

"Pemaquid," he said. "She liked it there. No, maybe that's not true."

"You are under oath, Mr. Lawrence." The prosecutor frowned. "As a judge, you know what that means. What is true?"

"I don't know." Dan studied his hands as if they might have an answer. Had she ever liked Pemaquid? She blamed him for taking them there so often.

"It took considerable planning on your part," Ansletter continued, "to get her body all the way from Miami to Pemaquid. Do you have friends on the bench in Maine?"

"No." He glanced at Monroe.

"Perhaps you wanted to be tried there instead of here."

"That never occurred to me."

"Ah, but you were a judge on a criminal court and you still say it didn't occur to you." Ansletter smiled as if he'd just pulled off a coup.

"Objection," Monroe said, "assuming facts not in evidence."

Judge Ogasaki called both lawyers to the bench for a private conference. Dan calmed himself by imagining what she was saying to them. He figured she'd sustain Monroe's objection and tell Ansletter to quit the character assassination. He could hear Ansletter's baritone whisper go up as he argued. Finally both attorneys returned to their places. The judge said, "Objection sustained."

Ansletter paced for a few minutes.

Dan knew Ansletter wanted to refute the no malice defense by harping on Maine. How could he counteract it? Intense heat radiated from his scalp. Monroe couldn't help him on this.

"So far we know all we need to," Ansletter said directly to Dan. "You helped kill your wife, as planned, and tossed her body out to sea. Therefore, I have no further questions." Ansletter waved his arm to encompass the whole court. "But I repeat. Good faith is not a defense for first degree, premeditated murder." He nodded toward the jury and returned to his table.

"Court's adjourned until tomorrow," Judge Ogasaki announced.

*   *   *

"It's too soon to worry," Monroe said after the judge left. "I'll be in the law library if you need me."

Dan nodded, appreciating Monroe's advice. Coming out of the courtroom he saw Ralph, Lucille, and a couple of news photographers rushing toward him. He felt like ducking the reporters.

"God, Dan, you worry me," Ralph said, reaching him first. "Why the hell didn't you tell the court about the Maine hurricane? And Buddy, for Christ's sakes? Our only chance is to get to the jury's guts."

"Shh. Let's get out of here before those damn reporters catch me. Come, this way." Dan unlocked the door to an anteroom and slipped in. "Monroe gave me the key," he said, closing the door behind them. "Have you seen Joanna?"

"I imagine she's in her cubby transcribing the day's irrational proceedings," Lucille said, raising her eyebrows. "Isn't that what court reporters do?" She placed her hand on Dan's forehead as if checking for temperature, or sanity. "You're avoiding Ralph's rather basic question."

"Yes, I am." He turned to Ralph and smiled at the big, worried face under the yachting cap. "This morning I relived the hour Buddy died. Bev and I were squabbling at the time. Ever since, I've blamed myself for his death. This morning I realized I blamed her, too, perhaps more than myself. For the first time, I wondered if my motive for helping her commit suicide was truly merciful."

Lucille's face sagged as she hugged him.

"So what if it was only half merciful?" Ralph said, blinking back tears.

"Let's get out of here," Dan said ignoring him. He opened the door to the hall and caught a glimpse of Beaumont Archer. Dan stiffened.

Lucille turned to look at the man standing by the courtroom entrance.

"Who's that?" she asked.

Beaumont's eyes locked with Dan's in recognition. Then he moved toward the far exit, laughing.

"Mean looking bastard," Ralph said. "I wouldn't want to tangle with him."

"Neither does Joanna." Dan watched Beaumont's retreating back. "That's her husband. I think I'll stay here a while, make sure he doesn't come back."

Ralph said, "I'll stay with you."

"I'm going to find Joanna," Lucille's said. "We must let her know."

"You do that," Dan said. "Then come back here and tell us when to pick her up. We'll take her to dinner."

*   *   *

Sweat beaded on Joanna's forehead. The sick air conditioner couldn't overcome the heat of lights in the tiny room behind the judges' chamber. She wiped her forehead with a damp Kleenex. It fell apart, dropping white fluff onto the keys. "Damn," she said under her breath. Little annoyances carry more emotional weight than life and death issues and murder trials, she thought. No, Sherri would be the one to say that, not me.

A knock at the door startled her. She saved her transcription then said, "Come in."

The door opened. Lucille decorated the opening with her great height. She wore a Kelly green silk dress and a camera bag. Wisps of graying red hair escaped their pins and, like moss, softened her prominent features.

"Hello, dear," Lucille said.

Joanna wanted to run into her arms, cry on her shoulder and hear Lucille say, "There, there, everything will turn out all right." But neither one moved.

"My, what a terrible place to work," Lucille said, surveying the room. "Similar to a darkroom without the excitement. Well, I suppose some trials are exciting. Never mind." She laughed, and then quickly sobered. "Dan and Ralph are doing hall duty. They sent me to find out what time they can escort you from these chambers to dinner with us."

"On, no, I don't think I'd better—"

"They're on a husband watch out there. Your husband."

"Beaumont's here?" She stood, ready to run. *But where?*

"Not anymore," Lucille said. "Dan out-stared him and he left. But he may come back, so tell me when and we'll pick you up in a black limo."

"Really?" Joanna felt her eyes open wide. She'd never ridden in one. She smiled at the Mafia-like specter of a limousine. "I should be finished here by six."

"Six it is." Lucille backed out. Holding the door, she said, "I do love intrigue. See you then, dear."

Alone, Joanna closed her eyes and sat as if in a trance. A strange twilight sleep came over her. Then a drop of perspiration landed on her upper lip and she came to. She felt a glow emanating from her center as she returned to her transcription. How wonderful Dan, Lucille, and Ralph are, she thought. I want to spend the rest of my life with people like them, yet I gravitate toward . . . She sighed. No more Beaumonst, Comps or Ricardos!

The transcript worried her. Dan hadn't defended himself in any way and his lawyer did practically nothing. Dan and Monroe were the most intelligent people she knew, but not today. Why? She couldn't help. She must help. How? She toiled and worried until Lucille came back and led her to a black limousine in front of the courthouse. Ralph and Dan stood beside it. Joanna laughed when she saw them, and shook Dan's friendly hand.

At that moment Beaumont and a blonde wearing purple plastic pumps walked past them. He had his arm around her hips.

"Hi, Babe," he said to Joanna, then turned to Dan and said beneath his breath, "Better watch out, old man. Snakes don't live long, and you're on borrowed time."

"You couldn't be more right, Mr. Archer," Dan said with a smile.

"Let's go," Joanna whispered to Dan, and dove into the limo.

Lucille told the driver to lose anyone who might try to follow them. He took them on a circuitous route down short, small streets, and back and forth over rivers and canals. Each time they took a curve to the right, Joanna leaned against Dan. She wanted to touch him, to sop up some of his strength even though he didn't seem so strong today. She wanted to cheer him on, yet she felt unworthy. As the limo bounced down a cobblestone alley, he patted her hand. His clean touch reminded her of how unclean she felt. She couldn't help but think of her passive, bewildering behavior Saturday night. How close she'd come to a *ménage à trois*, and how very far she was from developing a soul let alone a backbone. What if Dan found out? How could she possibly deserve his friendship now? She inched away from him.

Ralph and Lucille faced them, grinning as if all were right with the world. Lucille touched Joanna's hand.

"We're going on a wild goose chase," she said, "to a Venetian restaurant for dinner. Our pursuer, if we have one, will never find us there." She winked. "The driver and I planned the whole route."

"You're giving Lucille the time of her life, Joanna." Ralph said with a smile filled the limousine. "She's a born sleuth."

Joanna couldn't understand their levity. Even Dan smiled. Were they pretending the jury had acquitted Dan or were they so nervous they had to joke around? She longed to know but would not ask.

"You still haven't answered my basic questions, Dan," Ralph said. His smile had faded.

Lucille nodded. Joanna now knew they'd been pretending.

"Well, maybe Monroe will put me on the stand," Dan said. "Then I can provide the background—the hurricane, our attachment to Pemaquid, Buddy's drowning." His face seemed to darken.

Joanna recalled Dan's hurricane stories in that cathedral during Julio and the fact of Buddy's death at age four. She shivered all over and reached for Dan's hand.

Soon the driver stopped and opened the doors. They were next to a news kiosk. Joanna slipped out but stopped short when she noticed a familiar face on the front page of several papers.

"Ricardo," she gasped as she read a headline, "CHARITY RACKETEER BUSTED." Then another: "CHARITY THIEF ARRAIGNED." She reached to buy a paper and then stopped so Dan wouldn't wonder about her. She let her hand hang limply over the kiosk. Blood rushed to her face—fever heat and then shivers.

"Do you know him?" Dan asked.

"No, not really, well, I've met him." *Do I know him? Oh, God, yes.*

"Are you okay, Joanna? You look startled." Dan said.

Joanna felt his scrutiny. She wanted to hide.

"Well, here we are," Lucille said in a light-hearted tone. "I can smell the mussels already." Ralph opened the door to the restaurant. Lucille entered.

Joanna ignored the offer of Dan's arm and marched stiffly in ahead of him. She felt numb. Ricardo and Sherri . . . What a fool she'd been. *Racketeer, an actual racketeer.*

She glanced at Dan's cheerful blue eyes, Ralph's room-filling smile, Lucille's darting eyes framing and re-shaping all she saw. Shame flooded her. She ducked into the restroom and stared at herself in the mirror. A woman is known by the company she keeps, she thought. Or has kept.

She brushed her hair, let it hang over her cheeks and hoped to hide from Dan the consuming hatred she felt for Sherri Ann Taylor.

CHAPTER SEVENTEEN

Joanna awoke at five a.m. in a sweat, dreading her next encounter with Sherri. No dreams had relieved her shame. She lay still; imagined cutting up Ricardo's fancy suits, setting fire to Sherri's purple wig in the employee lounge, melting all her bracelets into an amorphous, ugly blob, jerking her hoop earrings until she screamed.

Shocked at herself, she slipped out of bed and re-routed her thoughts to Dan as she fixed a bowl of granola and milk. She ate absently, hardly tasting it, then moved around the apartment in a daze, slowly picking up dirty clothes and dusting the furniture with yesterday's stockings.

"It's still November. I really should put these ornaments away until Christmas," she said to herself, fingering the pearl studded ball she'd made so painstakingly her first year under Beaumont's thumb. And he'd made fun of it every year. But she set it back with the other ornaments surrounding her limp spider plant, threw on a purple print dress and headed for work early.

She noticed as she strolled toward the river that the morning sunlight, softened by a pitted cloud cover, gave the sidewalk a fuzzy texture. Her scuffed black pumps looked like slippers. For a minute she wanted nothing more than to go back to bed, to sleep away her whole life. She came to the river bank and stopped to sniff the air, fight off her drowsiness. You can tell it's fall in Miami, she thought, by the ever so slight change in the smell near the river, less seaweed, more motor oil. And, of course, hurricane warnings.

And hurricane friends. She sat on the low concrete wall, remembering how embarrassed she'd been to have Dan meet Beaumont. What if he were to meet Sherri? Or worse, Ricardo? The disparity among her post-Beaumont friends struck her. The kind of friends she wanted were not the ones she deserved. The ones she deserved, in terms of matching character, she now hated.

Slick psychological phrases came to mind: accept yourself as you are. Sherri's just being herself. Guilt is phony, just a way to keep you safe.

"Bullshit," she said aloud. "Guilt is real and Ricardo's an asshole." A woman passing by turned to look at her. Joanna blushed, ducked her head and moved on. Every damn generation, she thought, people struggle with sex and love and direction. Why shouldn't I? She stopped, dumbfounded, and knew she must examine her own direction. Or rather, her lack of it.

The early morning crowd near the courthouse thickened. She didn't notice the crowd until she was almost engulfed by it. The inner-city metro ground to a halt nearby. Two street vendors shouting in Spanish hastily packed up their wares and backed into a drugstore.

"What's going on?" Joanna asked a woman pushing against her.

"There's a nut inside the courthouse holding a judge hostage, and shooting at everyone else," the woman answered. "The SWAT guys are here, that's why the crowd's pushing us back. I bet Don Johnson's here, too."

"Who?"

"Miami Vice—"

"But it's not even eight yet. How could so many people be here?" Joanna clutched her purse against her chest so no one could steal it. Suddenly she thought Beaumont might do something stupid to get back at her. *No, it couldn't be Beaumont.* Still, she pictured him aiming his shotgun at her.

"It's been on the news since seven this morning." The woman craned her neck and peered toward the courthouse. "I guess everybody decided to go to work early and catch the action."

Joanna stood on her toes to see, but the crowd, a giant behemoth, had surrounded her and was pushing her backwards. A policeman with a megaphone stood on a wall and tried to disperse the curious crowd.

"What judge?" she asked but the woman had disappeared.

She became aware of the smell, a pungent, not altogether unpleasant scent of nervous sweat, stronger than the everyday Miami street smell. A tall, broad shouldered man directly in front fell back against her. She gasped and wiggled away only to hit a solid wall of flesh on her left. She felt a loosening in her stomach as curiosity turned to fear. Fighting to keep upright, she felt the panting breaths of those next to her and heard their voices over the din of police sirens.

A gigantic blast suddenly drowned out all sounds. It seemed more like a clap of thunder than a gun shot. The pockmarked sky certainly held no thunder. Cannon? Bombs? She felt herself being carried by the crowd, and clung to the suit coat of the man being shoved backwards against her, ready to crawl up his back if need be.

"They're blowing up the courthouse," someone shouted. "Look at them buzzards."

The sky filled with smoke and circling buzzards. Joanna suddenly felt the cool metal of a car against her right arm. She grabbed the door handle for leverage and the door opened a crack. She peered in. The car was unlocked, old, and empty. She noticed that the crowd surged in waves and waited, hoping to time the surge right to slip inside. It was an old Ford or Chevy sedan with torn upholstery and a cracked windshield. She figured the frame was strong enough to protect her from the crush of people.

"Get off my goddam foot," a large woman yelled, momentarily stopping the flow of the crowd. Joanna quickly slipped into the driver's seat. The crowd flowed by, yelling. A wail of pain pierced the vague roar of the crowd. It came from someone directly in front of the car, a scream so powerful it brought tears to her eyes. Peering through the windshield, she found the source. A boy, about ten, had tried to climb a telephone pole and had caught his leg on something, maybe a nail or spike. People pushing by squeezed him against it. Blood flowed from his leg.

He's literally crucified, Joanna thought. Can I do something? *Oh, please, somebody help him.*

She slapped her forehead. All her life she had asked others for help. Now, feeling the power of self-disgust, she dropped her purse on the floor behind her, shoved her way out of the car, and bending forward, arms outstretched into a V, plowed through the crowd to the boy.

"Stop!" she screamed. "You're hurting him."

She shouted until she was hoarse. A large man with dreadlocks heard her, glanced up at the boy, and then used his body to block the crowd. Joanna sent him a grateful glance and climbed part way up the pole. The boy had stopped screaming. Gently she pulled his leg off a large wooden splinter and helped him down to the sidewalk. Shouting, "Make way, make way," she and the man eventually got the boy into the back seat. Blood poured from his skinny calf.

Now what am I going to do? What would Dan do?

The boy just stared at her.

Using a tiny Swiss Army knife from her purse, she cut off the boy's shirt sleeve and made a bandage. She couldn't remember where to apply pressure to stop the bleeding. Images of the circulatory system came to mind. They were vague, but she remembered to press between the wound and the heart to block the flow of blood. The bleeding seemed to stop.

The boy grinned at her, despite eyebrows contracted by pain.

"Look, there's my father," he said, pointing toward small wiry man edging along a building toward them and scanning the crowd with a frantic look. Joanna squeezed opened the car door on right side, stood on the door frame and beckoned him over. With great relief she handed the boy out to his father and hastily shut herself in again. She looked in the rear view mirror to see if a person's face actually swelled with pride. She hadn't done much for the boy, but it was far more than she'd ever done on her own for anybody.

The car rocked as the crowd surged by. She peered out the window for an escape. A trash filled alley lay to her right. When the wave of the crowd surged again, she slipped out and worked her way through the much smaller stream of people who'd discovered the alley. She could hardly wait to tell Sherri. No, she remembered, not Sherri. Dan.

Safe now, Joanna ducked into a coffee shop for news she heard blaring from a small black and white TV screen. What judge would be in court this early?

The TV anchorman talked about the regular courthouse buzzards and interviewed an ornithologist. Joanna nearly hopped with impatience.

"What the hell happened?" she asked the black counterman.

"Some jerk tried to blow up the courthouse this morning." He wiped a glass as if he were being televised, and turned slowly toward her.

"Did he succeed?"

"Naw, just one courtroom. The SWAT guys got him before he killed anyone."

Joanna swallowed hard. "Who was it, do you know?"

"There he is now." The waiter pointed at the screen. "Well, if that don' beat all." The news showed two policemen escorting a small, dark skinned man wearing an orange cap into a squad car. "That's him there. Hell, that jerk was in here this morning—eating chess pie. I remember his cap. Ain't that something? By the way, what'll you have?"

Thank God it's not Beaumont, she thought, then noticed the man waiting for her answer.

"Coffee," she said, "black."

He poured her a cup of coffee, shaking his head. "Funny . . . I opened at five this morning and in walks this spic wanting coffee and pie. He eats without saying a word and walks out. Leaves me a quarter. Then right after I hear sirens, just as I'm turning on the news. Unbelievable. Takes all kinds." He handed Joanna the coffee mug.

"Thanks," she said.

"Yup, from seven on that little spic had them going. Drew the early morning crowd."

Joanna sipped her coffee and watched the screen. She gasped when the commercial ended and saw that Ogasaki was the judge the guy had kidnapped. Now, on screen, the petite judge wore a camera shy smile that surprised Joanna, warmed her. Ogasaki was her favorite—strong, sure, fair. A woman who'd made it in a man's arena. But camera shy? Heroes—heroines—can have feet of clay, she thought. I guess I can, too.

The judge told her harrowing story. She had gone in to work early and run into the crazed intruder in the hall. He kept a pistol aimed at her, tied and gagged her, then kept her nearby threatening to kill her. The police, at one point, held him in a lengthy dialogue. She managed to crawl into her office and hide under her desk. That's when he blew up courtroom twelve.

Joanna felt so weak she clung to the counter.

"You look like you've seen a ghost," the waiter said. "Anyone I know?"

"I work for that judge. Or did. I guess I'd better make a few phone calls."

He pointed toward the pay phone. She dropped in a quarter, punched the number.

"This is Joanna Archer, court reporter for Judge Ogasaki," she said to the answering voice. "Can I help? What should I do?"

The lady on the switchboard said she'd been instructed to tell all personnel for court twelve to stay home, in phone contact, until further notice. Joanna hung up and thought, I'll go home now. There's nothing I can do but sleep.

*   *   *

The clock hand aimed at two when Joanna woke from such a deep sleep she didn't know where she was. Dust laden sun rays slanted from the window to her clothes piled on the floor. It must be afternoon, she thought, and then remembered the wounded boy and her escape from the crowd. She smiled, feeling as if she'd just mastered a complex maneuver with her lasso. She used to be so good with a lasso she wanted to tell Dan about that, too. She reached for the phone and called him. He answered in full voice. She felt foolish and happy as she listened to his resonant response.

"Looks like we have a break from my trial for a day or two," he said. "Let's take advantage of it and do something interesting. What shall we do with the 'found' time?"

"Oh, I couldn't. Oops, there I go again. I guess I could play some. I've always wanted to—oh, never mind."

"Say it. What have you always wanted to do?"

She ran her fingers through her bangs then brushed the hair away from her face. "It's silly, but I think it would be fun to watch big fish like dolphins, you know, in their territory instead of places like Marineland." She paused. "I know it's—"

"Wonderful. We'll do it—fly to Nassau. Ralph will take us cruising in his boat. Of course, I can't leave the country until the trial ends, if then, but let's get together and plan it anyway."

Joanna held her breath. She had no excuses.

"Joanna, are you still there?" Dan asked.

"Yes."

"Good. Well, Ralph's going home soon. I'll call him and make the arrangements for next week, and hope we don't have to cancel them."

Joanna shuddered considering the possibility of conviction. She swallowed hard. "What about Lucille?"

"I'll ask her to come, of course. She's always ready for a lark. What do you say?"

"Why not?" Joanna realized that she'd been holding her breath. She let it go.

"Great. Meanwhile, I feel as if I've been given a last minute reprieve, somehow, and want to celebrate. How about a picnic with the gang tonight on Monroe's boat? I know he'll loan it to us and the weather's perfect now."

"That would be nice."

"I'll call you back as soon as I've made all the arrangements. Thank's for calling. I like the way you think."

A mixture of feelings flooded her when she hung up. She wanted to be with him and his hurricane buddies. Yet, how could she just up and go to the Bahamas? If it happens? Why the hell did she call him in the first place?

Well, so what? If she felt proud of herself for helping that boy at least she could feel deserving. Just deserts? False deserts? So be it. What's done was done.

She rifled through her closet and bureau drawers, but found no bathing suit, nor sport clothes of any kind.

I haven't played for so long. It's time to go shopping.

CHAPTER EIGHTEEN

"We're all set for the picnic tonight with Ralph and Lucille," Dan said when he called ten minutes later. "Ralph says he's eager to entertain all of us next week. Lucille says she'll tolerate Rosalie for your sake." He laughed. "You know how she teases Ralph about his 'society wife.' The trial should end Friday, Monday at the latest. Eastern was booked so I reserved seats on Bahamas Air for a noon departure on Tuesday and hope I don't have to cancel." He laughed again, a liquid note of delight. "That means we'll probably take off around two pm. Okay?"

"Wow, that was quick," she said, thinking that strong people make things happen fast.

"Time is of the essence. I don't have a whole lot of it left one way or the other."

"One way? What's the other?" She wanted to hug him.

"I may have to go to prison. Or better yet, I might fall in love and want to live forever."

"Well, you'd have to find a pretty strong woman, then." Only Lucille could fill that bill, she thought, but Lucille had been his friend too long to become a lover. It would've happened years ago if it were to be.

"Strength is relative," he said. "Everyone is both strong and weak."

"How are you weak?" she asked, lifting her shoulders.

His laugh this time carried the deep notes of a bass guitar.

"I expected too much of myself," Dan said. "At least that's what my wife used to say, and therefore expected too much of her. She complained that I wanted to be right all the time. I guess her complaints were justified."

"Well, at least you know what you want."

"Oh, my dear, I don't. I've never truly known. I'm usually weighing all the factors—looking for what I want. However, I do want to take you to the Bahamas and look for big fish on Ralph's boat. Just looking is enough. Finding is insignificant."

"I agree," Joanna said, and lowered her shoulders.

"See you tonight," he said. "I'll pick you up at five, okay?"

"Yes, I'll be ready." You're awesome, she thought as she slowly replaced the phone. Wise, gentle, handsome, and awesome. Finding really is insignificant. Did I find you, Dan? No, I wasn't looking. But I am now. I'm beginning to know what I want.

The doorbell rang. Dreamily, she opened the door to the length of the security chain. Sherri stood on the other side, her face mascara-streaked, her naked blonde hair hanging limply from her head.

Joanna felt a rush of pity at first, then revulsion and anger.

"What do you want?" she blurted.

"Ricardo's been busted, Joanna. I don't know what to do."

"I know." Joanna clutched the security chain.

"He's a charity racketeer, for God's sake. He was stealing charity money. Aren't you going to let me in? Or is someone with you?"

"Christ, you would think that." Joanna unhooked the chain and opened the door.

"This is some pad," Sherri said, sidling past Joanna. She wandered around the large living room, stared through the floor to ceiling window at the panoramic view, and fingered the art deco lampshades and yellow, corduroy-covered easy chairs. She turned, looked at Joanna. "Why do you have Christmas tree ornaments on a spider plant? Spider plants are ugly."

"I just dropped them there when I moved in—haven't figured out where to put them yet. Maybe they beautify the plant." She struggled with indecision—what and how to tell her off. Her mouth went dry. "Want a glass of wine or something?"

"Sure—whatever you have. I came here on an impulse—guess I should've called first." She looked strange, tattered.

"You're not on coke, are you?" Joanna backed into the kitchen.

"What's the matter with you?" Sherri asked, following her. "Of course I'm not on coke. I wouldn't spend my money on that stuff." She put both elbows on the kitchen counter and let her blonde hair hang forward.

So unlike her, Joanna thought. So like me.

"Hey, didn't you have a good time the other night?" Sheri asked, lifting her chin. "I thought you did. We didn't know he stole all that loot."

"Yeah, I had a good time . . . at first. But felt like dogshit afterwards. " Joanna filled two wine glasses with some California burgundy. *I can't blame her . . . Yes, I can.* She handed a glass to Sherri. "Here's the wine. Let's go out on the veranda."

The velvet air embraced Joanna, caressed her, almost soothed her. Sunlight filled the cloudless sky and a sliver of a moon showed its monthly promise. How could she hate Sherri?

"What's funny is I didn't know he actually was a charity racketeer," Sherri said. "I thought he was kidding."

"Me, too."

"You know, he . . . he loved me—and you, too." Sherri took a long drink. A sob escaped her lips.

"C'mon, Sherri, we were just two more notches on his remote control." She laughed bitterly. "How he controlled us. And I thought he had class. Must've been the booze and coke."

"What's with you?" Sherri asked, scrutinizing Joanna. "Where's the scared chick I used to know, the everything virgin?"

Joanna stood and leaned over the railing. *I could just shove her over the edge and listen to her scream all the way down. Why am I so furious with her?* She turned her back to the slanting afternoon sunlight. "What really matters to you, Sherri? What, deep down, do you think really matters?"

"I dunno. You're asking the question so you must want to answer it." She shivered. "Let's go inside. It's getting chilly out here."

"Afraid I'll push you off?" Dry mouthed, Joanna felt as if she were sucking rocks.

"Jesus Christ, Joanna!" Sherri stared at her then went inside. She perched on the arm of a chair and watched Joanna come in. "It's just as chilly in here. What the fuck's going on?"

"Okay, I'll tell you." Joanna began pacing, licking her dry lips. She stopped, glared at Sherri but could barely see her. "You seem to think that fun is the be-all and end-all. Empty, pig-headed fun. You almost got me thinking that way, too." She tossed back her hair. "You're a slut, groveling from bed to bed. You don't care about your kid, hate your parents, hate your job. Christ, you must hate yourself. Do you have any values?"

"What brought this on?" Sherri finished her wine in one gulp, picked up her purse and moved toward the door. Then she stopped, turned her head defiantly, "Yes, I have values. Friends, good times with them." She stared at Joanna. "And what are yours? You seemed to value Ricardo's luxury."

Joanna felt Sherri's words whip across her face. She collapsed on the couch and looked down at her helpless, dumb hands, fingers flopped on her lap like limp, overcooked fettuccine. Finally she raised her head to meet Sherri's stare.

"Touché . . . ah, Sherri, forgive me. I'm trying to find out what I think."

Sherri said nothing, kept staring.

"It's funny," Joanna said, "I told Dan I'd go to Nassau next week with him and Lucille—after the verdict if it's good. But I don't belong with them and I don't belong with you and Ricardo—or at bridge parlors." She opened her arms wide as she spoke, and then closed them tightly across her chest. "I guess I don't know where. I used to belong *to* Beaumont."

"If you weren't so damn critical all the time you could belong anywhere," Sherri said, moving toward the door. "I hate judges." She grabbed the doorknob.

"What do you mean? Dan? The black-robes we work for?"

"Man, you're obtuse." Sherri laughed. She let go of the door knob, moved to the center of the room and sat cross-legged on the floor. She pointed to her wine glass. "This is going to take a refill."

Joanna picked up the wine bottle and handed it to her.

"I don't like people judging me," Sherri said as she filled her glass to the brim. "Why do you have to?"

"Everybody judges." Joanna tucked her hair behind her ears.

"You're wrong," Sherri said, "I don't."

Joanna pulled her knees in close. She felt the anger dripping out of her drop by drop, and wanted to contain it—release it all at once. "Yes, you do. You make fun of me because I don't want what you want. That's a form of judging."

"I satirize—it's more fun. When you stop judging, you'll go for the fun, too."

"No," Joanna shouted, "No. I want to make judgments. I want to make my own decisions on right and wrong. I want to care." She dropped her voice. "I want to love people."

"So do I. But we don't need to judge in order to love." Sherri untangled her long legs and stood. She moved behind the couch and rested her hand lightly on Joanna's head.

"We don't need to fuck, either." Joanna stiffened at Sherri's touch.

"I didn't realize you were so conservative. Should've known, though, by the way you dress."

"Well, it's dangerous. I mean you could get AIDS. Do you know who else Ricardo's slept with? Who you have, for that matter?"

"Hey, Sweetheart, women don't go for assholes." Sherri lifted her hand from Joanna's head. "That's the only place you get AIDS. Ricardo's not gay or even bi. Sheesh, is that what's bothering you?"

"Sherri this is 1985! You work court cases! You know women can get AIDS! Joanna struggled to gather her thoughts. She knew she was straying from her real concerns by arguing about AIDS or the morals of the decade. She wanted to express them, discover them. Finally, she said, "When I was little, my mother went to bed, in my bed, mind you, with—and I hate to say this stupid fact—with the ice cream man. Don't laugh."

"I'm not laughing," Sherri said, staring at her. "Go on." She moved her hand lightly over Joanna's head again, smoothing her hair.

"I came home from school early with a fever and sore throat. And found them." Joanna continued, still stiff, but ignoring Sherri's caress as best she could. "His white uniform was crumpled on the floor on top of *my* Barbie dolls. For years afterwards my mother tried to bribe me. I don't know why because I never even threatened to tell my father. He'd have killed both of us if I had."

Sherri patted Joanna's head and then moved slowly toward the balcony. She kept her back to Joanna. "No fun. We all have stories, don't we?" She shrugged her shoulders. "When I was a freshman in high school," she said in a high voice, "I didn't fit in with the crowd. Didn't want to particularly. They were such rich prig—everything my parents wanted me to be."

Curious and feeling much friendlier, Joanna waited for her to continue.

"I had an art teacher at the time, Miss Rosenthorn. She admired my clothes every day." Sherri coughed, gulped some wine. "She said I had a flair for color. Anyway, to make a long story short, she seduced me soon after the basketball team gang-banged me in the back of Nathan's deli."

Joanna felt suddenly light headed. The scenes Sherri had just thrown at her wobbled like scrambled cable stations.

"My God, Sherri, that's awful."

"Funny, I still remember the Polish sausage they used to taunt me." Her voice had a dreamy quality. "So fucking typical."

"Jesus, why did those guys do that to you?" Joanna closed her eyes tight.

"Oh, probably macho shit. Besides, I like sex, unless it's cruel like that. Doesn't matter if it's with a male or female, or both." She glanced at Joanna and smiled.

"But what does all that sex do for you?" Joanna shivered despite the warm breeze blowing in. She pictured Egyptian mummies, leather-skinned, hollow.

"I just feel better." Sherri shrugged her shoulders. "Maybe I'm addicted to sex. Can't you see the serenity of the just-come look that gets in my eyes?"

"I'm not good at apologies, but I owe you one." Joanna put her feet back down on the floor, leaned forward, and cupped her chin in her hands. "I shouldn't have blamed you for my post-Ricardo feelings. You didn't betray me. I betrayed myself."

"It's okay."

"I'm straight, you know. I don't want sex with you." Joanna coughed this time.

"I know," Sherri said, turning back into the room. "That's okay, too."

Joanna leaned back into the couch. Her vision seemed clearer. The ornaments around her spider plant sparkled as if freshly sprayed with bottled water. She closed her eyes when she felt Sherri's hand on the top of her head again. This time she took the gesture as comforting.

"You know," she said, "the thing about my mother that's so sad, though, was what she told me the day I got married."

"What was that?"

Joanna felt the old lump in her throat. Her voice seemed out of control so she cleared her throat a few times.

"She said she didn't want to go to bed with the ice cream man, but he'd flattered her every day. Get that? Flattered her."

"Ricardo flattered us," Sherri said softly.

"Exactly, and I don't want to ever fall for that again, ever." She reached up and placed her hand on top of Sherri's, the one that lay so lightly across her head.

"Ah, but you will," Sherri said flatly.

"No!" she whispered," No!" It sounded like a scream in her head.

CHAPTER NINETEEN

Dan arrived soon after Sherri left. He carried an old picnic hamper reminiscent of Masterpiece Theater episodes—1920's picnics on the English moors. Some of the matting had broken and small pieces protruded dangerously here and there. The flat top had warped and curled up in one corner revealing the neck of a champagne bottle. He'd come by cab and they arrived at the Marina before Joanna could contain her grins.

Joanna gave him her hand to guide her along the quay. She felt strength centered in his palm as they headed toward the "Merci," Monroe's twenty-eight foot, teak sailboat. Glancing around, she suddenly remembered Sherri's comment about the old men at the marina who flew the cocktail flag so many times they "couldn't get it up anymore." She peeked sidelong at Dan, certain he'd have no trouble in that department. Then she realized her experience with older men, or younger ones for that matter, was severely limited—to Beaumont, basically, with a *soupçon* of Comp and Ricardo.

She eyed Dan in the fading sunlight of this stolen evening with more than a hint of lasciviousness, yet glad she wouldn't be alone with him long enough to reveal how she felt. And Dan, she knew, was too solid, too straightforward, to just flatter her the way Ricardo had.

"Watch your step," Dan warned, nodding toward guide ropes that extended from each boat—umbilical cords connecting the gently rocking boats to the mother quay.

"Good evening," a man sang out as he polished the chrome on his thirty-foot Chris Craft with short, rhythmic, and precise strokes. His stomach overflowed his red shorts. Though a good twenty years younger than Dan, the man seemed to be more of a specimen of Sherri's experience with the "old duffers" than Dan would ever be.

She smiled as Dan led her toward Monroe's boat with the assurance of a man who always knows what he's doing when he's doing it. He reminded her somehow of Cary Grant, although she couldn't see any specific resemblance—other than confidence shown by a focused concentration that amazed her. Or maybe his white cotton slacks and blue polo shirt.

The slowly setting sun warmed the back of her neck. A mild ocean breeze filled the air with the not unpleasant scent of decaying mangoes. Dan's fingers, gently caressing hers as they walked, sent tendrils of electric heat to her groin where her new jeans rubbed. She wanted to tug the jeans loose, but couldn't do so inconspicuously.

"Here we are." Dan set the picnic basket in the stern of an old wooden sailboat that creaked at each touch. "I'm pretending I maneuver this thing out of a crowded marina every day, and now I'm taking you for a cruise to see wild dolphins." He jumped aboard and reached for her hand. Sunlight shimmered on his thick white hair. In the southeast, above the Everglades, white thunderheads shone, too.

Joanna stole another glance at his blue eyes and caught them undressing her. He quickly looked away and helped her on board. She felt a moment's grace as if she, too, could know what she was doing at the moment, and why.

The boat rocked. She leaned on his arm and relished his scent: a combination of clean perspiration and faint aftershave lotion.

"When are Ralph and Lucille coming?"

Dan placed the picnic hamper at the galley entrance. He pointed to a cushion next to the rudder.

"Come, sit before you fall overboard," he said. "I'm pretending we're on the high seas."

Joanna sat as bid, trailed her fingers in the warm water, and waited for Dan to speak. She allowed herself one moment's adoration, and then asked again, "Ralph and Lucille?"

"I should have mentioned this before." His eyes held an apology. "I confess I was afraid you'd refuse to come here if I'd told you that both of them begged off this afternoon. Said they had too many things to do."

She felt the confidence drain through her pores and the familiar shyness return. She sat still, knowing any move would be clumsy.

"I guess that's okay," she said, lowering her head

Dan slid into the seat directly across from her and gently lifted her chin.

"You don't need to be afraid of me," he said. "I wouldn't hurt you for the world."

"Oh, I'm not afraid of you." *Of me. Much more afraid of me.* "It's okay."

"You're sure?" He let go of her chin.

"Yes, I'm sure. It's just, you know, what if someone from the court saw us here together—alone. I mean, couldn't that jeopardize your case?"

"No need to worry." Dan took her hand and kissed her fingertips, flailing nerve endings throughout her body. "First, it won't affect the outcome of the trial, and second, it wouldn't matter to me if it did." He grinned. "In other words, if it were a great risk to me having a picnic with you, I'd happily take the risk."

The teak hull squeaked as it rocked in the barely moving bay. Dan opened the picnic basket, releasing the scent of fresh Bimini bread.

"I was lucky this afternoon. I found a Bahamian bakery that was open." He tied a fishing line to the neck of the champagne bottle and lowered it overboard. "I'm going to try to re-chill the champagne and settle it down a bit."

"The water's kinda warm for chilling champagne, isn't it?" Joanna couldn't stop grinning.

"Bottom fishing," he said. "It's a tad cooler down there." He looked into her eyes. "As for the trial—has knowing me affected how you record or transcribe the proceedings?"

"I thought it would, but it hasn't."

"I knew it wouldn't," he said, releasing her with a slight narrowing of his pupils. Dan's blue eyes still held her. "You're too responsible, a pro."

Joanna felt a serenity she'd never before known as the boat rocked and the sun poured over them. She sat in comfortable silence, mesmerized by the moving patterns formed by sailboat masts against the blue sky. She felt so good, in fact, that her fear soon returned—the conviction that anything good is always taken away—and she began to feel normal again.

"What a beautiful day." Dan broke the silence with a cough and fished in the champagne. "I feel young and sentimental. Champagne's a little cooler."

Joanna felt a sudden and intense curiosity about Dan's life as she watched him open the champagne. She let it build in her until she could no longer contain it.

"What was your mother like?" she blurted.

"Fastidious." He leaned back against the gunwale. "She used to have fits over three cornered rips which I managed to get in all my clothes somehow. She was formidable. People were afraid of her, including me, but she actually was quite soft and dependent, especially on my father. He let her seem to be the stronger of the two. She wasn't, I discovered much later."

Joanna pondered this idea and tried to apply it to her own parents. Perhaps her father was the weak one after all.

A loud splash nearby caught her attention. A woman was treading water; three boats away, a man standing on the bow, stark naked stretched into a dive. He hovered for a second, his nakedness somehow natural against the blue sky. Then, with a splash, he joined the woman.

"Wow," said Joanna, "they're skinny dipping."

"Common practice here."

She wanted to hint they do the same, then, deciding to let him be the one to make such a suggestion, she returned to her questions. "Do you have any brothers or sisters?"

"No. Wish I did now, but when I was a kid I liked the freedom of being alone."

"Freedom's a paradox, you know." Joanna said, echoing Sherri.

"I know." He leaned forward, scanning her face.

She longed to kiss him, to feel his full lips under that soft white mustache, to touch the tip of his tongue with hers.

"Can you pour the champagne yet?"

"Sorry. You're so entrancing I forgot what I was doing." He unwound the wire around the neck of the bottle, reminding Joanna of her lassoing days. With his large thumbs exerting gentle pressure, he slowly pushed the cork out.

Admiring every move he made, she couldn't help smiling as she handed him two wine glasses from the picnic basket. The heat of his breath brushed her hand as he poured. Her hand shook.

"So, tell me about your mother," he said. "Is she beautiful, too?"

Beautiful? Too? She'd not thought much about her mother's looks.

"I guess she is. I mean there's nothing wrong with the way she looks. My father's terribly jealous, of both of us, actually." She pictured him in a series of scenes ranging from jealous rage to sneering as he insulted all who crossed his path. "Even when I was a little kid, he put my friends down. I'm sure he'd hate you on sight."

"I can understand that. What did he do to Beaumont?"

Joanna exploded in laughter. Embarrassed, she struggled to contain it. "They're so much alike. They hated each other for years, and then finally became friends." Sobering, she asked, "Are we doomed to marry replicas of our parents?"

"Only the first time," he answered. The noon sunlight sparkled on the dancing champagne. "Look at these bubbles, will you. Let's drink, but first let me make a corny toast."

Warmed inside from Dan and outside from the eighty degree temperature, she smiled.

"To your soul," he said lifting his glass. "May its wonder and strength reveal itself to you."

"Thank you." Tears sprang to her eyes, but she didn't hide them. She sipped the barely chilled champagne. Sounds of the naked couple splashing and giggling pleased her. The soft, seaweed scented breeze flowed over her. How she wanted to strip right then and there and dive in, too.

Dan pulled a small cooler from the basket and opened it. On a bed of shaved ice lay six giant shrimp, two cracked stone crabs and a small sushi tray with its dot of green horseradish and delicately curled ginger shavings.

"Ah," she exclaimed, feeling hungry for the first time. "Only you would bring such beautiful food to a picnic."

He smiled, broke open a stone crab and handed it to her. She inhaled the smell of the succulent flesh, watching him do the same while watching her. His eyes reflected hers reflecting his. She thought of nested Chinese boxes, Russian dolls inside slightly bigger dolls, and mirrors mirroring into infinity.

He dipped a raw tuna *tekka maki* in horseradish and fed it to her. She gasped, choked, laughed and gestured for more. He brushed a piece of rice off her chin.

Dan turned away from her in a quick move. He began checking the ropes and talking about sailing. She felt a chill, and wondered if she'd done something wrong. The thunderheads had moved in closer and the breeze had shifted from its usual southeasterly direction. It now seemed to be coming up from the Everglades.

"Storm coming?" she asked.

"Looks like it, but not for a while yet." He sliced the Bimini bread and neatly buttered the thick slices. "I hope you like this bread. It has a unique flavor." He refilled their glasses with champagne.

"I love to try new foods." She took a small bite of the soft, slightly sweet tasting bread. "It's good." Beaumont would hate it. She giggled, stretched her legs across to the opposite gunwale and leaned back, letting her hair fall back till it skimmed the water. The sunlight, though fading, now made her squint. She could feel Dan's eyes on her. At the same time she could hear him moving—washing up, re-packing the bread into the basket. She sat up, took another bite of her bread and stole glances at his face. Once she caught him with a private smile.

Finished with the tidying, he sat across from her again and sipped his champagne.

"You told me the night of Hurricane Julio," he said, "that you got tired of reading all the time so went back to school to become a court reporter. What did you like to read?"

"Everything and anything, I guess. I liked E.B. White's essays, and George Orwell's, but mainly I read fiction. I had no reading plan, as they say."

"Who are your favorite fiction writers?"

"Faulkner." She paused, stared at the thunderheads. "Don't care much for Hemingway. Ann Tyler. Tom Robbins, of course." She laughed thinking about Pan in *Jitterbug Perfume*, invisible but raunchy smelling. "Funny how some writers can touch you. Oh, Lawrence Durrell, actually, though he makes me work sometimes."

"Durrell, interesting. Ever read Melville?"

"No—not yet."

"Well, you're in for a treat."

"Have you read <u>Moby Dick</u>?" She raised her shoulders.

"Just once. I'm due for another reading." He looked up at the sky. "The whiteness of the whale compares to those thunderheads. Yes, Melville was a lusty character who could approximate in one novel all human experience. Durrell does that, too, only he takes five. Have you read the <u>Avignon Quintet</u>? I just finished it."

Tears filled her eyes again. She'd never expected to meet anyone who read those books she'd read in secret so Beaumont wouldn't broadcast how they filled her head with "bullshit notions." Scenes with Assad and Constance making passionate love in a steamy bathroom used to float through her mind when Beaumont screwed her. She glanced at Dan now, a little embarrassed by an intimacy she hadn't expected, the delicious one of shared literature.

He shot her a flirtatious look as if he'd read her mind.

Let me not get in bed with Dan too soon, she prayed, and lowered her head. *Let me know when it's not too soon.*

"Joanna, I'm very fond of you, more than I want to be . . . I realize I'm old enough to—"

"Sh, sh." She lifted her head and gazed at him. "Old enough to be my father? Is that what you were going to say? Well, I don't need a father." Her voice rose along with her sense of increasing power. "I don't want a father, and you don't even begin to look or act like any father I know."

"You know, I do feel like a young buck right now." He laughed. "It's been a long time." His pupils grew like a cat's in the dark. "So, you see me—uh—so, I'm not just, uh—." He grinned at her, red-faced.

She laughed and nodded. The wind suddenly increased in strength, fluttering flags and the edges of furled sails and rippling the water. The skinny dippers had climbed aboard their Chris Craft and were now wrapped in towels, nonchalantly drinking beer.

"I'm not very sophisticated, Dan," she blurted, "Sexually, that is—but I'm not exactly innocent, either."

"Does it matter?" He just looked at her with gentle love in his eyes. He smoothed his mustache with his thumb and forefinger. "I could say the same thing about me."

"When I was living with Beaumont I liked sex most of the time." Joanna spoke fast, breathlessly. "I mean he was passionate and not selfish in bed like some husbands. Still, I used to pretend it wasn't Beaumont in bed with me when I was mad at him—which was a lot of the time. That's the only way I was unfaithful, in my mind." She shivered.

"Are you cold?"

"No. A shadow just crossed my spine. I just shook it off. Did I ever tell you I used to be a champion with a lasso rope? Well, sometimes I wanted to lasso Beaumont." She twisted a clump of her hair. "Tell me about you. How was it with Bev. Listen to me. I feel as if I know her just from the transcripts. Pardon me for asking."

Dan reached into the cockpit and pulled out a thermos and two cups. He filled them with steaming coffee then laced the coffee with cognac from a small, silver flask. The air temperature had dropped ten degrees. He served the coffee at the right moment. Just as he does everything, she thought.

"No, you didn't tell me about that particular skill. I can see why you'd want to lasso him though." He laughed. "Clouds are moving in." He leaned back and squinted at the sky. "Actually, I'd like to tell you about Bev." He shifted his weight slightly, crossed his legs. "I used to believe in a rational world where only sex and death were mysterious, and neither of those was completely inexplicable." Head bowed, he sat as if in a trance.

"Go on," she urged, trying to curb her impatient curiosity.

"I was attracted to Bev from the moment I first saw her when the hurricane struck, a wide-eyed little French girl." He lifted his chin and looked out to sea. "I waited for her to reach the ripe old age of eighteen, and then married her before she had a chance to know other men. Aggressive son of a bitch, eh?"

"Did you ever have an affair with Lucille?" Joanna felt a jealous rush and gave her hand an imaginary slap.

"You're an intuitive lass." He laughed, a small trill of surprise. "No, never did. Often wanted to, but she never knew that."

"Do you still want to?"

"No, I don't think so." Dan furrowed his brows. "Over the years we've built a solid, platonic relationship. It would be like redirecting the flow of lava to begin a sexual relationship with Lucille."

"Okay, then, tell me about your marriage." The wooden hull, creaking as it moved, seemed as familiar and comfortable as an old aunt's rocking chair. Joanna pictured little cotton ties connecting homemade upholstery to the wooden dowels. A sharp crack of thunder seemed to bring the sky in closer. She felt strangely relaxed; secure . . . the cognac laced coffee, Dan's gentle blue eyes.

"Marriages, as you undoubtedly know, have ritual battles and ritual pleasures." He drained his cup and set it at the galley entrance. "Before Buddy died we had a marvelous sex life that balanced the ritual battles. But after that awful day at Pemaquid."

"He drowned at Pemaquid, didn't he?"

For a minute he didn't answer. Then he said yes.

"I thought so." She felt once again the enormity of his sorrow.

"After that we never forgave each other enough to truly make love." He ran his fingers back though his hair and rested the heel of his hand on his forehead. His face was obscured by his thick forearm. "We tried once a week to maintain some sort of marital illusion . . . created a new, unspoken ritual, and were faithful to each other in it until—until even as I speak to you now."

"Even now?" Joanna heard the barely disguised bitterness in his voice. She touched his knee.

"If you wear a hair shirt long enough, a silk one irritates your skin. I wore the hair shirt of Buddy's death, then Bev's disease. Gave up on ever feeling the silk one of pleasure again."

Joanna smiled, wanting to tease him into a lighter frame of mind.

"Come, now, Judge Lawrence. Tell me your dirt. Believe me, I won't record it for Ansletter's posterity."

He lifted her hand off his knee and kissed her palm, sending reverberations of that kiss throughout her body.

"Yeah," he said, slowly releasing her hand, "that poor, simple pilot trusted me, kept calling me a judge. At least you don't see me as a stodgy, moralistic, righteous old judge, do you?"

"No way, Mon." She dropped her voice, imitating the street vendors, but suddenly sat up straight. "That pilot. They're going to get you on that, Dan. Why *did* you take her body up there? Did she say she wanted to be buried with your son?"

He shook his head. His face grew dark as if airbrushed

"I'm not sure why. It has something to do with the hurricane. Doesn't make sense." He looked up at her and smiled. "Nor do I know why I've denied myself pleasure so long." The man in red shorts passed by and waved. Dan nodded absently. "You know, Joanna, respect from lots of people makes sexual deprivation possible, but now that I think of it, really stupid." Still holding her hand, he turned his face aside. "Still faithful, even now," he whispered.

A few fat, cold rain drops landed on Joanna's forehead and arms. Dan picked up her other hand and held both tightly. She realized from his grip that he really didn't know why and that he needed her. The thought gave her confidence.

"You once said that we, people, should need one another, and that it's good to." Lowering her head, she felt the old shyness constrict her throat. With all the courage she could muster, she said, "I would happily accept your need for me, whatever it is."

Dan bowed his head. More raindrops landed on her arms and hands. One of them was warm. He stood and pulled her up with him. Slowly he wrapped his arms around her and kissed her. She put her arms around his neck as much to brace her weak knees as to love him. He kissed her again and again, each time longer, softer. She parted her lips to let him in, feeling every part of her opening.

He pulled away, tore off his polo shirt and faced her, naked down to his white slacks.

"Let's go for a skinny dip," he said, "while the water's still warm."

Joanna felt her heart move. She looked around. Nobody out. She'd envied the skinny dippers earlier. Now was her chance, but still. She looked at Dan watching her. Patient. His chest with all that curly white hair—so sexy. She looked around again and then ripped off her blouse and bra.

"Last one in is a rotten egg," she yelled.

He gazed at her and slowly unzipped his fly. "I'll take my time. I'm used to being the rotten egg." Standing first on one leg, then the other, he pulled off his shoes and socks. Then, with a hint of a stripper's motion, he removed his white slacks and blue under-shorts at the same time.

"It's black," Joanna gasped. Like a theater backdrop behind his visibly swelling penis was a large patch of thick, black hair. An arrow of the dark curls spread to his navel.

"I'm still young down there," he said, pointing down.

Joanna laughed and then worried that others could be staring at him also. She quickly tore off the rest of her clothes and dove over the side.

The water, now chilly, felt like cool satin against her bare skin. She surfaced, enjoyed the raindrops on her face for a few seconds, took a deep breath and pushed herself downward, feet first. Then she saw the tiller of Monroe's boat about three feet away. Next, something grabbed her left foot. Instinctively, she pulled back and looked down. There, playing beneath her was Dan, a white-maned dolphin with a cute human butt. She surfaced to laugh. *I'm pretty darn sure I love him.*

She felt his hands slowly moving up the sides of her legs, stopping for a moment at her knees, then her hips. With a crash, he exploded above water as if wearing a jet pack. Drops glistened on his mustache and his blue eyes shone in the sudden reprieve of sunlight. She saw a double rainbow directly over his head, forming the top half of an elegant halo. She floated into his arms. *It's too soon.*

"I love you, Joanna," he whispered. "I want you. If it's too soon, I can wait." He reached up and grabbed the tiller.

She closed her legs and pointed her toes down to sink. Below boat level she felt her chest expand and pictured her heart opening, filling up with water, drowning. She hugged her chest. *One month, no, even one night, with him would enrich my whole life. I know I love him.* She pulled on an imaginary rope and surfaced. Spluttering and grinning, she threw caution to the gathering storm.

"It's not too soon," she whispered.

Lightening cracked, followed by an immediate clap of thunder and a downpour—beyond rain—as if some space creature had suddenly dumped a gigantic bucket of water on them. Dan climbed on board and reached over to help pull her on. She landed on top of him.

"Go below," he yelled over the roar of the downpour.

She slid off him and crawled down into the hold, to the tiny galley and a V-shaped vinyl bunk. Dan followed and pulled a navy wool blanket from a drawer which he wrapped around her. She crouched on the edge of the bunk at the base of its V, inhaling the scent of the damp wool. "It sounds like a waterfall up there."

Dan nodded as he spread a cotton sheet over the vinyl. She removed the hot blanket and stretched out on her back, warmed by his gaze. He sat on the opposite bunk dripping water from his mustache and the curls on his chest. Then he knelt on the floor beside her feet and began massaging them.

"I'm speechless, Jo," he said. "Satori."

The sound of the waterfall thinned to raindrops. The boat slowly rocked; the forward hold steamed. He caressed her arches. Her juices flowed. She wanted to stop him, make him climb into her and take her. Generosity permeated his every move, but the foot massage exceeded her ability to lie down and take it—like a woman. Still, somehow, she held back.

"What's Satori?" she asked.

"It's the essence of a kissed knee," he said, kissing her knee. "At the moment of kissing."

"How about kissed lips?" She opened her mouth, longing for his tongue.

"Patience, my love." He rubbed his face between her thighs. "I'm getting there."

She felt his hot breath on her wet crotch. Patience, she thought. I smell Pan, hear his footsteps on the bow.

Dan's hot, loving tongue entered her vagina. She quivered, arched her back. His hands covered her breasts; fingers caressed her nipples. She wished he had three mouths as she kneaded his shoulders. He pulled up beside her; she found his balls and gently rubbed them. He extracted himself from her grasp and rolled onto his back on the narrow bunk. With her eyes, she asked, *what's wrong?*

"This is too new to me, Joanna." He kissed her nose. "I'm not sure I can consummate this. I love your beauty, your body, your totality, but when you touch me, I'm suddenly . . . well, anxious. I'm brought back to my ego, as it were. My separateness."

"Oh, Dan, I don't care how old you are, how separate you feel or if you ever consummate anything." She buried his face in her breasts. "I love you, and just need to give back." She lifted his head and looked into his eyes. "I can't take from you all the time. I need to give, too. Will you let me?"

"I hope so," he answered in a hoarse voice.

"Well, roll onto your back, Sir, here comes your favorite court reporter." She massaged his feet and kissed the smooth ball of each one. Slowly she rubbed his thighs, enjoying his hair and thick muscles. He's a walker, she thought, a stair climber. He jumped when she circled the base of his penis. Gently she stroked it, feeling it harden and fill her hand. She licked her lips and bent over him, sucking gently. How she loved him. When she heard a sharp intake of breath, she lifted her head. "I'm climbing aboard your majestic sword now. You can do with me what you like."

He did. With a firm grip on her hips he controlled her movements. She reveled in his control, let go of her own and sank groaning into an abyss of pleasure.

She felt his increasing motion when her breathing returned to normal. Soon he erupted inside her. She pictured Vesuvius, felt his hot, life-giving fluid shoot into her. Briefly wondered if she was fertile. Didn't care. The word, "bliss" filled her consciousness. The smell of their mingled juices permeated the boat, enhanced by the receding storm and its residue of ozone.

"Genesis," he said, moving the damp strands of hair from her forehead. "I don't have the right to feel this good." He touched her lips. "My God, I forgot. Are you on the pill? I should've asked beforehand."

"Yes," she lied, remembering the moment she tossed her birth control pills in the river. "Don't worry." She stretched out beside him. "I love you, Dan. Will you let me just pour a whole bucket full of love on you?"

The wet look in his eyes at that moment, she knew, was seared in her memory for life.

"And I love you, Joanna. Have ever since Hurricane Julio." He laughed. "I told you about hurricane friendships at the time. Didn't warn you about hurricane love. I just hope I can wipe this silly grin off my face before Lucille sees it and starts shooting her camera at me . . . and before the trial resumes. This grin sure wouldn't help me in court."

"The trial may end tomorrow, if it reconvenes. Are you ready for the last day?"

"Sure, judgment day." His voice reminded her of fresh tar over gravel. On one final clap of thunder, the rain stopped and sunlight burst into the hold. "Ah, look," he said, spreading his fingers toward the fading sunlight, "Let there be light."

Joanna felt the light throughout her body, felt his love in every cell, and saw his love as a gigantic abstract sculpture representing hurricanes. She knew he hadn't flattered her.

She knew she could lose him.

CHAPTER TWENTY

Ralph Conscetti stood at the foot of Brickell Avenue admiring a multi-colored high-rise on the bay. Its pastel colors glistened with raindrops in the slanting rays of the setting sun. The colors changed at each floor. He held a small leather suitcase in one hand and binoculars in the other.

Hell, he thought, a drunk could find his way home by color. *Too bad Dan doesn't live in this building. I wouldn't have so much trouble finding him.*

The walk signal turned green. He could cross once again, but what would be the point? He needed to find Dan. Couldn't just leave without saying something. He regretted that Rosalie wanted him home for the art exhibit at the Governor's mansion and her damn garden party the next day. Of course Dan would say, "Go. Rosalie needs you, and I don't."

Damn him, he does need me. Ralph nodded his head, agreeing with himself. *Dan's so strangely passive in court the jury's bound to convict him. I've got to goose him. Yet, Rosalie . . . What the hell's so stupid about garden parties, anyway? To hear Lucille talk, Jesus. Not that I like parties so much—prefer one or two people to a crowd—but there's nothing wrong with them.*

Ralph peered through his binoculars hoping to spot Dan among the people moving along the sidewalk. A woman nearby with ill fitting false teeth chatted with her companion. Her mouth came into view through the binoculars. Quickly, he lowered them, wishing he could enjoy the results of his handiwork in people's mouths without having to listen to the people attached to them.

Still, I don't really mind the parties. Dan and Lucille like to make fun of Rosalie's social life. Are their lives so frigging significant? Where the hell is Dan? He crossed the intersection and pushed the walk button in case he decided to re-cross at the next light change. The five o'clock traffic spewed its exhaust on him. He decided to leave a note and grab a cab to the airport. A familiar voice caught his attention. Sure enough, Dan approached, gesturing with a picnic basket as he talked to his obviously absorbed and beautiful listener, Joanna.

"Hello there." Ralph called, hanging the binoculars around his neck. Neither one looked up. As they drew closer, he called again. Still no response. They moved as if encased in an impenetrable aura. Suddenly Ralph remembered the picnic on Monroe's boat and knew. He grinned. *Why, that old rake*.

"Good evening, Joanna, Dan," he said as they passed right by him.

"Ralph?" Dan looked up and blinked. He shook Ralph's hand and, to Ralph's surprise, hugged him. "What've you been doing?" Dan asked.

"I think I should be the one asking that question." Ralph leaned toward Joanna. "Hi, Jo. Did you enjoy the picnic?"

"Yes, thank you," she said. "Very much." Her olive skin reddened across her prominent cheeks. As she lowered her head, her hair fell forward like a curtain, but didn't hide the blush, nor the Cheshire Cat smile.

Ralph half laughed, half sighed, imagining Dan and Joanna making love. Then he remembered his task.

"I came looking for you to tell you I'm going home for a few days to see Rosalie. Unless you need me to stay till the end of the trial. I think I need to goose you to defend yourself better."

"Sure, go home," Dan replied. "I appreciate all the time you've spent here, but Rosalie needs you more than I do. I'll let you goose me from Nassau. When this necessary business is over, we'll all invade your breadfruit ranch and go looking for dolphins on your boat." He put his arm around Joanna's shoulders. She leaned into him.

"Well, then, I guess I'll catch the six o'clock flight. He waved at a taxi driver who screeched his tires into a U turn and stopped hard beside him. He shook Dan's hand. "Good luck, old buddy—be your most eloquent self tomorrow. Tell them everything, y'hear? I know you can get that jury on your side."

"I'll try."

Ralph squeezed his large body into the back seat of the taxi. He felt a wave of relief pour over him as he watched Dan and Joanna grin at him as the taxi pulled away. It seemed as if the trial had been settled already in Dan's favor. Joanna. Because of her, he thought. She loves him.

This feeling was so intense, he wanted to weep. Ralph couldn't remember seeing Dan glow like this. I love the bastard, too. How come?

He pondered this question as he paid the driver, trudged through the airport, fumbled in several pockets for his ticket, and rushed down the long corridor to the plane with less than five minutes to spare.

He peered through his binoculars as the Eastern flight climbed, enjoying again the teal, shallow waters of the ocean near shore contrasting with the dark blue of the deep. He thought of Pemaquid and the strange bond born there so many years ago, attaching him to Lucille and Dan. Not Bev, though, strangely enough. She was there, bonded with Dan, evidently, but not Lucille and him. Bev was too young at the time, too grouchy later. Did she feel like an outsider too, like Lucille's Arthur . . . and Rosalie?

How many times had they met at Pemaquid since? He started to count on his fingers, but stopped to admire his hands. Strong, square hands with deft fingers, neither slender nor stocky. Steady. Best hands in the business, and the worthiest part of him. The accident of good hands led him into dentistry. Dan had, in fact, suggested it when they first met at the Port Clyde Inn. Yes, long before he'd thought of a career, he'd been proud of his hands.

He recalled again when they first met in 1938 and calculated the years beginning with his left thumb. *Then we met there again in '40 and '41. Then the war. Didn't go back till '46. Then '48, '50 and . . . '52? No—Lucille and I didn't make it the year Buddy drowned. Not till '56, then '59 and just before Kennedy was killed, then '65.*

"Want me to take your glass?" A steward interrupted his reverie.

"Oh yeah, thanks," he answered. He felt foolish—caught counting on his fingers. The plane began its slow descent. He could see a long stretch of white sand on a deserted, index finger-shaped island. *So different from Maine. Benign.*

Most men love and respect one another from a distance, he thought, but Dan and I continue, year after year, to love one another close up. No wonder Rosalie doesn't like him.

Suddenly a conversation with Dan and Lucille at Pemaquid back in 'sixty-five popped into his mind as if it were yesterday, not twenty years ago. Just the three of them that year; Bev hadn't come. He and Dan in tweeds, Lucille so stunning in a black wool sheath she could've been the model instead of the photographer. She'd taken multiple close-ups of their hands. He smiled, remembering. Lucille was on the verge of becoming his lover.

The three of them stopped to rest near the lighthouse after hiking through the woods. He found himself talking about the bond that held them together, like strong parcel tape miraculously growing out of the Pemaquid rock.

"Well, Ralph, what do you think the genesis of human bonds might be?" Dan asked.

"I don't know, but just look around you—at us." He gestured with both arms, lifting them in a circle. "We meet here every other year or so as if we had no other lives, no other commitments or concerns."

Dan moved closer and looked up into Ralph's eyes.

"I think it's simply that we enjoy each other's company," Dan said, "and like this spot."

"You always did talk like a man with a mouthful of cavities." Ralph cuffed Dan's shoulder. "I think we meet here all the time because we're bonded by that hurricane."

"You two assholes arguing again?" Lucille closed her camera. Stop talking for a minute and breathe this glorious air. Pemaquid stays the same for us even as we change."

He and Dan obeyed and sat on the rock to watch the gentle waves. Ralph knew they were thinking of those other, ferocious waves.

Now, twenty years later, aboard an Eastern Airlines flight to Nassau, he caught himself jumping decades again to search for clues. There's more to that bond.

He gazed through the window at the outlying islands and expensive yachts sprinkled in the azure coves. Memory comes in waves, he thought. Yet, as many times as we talked about being bonded since that hurricane, we've never once mentioned our really shitty fight. *Verboten* subject. Strange.

He leaned back in his seat and rubbed his left hand as if the bruise were still there.

*   *   *

Ralph watched Dan fly out to sea still attached to the mast when that hurricane wind first hit their little craft. He'd grabbed Beverly by one hand just as the boat cracked open in the middle, but Lucille washed away from his grasp.

"Hang on," Ralph shouted, "keep your head through your preserver." A wave crashed over them, rolling them over and over and he lost his grasp on Beverly. He couldn't tell which way was up. He had to let the water take him where it would. He could see no trace of Beverly and, with despair, realized it was no use fighting.

The pressure in his lungs began to build, urging him to take some direction. He saw a large black bulk either beneath or above him, perhaps a whale. With all his might he swam in the opposite direction and broke through the surface just as his lungs seemed ready to explode. He gasped for air. Then he was thrown against the black bulk that he now saw extended above water. He could tell by its hard density and the pain in his knees that it was no whale. Rock. Black basalt and granite. He scrambled to the top hanging on by his fingertips as the waves crashed against him, inching higher as each wave receded.

He saw a flash of white to the south and wondered if it was Lucille's life preserver. The pewter sea swallowed it. Then again, he saw it. He climbed up the rock till he was free of the water, and peered out in all directions. North of him he saw Lucille astride a birch tree, riding it to shore as if it were a race horse. She waved to him as she rammed into the beach. He laughed aloud, and thanked God she would make it back alive. Turning south again, he thought he saw Dan, and tried to stand up, but the wind bent him double.

Then a particularly huge wave crashed against the rock where Ralph crouched and tossed Beverly almost onto his lap. He grabbed her skirt as the wave receded, pulling her with it. She was unconscious. Her full skirt, laden with water, ripped as he pulled her toward him. He took a chance, let go of it to grab her arm and managed, against the pressure of the wind and her dead weight, to lay her across the rock, away from the pounding sea. He placed himself lengthwise over her and used his body as pressure to give her artificial respiration. Water streamed out her mouth and she coughed.

"Dan, she's alive," he shouted again and again. He saw a life preserver bobbing south of the peninsula, a piece of white flashing in and out of sight. Then he saw Dan swimming toward the white. Or did he? When Ralph peered again he saw nothing but steel grey.

He held Beverly face down in his lap, and noticed how small she was. The white flashed again, and yes, that was Dan swimming toward it, away from them. "Dan," he shouted. "Over here. Lucille's on shore. Beverly's here." He looked down at her. Though unconscious still, she breathed.

The wind let up slightly. Ralph knew he couldn't out-shout it, but he could at least stand up. He worried that Dan would swim toward the life preserver thinking it was Lucille or Bev. He rolled Bev onto a flat spot and stood to wave. Dan disappeared and reappeared with the regularity of the crashing waves, but he made no sign of recognition. Instead he swam steadily toward the flashing white, moving farther south.

Ralph knew he had to get Dan's attention. He lifted Beverly and carried her to the south facing edge of the rock peninsula. He garnered all his strength to hold her up above his head, hoping Dan would see the white of her dress and swim toward them.

The winds howled louder than the devil in a fury as Ralph lowered Bev's small, unconscious body onto the rock. He caressed her forehead and brushed the hair from her face. Even though she had a woman's body, she was only fourteen and had a child's peaceful face. His arms shook from holding her over his head so long. But the ploy had worked. Dan had finally seen them and was swimming their way.

He scanned the horizon, relieved that Lucille, at least, was safe on shore, but he lost sight of Dan again. Suddenly a wave tossed Dan onto the lower edge of the rock ten feet away. He was limp, inert.

"Sweet Jesus Christ, what do I do now?" Ralph cried, his tone wavering between prayer and curse. Horizontal rain pelted him in sheets. Beverly lay unconscious beside him and Dan lay nearby looking every bit as young as Bev, though he was at least eighteen. Waves pounded the rock, threatening to take one of his charges out to sea—whichever one he left alone for the sake of the other.

The voice of his Italian grandfather singing, *La Donna e Mobile,* came to him as if from the wind, calming him. He half carried, half dragged Bev down the slippery rocks toward Dan, let go of her and made a quick catch of Dan's wrist just as a wave washed over both of them. He held on tight to Dan and kept his eyes on Bev until the series of waves let up. The sound of his grandfather's deep voice came back, this time whispering that powerful line from La Bohème, *Morte, Rudolpho . . . esperado.*

He knew he had to get Dan up higher on the peninsula, but he couldn't seem to pull him. Something interfered. When the waves slowed their bombardment Ralph saw a thin trickle of blood flowing across Dan's forehead. "Damn," Ralph cried, and tugged harder. Dan's belt was caught on a piece of shale.

He decided that Bev lay high enough from the waves to leave her for a second and unleash Dan. He surveyed the ocean through the rain, and then took the chance. While he lifted Dan to unhook his belt from the shale, Dan came to, and said, "Hey!"

"Thank God," Ralph whispered and let go of him to scramble back up to Bev.

Suddenly something grabbed his ankle.

Bastard," Dan shouted, "you threw her in. You killed her."

"Dan, she's here. She's okay. She'll come to," Ralph yelled at him, then felt a hard pull at his ankle. He twisted and fell on his back. The impact knocked the wind out of him. He tried to sit up, catch his breath. The wind howled around them.

"Why did you kill her, you murderer?" Dan shouted as he lunged forward and grabbed Ralph's throat. Blood ran down Dan's face.

It took Ralph a few seconds to realize that Dan was actually choking him, that he couldn't breathe. His strength returned with that realization. He knew he was larger and stronger than Dan so wrenched the hands from his neck and pulled himself to a standing position.

"You're crazy," he said, holding Dan out at arm's length—off the ground.

Dan flailed his arms and legs like a two year old having a tantrum, then grew limp.

Ralph lowered him to the slate. The waves pounded and crashed against the rock just as Dan bit Ralph's left hand.

He felt the piercing pain and screamed, "Christ, my hand." He threw a right to Dan's jaw. Dan fell backwards onto the rock.

"My hand. You bit my hand," he said, amazed and embarrassed by the whine in his voice.

Dan scrambled to a crouched position. "Son of a bitch! I'll get you." Now the blood streamed sideways across Dan's forehead. He looked so small and ludicrous; Ralph couldn't decide what to do. But his throbbing hand reminded him.

Dan made a flying leap at Ralph as a wave crashed over them; both fell. Wrestling on the slippery rock, Ralph felt his power building. Dan had definitely gone crazy. The possibility that Ralph's hand was permanently damaged infuriated him. He rolled Dan onto his back and pinned him, stretching Dan's arms above his head.

The storm ended as suddenly as it began. A gentle, almost mocking breeze caressed Ralph's hands. He pinned Dan's arms flat against the rock. Waves made a lapping sound in the relative silence and the sun appeared, obliterating the storm as sudden waking scatters a bad dream.

"You goddamn son of a bitch," Dan yelled, struggling under Ralph's grasp.

Ralph held steady. He knew he was stronger. Then from the corner of his eye he saw Bev move.

"She's coming to," he yelled, exultant.

"Mon Dieu! What are you doing?" Bev said, scooting toward them.

"Beverly? You're alive?" Dan cried.

"Why're you boys like that?"

"See. I told you." Ralph saw the change in Dan's eyes and released him.

Dan sat up, rested his bloody forehead on his knees and sobbed.

"I'm sorry, Ralph," he sputtered through dripping tears and mucous. "I thought you'd tossed her into the water."

"Why the heck would I do that?"

"Well, I saw you holding her up."

"I just lifted her so you'd see her and swim this way." Ralph rubbed his sore hand.

Dan blanched and looked away.

"Where's Lucille?" Dan asked. "Is she—"

"She made it to shore," Ralph said. "I saw her riding the mast like a bronco buster. She's probably gone in for help."

"Tu es hors de danger, mon cheri." Bev scooted beside Dan and put her arm around him. "Is okay. We live—we are all okay."

Dan squeezed her hand then reached for Ralph's. Wary still, Ralph moved away. His hand still throbbed from the bite.

"Come here, please," Dan said, standing. "Forgive me."

"Oui—yes, come closer, Bev said. "Give us your hand."

"You *bit* my hand." Ralph remembered Dan's comments about his hands just yesterday. How he could be a dentist or something with hands like his. That bite wasn't simply dirty fighting, it was an ultimate betrayal.

"Believe me, Ralph," Dan pleaded, "I thought you'd thrown her out to sea. I guess I thought that from what I saw." He spoke through a swallowed sob. "Forgive me, please."

Never trust a bantam cock, Ralph thought. But cocks don't have such snot filled voices.

"What the heck," he said, and punched Dan's cheek lightly.

Dan grinned and examined Ralph's bruised hand. Teeth marks showed, but the skin wasn't broken.

*   *   *

The plane landed with a jolt. Ralph rubbed the back of his hand and smiled at his memory. That was the only time he had seen Dan as a bratty, snot-nosed kid—no other time since. Still, the fight was the major source of their bond. He marveled at the thought. That's the genesis, he thought, that stupid fight. It made us brothers. Ah, wait until I tell that to the old bastard.

He pulled himself out of the seat and stood bent over in the habit of many tall men and readied himself for Rosalie. He saw her talking: nodding, smiling, her tiny hands punctuating monologues with graceful gestures, all caps here, italics there, irony and sarcasm differentiated with a look. Long red fingernails flashing in the sunlight. Talking. With sudden insight, he knew she was the most powerful woman on the island.

CHAPTER TWENTY-ONE

Ralph's Bahamian friends waved him through customs. His even darker gardener, Nigel, met him at the gate. Ralph began to relax in Rosalie's Mercedes convertible as Nigel drove through the silky air, down the narrow road to Lyford Cay and home.

"Welcome home, Mr. Conscetti," the entrance guard said as he opened the gate for this community of the discreetly wealthy of the world.

"Pull over to the shops, Nigel," Ralph said as he grinned and waved. "I forgot to get Mrs. Conscetti a present."

Several neighbors greeted him as he walked by the pink grocery store and ducked to enter the drugstore. He considered some gold earrings she'd like, but decided on perfume. She might have seen the earrings here and be ticked off that he didn't get her a gift in Miami.

He paid with a hundred dollar U.S. bill, stuffed his wallet with the colorful Bahamian cash, and then hopped into the car, whistling.

"Let's go," he told Nigel, "before Madame Giraux sees me and starts complaining again about her receding gums."

Ralph watched the sun color the white clouds a dark red then disappear, leaving a dusky rose glow that faded into darkness. Soon, though, the full moon rose, lighting a path on the water. Clumps of coconuts in the tall trees, outlined against the sky, reminded Ralph of the potent balls of jolly green giants.

"Ah, good to be home, again and feel that breeze," he said to Nigel. "Did you cut back the breadfruit?"

"Yes sir. Have to keep after them all the time. Planted some yellow roses along the west fence for the missus yesterday."

"Good, good."

Nigel pulled up to the black iron gate and honked the horn for his ageless wife who waved from the window of their blue clapboard garden cottage and came down to open the gate. Ralph thought gratefully of his investments over the years that made this paradise possible. Of course, if they'd had children, he probably wouldn't have taken the time to make so many investments, or cared. They might have been satisfied with less.

Nigel drove slowly through the gate and down the long concrete, oleander-lined driveway toward the sprawling one-story home with its blue tile roof and floor-to-ceiling windows offering views of both ocean and canal. The sloping lawn on the left led to his dock and new marlin fishing boat, "The Rosalie." He didn't really enjoy fishing, but Rosalie liked the looks of the cushioned swivel chairs anchored to the deck and the oversized trolling rod. He studied the boat now, looking forward to tinkering with its engine.

Nigel slowed to a gentle stop. Ralph let his eye and thoughts turn right to the ocean. He wanted to run barefoot across the beach and wade in to see if the red starfish still hovered ten feet from shore. Someone had raked the white sand that shimmered in the moonlight, inviting him. He resisted the urge and reluctantly turned toward the house.

Rosalie stood in the dining room. Light from the chandelier softened her features, her pursed lips. At fifty-eight, she looked barely forty. She maintained a youthful figure through an exacting regimen of diet and exercise with Rudolpho, her aerobics trainer. Now she stood with her legs wide apart, looking toward him with flinty green eyes. Light from the kitchen shining through her rose silk dress outlined the curves of her thighs. She wore no slip, knowing full well how it affected men, how it annoyed him in public, teased him in private. Her blonde hair, carefully colored every month, looped and piled atop her head. Long aquamarine earrings flowed down from her lobes like pristine waterfalls. The fine skin of her cheeks, taut since the face lift last year, was lightly rouged.

He opened the kitchen door and greeted her, annoyed with his usual coming-home trepidation. She ran to him, kissed him so quickly she barely touched his lips, then stood back to survey him.

"Ralph Leroy Conscetti, look at your clothes!" She frowned and pouted. "You're a disgrace. I can't let you out of my sight else you look like a . . . like a Sicilian." She hissed the word.

He glanced down at his black slacks and pastel plaid shirt. No tie.

"It's too hot to wear a tie, Rosalie."

"You're impossible, Ralph. Don't you know by now that you can't wear pastels with black?" She finally smiled. "Well, I'm glad you're home so I can dress you properly. Did anyone in Lyford Cay see you in that outfit?"

"No," he lied, and wrapped his arms around her. He always managed to embarrass her somehow, unintentionally. She needed everything to be perfect—Impeccable—the exact opposite of her childhood home in Trenton where she had endured being the eldest of ten children. He decided to be more careful about his clothes—to please her, at least on this score. "I'll go change. How are you, Sweetheart?"

"Well, I must say I've managed without you. Emily didn't show up again last Monday so I had to fire her and find a replacement. Nigel hurt his knee falling off the roof of his shack and couldn't finish grouting the tile in the guest shower. Tomorrow we go to the Governor's mansion. Two hundred people will be here for lunch the day after tomorrow. And you don't come home until now." She clicked her heel on the marble floor, accentuating "now."

"I would've come sooner, but Dan's trial isn't going very well." He felt a familiar dread as soon as he spoke. He'd learned long ago not to defend himself with Rosalie.

"Isn't Lucille there?"

"Yes." The question made him wary.

"Well, let her take care of him. He won't admit to needing anyone ever." She marched down the three steps to the polished ebony bar in the garden room. "I don't see why you had to go over there when there's so much to be done around here just overseeing the help. They're so impossibly irresponsible."

"Dan's on trial for murder, Rosalie." He lifted the binoculars off his neck and looked through them out to sea, enlarging the small waves cresting in the moonlight.

"Shouldn't he be?" Sarcasm rimmed her voice. To his surprise, she poured herself a crystal wineglass full of Chivas Regal and took an unladylike swig. This bothered him, for she rarely drank. She worried all the time about calories, and certainly needed nothing to loosen her tongue.

He backed away and took his suitcase into his bathroom, unpacked his toilet articles and washed his face in preparation for the tirade. *She'll be okay tomorrow, if she lets me make love to her tonight. But first things first.* Then he returned to the garden room, sat in his white leather recliner that somehow reminded him of a dentist's chair, and waited.

Rosalie sat on the brocade couch, her back to the window, the moonlit ocean.

"Are you hungry?" She asked in a softer tone.

"A little."

"Emily made some conch chowder before I fired her. I'll take it out of the freezer and heat it up for you."

"That would be nice." He looked at her a long time. "You really are beautiful, Rosalie. I'm glad to be home."

She took another large swig of the Scotch, set the glass on the ebony end table without a coaster—another surprise—and began complaining about Dan Lawrence.

"That so called friend of yours has no class. He lives in a condo in Miami of all places, yet looks down his nose at us." She crossed her legs with a flourish. "How dare he? He's a murderer!"

"Now, Rosalie, he just helped her . . ."

"Poor Bev. She had to put up with him all those years—suffering over Buddy's death while Dan went off to court every day, whistling, mind you."

She stood with a lurch, stumbled, and straightened. The words pouring out her mouth grew thick. Ralph stopped listening for meaning. How drunk was she? The glass was still pretty full. He stared at her. Her head bobbed as she spoke and her face was flushed. Suddenly her eyes widened and she stopped talking in mid sentence. She slumped onto the floor and stared at him. The right side of her face drooped as if the face lift had given way.

"Rosalie!" He fell forward out of the chair, rushed over to her on his knees, and checked her pulse. It raced—full throttle. "God, no—could it be a stroke? You're too young!"

She tried to speak, but could only moan gibberish.

"Sh . . . sh," he whispered, stroking her forehead. "Don't try to talk." Carefully he lifted her onto the couch. "Stay still now and rest. I'll call Dr. Bob and we'll get you taken care of."

One eye drooped. The other stared at him with such vitriolic power he thought of Lucille's portrait of an Amazon Yanomamo warrior, the one Rosalie would not let him hang. Now he knew why. He'd known all along. No amount of wealth can appease the anger of such a deprived child.

*   *   *

Ralph watched over her and waited a painful half-hour for the ambulance to arrive—watched her, loved her as he did the moment he first met her, the prettiest girl on the boardwalk. She, alone, continued to give him a hard on again and again—worth the diatribes. That and the fact she had always loved him. Thank God she never knew about his affair with Lucille.

The paramedics took her to Nassau City Hospital. Ralph called Bob Farnsworth, his neighbor, a heart specialist who played tennis with him every Wednesday, but he wasn't home. Servants tracked him down at the club, and he arrived at the hospital soon after ten. He confirmed Ralph's diagnosis: stroke on the left side of the brain.

"We'll do a cat scan and keep her here seventy-two hours to determine the extent of the damage," Bob said, "but don't worry, she'll survive."

"What's the prognosis—any idea?" Ralph swallowed hard.

"Too soon to tell." Bob put his hand on Ralph's shoulder. "It may take a good long while before she can speak again. It'll take some retraining—then I bet she'll be her old party-giving self, charming the pants off us all." He shook Ralph's hand. "Go home now and rest. I'll see you here tomorrow."

Tomorrow. Ralph wandered through the corridors absentmindedly seeking an exit. Tomorrow. Days ahead without Rosalie's words flowing over and around him. Without need for his silence.

He peered down a long corridor flanked by several closed doors and saw a string of colorless tomorrows. And he would live through them with her, help retrain her speech, regain her personality.

Tears streamed down his cheeks when he arrived home. He tore off the pastel sport-shirt, ripped off its buttons, stepped out of the black shoes and pants, and walked naked into the ocean. Light from the full moon helped in his search for that bright red starfish twice the size of his hands.

The cool water made him shiver. He thought about calling Dan, but it was too late. Besides, he shouldn't add to Dan's worries.

Tomorrow. Cat scan, governor's party, Dan's trial. All scheduled tomorrow. MacBeth. "To-morrow, and to-morrow, and to-morrow . . . creeps in this petty pace from day to day to the last . . . something . . . yeah, the last something of recorded time . . . and all yesterdays . . . all our yesterdays . . . have shown fools the way to dusty death." He let the tears flow.

"Life's but a walking shadow," he continued, struggling to remember the rest. "A poor player . . ." *What is it? Lucille would know.* "A poor player that struts and frets his hour upon the stage—yes, struts and frets and then is heard no more—a tale told by an idiot, full of sound and fury, signifying nothing."

Signifying nothing. Dan's hour on the stage is tomorrow. Rosalie's? Long after tomorrow.

He remembered he must cancel the garden party and pondered the irony that she should be the one to lose speech. He didn't like to chat—she lived to. The rough edge of the starfish scratched his toe. He gazed at it through the clear, still, moonlit water, and felt comforted.

Inside, in his bedroom, he called Dan, waking him.

"Rosalie had a stroke. She's in the hospital. She can't talk."

"I'll be there as soon as the trial ends," Dan said, "come hell or high water, conviction or hurricane. Keep the faith."

He hung up and lay on his back. In his mind's eye he saw Rosalie in a series of lovely dresses, talking and talking. Saying nothing much, but charming the ones she desired, chilling the ones she disdained. She's utterly powerless now, poor baby—powerless without speech.

Dan said to keep the faith. What faith? Life's a tale, told by an idiot, signifying nothing. Someone once said that faith's something only a few people manage to have—like perfect pitch. The rest of us flounder in the dark either looking for it or denying the need for it.

Faith peddlers make more money than call girls. Personally, I prefer the call girl.

I have faith in you, Dan. Jesus I hurt for Rosalie, for you, for Bev long ago, and now for me.

Is this the way the world ends, Rosalie? With a speechless whimper?

CHAPTER TWENTY-TWO

"How would you like your eggs?" the short, plump, waitress asked Dan.

Dan could barely take his eyes off Joanna. The waitress, a gnat-like intrusion, annoyed him.

"Cooked," he replied, brushing her away.

Joanna laughed in rippling, liquid sounds. He thought of a waterfall in Switzerland, and of fairies in old Disney movies.

"Your face sparkles," he said to Joanna.

"Dan, she wants to know how you want your eggs," Joanna whispered.

"Ah," he glanced up feeling a sheepish grin on his lips, "uh, poached, with grits on the side."

The waitress turned on her rubber-heeled shoe and left, shaking her head,

"Look what you do to me," Dan said. "I used to function quite well in a coffee shop. Now I'm so befuddled I need you to take me by the hand just to order breakfast."

"Guilty as charged, I hope." She grinned. "I don't know why I'm so damned happy. I should be worried."

He smiled back at her until he felt a strain in his cheeks and released the muscles.

"I know. I am, too, despite Rosalie's stroke and my trial today. How can we be so callous?"

Her face grew serious. She looked into his eyes for what seemed like several minutes. He grew uncomfortable.

"When I was under water beside Monroe's boat yesterday," she said, breaking the spell, "admiring your naked butt, I decided that one hour of mutual love with you would thrill me for a lifetime—that two would. I don't know. She lowered her eyes. "I'm lost. I love you. Forgive me, I can't think of anything else in the world now, not even your trial." Her eyes filled with tears. "We have half an hour more of this madness."

He reached for her hand but pulled back when the waitress appeared with their breakfast. Dan thought his whole being might turn into the steam rising from the dish full of grits she set on the table. He trembled as he spooned some onto his plate.

"A dollar for your thoughts?" Joanna asked, fork dangling from her fingers.

"You say the most profound, loving thing, and I think about steaming grits." He felt his face redden. "I'm sorry, dear Jo. I'm truly nonplussed." He felt the love in her eyes before he dared look to see it.

"You'll do fine in court today. I feel it." She pushed her hair back. Light reflected from it, reminding him of his mother's brown velvet sofa. "Nothing works better just before a battle of wits than losing them. The wits return on time, sharpened."

"Ah. Out of the mouths of gorgeous babes comes wisdom of the ages," he said, regretting the cliché. "Forgive my pompous response. My God, you're beautiful. It's as if I haven't really looked at you all along."

Reddening, she glanced away, and then gasped.

"Oh no, there's Sherri Taylor and she's spotted us."

"Who's Sherri?"

"Friend of mine, sort of. Court reporter."

Dan stood as the tall blonde, wearing a turquoise cotton suit and a mischievous grin, reached their table. Joanna introduced them.

"My pleasure." Dan said as he shook Sherri's warm hand.

Sherri looked him over. Releasing his hand she turned to Joanna, still seated.

"So this is Dan," Sherri said in a low voice. "Man, what a hunk. I thought he was just some old fart who murdered his wife."

"Hush, Sherri." Joanna said, frowning.

"Care to join us?" Dan asked, although somewhat shocked. Nevertheless, he smiled and held a chair for Sherri.

"No thanks." Sherri touched his arm with her forefinger. "I'll be late for work. Just wanted to meet you and ask Joanna to give me some of her time." She glanced down at Joanna. "I need a heart-to-heart soon, okay?"

"Sure," Joanna replied. "I'll call you first chance I get."

"From the looks of you two from way across the room, I won't hold my breath." She backed away, waving. "But do call," she shouted and went out the door.

"Watch out for her." Joanna said. "She'll put the make on you and you won't even know it."

"If I don't know it," he teased, "I won't have to watch out, will I? Besides," he said changing his tone, "I'm unable to envision anyone but you, and she seemed to be truly in need."

"I know, I know." Joanna looked contrite.

Dan felt a sudden urgency, fear that his time with Joanna was up for good and that he should be planning his defense.

"There's an anteroom to the right of the courtroom entrance that's usually locked. Monroe gave me the key to it. Do you know where I mean?"

She nodded.

"Meet me there at the recess. I'll be inside waiting for you." He checked his wrist only to find it watch-less. "So little time," he said, taking the first bite of his eggs which had grown tepid. "All of a sudden the thought of constricted time feels like peanut butter in my throat. I feel as if I'm squeezing out words with one of those gadgets you use for decorating cakes."

"What would you like to say to me now?" Joanna set her forkful of scrambled eggs back on her plate. She gazed at him from those wide hazel eyes.

Staring into them, he relaxed.

"For starters, I love you—deeply. I think I've loved you from the moment I met you. Do you remember the shuddering elevator during Julio—your wet nightgown—the night in the cathedral?"

"I'll never forget that night."

"We've talked of our age difference so much it no longer seems to exist," he said. "But it does. What future can you have with me?"

"I have now," she replied, smiling. "That's my future, a series of nows." She looked at her uneaten breakfast.

"Through you, I've discovered my own need." He let his eyes meet hers, glanced away, then back again. His head swam. Her eyes asked for more; he searched for answers. "God, I need you." He laughed. "Wow, if Lucille and Ralph heard that they'd cheer from Maine to Miami."

"Speaking of Ralph?"

"I'm concerned about him. Rosalie's stroke was in her left brain. She can't talk, which is a really tough situation for her. I'd like to rush to his side, as he did mine, but of course I can't. Since yesterday, since loving you completely, I want to live—with a passion for life I haven't felt in years. I should be planning with Monroe right now."

Joanna reached across the table, stroked the back of his hand.

"But there's an absurdity in urgency," he continued, turning his palm to hers. "No amount of planning will get the jury to acquit me. There's absolutely nothing I can do for Ralph today. And, I can't marry you and take off for a honeymoon in the Himalayas."

"Guess I'll have to get a divorce right away," she said. "Actually, I've already started the process. Beaumont's been served, and I don't think he'll contest it."

"I wouldn't be too sure. He may not contest it in court, but watch out for him outside." Dan glanced around suddenly worried Beaumont might see them together.

"Lucille would say, 'There's a divinity that shapes our ends, rough hew them as we will.'" Joanna said.

"You're so right. She would." He swallowed a spoonful of cold grits, feeling the contrasting warmth of his affection spread to his fingertips. "I keep on rough hewing, but certainly see how pointless my efforts are." He stood and gestured for the bill. "Nonetheless, I'm ready—hand me my saw." *Brave words from one with a stomach hollowed by anxiety.*

He placed his hand firmly on Joanna's elbow and steered her across Flagler Street, attempting from habit to hide his fear. He stared up at the buzzards ensconced as usual in their daytime perches on the courthouse, waiting for the morning sun to burn off the chill, and felt a comforting connection with them.

But then he saw a man on the courthouse steps wearing a plaid cowboy shirt and a belt with a huge metal buckle. He stopped, let go his hold on Joanna.

"Is that him?" he asked.

"Who?"

"Beaumont."

"Oh, God, it is." She gasped. "What's he doing here?"

"Skulking as usual—forget him." Dan continued walking, carefully separating himself from Joanna. "Don't worry; he's probably here for some violation. When did you have him served with divorce papers?"

"Just the other day—before our picnic."

"Shoot—the world's too much with us. There he goes. Didn't see us," Dan said. They entered the courthouse. The corridor looked empty. "I just want to sit on the seashore with you and listen to the waves—watch the birds." He glanced around again and then touched her chin briefly.

Joanna peered up and down the corridors then pressed his hand against her cheek.

"I wouldn't put it past Beaumont to testify against you somehow," she said.

"He can't hurt me as much as I can hurt myself on the stand," Dan said, surprised, but pleased by her fear. He touched her lips with his forefinger just before they reached the courtroom door.

"Here we are," she said. Her voice sounded prayerful.

He felt a rush of warm, stale air when he opened the door—and a rush of fear. He could not control anything anymore. Anymore? Had he ever? No, he'd had only the illusion of control, even with Bev's illness.

"We're early," he whispered.

"I know. I have an appointment with the new recorder on this case."

"Why a new one?" he asked. He felt a range of emotions wash over him. Was she deserting him now?

"Remember how it's bothered me all along? Knowing you, yet recording your trial?" She smiled gently at him as if he were a little boy.

"Yes."

"Well, I managed while just being your neighbor, but now, loving you? I love you to the tips of my fingers, and they're supposed to hit the right keys. I called Ogasaki right after we got back from our picnic yesterday. Gracious as usual, she accepted my resignation. Of course I didn't tell her why." She touched Dan's arm. "I don't have to sell my soul for a soul now." Smiling, she tossed back her hair. "I'll be sitting in the back with Lucille. Good luck, my love."

As she moved away he felt his courage draining as if she held a string that unraveled him.

CHAPTER TWENTY-THREE

Dan had regained his composure by the time Judge Ogasaki called the court to order. He noticed a new tightness around the judge's mouth. Nothing else revealed her ordeal with the terrorist. He knew she wouldn't mention it in court, though he could feel the curiosity in the room.

Ansletter's hair sprouted more than usual. He drummed his pen on a legal pad, fidgeting like a student before an exam. Monroe sat calmly beside Dan, cleaning his glasses with a handkerchief.

"All set?" Monroe asked, looking at Dan with gentle, myopic eyes.

"I think so," Dan replied, "but you back me up in case I fumble."

"You won't fumble." He put his glasses on, stood, and called Dan's former maid, Maria Aviota, to the witness stand.

A short, round woman moved down the center aisle emitting a strong scent of whatever perfume she wore that had always irritated him and warned him of her presence. It wasn't the sugary scent that bothered him; it was the amount she wore. It gave him a headache. He remembered now that he'd noticed it during that bright, horrible slice of time when he gave Bev that tumbler full of vodka. He should have known Maria was there. But what difference would it have made in the long run?

"Please describe Mrs. Lawrence as you knew her." Monroe said.

"Ah, she was young to be sick like that, but you know, she sometimes made sense." Maria glanced at Dan, then back to Monroe. "Most of the time, though, poor Mr. Lawrence had to either chase after her or listen to her harp on and on. Man, she had bitching down to a science. And she was always hiding things. I found her wallet in the toilet tank one day when I lifted the cover to check why it kept running." She paused, rubbed her chin. "And Mr. Lawrence's eyeglasses in the flour canister and a bunch of her makeup under the—" She clamped her mouth shut as if suddenly aware of her audience and studied her hands clasped in her lap.

"During the two years you knew the Lawrences, you worked in their house at least three hours a day, five days a week. Is that correct?" Monroe asked her in a gentle tone of voice.

"Yes, Sir. I cleaned and picked up. Sometimes cooked."

"Then you were able in that time to observe Mr. and Mrs. Lawrence together."

"It was a zoo." She smiled, quadrupling her chin.

"Please go on," Monroe urged. "How was it a zoo?"

"Mrs. Lawrence was always on his case. The more she ragged, the less he said. She followed him around, shaking her finger at him, sometimes even hitting him, screaming about this, that, and the other thing, but particularly about Pemaquid. Sometimes she thought he was her mother and yelled at him about her childhood. I was scared she'd think I was her mother and spit some of that venom on me, but she didn't, thank God. I couldna stood it. I don't know how he did." She nodded toward Dan.

"Please describe Mr. Lawrence's behavior."

"He was a saint . . . most of the time. But he's human. There's just so much a person can put up with, you know. Every once in a while he'd blow it." She grinned then clapped her hand over her mouth. "Actually, he hardly ever raised his voice."

Dan felt again the drudgery and pain of those days. Living in the proverbial trenches. He hoped Monroe would redirect the testimony so the jury wouldn't think her behavior drove him to kill her.

Monroe took off his glasses and held them up toward one of the ceiling lights. Slowly he pulled out a handkerchief and methodically cleaned each lens. Dan wondered what he was planning.

Monroe put his glasses back on and peered at Maria. She wiggled in her seat.

"Was she like this every day?" Monroe asked.

"No, not all the time." Maria looked upward for a moment. "You tend to remember the worst times. Actually there were days, not many, mind you, when they seemed normal and happy with each other."

"You described to the court last week," Monroe said, glancing at the jury, "how you happened to be in the Lawrence house on that weekend you saw Mr. Lawrence pour a glass full of straight vodka and hand it to his wife, knowing full well with the pills she had taken, it would kill her. Did you ever wonder why he did that?"

"No, sir. I figured he couldn't take it any longer."

Ansletter grinned.

"Did you ever hear of any plans they had made for her death?" Monroe asked.

She stared at the ceiling a few moments, then looked again at Monroe.

"I didn't hear any specific ones, you know, thought out plans. I heard her rant and rave about him going to Hell if he died before she did. Called him a coward for not killing her. And once I heard her yell she didn't want his f-ing sleeping pills."

"Thank you. No further questions." Monroe nodded to Ogasaki and returned to his seat.

Dan glanced back at Joanna to reassure himself that his current love had nothing to do with Bev's death. Yet, in a way it did. Her death made love possible. The very trial here made meeting Joanna possible.

He used to be so sure of himself. Now he knew that guilt or innocence depends on the perspective you take. From one point of view, he did his duty as promised. From another, he made love possible again. One last fling. One more chance for happiness that Bev could not have.

If point of view determines guilt, how can anyone find justice? Truth, beauty, and justice, and the rarest of these is justice. His eyes burned. He caught Joanna's eye and felt encouraged to shift his perspective again, back to his promise to Bev.

Ansletter paced in front of the witness stand then stopped abruptly. Maria looked frightened. Dan sent her comforting thoughts: *don't be afraid, Maria. He's all bombast with no balls. A court eunuch with a cowlick.*

"A few minutes ago," Ansletter bellowed, "you said, and I quote, 'I figured he couldn't take it any longer.' You described the Lawrence household as an emotionally charged zoo. Is that correct?"

"Yes, sir."

"Would you say this zoo was so intense it could induce murder?"

"Objection, your Honor." Monroe jumped up. "Speculation—assumes facts not in evidence."

Judge Ogasaki didn't respond for a minute, as if sorting her thoughts. Dan wondered if her ordeal had affected her confidence.

"Objection sustained," she said with a fragile note in her voice that unnerved Dan. Monroe shot him an anxious look.

"Let me rephrase." Ansletter bowed his head. "Ms. Aviota, look at the defendant over there, Judge Lawrence. Do you see any physical evidence of Mr. Lawrence being under great strain?"

"No." She glanced furtively at Dan. "He looks a whole lot better now."

"How did he look then?"

"Objection." Monroe stood again. "Irrelevant."

"Objection sustained," Ogasaki replied in a stronger voice as if she had found focus.

Ansletter grunted and paced toward the jury.

"Is it true," he asked in a softer voice, "that you actually saw the defendant fill a tall glass with vodka and hand it to Beverly Lawrence?"

"Yes." The blood drained from Maria's round face.

"Did he tell her to drink all of it?" Ansletter had his face so close to hers she leaned back. He turned to look at Monroe as if expecting another objection. Dan marveled at Monroe's placid demeanor.

"No sir. It was her choice."

"Would you make such a choice?"

"I doubt it." Maria sighed.

"No further questions." With his usual flurry, Ansletter sat.

"Your Honor," Monroe said, "May I redirect now?"

The judge nodded and Monroe strolled up to the stand.

"Ms. Aviota," Monroe said, "You heard Mrs. Lawrence call Mr. Lawrence a coward for not killing her. Is that right?"

"Yes sir. Lots a times."

"Do *you* think he killed her?"

"No. She drank the vodka. He just gave it to her."

"Thank you." Monroe bowed slightly and said, "No further questions."

"The witness may leave the stand," Ogasaki said in full voice.

Dan tried to catch Maria's eyes and nod at her as she passed, but she didn't look at him. He had a strong urge to grab her arm and tell her she did fine, that she didn't hurt his case in any way. Some day he'd tell her.

The judge asked for the next witness; Monroe called Judge Lawrence. Dan could hear Ansletter breathing as he moved to the stand. He glanced back at Joanna, and then spotted Lucille in yet another bright green dress. He smiled inwardly, knowing her mind. "Hey, sweet asshole," she'd say, "tell them everything. I mean everything." He nodded to her.

"Judge Lawrence," Monroe began, "please reiterate for the court the steps that led to the death April 5, 1983 of your wife, Beverly Duvoir Lawrence."

Dan gazed at Lucille, raised his eyebrows. *Everything?*

"Please tell the court how your wife came to make this strange request of you." Monroe spoke in his usual soft voice, yet his words carried.

"Okay." Dan cleared his throat. "Mrs. Lawrence was a very shy person," he began. "She didn't make friends on her own, probably because she distrusted strangers." He surveyed the jury, studying their faces. "When we were first married, her father died, only forty-eight, leaving her mother to exist on a small pension. Women weren't expected to make their own way in those days." He paused, thought of the many times he'd watched Joanna's skillful fingers, her unpolished, short nails tapping away.

"Your Honor, we don't need a dissertation on society here," Ansletter interjected. "Could we have more direct questioning?"

"Continue Mr. Lawrence," Ogasaki said, ignoring Ansletter's complaint.

Lucille gestured with open palms, *Tell them everything.* Dan appreciated her long face nodding encouragement, and missed Ralph with a sudden poignancy.

"Beverly's mother probably had Alzheimer's disease, too, but it was called early senility in those days." Dan rubbed his damp palms on his pants. "She lived in the best nursing home we could find in Buffalo. Think I mentioned this before. We visited her regularly. At that time Bev made me promise that if she were ever sick like her mother that I would help kill her and not sentence her to live out her years in a nursing home." He took a sip of water.

"Go on," Monroe urged.

Dan could hear a cricket somewhere in the quiet courtroom reminding him of the opening day of his trial. *Is it the same cricket?*

"I promised her," he said, pulling himself into the present. "She also asked me to smother her so she would experience something similar to death by drowning. She had the strange notion she could get closer to our son that way."

A woman in the jury gasped, making him realize how macabre this sounded. He had lived with her smothering plan so many years, the thought had become commonplace, even though he knew he could never do it.

"In March of 1983," he continued, "I was able to convince her that barbiturates and vodka, taken together, would give her a similar experience, easier than smothering. I promised to give both to her on her mother's birthday in April. Also, she asked me to give her the final choice."

"If she wanted final choice, why didn't she just commit suicide?" Monroe hung his thumbs just inside his pants pockets.

"She insisted I help her do it." Dan let a weary sigh escape, and then straightened his shoulders.

"And why did you take that responsibility?"

"Marriage is wonderful and difficult," he said, trying to gather the thoughts racing through his mind. "You can't change the person you marry, and sometimes you have to go against your will for the sake of the commitment." He felt a sudden embarrassment—almost shame. "I took the responsibility for her life because she gave it to me. And I had let her down before."

"How did you let her down?" Monroe's voice carried genuine curiosity.

"Buddy." He lowered his eyes and swallowed hard. He concentrated on the sound of the cricket.

"Buddy was your son."

"Yes."

"And he drowned at Pemaquid—when he was a little boy." Monroe's voice was soft, yet thick with affection.

"For years I thought I let her down by taking Buddy to Pemaquid in the first place. Actually, it was just an unfortunate accident—neither of us to blame. We didn't recover from it very well." He crossed and then uncrossed his legs. "She grew even more dependent, and I carried an unwarranted load of blame. You see, I couldn't continue to refuse her requests for her life, or for her death. At the time I believed they were valid."

"When you were a Supreme Court judge in Buffalo, New York, you earned the reputation as a fair but very stern judge." Monroe glanced at his notes. "Did you ever sentence anyone to death?"

"Objection. The defense calls for irrelevant material."

"Objection overruled," Ogasaki said, and turned to Monroe. "Please establish relevance here, Mr. Cort."

"If it pleases Your Honor, I'd prefer to give Mr. Lawrence the opportunity to do just that in his response." With his forefinger Monroe pushed his glasses higher onto the bridge of his nose.

She nodded.

Dan cleared his throat. He glanced back and saw Lucille's wide grin, Joanna's raised shoulders.

"No, I never sentenced anyone to death," he answered. "I don't believe that the state, as a rational agent based on civilized law, has the right to take human life. I don't believe anyone has the right, with malice aforethought, to take human life, including me." He glanced at the jury. "However, individuals do act from private motivation and sometimes will take lives out of decency, compassion, and commitment." His voice broke.

The silence in the courtroom touched him. Even Ansletter stood still. Dan cleared his throat again, and spoke louder.

"A court of law must act on higher moral reasoning than any individual might. Because it represents a collective group, it should reflect the highest collective reasoning, not the lowest. I helped my wife die for individual, personal reasons. As judge in a court of law I could sentence a murderer—one who killed with malice aforethought—to prison for life, but could not presume, as a representative of a civilized state, to take his life."

Monroe clasped his hands as if stifling spontaneous applause.

"Why, then, did they call you the hanging judge?" Monroe asked.

Surprised, Dan glanced at Ogasaki, and then answered.

"I wasn't aware of the nickname. I suppose people called me that because I sentenced murderers to life imprisonment without possibility of parole—which to them was worse than hanging." He recalled the agony of some of those decisions and wondered what kind of sentence he would get. Which one would he prefer?

"No further questions at this time," Monroe said. Dan saw a smile tugging at the corner of his lips.

Judge Ogasaki hit her gavel twice and called for recess. Dan turned around and faced Joanna. He felt drunk from the look in her eyes. Dare he hope?

*   *   *

Dan unlocked the anteroom and slipped in. He leaned his back against an old oak desk in the musty room, swallowed a nitroglycerin tablet to be on the safe side, removed his glasses, and rubbed his eyes with the heels of his hands.

He heard the door open and shut fast then felt Joanna in his arms before his vision cleared enough to see her. So young, so frail—yet she sent strength coursing through him as if someone had shot his veins from Ponce de Leon's famous fountain.

"You were magnificent up there." She kissed his lips and his neck and whispered in his ear, "I knew you would be."

He held her, silently soaking up strength, until the first chime sounded to resume court. He studied her radiant eyes a moment, and then released her.

"Ansletter's been wounded." He stood up straight and said, "He'll come back vicious, you know."

"Are you afraid?" she asked.

"Oh, my darling, yes." He pulled her to him, felt his naked need. "I want so much to be free to be with you, I'm scared to death."

"You'll be free." She ran her fingers through his hair. With a quick kiss, she backed away. "I love you," she whispered and slipped out, closing the door softly behind her.

There's such finality to the sound of a closing door, he thought, and opened it.

CHAPTER TWENTY-FOUR

Monroe opened the door to the anteroom and beckoned. Dan stood and smiled at him, feeling confident again.

"Court's in session. You're still on," Monroe said. "I need to pull the whole story out of you."

Judge Ogasaki granted permission for Dan to re-enter the stand. He promised Lucille in a quick glance "to tell all."

"So far, Judge Lawrence," Monroe said, "the evidence shows you first planned, and then helped your wife commit suicide, essentially because she asked for it many times. That you then flew her body to Maine and buried her at sea, much as a sea captain might." Slowly he strolled toward the center aisle, encapsulating previous testimony for rhetorical effect and rubbing his red mustache. "You were a Supreme Court judge in Buffalo, New York for twenty years and you know the law. Kindly tell the court why you are not guilty as charged."

"I plead not guilty—I repeat—because my intent was honorable." Dan glanced at Joanna and Lucille and then looked at the second juror in the back row whose deep brown eyes seemed sympathetic. "I have always believed it's wrong to take another person's life. That's why the last two years of Mrs. Lawrence's life were so hard on both of us. I consistently refused her request."

"Yet, in the end, you felt compelled to acquiesce to her wishes. Correct?" Focused on Dan, Monroe's blue eyes softened with compassion.

"Yes. You see, I took a vow when I married her," he said, struggling to control his feelings, "to love, honor, and cherish her, through sickness and health, till death do us part." He raised his voice and repeated, "till death do us part. Finally, I had to honor her request. As I've told the court, I had a heart attack in January of '83. The doctors told me I could have another at any time. So, I finally agreed to help her die." He glanced at Lucille and met her eyes. "We had a pre-arranged finger symbol. If, after she drank the vodka, she changed her mind and she made that signal, I would rush her to the hospital and have her stomach pumped. Thus, at the final moment, her death was her choice."

"And what was this signal?"

Dan closed his eyes.

Monroe repeated the question.

"She was to raise her middle finger and flip me off."

A nervous laugh from the spectators momentarily drowned out the cricket.

"But she didn't do it, right?" Ansletter jumped up, bellowing. "This is beyond belief!" He shook his head. "Were you watching her hands while she drank, watching her die?"

Ogasaki reached for her gavel.

"I watched them every minute, Mr. Ansletter. To tell the truth, I couldn't stand the thought of her drinking that much straight vodka. I didn't think she could keep it down. So I watched her fingers. She had insisted for so many years, and I grew accustomed to the idea, desensitized, I guess." The cricket noise grew louder and the white light of that day seemed to invade the courtroom. His mouth remained dry despite several sips of water. He wondered if his birds of paradise were thirsty.

Ogasaki let go of the gavel. Ansletter sat. Steam seemed to come from his whole being.

Monroe stroked his red mustache and then resumed his questions.

"Was it symbolic of your relationship," Monroe asked, "that she flipped you off regularly?"

"No, not symbolic—actual. Because of her illness she often became that angry. Irrationally so. The finger was her idea." Dan felt vulnerable and ashamed. What would Joanna think of him? Then he remembered Beaumont. We are not, he reminded himself, who we marry.

"And afterwards, you took her body to Maine. Was there some relationship to your son's death there?"

"In a way, yes. My son had drowned there years before. She," his voice broke. "She wanted to be with him. I realize it doesn't make—"

Dan took another sip of water and collected his thoughts. The members of the jury leaned forward as one. He spoke directly to them.

"Each of us has a reptilian brain at the base of the head, just beneath the evolving human sections. I can only hypothesize that the part of my brain that feels terror and spirituality in great beauty motivated my actions that day. I did not plan to take her body to Pemaquid." He turned to Ansletter. "From the testimony so far—especially Maria Aviota's—it's evident that my life with Beverly was hellish toward the end. Actually it grew increasingly worse each year."

Dan rubbed his temple and surveyed the room.

"If any one of you has ever tried to care for someone with Alzheimer's, you would know that my reasons for helping her die were not pure. It was my impure motives—those moments of hatred and despair and helplessness—that kept her alive. It was the idea I'd failed her, or she me, that kept her alive. It was the fact I had changed over the years while she clung fearfully to the memory of a dead son that kept her alive, a memory I resented because she blamed me for his death." He paused, glanced sideways at Joanna. "It was loss of love that kept her alive. It was true, committed love that finally poured the vodka."

The silence in the courtroom seemed thick, barely penetrated by an occasional cough.

"And Pemaquid?" Monroe asked gently.

"I intend to clarify that," Dan replied. "Bear with me." He adjusted his tie. "You see, I first met Bev at Pemaquid when she was only fourteen and I was seventeen. We, new friends that I'd just met and I, were caught at sea in a hurricane and tossed from the boat. For a long time I swam around in that wild water trying to find them, but mostly trying to save my own skin. Then I saw Ralph Conscetti on the rock holding Bev's body over his head as if he were about to toss it into the waves. I thought she was dead. In fact, I was so sure he'd tossed her out to sea, I attacked him, for which I am still very sorry." Tears filled his eyes. He took a deep breath. "Anyway, I took her body to Pemaquid because," he said, raising his voice, "it's a beautiful and terrifying place, and that's where she belonged."

Monroe turned to Judge Ogasaki. "No further questions, Your Honor."

The judge tilted her head to Ansletter who stood and looked straight at Dan.

"And that's where she belonged, Mr. Lawrence? No punishment? No malice?" He turned to the judge. "No questions, Your Honor."

"Your Honor," Monroe said, "I'd like to make a point here. Our defense includes no malice aforethought. In the case of the state versus Robert Mather—"

Ansletter jumped up as if on a pogo stick.

"Out of order," he shouted. "Other cases are not part of this trial."

Dan had figured Ansletter would object to this part of their defense plan, yet felt his heart sinking in disappointment.

"Release the witness," Ogasaki said, "and approach the bench."

Monroe, dwarfed by Ansletter, stood beside him before the bench, whispering in staccato bursts.

Dan returned to his seat. He glanced around and thought he saw Beaumont enter. He surveyed the back of the courtroom. There stood Neanderthal Man dressed in a plaid shirt open at the collar. A gold chain nestled among black curls that almost covered his Adam's apple. Beaumont frowned at Dan, staring at him from those deep-set, almost black eyes.

Joanna's eyes widened in recognition, but she remained motionless. Dan admired her while he felt his whole body turn to fluid. He imagined Beaumont on the stand, Joanna near the bench recording the trial and Ansletter brushing back his cowlick, asking him to describe for the court her relationship with the defendant. And Beaumont clearing his throat—more a hacking sound before saying he didn't have a relationship with the defendant but that his wife does.

Dan pulled himself out of this scenario by pressing his legs against the rungs of his chair. He didn't want to look at the jury, but he did. Their faces were open, questioning; he examined each one, feeling once again he was in the right. Then he glanced back to find that Beaumont had disappeared. But Dan knew the guy would come back to haunt them—somewhere, sometime.

The lawyers returned to their seats after a lengthy whispered consultation with the judge. Ogasaki picked up her gavel.

"The Defense requests we retire to chambers for a private conference," she announced. "Request granted. Only the prosecutor, defense counsel, the defendant co-counsel and the recorder need be present. Final evidence and closing statements will be presented tomorrow, at nine." She hit the bench with the gavel. "Court adjourned."

*   *   *

"We are meeting here," Judge Ogasaki said, "outside the presence of the jury at the request of Monroe Cort and Daniel Lawrence to include relevant cases in the record." The new recorder's long, red-polished nails flew across the keys.

Dan waited for Monroe and Ansletter to speak and listened to his heart both metaphorically and literally. He concentrated on deep breathing until his heartbeat seemed to find its normal rhythm and his thoughts some clarity of purpose.

"Mr. Lawrence, will you begin?" he heard Monroe ask in a gentle voice that encouraged him.

Dan stood and described in detail a recent similar case in Florida: The State versus Robert Mather. Mather had shot his wife when her pain from stomach cancer could not be relieved by medication.

"The jury convicted Mather," he said, because the poor guy showed no remorse. Is that justice? He did what he felt compelled to do. How could he feel remorse?" Dan wondered if his contempt for that jury showed in his voice. He modulated it, paused and rubbed his brow. "In the Netherlands, euthanasia is common, and accepted with the terminally ill. I realize this is a different jurisdiction, but we could do well to examine this civilized country."

Judge Ogasaki turned her head as if to hide her expression. Dan suddenly remembered her daughter had married a Dutchman and hastily changed the subject.

"In the case of the state versus Radelow, 1984," Dan continued, "the jury acquitted Radelow because his wife was unable to take her own life, was terminally ill, and suffered the pain of multiple sclerosis. Or, did the jury acquit him because, unlike Mather, he wept in court?" He stared at Ansletter. "Given a similar situation—a loved one begging for death—what would you do?"

Feet wide apart, wrists crossed in front of his groin, Ansletter pursed his lips, rocked on his heels, but said only, "It's against the law to kill anyone."

But not to kill civilians overseas, Dan thought.

"If the criterion for acquittal," Dan said to Ogasaki, "is terminal illness of the deceased, the inability to commit suicide, and extreme pain, then I, too, should be acquitted. If it's weeping or remorse, then I am guilty. Tears for my wife have been long spent. I have no more." But as he spoke, he felt them forming behind his eyes.

"If, as the district attorney suggests," Dan continued, raising his voice, "an acquittal now would set the precedent for spousal murder, why has there not been a sharp increase in such crime since the Radelow decision? If I thought for one moment that not helping her die would save my freedom, I would be guilty of the lowest form of human consideration." He knew Judge Ogasaki would understand, but his heart pounded in an irregular beat. He reached for water.

"If Judge Lawrence were sane at the time of the murder," Ansletter said, glancing at his notes. "and he has not pretended otherwise despite his reptilian brain theory, then there's no doubt he's guilty. The rate of spousal murder is irrelevant. Taking one life is enough."

Judge Ogasaki studied each one. Dan felt her gaze and wished he could reassure her.

"There is no more to be said here," she said. The jury will have to decide."

"We've reached impasse," Monroe said. "Thank you for including this in the record, Your Honor."

Outside, Monroe's eyes were glazed and he stood so still Dan wondered where he'd gone. He touched Monroe's sleeve.

"We have one more witness tomorrow—Bev's doctor," Monroe said without moving or blinking away the glaze. "I'll follow Ansletter's summation. We don't need legal strategy anymore—just guts." He slapped Dan's knee. "Let's go."

CHAPTER TWENTY-FIVE

Dan felt rested the next morning and filled with love after dinner with Joanna, Lucille and Monroe, a spectacular sunset, and a long delicious night with Joanna.

"Delicious?" Joanna asked, grinning as they approached the courtroom.

He shrugged his shoulders and blew her a kiss. A resurgence of hope filled him as the trial resumed.

Monroe called Dr. Denis Bouculat, Bev's doctor, to the stand. The Frenchman had pursed lips, a slight build and a slow rolling gait. He was often heard to say, "In France, time is not money." Beverly had found him soon after they'd moved to Florida. He nodded to Dan in greeting and entered the stand.

Monroe established the doctor's credentials for the court: general practitioner whose patients varied from children with measles to adults with confusion. Doctor Bouculat folded his hands in his lap and awaited all questions with an equanimity Dan attributed to French *savoir faire*.

"Are you familiar with this case?" Monroe asked.

"Yes. I've known the Lawrences for four years." He crossed his legs at the knees.

"Mrs. Lawrence was your patient. Please describe her symptoms and your diagnosis."

"Her symptoms were typical of Alzheimer's, beginning with loss of memory and coherent thought, then hallucinations. Once, in my office, she imagined and fell in love with a multi-colored cat wearing mirrored sunglasses." He paused, looked at Dan. "And, she said she both loved and hated her husband."

"Did she let you know why she hated him?" Monroe fingered his mustache.

"Ah, yes," he replied with a smile. "Quite clearly. Often she complained that he wouldn't do what she said and that he would not smother her."

"Smother?"

"Yes. She wanted him to smother her with a pillow." The doctor shrugged his shoulders.

"How did you treat Mrs. Lawrence?" Monroe ran his fingers through his red hair.

"I couldn't treat her," the doctor replied. "There's no cure as yet. I spoke to her in French. That's all I could do."

"That was a lot," Dan said under his breath.

Monroe stifled a smile. Ansletter raised his eyebrows.

"In your opinion, Doctor," Monroe asked, "could she have made plans for her death specific enough to include when and how?"

"Mrs. Lawrence was an unusual case," he replied. "I diagnosed Alzheimer's at first from her many symptoms. However, she was young for such a disease—not yet fifty, I believe—and had many moments of clear thinking despite its progression by the time she came under my care." He turned toward the jury. "I sent her to the hospital for tests. I suspected a brain tumor, but the tests were negative." He gazed at the ceiling. "*Mon Dieu.* I did not believe those tests." Looking back at Monroe, he said, "To answer your question: Yes, she could, and did, plan her own death specifically."

"Thank you. No further questions." Monroe returned to his seat.

Ansletter approached the stand. His shoulders, hunched forward, raised the hem of his suit coat in the back. Dan felt inexplicable warmth for the prosecutor. It's a heartless job, he knew from experience, representing the state. Much easier to defend a visible, warm blooded murderer than an abstraction called "the State."

"Dr. Bouculat," Ansletter began, pronouncing the t in his name as if on purpose, "you seem to have some confusion about your diagnosis of Mrs. Lawrence's illness. Did you ever send her to a neurologist?"

"No. I saw no reason."

Dan was amazed at the doctor's ease.

"Yet you, yourself, weren't sure what she had?" Ansletter raised his eyebrows.

"I was sure she was very ill with an incurable, mentally debilitating disease."

"You said she could decide how and when she would die. That's more than most of us in sound mind and body can do," Ansletter said with an almost imperceptible sneer. "You are just a general practitioner—right?"

"Yes." Bouculat smiled. "Just a general practitioner."

"Then how could you know Mrs. Lawrence was capable of planning her own death?"

"I just received this letter from the wife of one of my patients whom I referred to neurologists five years ago." He pulled a handwritten letter from his breast pocket and looked at the judge. "It's pertinent. May I read it?"

Judge Ogasaki nodded.

"My husband has Alzheimer's, as you've known all along, Dr. Bouculat. I've been told by three doctors there's no cure. He's gone through many phases by now, hallucinations, angry pacing all night, hiding things. Then slowly he lost all his functions, the ability to write and speak, stand up without falling, etc. Finally, a blocked urinary tract and fever put him in the hospital. Pneumonia. After massive doses of antibiotics he was cured of pneumonia, but could no longer swallow. So they inserted a naso-gastric tube." The doctor paused and looked directly at the jury.

"I begged that they not keep him alive," he looked down at the letter and continued reading. "What a farce it is to sign for no heroic measures! They continue to feed him—and his heart is strong. Dr. Bouculat, that was three weeks ago and he is still alive! Today, while looking for a comb in his hospital bathroom I was temporarily out of sight when a hospital administrator and two doctors stood at the foot of my husband's bed discussing him. The administrator said, and I quote directly since it's burned into my brain, 'We need to keep this one alive and let the one in 220 A go. This one has insurance above Medicare. The other one is costing us eighty dollars a day.' Dr. Bouculat, what can I do except curse the fact we have insurance?"

The doctor slowly folded the letter and pocketed it. He looked up at the prosecutor.

"I have no good answer for her," he said and held out his arms for a second.

"That's a sad story indeed, Doctor," Ansletter said with a sigh, "but it's not relevant here, and may not even be true."

"Yes, it is," he interrupted. "Both relevant and true. I've sat in on hospital death committees. It's a matter of pure business who lives and dies among the terminally ill. Dan Lawrence has insurance. His wife would be alive today living in the horror she most feared if he had not helped her die. Judges can't play God in America, but doctors can—and do."

"That's a goddamn lie," a man in the audience shouted. Others began shouting back at him.

Ogasaki pounded her gavel.

"Court's adjourned until two o'clock," she said when the noise subsided.

*   *   *

Dan felt weariness in his bones. Ansletter's summation seemed long and repetitious.

"At least you won't put the jury to sleep," Dan whispered to Monroe.

"I'll be fast," Monroe replied, "but after Ansletter rebuts, I'll take my time with the summation, lots of time." He grinned. "Remember, the quality of mercy is not strained through a brief legal brief."

Monroe stood and delivered his summation; Ansletter rebutted in only two minutes for a change, reiterating the facts that weakened Dan's defense: premeditation, burial at sea.

Dan glanced at Joanna. She sat very still, statue-like, hands poised as if she were still recording. A sturdy geranium, he thought, in orchid clothing. Then he studied the jury. He'd seen thousands of cases and all kinds of jurors, but this felt like his first time in court. Here were twelve varied characters, plus two alternative jurors, who gave up their time to serve justice, at best, or to have something to talk about when it was over, at worst—maybe a little of both. Three jurors on the far left of the front row, two men and a woman, had formed a clique. They smiled in unison now and shot each other knowing looks.

Monroe smoothed his red mustache, took a deep breath, and began his generalized rebuttal.

"Ladies and gentlemen of the jury, I submit to you that my client, Daniel Briggs Lawrence, is not guilty of murder in first degree because the premeditation was hers, or second degree because he had no malice toward his wife, no criminal intent. She was terminally ill. The decision you make on this case will establish precedents of mercy and compassion."

One of the jurors in the back blew his nose loud enough to stop all action. Joanna put her hand on Lucille's arm. Judge Ogasaki grabbed her gavel. Monroe acted as if he ignored it.

"I'd like to relate a true story that has bearing on my case," Monroe continued. "My aunt, a District Attorney in Tampa, happily married with two grown children, was rediscovering privacy and music with her husband when he had to have open heart surgery. He survived the surgery and she retired to spend more time with him. Then one day he grew alarmingly ill and she rushed him to the hospital. He had pancreatic cancer. The doctor said her husband had only a few months to live, that during those months he would suffer excruciating pain. Because of his heart condition, pain medication would probably kill him. Unwilling to play God, this doctor told her she must decide whether or not to ease his pain."

Monroe paused, stared at the floor. Over in the corner the cricket sounded. The new court reporter's red fingernails hovered over the recorder, waiting for the next syllable of sound.

"That night," Monroe said, "she called her adult children, my cousins, to help her with the decision. They supported her choice to take a chance on medication. At his first piercing scream, she called for it. They injected morphine, and he died."

The members of the jury stared at Monroe as one.

"My aunt, a prosecuting attorney much like Mr. Ansletter here, suffered terrible guilt for three years afterwards. You know why?" Monroe's voice grew hoarse. "The doctors didn't ask her husband. They gave *her* the decision! I suspect they gave it to her so she wouldn't litigate against them. The dead don't sue. But it should have been *his* decision."

"Beverly's death was her decision even though his hands helped to carry it out. Unlike my aunt, he doesn't feel guilty. He is not guilty. Monroe glanced at Dan then turned to face the jury. "When the quality of life becomes not just meager, but torturous—either through pain as my uncle's case in Tampa, or through fear as in Beverly Lawrence's case—the quantity of life, length, duration, and a so-called natural death cease to matter. After Judge Lawrence had a heart attack, Beverly Lawrence tortured herself with the fear that he would die and leave her alone in a nursing home."

Dan saw the second juror in the back nod.

"If you believe that quantity of life is more important than quality," Monroe continued, "then he is guilty. Ladies and gentlemen, justice is an abstraction. Among other things it means that everyone is equal under the law. The law in Florida states that murder in the first degree is 'the unlawful killing of a human being when perpetrated from a premeditated design.' In the letter of the law he may be guilty. But is the letter of the law the same as justice?"

Dan saw the grey haired woman taking notes. She stopped writing, finally, and looked up, meeting Dan's gaze. The three-juror clique wore identical dour expressions. He wanted to shout at them, 'The law is not a Procrustean bed,' but knew better. Metaphor is best left to the poets.

"Through legislation," Monroe said, straightening his shoulders, "we strive for justice, but don't always make it." He strolled to the end of the jury box, then back to the middle. "It's the cases—trials like this—that help us achieve true justice, an abstract concept impossible to define except through specific cases."

Amen, Monroe. We don't stretch or shorten people to fit a bed, we change the size of the bed to fit the people, Dan thought, still wishing he could shout the Procrustean metaphor.

"We weigh the facts of each case, and the intent," Monroe continued, "in light of the abstraction, and then reach a just verdict. We trust you to do that. You see, I'm not pleading for Dan Lawrence alone. I'm pleading for each one of us in this courtroom who, because of advances in medical science, must make decisions that fate used to make for us—before there were medical plugs to pull," he lowered his eyes, "or not pull." Then he looked squarely at the jury. "I'm pleading for premature babies forced to live mentally and physically handicapped lives because science kept them alive."

Dan heard a woman gasp.

"I'm pleading for you and you and you," Monroe said, nodding toward the bald man, the second juror in the back, and the grey haired leader, "when the time comes for you to defend yourself before a jury because you did what was right in your heart for someone you love. I'm pleading for justice for all of us. He is not guilty." Monroe lowered his eyes. "Ladies and Gentlemen, I rest my case."

Dan felt Joanna's gaze, heard Lucille's silent applause. Speechless, he shook Monroe's hand.

Ansletter stood to rebut with his usual flurry, paced toward the jury, stretched his arms wide as if to encompass all of them, and then leaned forward, hands on the rail.

"The burden of proof, Ladies and gentlemen of the jury, is on the state. But there's not much to dispute, is there? Let's take a look at what's been going on here." He adopted a conspiratorial tone. "My colleague, Mr. Cort here uses a lot of big words. Hell, I've been to college and I don't know half of them. I'm going to speak to you in plain English. Do you know what an abstraction is? He scratched his head. "Pretty vague." A few members of the jury smiled.

"I know this." Ansletter stood straight and bellowed with all his vocal force. "The law is the law." He paused, surveyed the jury, then lowered his voice a few decibels. "Mr. Lawrence admits that he knew the law—that he broke it. He deliberately broke it. And his lawyer speaks to you of justice. But justice is served when those who break the law are punished." He drew out the last syllable of punished into a hiss. "If not, we would live in anarchy, or martial law. Would you like to live with armed soldiers watching your every move? That's martial law. Would you like to live where neighbors shoot at each other and loot? That's anarchy. Without law we fall into either extreme. Mr. Lawrence broke the law—one he knows well. True, he had his reasons. Even I have been known to rationalize a misdemeanor or two."

Two jurors in the front row smirked.

"But I don't play God! Nor do doctors—and they are not on trial here." Ansletter twirled around and stared at Dan. "Anyone acting above the law thinks he's God. Ladies and Gentlemen, he isn't." He slammed the railing with his fist. "The United States of America is a great nation because its people are law abiding, voluntarily so, because its judicial system is made up of ordinary folks like you and me who don't pretend to be better than others, above the law, and because its deeply religious heart still beats." He paced in front of the jury. "We may not go to church so often, and we may doubt some of the sayings of those old time religions, but we still know right from wrong."

Dan watched the show, wondering if Ansletter's theatrics affected most of the jury. He realized it worked on some.

"Murder is wrong," Ansletter roared, pounding his fist on the railing, "even perpetrated on the least favored among us. When—at what stage of terminal illness does a person cease being fully human? Who can say?" He raised his right arm. "I say, and I say with a full human and God-fearing heart, death by another's hand, even in compliance with the victim's hand, is still murder."

He's pushing too far, Dan thought.

"Ladies and Gentlemen, if you find Judge Lawrence not guilty of murder when it has been shown beyond all reasonable doubt that the administration of lethal doses of alcohol killed his wife on April 5, 1983 and that he threw her body out to sea, then you do not have religion or patriotism or justice in your hearts, and risk—by acquitting one who thinks he's God—true anarchy. Think about it, Ladies and Gentlemen." He paused, crossed his hands behind his back, and rocked on his heels.

The three jurors on the left looked like they were about to applaud, but stilled their hands. Dan wondered how many of the rest felt that same urge, but their faces were expressionless.

"Anarchy, I repeat, anarchy. Let justice be served." Ansletter twirled on his heel and returned to his seat.

The courtroom seemed to echo with his words. Dan heard reporters' pens scratching across pads.

Judge Ogasaki turned to the jury and, in a monotone, read the Florida definitions of first, second and third degree murder.

"You are to consider all the facts in evidence carefully," she said in a soft but impassioned voice, "but remember, unless you do find malice aforethought, there can be no murder in the second degree. Court adjourned."

Dan saw one of the clones in the jury mouth 'anarchy' as the jurors filed out.

CHAPTER TWENTY-SIX

Joanna stood on Dan's veranda watching a brilliant sunset when a sudden squall soaked her. She backed under the overhang and looked for Dan to ask for a towel. He had his back to her, sipping Retsina wine as he created moussaka, his favorite Greek recipe. After he put it in the oven, he turned to her and then rushed out with a dish towel and umbrella. The sun came out and formed a rainbow. Dan sat beside her on the bench, kissed her cheek, and then stroked the stem of a bird-of-paradise.

"Your moussaka smells wonderful," Joanna said as she dabbed her hair and face with the dish towel.

"So do you."

Just then another cloud dropped its cargo. Joanna opened the umbrella and held it over both of them.

"Listen to the rain pound," she said. "Sounds like a Louis Bellson drum roll."

He smiled at her.

"Did anyone ever tell you your mustache smiles?"

"Yeah. Lucille. According to her it also frowned and showed I was in love with you before I even knew it."

Joanna laughed and leaned her head against his chest. She noticed the pills in his shirt pocket and remembered. Heart. Her stomach jumped and she sat up to scrutinize him. He seemed invincible. Yet?

"Shouldn't you be on a special diet of some sort?" she asked.

"Why?" He kissed her fingertips and looked slyly at her.

"Your heart."

"My heart's so full right now I can't protect it by anything, let alone diet."

"I'm serious." She gazed into his eyes.

"So am I."

The rain stopped; the dark clouds slowly dissipated and the sky resumed its colorful sunset show. Dan folded the umbrella, leaned on the railing with his back to her. "Remember when we first met—in November only, but it seems like years ago—and the elevator stopped? You were scared."

"Yeah, that old English proverb, 'Death comes either too soon or too late'."

"You remember!" He faced her with a big smile and then sobered. "Control over death is an illusion." He patted his shirt pocket. "But as you see, I'm a cautious risk taker." Turning back to watch the sky, he continued, "I knew when I finally agreed to help Bev die that I had no real defense in court. But I wanted to raise the issue—"

"Hey," she interrupted, "it's been eight days already and they're still deliberating. That's an unusually long time. Someone on that jury's fighting for you."

"—and I was willing to risk a jail sentence rather than deny her—rather than avoid the issue. Even though now I long to be free to be with you, I don't regret taking that risk. Hell, I risk death every time I make love to you." He laughed, a soft exhalation. "Actually I do have an awe-filled intimation of death each time, a foreshadowing, as it were, complete with the opposite feeling of creating life." He swiveled around and looked into her eyes. "Are you—could you get pregnant?"

"I stopped taking the pill," she whispered. She felt her whole body blush. The horror of her night on Ricardo's black satin bed with Ricardo and Sherri washed over her again. How close she'd come!

"Do you want me to use a condom?" Dan asked

She uncrossed her ankles and shook off her shame. She pushed herself up to hug him.

"Oh, my dear, no," she said. "I'm a risk taker, too. Finally."

She felt his hands cup her rear as he pulled her in tight. The soft, moist breeze seemed to wrap them in a wet silk sheet. His love, so straightforward and gentle, melted her once again. She succumbed with pleasure.

*   *   *

At four in the morning Dan's phone rang, waking Joanna with a start. Dan answered.

"It's Sherri," he said and handed her the phone.

Sherri told Joanna she was sorry to wake Dan but she'd called her place first. She was downstairs in the lobby and desperate. Joanna invited her up. Leaving Dan asleep, she slipped across the hall to her aunt's condo. She felt too deliciously loved to empathize with Sherri's latest disaster, but she could, at least, listen.

Sherri fell into her arms sobbing, blonde hair matted, make-up washed away. Wearing faded jeans and a paint spotted T-shirt, she looked strangely young and innocent. Joanna held her, crooning. Something was radically different and wrong. She led Sherri to the sofa facing the veranda and the black sky, and then sat beside her.

Sherri swallowed hard and stared straight ahead.

"Remember the bruise on my arm a few weeks ago? Sherri asked. "You asked about it the night we went to the bridge parlor and I told you the Red Cross is always calling for my blood."

"Yes. I remember. It was that awful night with Comp." Joanna shuddered with the memory.

"Well they called me last week. The Red Cross has just started a routine screening for AIDS and I've—" She burst into tears again.

"You—you have AIDS?" Joanna jumped up, backed half way across the room.

"No." Sherri yelled, and then continued in a lower tone. "According to them I don't, but I may be a carrier. I can infect others. Maybe, but that's enough." She pulled a ragged tissue from her purse and blew her nose. "I have to test again in six months. My blood showed a—a human immune deficiency disorder—they called it."

"Oh my God. That means Ricardo? Could I get it?" The horror traveled her body in waves.

"No, Joanna." Sherri reached out her arms. "No. You ran, remember? You don't have to worry. And I told Ricardo already—and the others I've balled in the last six months—ones I could find, anyway. They check out negative. Besides, you didn't come close to having sex with Ricardo."

Thank God, Joanna thought, but so perilously close—Ricardo naked.

"It all happened so fast." Sherri stood and headed toward the bathroom. "The last few days have been sheer hell. I needed to see you bad, but wouldn't ask till I knew for sure you would—" She buried her face in her hands. "And until I believed it was real. That was four o'clock this morning."

Joanna trembled all over as she made coffee. As her own fear subsided, she began to think of Sherri. *Carrier. How can you be a carrier and not get it eventually?* She knew too little about AIDS. The world knew too little.

"They're my whole life—men are." Sherri circled the living room. "I need them," she said, facing the kitchen.

"I thought you liked women, too." Joanna returned to the living room and set the tray of coffee, cream, and sugar on the table beside her spider plant, accidentally knocking a Christmas ball on the floor. It rolled toward the veranda.

"Well, yeah. You. I love you. But men, Jesus, they're my life blood. Without them I'm, I'm, what the hell, I'm inert. You might as well plant me in your yard and turn on the sprinkler once a day. You'd have to turn it on since I won't turn anything on any more." A deep sob rumbled in Sherri's throat. Joanna felt one growing in hers.

"You know what it's like to be deadly?" Sherri asked. She sat on the sofa and smiled without humor or joy. "You could use me as a Hit Woman. Sic me on Beaumont."

Joanna realized at Sherri's comment that she didn't hate Beaumont, but she didn't say anything. She sipped her coffee. It had grown cold. She set her cup down as thoughts careened through her mind.

The black sky outside took on a lighter hue.

"The darkness before dawn just died," Joanna said, embarrassed by the alliteration and triteness of her comment. She reached over and touched Sherri's arm, hoping the touch wouldn't interrupt or trivialize Sherri's feelings. "Watch," she whispered.

Sherri looked out at the sky. Silently, for a good half hour, they watched it turn gray, mauve, pink, almost white, then blue, each shade imperceptibly melting into the next. Sherri broke the silence.

"God's sure a master of the palette."

"Yes, and the palate, too." Joanna's eyes stung. Dry too long. "Also the puppet." She recalled Lucille quoting Lear. "And he kills us for his sport."

"Or, in this case, my sport," Sherri whispered, and then let out a bitter laugh, breaking the spell.

Joanna stretched and felt a twitch in her abdomen similar to what she felt each month between periods when she suspected ovulation. Each time she felt the twitch she imagined a pin ball machine. Pull the lever, release the ball and let it bounce down the tubes. Unless, of course, some barrier stopped it, like a fire hose shooting in streams of curly tailed sperm. The twitch subsided and she settled into the chair.

Sherri handed her a fresh cup of coffee, patted Joanna's knee then began circling the room again.

Joanna watched her, wondering what it was like to be her.

"Tell me about men, Sherri. I've known only two men intimately—Beaumont and Dan. I was too chicken to know more."

"What do you want to know?" Sherri's voice sounded contemptuous, almost bored.

"Hell, you don't need to tell me anything. I was just curious about differences in bed, and my own responses."

"I'm sorry, Jo." Sherri stopped in front of her.

"Quit apologizing. Women always apologize." Joanna said in a sharp voice, hoping to pierce something.

"And men never apologize?" Sherri asked. "Now, can you cut the crap with always and never? Ready to hear about my personal experiences? Which are unlike yours except for Ricardo—and you saw that he was nothing but a performer."

"Right on." Joanna laughed, glad that Sherri had snapped back at her. "He choreographed every move, like the laser video dancing. And I thought he was so smooth, so sophisticated."

"Yeah. He was good, all right. One of the best. He could get his dick hard on command and keep it that way to make sure he was in control all the time. Choreographer is right."

"Beaumont could do that, too. I thought he was such a great lover. He was my first. He deflowered me, as he used to say. God that hurt. But he stayed in control—stretched me out to accommodate him, the prick."

Sherri choked on her coffee.

"Seriously," Joanna continued, "I'm so in love with Dan I think he's the greatest lover in the world. Yet sometimes he's so—" She held her palms up in front of her. "So inept, almost, and innocent. I adore him."

Joanna felt Sherri's eyes on her. She looked up. The bright light of dawn haloed Sherri's hair.

"Never thought I'd say this, but I truly envy you." Sherri shook her head. "I gave up on love years ago." She glided over to the veranda, opened the door to let in the fresh morning air. "This isn't the time or place to tell you my bedtime tales. We should be drinking rotgut whiskey in an empty dive somewhere."

"Still, sordid tales can flow in nice settings," Joanna said, heading for the kitchen. How about me fixing you some toast and honey to fortify you and you can ramble on till you get sleepy?" She remembered lots of rambling, inane conversations at funerals, understanding them now.

As Joanna fixed the toast, Sherri moved slowly from room to room, speaking in a monotone.

"When I was in high school I had a crush on the basketball center, a tall blonde Viking, like Ricardo, sort of. He didn't look once at me, let alone twice, though lots of other guys did. So I started sleeping with his best friend—get this, Jobiah Shaw. He had the hots for me. Claimed he was in love. I didn't feel much for him one way or another."

Joanna handed her a plate of toast. She realized how naive she was about women and wondered how Sherri came to be so sexually free, yet somehow not right with herself.

"Thanks, Jo. Anyway, one day the three of us were in Job's bedroom listening to the latest Yoko Ono crap. Jobiah and the Viking sat on the floor and I lay on my stomach across his twin bed. Plaid collegiate looking bedspread. Innocent was I? Shit, no. I asked the Viking to toss a blanket over me. He did. Then,while Jobiah kissed me, the Viking, under the blanket, slowly rubbed my back—lower and lower until he had me on fire. I'd have fucked him in a minute if I'd had no couth at all. But I had couth." Sherri chewed thoughtfully on the toast. "Ha. Poor old Job thought my passion was for him. His mother came home before I had a chance to get myself in real trouble."

"Were they on the same basketball team that—that raped you in the deli?"

Sherri looked up with wounded eyes.

"Yes . . ." She sighed. "You know, puppy love is something else. You never forget it." She put her toast back on the plate and rested her head on her knees. "The Red Cross told me I won't die from this. Guess my sentence is a broken heart."

"Tell me about the father of your child." Joanna stroked Sherri's hair.

Sherri raised her head. She wiped away the fresh tears with the back of her hand.

"Love doesn't make sense—not one bit. I've had so many really good lovers, ones who can play my body like a fucking harp." She smiled. "Old Ernie, the asshole who ran out on me, must have learned about sex from nerds. He thought foreplay was something golfers did."

Joanna laughed. Even in tragedy, Sherri's wit flowed.

"And he was skinny and going bald," Sherri continued, sniffing like a kid with a runny nose. "No great catch, that's for sure. But here's the funny part." She looked directly at Joanna. "I'm pretty slow to come—with man or woman. Sometimes I don't make it at all. That's why I like lovers who know how to pluck my strings. Yet Ernie, he'd undress by himself, rarely touch or kiss me, jump into bed, roll on top and stick his dick in me without so much as a how-de-do. And get this. I'd be dripping wet and would come before he did. Can you beat that?" She stared at Joanna, shaking her head. "Then the fucker left me as soon as he knew I loved him. He never did know I was pregnant by him. I wonder if she looks like me."

"Do you have any idea why you loved him?"

"Who the hell understands love? I needed him in some weird way and I really got off with him. Ha. Uncle Ernie. Maybe he reminded me of a friend my father had when I was little. Stock broker. Used to hold me on his lap. "She slapped her forehead. "No, it wasn't that guy. Ernie looked and acted just like my old man when he was young. Isn't that something? And he abandoned me just like my father did whenever I spontaneously adored him."

"I thought your father was in New York with your mother." Joanna pictured her own parents still together—glued together.

"Yeah, he still is, in flesh if not in spirit. Anyway, Ernie had a leather box of cuff links. Never wore them, of course, but he treasured them. My father had a box for his tie tacks and cufflinks, too. When I was little he'd let me play with them." She walked out on the veranda and then came part way back to the sofa. She collapsed to the floor and sat cross-legged, silent.

Joanna waited patiently, wondering how best to help her, deciding again just to listen.

"I was practicing counting." Sherri cleared her throat. "Had the cuff links lined up on the floor. My dad came in and sat down to watch. I jumped into his lap and kissed him. Even told him I loved him—and I did at that moment."

Tears filled Sherri's eyes again. Joanna ached. If she'd had tender moments with her dad, she couldn't remember them.

"Then the bastard shoved me off his lap and told me to pick up his cuff links." Sherri shrugged and smiled. She turned to Joanna. "Yup, he's still around—with my mother. He's been physically there since, but he left me at that moment, and never really came back. Never got mad at me after that either. Never touched me. Flinched when I touched him. Wait a minute. I started out to tell you about my sex life and got sidetracked."

"Not really."

"Ernie didn't like to touch me either. Shit, I hate psychobabble, but is Dan anything like your dad?"

"No, but he's similar to my grandfather—gentle, warm, alive. Grandpa's face showed the complete range of human expression. So does Dan's."

Sherri frowned. Tiny ridges followed the arcs of her blond eyebrows.

"What am I going to do, Jo? I wouldn't even think about the AIDS shit for two whole days, and then when I did I told myself the test was bogus. Classic denial, right?" She uncrossed her long legs and rose gracefully. "Almost got laid last night, but told him at the last minute. The dick slapped me. That's truth for you."

"Can you blame him? My God." Joanna jumped to her feet. "I don't mean to scold you, especially now, but think, Sherri. You led him on, and then told him. Timing is mighty important for truth-telling." *So many cowardly years I lied to Beaumont.* She fingered the Christmas ornaments around the spider plant, and then slowly, deliberately, threw each one over the veranda railing, tossing away each year of her stupid marriage. She heard a satisfying splash as the big, sequined one she'd made especially for Beaumont hit the canal. "You have to make a decision, Sherri. Either you continue pretending you're not carrying a deadly disease, or you change your habits completely and find another way to go. In fact, this may be what my mother would call a godsend."

Joanna continued tossing the ornaments as if it were a mundane task.

"Yes, timing," Sherri said after a while. "I have to go back in six months to re-test. The counselor did say it may be a fluke. I could be clean after all."

"So give yourself six months without sex."

"But what'll I do?" Sherri let out a mournful wail. She collapsed to the floor in front of the veranda.

Joanna sat beside her, picked up and rubbed Sherri's white knuckled hand. She considered suggesting masturbation, but realized Sherri's need was not so much for sexual release as for some kind of affirmation.

"Anyone who can fight for life after the knocks you've had," Joanna said, "will still fight for life. You'll know what to do."

"And not do. I'm thirty years old. They told me carriers don't come down with AIDS as far as they know, now. But I know better in my heart." The new, soft resonance in Sherri's voice raised goose bumps on Joanna's arms.

Sherri looked at her. Joanna studied her face remembering the make-up, the wigs, the brazen talk. Now she saw a strange serenity. Clear blue eyes, calm breathing.

"I'm thirty years old," Sherri repeated. "I've never thought much about death. I assumed I'd live to be seventy-five, at least, with lots of bittersweet laughs along the way. Now I know better. A deadly virus is a deadly virus. I may have a terminal—" She broke off with a laugh. "A terminal. Isn't that funny? A bus terminal for this Greyhound half-way across the country. To make it all the way to California I'll have to start noticing nanoseconds." She turned to look at a sparrow perched on the veranda railing. "I'm just beginning to peer into the void."

Joanna recalled Sherri's goal to save five hundred a month to buy her own club and then move to L.A. or Houston, somewhere young, and open up a night club.

"You could still buy a night club here, Sherri. Hire musicians. Be a charming hostess who rebuffs all overtures except musical ones."

"You nuts? In Miami? All my customers would be Geezers or Cubans who hate punk."

Joanna thought that wouldn't be so bad. What did Sherri need most? Punk? She recalled Dan admitting that he needed her, that he hadn't allowed himself to need anyone before. Was Sherri's need for sex any different from her own need for gentle stability? *And the fact is, we're all in limbo*.

Sunlight streamed in, lighting dust particles in the air. Joanna stood, pulling Sherri up with her, and picked up her spider plant.

"Ugly thing, isn't it? Sums up my life of lies. Here's to this nanosecond." With a hefty swing, she threw it over the railing. It hit the water with a great splash. They leaned over the railing and watched. A caretaker on the walk below shook his fist at them.

"I can sleep now," Sherri said with a smile, and curled up on the couch

Joanna covered her with an afghan and felt that strange twinge in her stomach again. Tomorrow, she told herself, I'd better take that pregnancy test.

CHAPTER TWENTY-SEVEN

Joanna and Monroe sat on a bench by the river two blocks from the courthouse where the jury deliberated. They watched the river easing along. It looked as if nothing else in the world mattered. They waited for Dan who had opted for a haircut and mustache trim.

"Do you think it will be a hung jury?" Joanna asked Monroe, fascinated by the sunlight playing in his bright red hair. He looked disarmingly young for a trial lawyer. Did he have enough experience to protect Dan? She shook off the question for she liked waiting for Dan with Monroe because she could tell he, too, loved Dan.

"Hung jury? Hell, I don't know," Monroe said. He stood and faced her. "The fact that it's taking this long is good for us."

A pelican landed on the river with a splash. They both watched it; Joanna giggled like a little girl and moved closer to the river's edge.

"They're so clumsy when they land," she said, "yet so graceful in flight."

Monroe nodded. He sat on the concrete wall, back to the river, nibbling on a stone crab he'd bought from a fish vendor going by.

A huge ray, slinking along the bottom of the river caught Joanna's attention. It looked like the reflection of a white cloud yet with muscle, tissue, and purpose. She shivered.

"How long have you known Dan?" she asked Monroe.

"All my life, though I met him only two years ago." He smiled, wiped his fingers on his handkerchief, and adjusted his glasses.

"What do you mean?" She sat beside him and noticed his redolence: stone crab and clean sweat, a strangely pleasant combination.

"This may sound odd, but I'm an honest man. Early training." He looked straight at her. "Diogenes would have said on meeting me, 'So, it's you.' But I'm not proud of my honesty. It doesn't get me what I think I want—in fact it gets me into a passel of trouble, especially with women." He tossed the empty crab shell into its bag and lapsed into silence.

"Diogenes? Is he Greek?"

"In Plato's time." Monroe laughed. "He was a cynical nut, basically, but he's famous for prowling through a crowd saying, 'I'm looking for an honest man.' The best thing honesty got me was Dan's friendship. That's why I say I've known him all my life. Actually, honesty is not so much a virtue as a habit, like deceit, or gambling. Sometimes being honest is as much a pain as compulsively doing anything."

"Maybe we should start a chapter of Honest Anonymous where you learn how to lie."

"Yeah, as a good lawyer should," he said with a laugh. "Dan could be a charter member." He turned and stared into the river. "We all like mirror images of ourselves. That's not bad for starters in this crazy world."

Joanna pictured Sherri in the employee lounge, layering on bracelets and make-up, transforming herself in order to stay the same. *My mirror image?* She touched Monroe's sleeve.

"I'm pregnant. I'm going to have Dan's baby."

Monroe jumped up and grinned at her.

"Some things are so fantastically right in this world," he said in a reverent tone of voice. "What did Dan say? Man, I can picture him melting like a snowball in Miami Beach."

"He doesn't know yet. I just found out from one of those take-home tests, so don't know for sure. But I feel it."

"Tell him, tell him. Watch him dissolve like an ice cream sundae in a hot oven."

"Monroe, cut the similes. What if the verdict is guilty?"

Monroe's red mustache drooped. He rubbed his eyes.

"We'll appeal."

"Chances?"

"Dan's chances of acquittal aren't good, despite the long jury deliberation." He reached out and touched her shoulder, turning her toward him. "Florida law demands a minimum of twenty-five years for first degree murder and there's no provision for a mercy killing defense. In fact, just last year the appeal didn't work for a man who shot his wife. A three judge panel wrote that the question of mercy killing had to be decided by the legislature, not the judicial branch." He stood and stretched his slight frame. "In practice, though, judges and juries have gone outside the law to show lenience to people who kill terminally ill relatives. That's our best hope."

"Look, here he comes." She grabbed Monroe's forearm. "I've known him for such a short time in terms of the calendar, yet, like you, I've known him all my life."

"How do I look, clean cut or guilty?" Dan asked, waving at them.

"You look wonderful." Joanna wrapped her arms around him and kissed his neck, inhaling the barbershop aroma that blocked his usual scent. "Our redheaded Diogenes here says he'll appeal if they find you guilty." She grabbed both their arms and wished she were Dorothy heading home from Oz rather than Joanna making quips to hide a heavy heart. "Let's go eat. I'm starved."

"Hey Dan, which one of us is Diogenes?" Monroe shouted over the noise of a helicopter and followed Dan and Joanna heading toward the sidewalk café across the street from the courthouse.

*   *   *

Dan felt his anxiety draining with each phrase of conversation, each bite of food and warm smile or touch under the table. It came back with daggers when he saw Beaumont Archer slip into a restaurant across the street. His heart raced. Joanna sat directly beside him. He wondered if she'd seen Beaumont.

"I've ordered champagne," Monroe said. "I hope you don't mind. For a special toast."

"Bit premature, don't you think?" asked Dan. "They may take another week coming to a verdict."

"Who says we're toasting a verdict?" Monroe asked. He turned to Joanna. "Your turn."

She turned a beautiful shade of crimson. Dan wished he could capture in full color the expression on her face at that moment, enlarge the image and paste it over the courthouse doors as a reason for all that goes on inside.

Joanna smiled and cleared her throat.

"You and I," she whispered and cleared her throat. "We are going to have a baby."

Dan knocked over his water glass. *A baby! Like Buddy? Or a girl? Oh my God how wonderful. A baby!*

"We're going to have a baby?" Dan grabbed Joanna's hands, kissed each one, and then turned to Monroe. "I don't know who God is, but will you be our baby's godfather? Where's Lucille? We've gotta have a party. Life's too short to put off celebrating." He guffawed and then burst into tears.

He felt Joanna's arms around him and wiped his tears with a table napkin. It took him a while to feel composed enough to do a little soft shoe shuffle on the sidewalk.

"I'm not one for giving thanks to God, but Thanksgiving this year will really tax my professed incredulity." He grinned broadly. "I'm going to have a baby!"

He heard Joanna's and Monroe's laughter as a single, harmonic, hymnal phrase. The buzzards perched on the upper quadrant of this Mesopotamian courthouse seemed as benign as mourning doves. And of course, Dan thought, they are.

Sherri Taylor, wearing a conservative blue linen suit, approached them.

"Isn't that your friend coming—the one who'll put the make on me?" Dan asked Joanna.

"She's changed." Joanna said. She waved and beckoned to Sherri who responded with a nod and joined them without smiling.

Dan wondered how one so young and pretty could be so sad. He noticed Monroe studying her and a delicious matchmaking notion entered his mind.

"They're still deliberating," Joanna said and grabbed Sherri's hand.

"I heard." Sherri shook Dan's hand. "Good luck, Sir."

She seemed like a different woman. Her touch had no hint of flirtation now. Dan introduced her to Monroe who stood to greet her, looking pale and ill at ease, as if he didn't quite fit into his small body right now.

"We've seen each other around the courts," Monroe told Dan, then turned and said, "Hi, Sherri Taylor."

She nodded in recognition.

Dan knew Monroe had trouble with women, but not how or why. Monroe had once confessed he had great desire for them but couldn't conjure up the right moves or phrases to get beyond awkward moments. Soon each woman gave up on him and left. Dan wished Monroe would have patience with himself. He leaned toward Joanna and whispered.

"Let's back away slowly. Give Sherri and Monroe a chance."

"No chance." Joanna's eyes flashed.

Dan wanted to ask why but Sherri looked directly at him.

"Sherri, come with us to my place," he said. "We're going to celebrate with champagne and Beluga caviar—whether you like it or not." Unable to contain his grin, he turned to Joanna. "Tell her." He felt his heart racing.

"Tell me what?" Sherri, too, seemed out of place in her body. With an awkward lurch toward Joanna, she asked, "What on earth can we celebrate now?"

"I'm pregnant." Joanna smiled, and then dropped her head forward letting her hair hide her face.

Sherri slowly rubbed her chin. Tears filled her eyes. She blinked, shook her head angrily as if to sprinkle the world with her tears.

"I'll be damned," Sherri said in a loud voice. "Of all the luck! Shit, I'm turning green." She turned her back to them and paced a few steps away. Dan wondered what was wrong. Then Sherri hit her head on both sides, returned to the table and said, "Hey, we're all gonna raise this kid, even you." She pointed at Monroe. "Give it the best damn life five or six parents can provide."

"Of course," Monroe said, nodding.

A sudden breeze from the east blew Joanna's hair off her face. Dan noticed her blush had faded. He felt a sudden need to get out and absorb his good fortune as well as increased anxiety that he might not be able to raise his child.

"Let's go call Ralph and Lucille and get this celebratory show on the road," he said. "At least Lucille's available. Taxi!"

*   *   *

Monroe stood alone on Dan's veranda among some gaudy birds of paradise. The party inside didn't match his mood. Reflecting on the trial, he realized he'd done little to affect the verdict. Other times in court his reticence turned out to be a virtue. With women like Sherri Taylor it was more than a fault; it was a default in the program.

He watched a falling star and remembered making wishes on them. What would he wish for now? Each time he had a woman in his life he wished for solitude, and now that he had solitude he wished for . . . for this new one, Sherri? He pictured his most recent girlfriend but couldn't think of her name.

"You're so honest and sweet, Monroe," she'd said as she packed her suitcase for bigger fields in California, "but that shit suffocates me." Sweet? What did she mean?

He did remember the name of his last year's love. Arlene. She left him claiming he'd raped her. She didn't think he was sweet. Hell, they were almost living together. He was inside her ready to explode when she told him to stop. She wasn't up for it that night. But it was too late. He couldn't stop. How could that be rape? He loved her. God he missed her, despite the fact she betrayed him like that. Faith in the judicial process, working with it every day helped fill the void. And talking with Dan. Dan didn't know anything about Arlene, yet what he had to say soon after reverberated.

"We need to put practical limitations on ideals," Dan had said. "Limitations are useless without ideals pushing against them. And, ideals need limits, too. Can't have one without the other. Like men and women, they need each other."

Monroe had often thought of his words. Men and women do need one another, yin and yang.

"Excuse me," Sherri said and stumbled onto the veranda, interrupting his reverie. "I didn't mean to trip into your space."

"Welcome. It's a great view out here. Look at all the stars."

"I've spent a lot of time on these verandas lately, it seems." She scrutinized him. "You're short."

"I'm as tall as you," he answered, straightening.

"That's short for a man. Course, I'm tall for a woman."

He stared at her, mesmerized by her good looks: fierce blue eyes, unpretentious natural blond hair hanging like milkweed beside the clean, clear skin of her oval face. No make-up. Full, enticing breasts and long legs that could almost wrap his frame twice.

"Tall is as tall does," he said.

"That's supposed to be handsome is." She laughed. "You have nice freckles. Dan says you're the best defense lawyer in Miami. I'd like to fuck you, but I won't."

"Why won't you?" he asked, delighted.

"I have a deadly virus called LIV" Sherri lowered her eyes. It means I'm an AIDS carrier."

Her words felt like the blow of a fist to his solar plexus, painful, yet strangely refreshing.

"How do you know?"

"Gave blood to the Red Cross. They've just started routine screening for AIDS. Called me in." Her voice was flat. "I don't have it, but I could give it to you."

"Even through a condom?"

"I'm allergic to 'em and can't trust my germs—I'm on the pill." She burst into tears.

He reached for her hand but she pulled away.

"I'm sorry," he said.

"I had a baby once. Gave her up. Joanna's so fucking lucky."

Noises from the party inside filtered through Monroe's consciousness. The joy inside was such a contrast. Sherri's blue eyes had a piercing clarity that reminded him of stained glass windows, eyes of saints. He lifted Sherri's hand to his lips and kissed it. This time she let him touch her.

"Has Diogenes found you, lovely woman?"

"Who? Are you for real, man?" Sherri shuddered, backed against the railing and stared at him. "You're supposed to slap me, call me a prick tease."

"I call you a rare and beautiful woman," he said, surprised at the strength of his interest in her, and his own eloquence. "I'd like very much to get to know you, even though we can't make love."

"I'd have to wear flat shoes."

"So what?" Moonlight angled, in throwing long shadows of Dan's bird of flowers against the stucco wall.

"Even though no sex?"

"So what's new? I don't score anyway. Can't make an athletic contest out of it."

"I've scored too much, obviously, some fag in the woodpile." A hard edge came into her voice then melted with a sudden look of contrition.

He stared at spots of light on the black water nine stories below and listened to her soft breathing. The enormity of her problem finally seeped into his consciousness. He could no longer be light-hearted, yet he felt a tug pulling him toward her the more he thought about pulling away.

"What irony," he said. "I bet you could be the woman of my dreams. I want to make love to you and live to tell about it. And I want to live so I can get to know you better. That's my choice. Platonic love. What do you say?"

"Shake, partner." Sherri lowered her eyes. "I'm up for a different sort of grab-ass. Do you think we can see each other and maintain? I get hot for short freckled geniuses, too."

Someone inside turned up the music. The Beatles in full chorus: *Will you still need me, will you still feed me when I'm sixty-four?* Monroe peered in. Dan and Joanna were dancing. He turned to Sherri.

"Come on, tall beauty, let's dance."

"It's hard to dance with bended knees."

"Then straighten them. Why does a man have to be taller than a woman?" Monroe put his arm around her shoulders. He felt his chest expanding with affection. What a woman. "C'mon, Sherri, let's innovate."

"Innovate?" She shrugged. "Might's well, can't fuck."

A camera flash lit the room as they entered. Lucille, Dan's photographer friend, grinned at them and gestured with her camera.

"I've just caught your souls on film, but don't worry, I won't sell them without your consent." She extended her right hand to Sherri. "I'm Lucille MacIntosh. I sneak into people's lives through this little black box."

"Can it see my virus?" Sherri asked, her blue eyes wide open, clear, innocent as a child's.

Monroe appreciated Lucille's quick glance to include him before concentrating on Sherri.

"No, my Dear. If you have a virus, you wear it well. It's transparent."

Sherri smiled at Monroe. He felt it in his groin. *This isn't going to be easy.*

"Monroe," Lucille said, "Dan has a terrible quandary. He's excited about Joanna's pregnancy but fears, I'm sure, that he won't be able to support a child, emotionally that is. You can't rock a baby in jail. Do you have any sense of the outcome of this trial?"

"I'm sorry, Lucille. It doesn't look good. We can only hope." This time Monroe had to blink away tears.

CHAPTER TWENTY-EIGHT

Joanna awoke as rays from the morning sun beamed through the Venetian blinds on Dan's bedroom window and spread across the sheet covering them. She watched the contoured patterns the light made over the terrain of their bodies, across Dan's suit coat hanging on his clothes press. She smiled remembering the first time she'd seen this wooden apparatus with the pants hanger and tray, like a butler waiting for the contents of his pockets. She'd asked him what it was. So many things about him reminded her of Masterpiece Theater episodes.

She touched Dan's forehead with her fingertips. He wouldn't wake up grouchy. He wouldn't threaten her. He wouldn't injure her. She lay there listening to him breathe, wallowing in her fantastic luck. Here she was, in bed with a wonderful man who loved her and pregnant with his child. Feeling worthy, too. She remembered the many times she'd told herself she didn't deserve to know Dan, let alone love him. Then everything had happened so fast. She'd helped a kid in the crowd and discovered she wasn't a total wimp. She'd fought out her anger at Sherri. Even let Sherri get to know Dan, expecting a collision all the time between the two sides of herself.

"And they lived happily ever after," she whispered in Dan's ear.

He opened his eyes, patted her stomach, and kissed her ear sending delicious little twitches down her side.

"Don't you think we ought to get married before you start to show?"

"Can't do that," she said, "until my divorce is final. Six more months."

"Beaumont." Dan rolled his blue eyes. "Somehow I keep forgetting about him. At least wanting to."

"It'll be wonderful when we can forget him, even if we're stuck here waiting for an appeal." She smoothed his sleep rumpled mustache. "In fact, today I'm going to the courthouse to make sure the divorce papers are being processed as I intended."

"And what else are you going to do there?" The mischief in his eyes made him look young.

"Take a pregnancy leave. Tell Judge Ogasaki the whole truth. I think she'll like it even though the jury's still out." Joanna swung her legs onto the floor. She felt Dan's eyes on her as she stretched her naked body and slowly weaved her way to the bathroom. She returned refreshed, face still wet, and pulled her bra. "You like to watch me dress as well as undress, don't you?"

"You're a mobile work of art in all your forms. But it's that soul you bought with your soul that I really love."

"Hunh?"

"Remember the night we were trying to define soul and you—"

"Oh yeah. Okay, now that I have a soul, I do my laundry regularly." She tossed a pillow at him. "Speaking of that, I have to finish moving out of Aunt Martha's place. She'll be coming home from Africa any day now. God, I can hardly wait for you to meet her. She's the Mona Lisa of my family."

"What was she doing in Africa?"

"Shooting elephants Lucille style." She lay back on the bed and pulled on her pantyhose with her legs straight up in the air. "So, what are you doing today?"

"I'm going to read some of Auden's early poetry, make reservations for *The Tempest* now playing at the new Old Globe in Coral Gables, hope against hope Monroe calls saying they've reached a verdict, make love to you, call Ralph and have lunch with Lucille, not necessarily in that order. I'm a lucky man." He rubbed the top of her head.

"You *hope* Monroe calls, I'll pray." Joanna struggled into her brown turtleneck shirt and spoke through the fabric. "That's right, Lucille's going to New York for her new show. She's something else. And Ralph?"

"Rosalie's home from the hospital now and he's taking care of her. One day at a time."

The weariness and pain in Dan's voice reminded Joanna of his experience with Bev. She knew she had yet to know that kind of care, and prayed Dan would live long enough to need it.

"Would you kill me if I had a debilitating stroke?" Dan asked as he rolled out of bed.

God no! The thought sent chills to her toes.

"No, never," she said aloud. The depth in her voice surprised her. "Then I won't ask you to. Now or ever."

*   *   *

Judge Ogasaki invited Joanna into her office and sat beside her on a brocade settee. "Your replacement is working out well, Joanna, but I'm happy to see you. Is everything fine for you now?"

"Oh yes, Your Honor, I came to tell you that I want to apply for a pregnancy leave."

"I thought you filed for divorce." Ogasaki straightened her back and looked at Joanna sideways.

"I did. I had to get out of that marriage. It was awful. I didn't really know how awful until I met Dan—"

"Then who is the father?"

"Daniel Lawrence."

"You know you shouldn't be telling me this."

"Why?" Joanna studied the woman's face for clues.

"Mr. Lawrence may have had other motives for helping his wife die."

"No, Your honor!" Joanna jumped up and cried out, "No. He didn't even know me until Julio. We met during the hurricane just before the trial began. He's my neighbor. We had to evacuate the building together. We fell in love in a cathedral. I didn't even know he was on trial. He didn't know I was a court reporter." She collapsed on the settee and covered her face with her hands.

Ogasaki did not move or speak.

After a few minutes Joanna felt a hand on her shoulder. She looked up.

"Come see me, Joanna, after the verdict is in. I want only the best for you. I can say no more now. And, I accept your application for leave. Of course, you must put it in writing."

Joanna left feeling like a little kid, an embarrassed but accepted little kid. She wavered as she walked between panic and confidence, ending up at a hardware store on her way home. There she felt calm and bought a rope to string a clothesline from Dan's veranda into his kitchen.

"Some things don't dry properly in commercial dryers," she explained to the clerk and wrapped the rope around her elbow as she had as a child when she'd practiced lassoing. The rope brought back body memories. She could feel the rope hit and wrap her target. What fun! She smiled and told the clerk she'd eventually be hanging diapers on this line. No diaper service for her. No Velcro Pampers either. Just sweet smelling, air-dried diapers.

"Today is the day they give babies away with a half a pound of tea," she sang to herself. "If you know any ladies that want any babies, just send them here to me." White cotton clouds floated overhead. She felt blessed by them as she sang her way home, mission at court accomplished, laundry and love ahead.

Dan showed up at her aunt's place at three and watched Joanna gather the laundry. He told her about his conversation with Lucille at lunch.

"Lucille agrees with me that Ralph doesn't want her to go down to Nassau now. He needs to work with Rosalie alone, help retrain her ability to speak." Dan picked up the basket of clothes. "Here, let me help. Poor guy. We've always known he loves her, though we couldn't figure out why. I couldn't stand Rosalie's tongue for a day, let alone a lifetime."

Joanna decided not to tell him now about her conversation with Ogasaki just yet. She took the basket from him and handed him a compact disc.

"You stay here and listen to the opera. I'll be back in a few minutes." She started out, then stopped and tucked her hair behind her ear. "There's a mystery to love. How could I think I loved Beaumont enough to marry him when it's obvious my heart cried out for someone like you?"

Dan caressed her arm with his left hand and her heart with his electrified blue eyes. He kissed her, then looked away and rubbed his chin.

"You know, Joanna, Ralph had an affair with Lucille in the sixties, he said. "Arthur,

Lucille's husband, never knew, of course. Neither did Rosalie. But I did, and felt jealous." His eyes faded in a far-away look. "We've both loved Lucille in different ways for years. The affair ended and they stayed friends. Amazing, what?"

Joanna's stomach tightened with jealously. *Don't be foolish.*

"But that's old stuff," he said, kissing her cheek. "Right now I'm madly in love with a pregnant woman who has gorgeous cheeks." He hugged her across the laundry basket. "Want some help with that?" he asked tugging at the basket.

Joanna felt her muscles soften. *Pianissimo.*

"Laundry's mine, job's mine. Your job is to listen to Ernani and tell me what's happening. I'll be back in two shakes of a lamb's tail. No, in two choruses."

As the elevator descended she heard the second elevator going up and compared the movements with termites scurrying in a mound. She heard the other elevator stop and wondered if Aunt Martha had returned. She expected her any day now.

The smell of spilled bleach in the laundry room choked her. She pulled out the wet clothes onto a table and then shoved them into the basket. These things will dry on a line nicely today, she thought. Tugging and then pushing, she rolled the basket onto the elevator. *That didn't take long.* She pushed the button for the ninth floor. *Maybe just one duet and a chorus.*

The same mirror in the elevator cabin that had reflected her shame so many times before, now, like magic, simply reflected her face. I really am pretty, she thought as the doors opened on the ninth floor. She draped the clothesline rope around her shoulders and tugged the heavy basket toward the open apartment door. She stopped half way to figure out an easier way to transport the load when she heard a man's angry voice.

"Cut in on my territory, will you!" Then something crashed hard against the wall.

She felt a sinking in the pit of her stomach when she recognized Beaumont's voice.

"Leave him alone," she yelled and ran into the apartment without the laundry.

Beaumont turned at her voice. Dan hit him on the chin, spinning him.

"Dan, don't. He'll kill you."

Beaumont came out of the spin and shoved the dining room table at her, pinning her against the wall.

"Hello, Darling. How's my little wife? My true Babe? I got your papers. Going legal on me, now? Didn't think I'd find you, did you?" Sour mash breath carried his words, dropping them on her like pigeon shit. "You under-estimate me, Joanna Archer."

The table bruised her hip bones. *Oh God, my baby!*

"Just neighbors, old man?" Beaumont hissed to Dan. "I told you—you're living on borrowed time." He moved toward Dan, massive shoulders hunched forward. "My fucking time and I didn't lend it to you." He swung his arm. His fist hit Dan's right eye, twisting his glasses.

Dan landed a blow to Beaumont's gut.

"Stop!" Joanna screamed. "Both of you stop!" Shocked, and pinned by the table, she watched her huge husband pound the older man. The veranda door was open behind them. "Look out, Dan!" she yelled. "Get away from the veranda." Verdi's crescendo echoed her scream. Her heart pounded in her ears.

Dan jumped away from the veranda and punched Beaumont's chest like a drummer.

Beaumont kneed him in the groin. Dan sank to the floor, curled up in pain. Beaumont kicked his back. Joanna saw the cords standing out on Dan's neck. His eyes bulged as if the pain literally blew him up. Furious, she slid under the table and crawled out behind Beaumont's back. She grabbed the rope off her shoulders, wrapped it around her elbow, knotted the end, and then lashed out with it.

"You stupid bastard!"

Beaumont looked startled by the rope. He stopped kicking Dan and laughed.

"What's this, Babe? Want to lose another fingernail?"

She jumped back and rewound the rope. Body memory from hours of practice. Beaumont lunged at her and she let the rope fly again, bullwhipping his eyes. He dropped to his knees and covered his eyes with his hands.

"You blinded me," he groaned.

Joanna ran behind him and coiled the rope around his neck. Bracing her legs against the table, she pulled the rope tight.

"Don't you dare move, Beaumont Archer, or I'll strangle you and shove your stupid body over the veranda. I've already tossed the spider plant and Christmas ornaments." Fire raced through her body. She held the rope twisted around her wrists. It was her life line. She hated his thick, hairy neck and knew the desire to kill, knew she could do it easily, could get rid of this sour-mash stinking creep for good.

Each time Beaumont moved she put enough pressure with the rope on his carotid arteries to force him into a slump. Dan called her name, diffusing her anger. Holding tight to the rope around Beaumont's neck, she watched Dan pull himself up. The blood had drained from his face. Bruises began to show, but his eyes were clear. She knew he had his wits about him. He nodded at Joanna and picked up the phone. She studied his face as he gave the police the address, knowing he knew how close she had come to killing Beaumont.

"They're on the way," Dan said.

With renewed effort, Beaumont used his head as a club against Joanna's hip. She kneed his back, tightened the rope till he passed out. Dan came over, trussed him like a pig, and revived him with a slap.

Forming what Dan called "a macabre tableau," they waited for the police. Again, she admired Dan's caution. A macho guy would have tried to take over, and in a transfer of power Beaumont would've escaped. For ten minutes no one spoke. Beaumont struggled briefly against the rope, and then gave up. He closed his eyes as if in weary shame, as if he knew how close she'd come to killing him.

Pounding footsteps signaled the arrival of the police. Two large cops entered, one white, one black. Both wore high boots. They filled the room with their massive presences. The white one, a potbellied, ruddy-skinned blond, looked first at Beaumont, then one by one at Joanna and Dan.

"Okay, give me names," he said, uncorking a well-chewed ballpoint pen.

Beaumont groaned. The black cop un-trussed him, and then handcuffed him.

Dan spelled out their names for the officer taking notes.

Joanna watched the white cop writing. She worried where the report would go. To the press? How would this look to the jury on

Dan's trial? She could picture the headline on the Miami Herald, MERCY KILLER ATTACKED BY JEALOUS HUSBAND.

The doorbell rang, startling them. The black officer opened it on a little, white haired lady in a bright red dress and backpack and carrying a camera bag

"I'm home, Joanna," the lady said.

"Aunt Martha," Joanna ran to greet her. Her arrival at this moment struck Joanna as a contrived ending to a play.

"Have I missed something?" Martha asked, "Why Beaumont, is that you? What on earth are you doing in my apartment?"

*   *   *

The morning sun had almost reached the top of the sky when Joanna finally awoke. The walls of Dan's bedroom seemed to expand to contain the sunlight, much like a balloon taking in air. She inhaled the light, gazed at his clothespress, then bolted. The bed was empty. "Dan?" she cried.

"Morning, sleepy head." He limped in with a tray of coffee and hot croissants. The left side of his face was puffed and bruised, sending his mustache askew.

"You look like a kid with mumps who fell off a monkey bar," she said, giggling with relief. Sobering, she asked, "How do you feel, Honey?"

"I hurt, Madame." He set the tray on the end table and groaning, crawled into bed. "I hurt all over. I lost a fight." He took her chin, turning her face toward his, "and you won the championship bout. A ninety pound weakling just beat the guy who kicked sand in her face for so many years." He kissed her. "You were magnificent. And you didn't kill him. Now that shows real class. *Savoir faire*, my love, true *savoir faire*. Where'd you learn to handle a rope like that?"

"Kid games . . . Actually, I practiced lassoing a fencepost for years—pretended it was my father." Sipping her coffee, Joanna pondered his words. My mettle's been tested, she thought. "If you'd asked me yesterday," she said, "what I'd do if Beaumont finally found out where I lived I might come up with a bunch of possible moves, but not one would be whipping him blind with a clothesline."

She settled back against the pillows and let the glow of pride, the kind that doesn't go before a fall, warm her. She'd truly done it. "This is my Independence Day, isn't it?"

He applauded and leaned forward to kiss her when the phone rang. He let it ring for a quick kiss then answered. She heard him say, "Ralph? Ralph are you at home? Oh no . . . Oh no, Ralph, why the hell didn't you let her go?" His voice: cinders grating on ice.

Joanna tensed for this new tragedy. Dan slowly replaced the phone.

"Rosalie took an overdose of sleeping pills. Ralph found her passed out and had her stomach pumped. She hates him." He raised his fists above his head and looked straight up. "Why didn't he let her go?"

Joanna felt the anguish in Dan's voice, one hard pluck of a cello's bass string. She felt naïve hearing the intimations of issues way beyond her.

"We need to get to Nassau," Dan said, "if only I could leave the States! I have to get there soon, be with him, and keep my mouth shut. But I can't! We've been through too much together. Oh God, Ralph."

CHAPTER TWENTY-NINE

Lucille stepped out of the taxi in front of Kennedy Airport, stretched her wool scarf over her mouth and wondered why the hell she'd come back for her show. She headed for her flight south thinking that waiting for a verdict in Miami was another form of hell. The January air here hurt her teeth. She wondered if people with small teeth had the same trouble in cold weather. She headed toward the shelter of the terminal and stopped to examine a milkweed growing between two discarded concrete blocks, one block tilting precariously against the other. She removed her lens cap to shoot it, and then noticed an old man struggling to climb out of a cab, using his cane to fend off two young men offering help.

A bag lady sitting on the curb nearby cackled at him. Lucille took a few shots of the woman's toothless mouth. The old man thrashed his way toward the terminal, oblivious of his audience. Lucille regretted, for a second, her Manhattan persona—no feeling.

Lucille replaced her lens cap at the sound of a jet turbines winding up. She hurried inside, feeling the excitement of imminent take-off and returning to await the jury with Dan, and yes, Joanna, newly pregnant and a most welcome member to the family.

She wondered, once airborne, about her eagerness to see them. Ralph and Dan, more family to her than her own relatives, wouldn't even know about the rave reviews of her show in the New York Times. Dan hadn't even seen his mustache shots. It didn't matter. Public adoration is fun for awhile, she thought, but intimacy is what I crave. Too bad I didn't realize that before Arthur died.

She pulled out the letter Arthur's sister had slipped to her yesterday.

"Your show's impressive," she'd said with a rough edge to her voice. "But is it worth it, Lucille?" She handed Lucille the letter and continued, softening, "Here. I found this in a drawer in Arthur's apartment right after the funeral. I kept it in case I ran into you. Since you wrote it, it's yours."

Was it worth it? The letter, written in her back-slanted hand, was dated July 4, 1978.

"Dear Arthur,

This is the Fourth of July, and I'm making my final declaration of independence. Goodbye, again, my love, my last goodbye. I can't be what you want. I see. You listen. You hear what the slightest catch in my breath reveals. I see the small muscle strain around your eyes. We cannot mask ourselves. Perhaps that's my problem. I refused to have children—robbed you of immortality while trying to build my own. Dear Arthur, forgive me if you can. I refused to take on the role of aunt to your nieces and great-aunt to their children, even though I know how important they are to you.

My darling, I'm so sorry, yet unwilling to change. Tomorrow I'm going to Nassau with Dan and Bev for a few days, despite Rosalie. Her nebulous natter will focus my anger on her and free me to mourn the death of us. Though I must leave you or die, I love you. But, then, you've always known that."

Tears sprang to her eyes. She folded the letter into a tiny square and put it in her purse. She closed her eyes and saw Arthur scolding her. Then she relived the waves at Pemaquid, herself at fifteen meeting Dan and Ralph at the Port Clyde Inn. She opened her eyes and thought how naive she'd been asking them to help her find Gus. And her father was an innocent, too. How could it matter if Gus were a Communist? Shoot, she thought, nodding her head as if conversing with someone, we've spent half a century worrying about communists when it's our neighbor, our staunch, conservative, capitalist pal, who fucks us over. In Russia it's probably some comrade who betrays his neighbor, not one of our CIA agents.

The captain's voice interrupted her thoughts. While he read a commercial for Eastern Airlines, she stole another glance at the New York Times on the empty aisle seat beside her. She'd folded the paper with the review of her retrospective on the outside, face up. An ad for "The Tempest" playing in the Village ran in an adjacent column. Shakespeare's last play, she thought, a farewell to his audiences. Maybe he knew his magical powers had waned. Maybe this should be my last show, until I come up with something new, anyway.

The seatbelt light went out; the click of belt buckles and sounds of people moving seemed to lighten the atmosphere in the cabin. She dozed for an hour or so. Then a tall young man with a blond beard and intense blue eyes leaned over the Times review. "Are you Lucille MacIntosh?"

"Yes, I am. Do I know you?" Wide awake now, she studied him.

"We've never met. I don't want to intrude, but when I saw you get on the plane I hoped it was you." He rubbed his beard. "Well, I just wanted to tell you I'm a great fan of yours, your work. I saw your recent show several times. The mustache series is absolutely stunning. What power! Is it your husband's? I shouldn't ask." His words tumbled over her, a refreshing waterfall.

"Thank you. Take a breath and tell me your name." She reached up and shook his hand.

"I'm Leroy Battin-Jones, working to be an artist." He grinned revealing bright, uneven teeth. "Like you, using photography now. Do you do all your own printing?"

She moved the Times and invited him to sit, delighted with his youthful brashness. He squeezed into the space airline manufacturers create for pygmies.

"No," she said, "the mustache is not my husband's. It adorns the face of a dear old friend." *Whose life is still in jeopardy.* "My husband's dead. And, yes, I do all my own printing. Do you?"

"Yes, of course." He reddened. "Pardon my questions. It's just I've admired your work so many years I feel I know you well enough, I mean—"

"It's okay." She restrained a motherly urge to pat his bony knee. "Have you entered any competitions?"

"I did a series on New England barns falling down, black and white." His lips formed a wavy, embarrassed smile. "One piece in the series won second place in the Los Angeles Times annual competition. Mainly, I've been honing my skills, trying to get control of the craft." He coughed, rubbed his Adam's apple. "You need that before you can do the art, don't you think? Of course, you have both."

Lucille smiled, aware, though, of her sadness. *New England barns. Dull. Dead as my barn series, or mustache series. I need a radical change, a new vision.* Looking out the window, she noticed the reflection of her face in the cloud-backed glass. She tucked a fading red wisp of hair back into the coiled bun that Arthur MacIntosh loved to uncoil. Why had she hurt him?

"Do you want me to leave?" Leroy asked.

"You are a sensitive young man," she replied, feeling suddenly generous. "Soon, but not yet. I was thinking just then of my husband. He died three years ago."

"Sorry." He cleared his throat.

"We were divorced, though." She laughed. "More than once. He wanted children." She laughed again, lightly, sadly. "His name was Arthur MacIntosh. It occurred to me again, I chose art over Art. Pardon the pun." She turned to look at Leroy. His face was open.

"I want to know everything about you," he said with the earnestness of youth. "No, I don't mean to pry. Your work stands alone, moves me. Tell me how you got to be so, you know, famous." He inhaled as if he'd been swimming under water and had just come up for air.

"Famous?" Lucille relaxed into laughter that brought tears to her eyes. "I suppose in our little specialized world I'm famous. Actually, you're the first fan I've met on an airplane."

"Blows you away, huh? Sure blows me away sitting here talking with you."

The cocktail cart came by. Leroy asked for champagne for two.

"To celebrate the moment," he said. He grimaced when he had to settle for Navalle white. He gave the stewardess a twenty dollar bill, poured the wine, lifted his plastic glass to Lucille's, and toasted, "Cheers."

She enjoyed his banality. They touched glasses.

"Listen," she said. "The squeak of our plastic containers trying to clink could be symbolic of a society where soft, squeaky convenience items replace hard reality." She smiled at him. *Jesus, I really do need a new vision. Ordinary portraits? Baby pictures?*

"When did you know, I mean really know, that you wanted to be an artist?" he asked. He drank his wine and stared at her like a puppy, a blue-eyed puppy.

"When I was fourteen or fifteen. I intended to be famous—like Stieglitz. It took me a while to give up the fame part of my ambition, but never the art. Most of my life I've questioned my motive." She pictured her tall, redheaded Arthur leading her to bed, murmuring sweet Gaelic sounds. Abruptly, she turned and looked directly at Leroy. "I've paid a price for my ambition. Yet, each time I questioned myself, I answered, 'Yes, well, it's what you consistently want to do, so do it.'"

"Man, that's what I needed to hear." He finished his wine in one gulp, crushed his glass into the magazine pocket.

"It's artsy to call a passionate interest an art, whatever the form it takes," she said. Her words surprised her. Hadn't she sacrificed for art? Made the holy pilgrimage? Forged her way to recognition? Spent a million hours in a damn darkroom trying to capture the light? She looked out at the clouds now, studied them from varying angles. *My pleasure, she thought, is sifting the reams of visual impressions assaulting us each day and finding one that sings an aria.*

"What are you thinking about?" he asked, staring at her.

"My passion for a good focus." *A good fuck?* The thought brought heat to her face. "For instance, I'd like to take a shot of your hands right now. They show a state of tension my camera would, as a spy, capture. Your hands, plus the genius of Nikon and my choice of focus, would create a piece that speaks of the diminishment we experience while conversing with an imagined guru. Of course, not every viewer would catch my intent, but they'd get the tension."

Leroy unclasped his hands and rubbed his palms on his thighs. Slowly he stretched one leg into the aisle. The plane slowed and banked to the left. The fasten-seatbelt-light came on.

"Thank you, Lucille MacIntosh," Leroy said. "We're starting to land. I'd better go back to my seat." He hauled himself awkwardly into the aisle, turned toward her and shook her hand. "I'll never forget this."

"Neither will I, Leroy Battin-Jones. I'll be looking for your work. Keep shooting from the heart."

The captain's voice came over the loudspeaker announcing the plane's approach to landing.

"Temperature in Miami this afternoon is a pleasant seventy-two degrees and dry with thunder showers forecast for late tonight."

Over the noise of the captain's broadcast Leroy mouthed to Lucille, *I will,* and disappeared down the aisle.

Lucille felt relieved to be alone again despite Leroy's ego strokes. She admired the whiteness of the thunderheads and compared them with Dan's mustache. The series had really worked. She knew the craft, as the kid said, and felt the art. Had felt it. What now? She glanced at a young couple with "honeymoon" stamped across their features. Sex is usually for peers, same age types. Dan and Joanna not only cross generations, they skip one. Two generations if you think of hormones sprouting at fifteen. What now with them? Wait and see.

She remembered being fifteen and jealous of Bev's petite beauty. Dan, faithful to Bev, and miserable. Such a cold woman. He wanted me, she thought, but wouldn't act on it. Ralph acted, thank God. Though sex with Ralph was always a bit off, as if neither of us knew what we were supposed to be doing. With Arthur it was a ballet. Ralph must love Rosalie from some deep sexual draw. What else could keep him with that harridan? How is he now with her? Wait and see. The plane taxied to the gate. Lucille felt her chest expand. Soon she'd see the two men left in her life she dearly loved, first

Dan in Miami then Ralph in Nassau, with Dan and Joanna if the verdict is, as she prayed, not guilty.

Reviewing her loves, she decided she'd loved Gus as a child, Ralph as a lover in the sixties, sisterly ever since, Dan always, even worshipped him at times. But it was for Arthur MacIntosh she opened her legs and heart at the same time. How that unnerved her! At least in the darkroom she had some control. And she'd believed all along her obsession with photography took courage.

"Bullshit," she said, beginning to see.

An old lady in a green hat glared at her. Lucille nodded toward her and smiled.

"One of the most underrated pleasures in this life, she said to the green hat, "is discovering your own lies, don't you think?"

*   *   *

"Miami Airport looks like every airport in the world. Whatever happened to local character?" whined a bald man wearing a tweed jacket with brand new elbow patches. He traversed the corridors near Lucille. She turned to see if he was addressing her. He seemed to be grumbling to himself, but she answered anyway.

"You have to look harder in airports for local character," she said. "Each terminal is different. Smell, for instance. Accents over the P.A. system. Wall advertising. Pace of the travelers."

"Huh? Are you talking to me?" asked Elbow Patch.

"No, I suppose not. Excuse me." She smiled at him; they moved apart. *We do talk mainly to ourselves. The world's full of monologists. When our words meet, touch, and dance into dialogue, it's such goddamn fun.*

"Lucille—over here."

She heard Dan's warm, resonant voice echoed by Joanna's light one, and felt her heart expand. She hurried toward them, glad to leave Elbow Patch in the dust of his arid existence.

Lucille gasped the minute saw them. Something was wrong. They stood stiffly apart, like stick figures. Neither smiled. She rushed toward them with a catch in her throat. *Oh God, they found him guilty.*

A crowd of short, Middle Eastern tourists cut Lucille off. They smelled of hummus and spoke in a language she could picture. She made her way through and realized that Dan's face was badly bruised.

He kissed her cheek and took her suitcase. Joanna hugged her.

"What's happened?" Lucille asked, feeling a hole in her chest.

"Ralph didn't let her go," Dan said.

Confused, Lucille looked to Joanna.

"Rosalie tried to commit suicide," Joanna said in a rush. Sleeping pills. Ralph found her in time, had her stomach pumped. She's alive but worse off. She lost all the speech she'd regained and Ralph says she hates him."

"Poor Ralph," she said, feeling relieved that the problem was Rosalie. People crowded by. She smelled stale beer on someone's breath. A woman who'd bathed in Chanel edged by. Lucille covered her nose and turned to Joanna. She noticed that Joanna's eyes were especially clear and shining. Joanna looked pleased with herself. "What else? A verdict?" Lucille asked. "Why the bruises, Dan? Did you fall off the bench? I sense some good news with the bad."

"No verdict yet and I fell off the bench a long time ago, as soon as I knew I could never be truly just." Dan chuckled, hugged Lucille and beamed at Joanna. "This pregnant young lady lassoed the beast, Beaumont. Protected me and restrained herself from killing him when she had the rope around his neck."

"Joanna Archer, Joan of Arc. Well, well." Lucille grabbed Joanna's hand in awe. "I want to hear about it in detail. Let's go get the rest of my luggage." She swung her camera bag over her arm and led them in full stride. They spread out beside the carousel to catch her luggage. When her two small suitcases came by Lucille caught one and Dan the other.

"Dan, why did he have her stomach pumped?" Lucille asked as they headed outside.

"I don't know. You can imagine how I felt. We're bloody opposites."

"He needed her alive," Joanna said softly.

"Rosalie needed Ralph." Lucille let out a low whistle. "I suspect he needs that specific need just to feel whole."

"Thanks for that, Lucille," Dan said. "I confess I've been judging Ralph unfairly."

Lucille walked ahead, silently worrying about Ralph. She stopped and turned back to Dan.

"Somehow I'm reminded of *The Tempest*. Remember Prospero destroying his book of magic?"

"Sure do. We saw the play recently."

"I may be talking about myself here, as usual," Lucille said, "but I think Shakespeare, through Prospero, wanted to return from the magic of art to the wonder of life itself." She looked right into Dan's eyes. "I do, too." She stopped. "Look." She pointed at a tiny, old black lady bent double over her cane who stood next to a water fountain. A red headed toddler wheeled by in a stroller, eye level with the little bent woman. Lucille grabbed her camera and in a split second removed the lens. The green-eyed baby stared solemnly into the old lady's eyes. She stared back. They seemed to understand one another. When the baby and her oblivious mother disappeared into the crowd, the old lady grinned, her toothless mouth a cavern of mirth. Lucille shrugged her shoulders and replaced the lens cap on the camera. "Instinct. See why I'm packing away my Nikon, Dan? Polaroid shots from now on—of your baby. I'm going to be a true godmother. Ripeness is all, as the bard says."

"You can't stop now," Joanna cried. "You're on a roll."

"You're right. A child is a wonder." Dan patted Joanna's stomach. "One we can give to Ralph and Rosalie, too." He looked at Lucille. "Are you really giving up your art?"

"Whoa." Joanna stopped suddenly, turned to Dan. "Don't expect a baby to solve adult problems."

"Don't worry, Sweetheart, I don't." Dan put his arm around Joanna's shoulders and smoothed his mustache, eyes glazed in thought. "Children do bring a fresh perspective to the world, though."

A combination of excitement and dread washed over Lucille. She moved in front of them, faced them.

"Art, or the arts, if you will, are to adults as toys are to children, a means to rehearse life. As children outgrow toys, people outgrow art."

"So, now you're no longer a child," Dan said, "you're going to put away childish things?"

Lucille laughed, and then turned toward the exit. Wait and see, she thought. *Keep seeing.*

Dan and Joanna sat on the orange plastic seat of the airport shuttle going into town. Lucille faced them, and for a half hour, listened to the Beaumont tale told in tandem. She then gazed at the sky. Clouds had formed a zoo of stuffed animals. She wanted to photograph them for wallpaper in the baby's room. She turned back to Dan to continue their earlier conversation.

"An island can be a symbol of birth, or rebirth," she said to them. "And a baby, like Ariel, stands for both male and female elements of the psyche." She paused and laughed at herself. "I have a new vision. I believe I'll actually like Rosalie."

"You hot ticket. You're right." Dan said. "I bet I will, too, and be glad he kept her alive."

Joanna yawned and leaned her head on Dan's shoulder.

"We are such stuff that dreams are made on," he sang as the bus driver called their stop near the courthouse.

Lucille smiled at the familiar words and moved into a line of brightly clad Miami tourists waiting to exit.

"And our little lives are rounded with a sleep," she said. *If one lets you sleep. Ah, Ralph, my dear friend, erstwhile lover, you must be torn in two.*

Then she looked at Dan aglow with love for Joanna and shuddered. *He has so very much to lose if they convict him.*

CHAPTER THIRTY

Sherri Taylor roamed the Miami streets every day now that she was no longer employed. There was nothing to do but wait for the jury's verdict and it was taking way too long. Monroe worked every day on possible appeals if a guilty verdict came down. So she roamed and watched the Cubans decorating their city for Christmas, shouting in Spanish from open windows. Big plastic crèches blocked the sidewalks.

One day, when the clouds skittered across the sun causing startling contrasts of light and dark, Sherri stopped before a shabby, three-by-four foot crèche. The paint was peeling on Joseph and Mary and the Christ child had lost an eye. A little girl, no more than three, with gold studs in her ears, poked her finger into the empty eye socket of the Baby Jesus.

Sherri slowly surveyed the scene and spotted the missing eye, a brown speckled marble, nestled against a camel's leg. Thinking it might not be such a good idea for a blonde Anglo to touch the crèche, she moved on. Then she stopped, returned to the crèche, and spoke to the child in Spanish. She knelt to place the marble in the Jesus doll's eye socket and felt people watching her. The little girl reached over and touched Sherri's cheek with the curiosity of a kitten.

Sherri imagined kneeling there forever, entombed in this tattered crèche on a side street in Miami. The idea appealed to her. She could be embalmed as the Virgin Mary. Her given-up daughter might happen by in the Twenty-first Century and recognize her. Not totally, of course, but in a haunting way.

Nearby, several men were stringing colored lights across the street from second story windows, laughing and chattering, emitting round syllables that simmered in the warm Caribbean breezes like fresh oysters in butter. Sherri relished the sound. Then, to cut off the pleasure of the moment—not a habit with her she realized—she started walking fast, as if she had a destination. She pictured Dan Lawrence, so free of small fears he could discuss his large ones. Dan: the Santa Claus of mankind with his white hair and gifts that fell out of his mouth like toys out of Santa's sack. He said so little, yet each phrase held value. No wonder Joanna thrived despite the threat of a guilty verdict. *When will we know? Poor Monroe.*

She thought she saw Monroe's smiling face reflected in a store window, but soon realized it was her imagination. Monroe was the least likely person to become significant in her life because he was short. Yet, as it turned out, he was the most likely one she could love. It dawned on her that since the night of Dan's party she'd seen Monroe almost every day, if not for dinner, then for lunch, his push. And she'd see him again tonight.

The clouds melded together, darkening the sky.

"First light, den dark," a wizened old black man said, staring at the sky. "Yo clouds oughtta make up yo mind."

A sudden downpour soaked them. Sherri strolled on for three blocks, lifting her face to the rain, letting it wash her, knowing that nothing, not even God's sweet dew, could cleanse her now. She thought of the Middle Ages, the Black Plague, of gonorrhea and syphilis. She practiced a speech for Monroe. *You claim you have trouble talking to women. Yet you speak freely to me. What the hell am I but a deadly disease? What can you possibly want with me?*

A taxi horn blasted. She jumped onto the sidewalk, barely escaping the taxi's onslaught. A bull. She was the picador. Monroe the toreador? She shook her head in disgust. "Shit, I'm beginning to feel fucking sorry for myself."

She ducked into a discount department store and weaved her way among the Christmas shoppers buying plastic fir trees and giant tins of candy. A ten-inch high reindeer with a flashing red bulb in its nose nodded at her. Tinny sounds from a tape player in its stomach hinted at the myth of St. Nick, modernized by Rudolph. She remembered riding the huge Rudolph in Macy's the year she was three. *A damn bucking bronco to a three-year old*. Her father had dropped a quarter in the slot, set her on Rudolph's back and laughed while she clung to Rudolph's ears in terror.

Sherri now wondered why her father had laughed at her terror. She moved down the aisle away from the nauseating scents of the perfume counter. A two-foot square Amazon rain jungle, replete with plastic trees, parrots, vines, monkeys, tigers, and boa constrictors, blocked her progress. Grubby little fingers on each side of it were slapped by varying mothers or caretakers. "Don't touch," each slap said. Sherri didn't touch even though the tiny plastic victims of the larger predators looked terrified.

She remembered a handsome Florida State Lambda Chi she'd picked up at a rock concert, the look in his eyes when she'd sucked his finger and then bit it, the power she'd felt from his fear.

My old man was powerless. The thought came crashing down on her. *It's a fucking equation. So simple. Tyranny of the terrified.*

The memory of her father berating her mother in his perfectly articulated and smooth voice drowned out the sounds in the discount store. Her mother alternating between screaming and sobbing. Her father in control. The man of the house. The powerhouse. He knew better than to reveal his terror. It's the law of the jungle.

"May I help you, Senorita? I think it's your turn." A short, round woman looked up at her, unnerving Sherri with gentle brown eyes.

"Just looking, thanks." *She knows.* Sherri weaved through the crowd toward the nearest red exit sign. She avoided touching anyone, raising her arms above her head when necessary. The saleslady's eyes, much like Monroe's, held no terror. They could melt anyone's sadistic impulses—hers, her father's, or his father's before him.

She knew, outside in bright light again, that she must give up Monroe. She ran five blocks and up four flights of stairs to his office with a burst of resolve and collapsed on the settee across from his new young and healthy secretary.

"Hey, it's a jungle out there," Sherri said to her with a smile.

The secretary nodded and raised her plucked eyebrows and then looked down at her desk calendar.

"Do you have an appointment with Mr. Cort?" she asked in a haughty tone.

"Forgive me." Sherri swallowed to contain either a loud guffaw or a sob. "I come gasping in here—probably wild-eyed, Grinching out Christmas, so to speak, and neglect to tell you that yes, I have an appointment with Mr. Cort." But not now, she thought.

"Your name?"

"Sherri Ann Taylor."

"I don't have you listed. Are you sure—?"

"He probably forgot to tell you. I'm a friend of Dan Lawrence."
The secretary looked her over.

"He should be free soon," she said and turned to face her computer.

"Thanks." That's a powerful name to drop, she thought, leaning back on the leather settee. A new thought teased her mind like a buzzing mosquito. She needed to catch it, but couldn't. Her father's perfectly modulated voice echoed around the mosquito. She saw him adjusting the collar of his big overcoat, making sure it was neither too close nor too far from his neck. *He couldn't take one fucking chance, risk making the smallest mistake!* The mosquito buzzed louder. *Tyranny of the terrified. Ha, I represent tyranny of the reckless. There's an unhappy medium here between being wimp-like and rambunctious, one I need to find.*

Monroe opened his office door. A sullen-eyed young man with a patchy black beard dragged his way out.

Sherri saw Monroe's welcoming smile and felt it to her toes.

"Sorry to bother you." She stood, smoothing her skirt. "I just had some ideas I wanted to explore with you when you have time."

"I'd always have time for you." He took her hand and led her into his office. "You don't know what a relief it is to find a gorgeous wildflower among the rusty and twisted frames of my junkyard." He closed the door behind them and then backed away—behind his desk.

A sudden love hunger made her feel weak all over. She collapsed into one of the client chairs facing his desk.

"You okay, Sherri?" He leaned forward. "Can I get you something?"

"I'll be all right. Cupid's arrow just pierced me."

"Wow." Monroe beamed at her. His red mustache shook as he leaned back in his chair and clasped his hands behind his head. "Start exploring," he said. "I'll follow."

She stood, moved to the window, and looked out on seagulls circling the parking lot.

"I had a baby, a girl, four years ago. Guess I told you already. Anyway I gave her up for adoption at birth. I keep looking for her." She swiveled toward Monroe. "I was never afraid of anything. Reckless, you know?" She laughed.

"Go on."

She stared at him briefly, grateful he didn't question her nor demand logic, and then looked out the window, seeing nothing.

"What I always liked about Joanna was her honest fear," she said. "She never tried to gloss it over. You don't either. I didn't think I hid from my own fear—just didn't feel any."

She moved behind Monroe and put her hands on his shoulders. She could smell his clean, healthy body and wondered if he could smell her disease.

"Now I am truly afraid," she said.

"Yes. I am, too." He caressed her hands without looking at her. "It sneaks up on me like a cat. Pounces when I least expect it. I'm okay now, though."

She pictured his slight, wondering frown and rubbed her cheek against his red curls. "This is as close as we have ever dared get. You should be wary of me." She leaned on the edge of his desk. "Anyway, my father was afraid of my mother, of me, of imperfection, of shit. If you're afraid of shit, you're afraid of death. Well, I don't give a shit about shit, but I'm fucking scared of dying, and scared to death of infecting you."

He swiveled his chair to look up at her, then reached out and pulled her onto his lap, burying his face in her breasts. The heat of his breath pierced her shell, raced throughout her body.

"Monroe, please. Don't. I'm a leper."

"Hush." He held her tight.

"A leper with no religion. No opiate. No true sense of sin, just stupidity." She looked into his eyes then turned her head away. "I fucked around a lot. Christ, one week I went to bed with six different men. Rested on Sunday. I suppose I figured deep down I might get the love that my old man was too scared to show or feel." She stood and kissed the top of Monroe's head. "I feel more love from you than I've ever known. There's the cross of irony I bear."

"Explain."

"I'm super hungry for you and must not get close to you. I may have created my own tragic opera, but I won't give you a part, not even a role in the chorus." She escaped his embrace in a sudden move. "I won't be seeing you anymore." A sob stuck in her throat.

"Hold it." Monroe raised his hand and waved it like a schoolboy with the right answer. "You say your father was afraid of life. Right? He covered up his fear. Don't you suppose he learned that habit somewhere?"

She opened her mouth to speak, but he silenced her with outstretched hands, palms facing her.

"You say you weren't afraid, denied it to the point of not knowing you were denying. Now you feel it." He stood, moved around his desk and put his arms around her. "I'm scared, too, but I'd rather risk death than life without love—your father's choice. You see, I realize now that before I met you I was afraid of love. Your virus gave me the barrier I needed to risk feeling passion from my heart . . . instead of my dick." He smiled like a small, shy boy. "Now I'm ready to risk infection, too, I think."

"No!"

He put his hands on her cheeks and turned her face toward his as if he wanted to kiss her lips. His eyes flickered.

"You have courage," he said. "Anyone can summon up courage to face the known." He let go of her face, dropped his hands to his side. "Besides," he said grinning, "I have condoms, and they're ninety-five percent safe."

"Have you ever used one?"

"No. You and I came of age with the pill. Hell, I didn't even carry one in my wallet, which was de rigueur half a generation ago."

She didn't know whether to laugh or cry. Should she let him risk with her? True, he needed her. He admitted that. She definitely needed him. He took the edge off her self—loathing. Made her forget. Made her think she'd just had a run of bad luck, nothing more.

"Do you know how to use one?"

"I'll learn. I saw a TV program on AIDS that showed you how to put a condom on a banana. My dick's a bit smaller than a banana, so it should be easy."

She laughed. Theater tragic-comic masks came to mind.

"I have to think." She stared out the window again, watching cars pull in and out of diagonal spots. "If I have five years to live or five days, I might as well live each one with as many senses as I have available to me. But . . ."

She heard Monroe pick up the phone and tell his secretary to re-schedule the rest of his appointments, then close up the office for the day.

"Christmas shop," he said to her, "if you're in the mood."

Sherri turned and watched him replace the phone.

"I saw a one-eyed Christ-child in a crèche today and found its lost eye near a camel. I replaced it. This little Cuban girl touched my cheek . . . You do have the courage, don't you?"

"Sure."

She thought she heard a catch in his voice but when she listened to his breathing, it had the soothing, haunting sound of a distant train. She watched him search the middle drawer of his desk.

"Ah, here it is," he said. "Hell, it takes courage to chance shrinking a decent hard-on by messing with one of these things . . . especially in the presence of a sexy woman. Still, it's okay. I've been reading Jolan Chang."

"Who?"

"He wrote the Tao of Sex and Loving, advising men to save their ching." Monroe studied the package, tore open a corner.

"Ching? What a great word."

"Semen. Source of life. In other words, don't ejaculate every time you make love so you can truly love a woman again and again without fear of impotence. And, if you're not hard, so what? With the soft entry technique and true affection, you'll soon be plenty hard."

"Save your ching? How?" Sherri stood absolutely still.

"Special technique for control." Monroe placed the opened package on the edge of the desk, closed the draperies, and embraced her, resting his cheek lightly against hers. She knew the moment called for a kiss. As she turned her lips toward his, she felt him draw back even as his arms tightened around her. She knew he wanted her, knew she could make him cross that deadly line. She could shame him into it as she'd almost shamed Joanna into bed with Ricardo and countless others into bed with her. His rock hard penis rubbed her pelvis. Go for it, she thought, just don't kiss. She felt his hand tracing the dangerous split of her body.

"Taking chances with you beats the best rollercoaster ride in the world," Monroe whispered in her ear.

Her muscles contracted.

"No, my love, it's time for me to stop riding roller coasters, especially on your dime." She withdrew, feeling the velvet gown of her life-long hedonism unraveling, slipping off. "No, I won't do it."

He dropped his arms, turned toward the window, and hung his head in silence.

"All my life," she said," I got what I wanted—just didn't know what to want." She heard petulance in her voice and shook her head, angry with herself. With his back to her, he waved at her, his arm thrust awkwardly behind him. Tears blurred her vision as she pushed his hand away. "I won't let you risk your life for my needs, for, you see, I love you."

He turned. The features of his face seemed to be melting together.

"Forgive me, Sherri. I'm such a fucking wimp—couldn't kiss."

"No!" She flattened her hand toward him like a traffic cop. "I may not have long to live, but I intend to live with myself every goddamn day. If I infected you I couldn't live with myself a minute."

Monroe tossed the package of condoms onto the desk and moved over to the window.

"Will I still see you?" he asked, his back to her. "Will you still see me?"

"Who knows?" Her voice cracked under affected bravado. "Let's just wait and find out. Tomorrow we may enjoy one another as we have for the past month. The next day we may let our love freeze to death like a street person in Buffalo. Or, we may decide love without touch is better than . . . than splitting.

He remained silent, unmoving. She stared at his back with affection and wonder. His slight rounded shoulders began to heave. She watched him dry-eyed, knowing this ache dug too deep to cry, knowing he had to be strong to plea Dan's case. *Why did I let him love me? I've fucked up everyone I know!*

CHAPTER THIRTY-ONE

Dan had just finished a lunch of leftover moussaka when the phone rang. He left the table to answer it and heard Monroe's voice, strange and harsh, barely recognizable.

"Dan," he shouted. "No hung jury! They've reached a verdict. C'mon down."

"They've reached a verdict, Joanna! They've reached a verdict!" Dan spun around to face Joanna who was clearing dishes from the table. To Monroe he said, "We'll be right there."

Joanna dropped the plates onto the table and clapped her hands, and then held them in silent prayer.

"Andiamo, Sweetheart." Dan said as he checked his shirt pocket for the nitroglycerin tablets and donned his suit coat. She grabbed her purse. He took her arm and headed for the elevator. The door opened revealing a scent of lavender. It reminded him of his first meeting with Joanna. He smiled. "Remember our first trip down this elevator when we had to evacuate the building? And the elevator stopped half way down?"

"I sure do," Joanna said. "You said, 'Death comes either too early or too late.'" She punched his shoulder and kissed him as they descended.

"Well," he said, "I'm repeating it now and, among other judicial and eternal pronouncements, I love you."

*   *   *

A cricket called for a mate in the hushed courtroom. Dan turned to look in its direction. His heart raced. Joanna sat directly behind him with Lucille. Sherri Taylor sat across the aisle. He noticed Monroe glancing at her several times. The cricket called again. *We're all in a mating dance. Beaumont, Joanna, Rosalie, Lucille, Ralph, Monroe, Sherri. Me. We're all rubbing our legs together, calling for mates. To propagate. To counteract the inevitability of death.*

A door beside the bench opened and the jurors entered, single file. Dan thought he noticed an atmosphere of shame coming from them. Not one would look at him. The curly haired lady held her chin high. The three clones marched single file, in step. When they were all seated Judge Ogasaki asked the foreman to stand. He turned out to be the sympathetic brown-eyed man in the second row instead of one of the clones, to Dan's relief. But the clones outweigh him.

This is it. Ogasaki will take a couple of weeks before sentencing. Gives me two weeks more to live. Two weeks with Joanna, more real life than I expected, certainly. More than I've ever had. He felt an eerie weightlessness.

The foreman handed Judge Ogasaki the folded slip of paper. She opened it and read it without looking up or changing expression. Dan remembered how had he handled this moment in the past, maintaining his own straight face.

"Please read the verdict," Judge Ogasaki said in a clear, strong voice.

The foreman opened the paper. Dan grew aware of a rustling sound—people shifting in their seats. He held his breath.

The foreman lifted the slip of paper high, adjusted his glasses and read, "We, the jury of the State of Florida, case number 537902, regarding the charge of murder in the first degree of Beverly Lawrence, perpetrated from a premeditated design—" He cleared his throat and looked straight at Dan and continued, "find the defendant, Judge Lawrence, not guilty."

Dan wasn't sure if he'd heard correctly, but he couldn't ask in the uproar surrounding him. Reporters rushed out through the back door. He stood there numb when Ansletter shuffled over and shook his hand. Lucille took their picture. Weeping and grinning at the same time, Joanna threw her arms around him.

"You're going to help me raise our child," she whispered in his ear.

Her words penetrated, touching off a geyser. A sob escaped his lips and tears overflowed his automatic attempt to restrain them. He shook his head. *God damn it, I'm crying like a baby in public.* Lucille hugged him. He felt her camera hit his leg and he laughed, and then sobering he asked, "Will you call Ralph?"

"Of course, you idiot," Lucille said. "Here I go. He'll be waiting, I know."

*　　*　　*

Ribbons of white beach outlined the amoeba-shaped islands stretching across the patchwork sea, blue and translucent green. Dan leaned across his sleeping beauty to look out the small airplane window, chanting his mantra, *Truth, beauty, justice, love, wonder.* He touched Joanna's cheek to waken her, knowing she'd fall asleep again as quickly as a kitten. Lately she slept more than twelve hours in the twenty-four. It seemed to be the only symptom of her pregnancy. Bev, he remembered, had had morning sickness day and night and hardly slept at all.

"Look at the islands, Jo," he said. "They're beautiful." Joanna lifted her head, smiled at him, then peered out the window. She clapped her hands.

"Magic. Why do islands seem enchanted, especially tropical ones?"

Lucille leaned forward from her seat behind them and patted Joanna's head.

"I saw an enchanted island in the middle of a lake in Ireland," Lucille said. "Rain forest, ancient Celtic crosses, druids behind every tree."

"Think we should hold our wedding here?" Dan asked Joanna and grinned at Lucille.

"I don't know." Joanna squeezed his hand. "But I'd marry you anywhere—that island in Ireland or even Las Vegas. I hear they have Disney-like wedding chapels for instant ceremonies."

"For people who fear they might change their minds if they don't get it over with fast." Lucille said. She leaned back and buckled her seatbelt.

Dan pushed back Joanna's hair so he could admire her profile. He hoped for a baby girl with cheek bones just like Jo's.

"I may be eight months along before I'm finally free of Beaumont and able to marry you legally," Joanna said. "Won't that be a wedding? What would I wear?" She laughed a melodic trill.

"Maybe we should get married on an island. Aunt Martha would like that."

The plane banked for landing. Dan felt a rush of blood to his skin and a moment of fear. Of what? Death? No, fear of loss now that he had so much to lose. He felt Joanna's eyes on him.

"What's the matter, my dear Daniel Briggs Lawrence?" she asked.

"Nothing. Just scared for a moment there."

"You scared? What are you scared of?"

He pulled out his handkerchief and wiped his forehead. His skin burned. She placed her cool palm on his cheek. The fear subsided. He gazed out at the greenery coming up to meet them.

"Losing," he said. "Losing what I recently acquired: justice, love, wonder."

"Clarify please, for the record, your honor," she whispered.

"I'm so damn happy," he answered. "I expected to lose my freedom after the trial, and I didn't. Who would've thought I'd fall in love at my age? I'm overwhelmed by it. And there's nothing more awe inspiring than a baby."

She kissed him.

The plane landed with three distinct bumps and rolled to a stop. Lucille stood in the aisle before the pilot turned off the seatbelt light.

"I think I see Nigel leaning against the fence," she said. "Yes, that's him. Some things never change."

Dan felt a flush of excitement. His legs tingled. He rotated his ankles to wake them up.

"I haven't seen Nigel for a few years. Didn't realize how much I missed him," Dan said. He watched a team of black men rolling a silver stairway toward them.

"Hey," Joanna said, "I'm the new kid. Who's Nigel? Clue me in or I'll fall asleep again."

"Nigel is Ralph's gardener," Lucille explained to her, "and has been for twenty-five years. Lives with his wife, Annabel, in a cottage on Ralph's land. She's Rosalie's housemaid and hairdresser. She'll do your hair, too, if you want. She's really good. And Nigel meets guests at the airport. He has a wonderful accent: combination of British aristocracy and African Black."

"He'll speed us through customs, too," Dan added as they descended the silver stairs and, bent into the wind, headed for the terminal.

Nigel greeted them with the grave face of a basset hound. He shook Dan's hand, kissed Lucille's, and bowed to Joanna. His long, lanky frame was, as usual, ramrod stiff, though his tight curls had turned gray. His white teeth flashed lightning bright against the inky blackness of his skin.

Dan watched the play of expressions on Joanna's face as she looked at Nigel: pleasure, respect, amusement, even wonder.

"How's Mrs. Conscetti?" Joanna asked him.

"Not well." Nigel lowered his head. He opened the back door of the royal blue Mercedes convertible. "Not well at all," he said under his breath. "Can't flirt."

Lucille guffawed and climbed into the back seat, beckoning Joanna to join her.

"The mister will be glad to see you," Nigel said as he stowed the luggage in the boot.

"Will you feel this air?" Joanna said, sliding in back with Lucille. "Light—yet sort of wet—like a luxurious body lotion. A satin sheet." She laughed. "I feel like doing a commercial for the air alone. How come I've lived thirty-four years near this magic place and never knew how it felt?"

"Don't need to regret seeing and feeling things for the first time," Dan chided from the front seat. He grabbed the front seat divider when Nigel swerved, just missing a bicyclist on the narrow road. When Dan leaned back and scanned the horizon, he began seeing the familiar route through Joanna's eyes: lush vegetation; tiny, ramshackle churches, extremes of wealth and poverty blurred by benign weather. We've truly crossed the border, he thought, looking at remnants of the New Year's Junkanoo parade piled beside a tar paper shack: brightly colored cardboard pieces in varying shapes decorated with primitive designs. Or abstract. He wasn't sure which.

"Are those leftover Mardi Gras costumes?" Joanna asked, pointing at them.

"Would you explain Junkanoo to Joanna?" Dan asked Nigel. "She's new here."

Nigel flashed his magnificent white teeth at Dan, suddenly losing all traces of servile solemnity.

"Sure. I be glad to." He drove the next few miles looking back at Joanna with only occasional glances at the road ahead. "We do Junkanoo every year—Boxing Day and New Year's. Great parade. Too bad you just missed it."

Joanna leaned forward on the leather seat. The wind blew her hair against Dan's face. He noticed a faint scent of mint as he watched Nigel's animated face explain Junkanoo. Dan held the moment, as if Lucille had photographed it. It would replay in his mind he was sure as persistently as the image of Ralph holding Bev's limp body high above his head. It took Bev's burial at Pemaquid to erase that. This one he'd happily keep: tasting Jo's hair, breathing in the tropical air that goes down like gelato on a hot day, watching the kaleidoscope of greens against the cerulean sky, listening to Nigel's sonorous British voice laced with black vernacular. Joanna sat back. Her hair trailed off his face, tickling him.

"Junkanoo named after John Canoe, the bloke who started it, but we can't quite remember what he did. When I's a child, Junkanoo be simply a street dance. No competition or anything. Just cowbells and drums. No brass like now. No organizations, but jolly good fun. Now, of course, it be better. I happy to show you costume I wore this year."

"Oh, do. Wear it," Lucille pleaded, "re-enact your part of the parade. What were you this year?"

Swerving to avoid a pedestrian carrying a basket full of bananas, Nigel turned to watch the route ahead.

"I be a man-beast this year, a lion from the book of Daniel. My brother be beast from Revelations."

Dan felt Joanna's fingers caress the top of his head. They felt so cool, he wondered if he had a fever.

"What do you say about lions, Dan?" Joanna asked him,

"I suppose it's a good idea to lie down with lions." He turned to look at Joanna's and Lucille's windblown, bright-eyed faces. "Seriously, last year I met a professor from Chapel Hill who likes to play with wolves. He visits the wolves every year and lies down nearby. Now they know him and play with him."

"Like playing with dolphins?" Joanna asked with a lilt in her voice.

"Right." Feeling strangely light headed, Dan continued, "Once, though, in the northwestern woods, he came unexpectedly face to face with a grizzly bear. Had no way to escape, so what did he do?"

"He fell to the ground," Lucille guessed.

"Right. Actually, he sat down. And the bear, get this, came over and patted his shoulder then wandered off. I guess that's what won those lions over for Daniel. He just lay down with them. Saved his hide."

"I heard it was God's intervention," Joanna said.

"I think the book of Daniel was written after the New Testament," Dan said. "Perhaps it shows Greek influence. I've heard that some of the early Hebrew tribes didn't believe in an intervening God, nor life after death." He thought of his birds of paradise parading on the veranda and wiped his brow. They were so garish, so eager for life, and when they died, they died fast. *This can't be another heart attack. Doesn't feel like one. Probably coming down with the flu.*

"The Greeks," Dan continued, struggling to feel normal, "had the universe peopled with active gods constantly interacting with humans. Maybe they influenced whoever wrote Daniel."

"Mr. Lawrence, which you believe be true, Greek or early Hebrew?" Nigel asked as they stopped at the entrance to Lyford Cay just long enough for the guard to wave them through the gate.

"Personally, if I'm caught in a den of lions," he said smiling, "I'm going to lie down and pray for God's help."

"We be soon in similar den," Nigel said sadly.

*   *   *

While Dan napped, Joanna strolled the grounds of Ralph's estate, amazed at the extravagant cleanliness and beauty, astounded with Ralph. She hadn't pictured him in such lush surroundings. Now, here, she thought, his face drooped and his deep set brown eyes seemed to strain against the feelings behind them. She remembered his elevator-filling smile and mismatched clothes and missed them. Here he was tidy and even color coordinated.

She let her eye follow the curve of the oleander-lined driveway. White cement swept clean. Not a trace of oil. Did Nigel bleach it? Garden spanning the hundred or so feet between the ocean and canal. House all blue and white. Lots of tile and window walls, shiny clean. The cleanliness of the place overwhelmed her. What lay beneath?

Nigel and Annabel, servants, yet masters. Joanna surveyed the garden, a garden more like Eden than any she could imagine. Rich with exotic herbs, fruits and vegetables: red, lime green, and dark blue grapes, pale green endive, burgundy and green basil, dark green escarole, purple cabbage, Kelly green snow peas, yellow breadfruit in the trees, and many more plants she'd never before seen, let alone heard named. Though she detected the scent of anise, she couldn't spot it in the profusion of plant life. Behind the garden, near the vine-entangled arch, a marble fountain splashed water over a kneeling, winged nymph. Angel? Ariel?

Nearby, Rosalie stood silently under an arboreal arch, the perfect wedding spot. Cautiously, Joanna approached her, recalling how Rosalie had laughed hysterically when Ralph first introduced her, then lapsed into ominous silence. Fifty feet away from her, Joanna stopped, not wanting to intrude, yet curious. She studied Rosalie's Picasso-face that wore two expressions. The good side showed anger. The bad side drooped in despair.

Suddenly Rosalie turned and glared at Joanna. Annabel, stooped and skinny, materialized beside Rosalie.

"Come, missus," she said to Rosalie, "time for tea and your favorite coconut biscuits."

Mute, Rosalie stared at Joanna. Annabel cupped Rosalie's chin and turned her head away. Rosalie dissolved into tears that stopped as abruptly as they began. She let Annabel lead her into the house.

There, but for the grace of God, goes Dan, Joanna thought, shivering in the balmy velvet air.

*　　*　　*

Annabel ran her arthritic fingers over Joanna's head, lifting and dropping thick clumps of hair.

"What style you want?" she asked Joanna, sharpening scissor blades on a whetstone.

"I'm ready for short hair, not severe." Joanna looked at Annabel's tiny black face in the mirror, the pointed chin, the inscrutable expression. "Ralph told me to give you free reign. Said you were a natural stylist. What do you think I should have?"

"Face like yours be best without much hair." She brushed Joanna's bangs straight back. "See? I cut now." Joanna let go of her hair with the realization that it took an inordinate amount of will to do so. Annabel finished cutting and pulled the towel off Joanna's shoulders. "Go show your face. Beautiful picture needs plain frame."

When Joanna came out of the cottage she saw Rosalie standing in the driveway. Rosalie pointed at Joanna and laughed silently with one side of her face. Joanna ran through the back door of the house, down the marble hallway to the guest bedroom she shared with Dan. He was, strangely, still asleep. She decided against waking him, and gazed out the floor-to-ceiling window, watching Rosalie and Lucille approach each other from opposite sides of the garden. Then she looked in the mirror and played with what was left of her hair. It didn't cover as much as an inch of her face. She laughed aloud and woke Dan.

He frowned, rubbed his face.

"I had Annabel cut my hair." She kneeled beside him

"What the hell did you do that for?" he growled. Astonished, she tensed her muscles, and then took a deep breath.

He smiled as if he'd not rebuked her and ran his fingers over her head.

"You look stunning. Older somehow, and gorgeous." He winced.

"Are you okay?"

"Have a touch of flu, I think. Not bad, just out of sorts."

"Not your heart?" She caressed his chest.

"Don't be stupid," he barked, then shook his head as if to clear it. "Sorry." He covered her hand with his. "Still here. Still beating for you. No, don't worry. I know heart attack symptoms." He sat up. "I do like your haircut. Now everyone will be able to see your lovely cheekbones."

She felt her face flush. It was definitely naked now.

"Hey, I'm the one supposed to be sleeping all the time, not you," she said and turned away so he would not see the panic in her eyes. *There's no more hair to hide them and they reveal everything. My God, what can I do for him?*

CHAPTER THIRTY-TWO

Joanna sat at the dining room table brooding when Dan came bouncing in and gave her a quick kiss. Strange, she thought, he seemed so sick, so unlike him but now he seems fine.

"So, what's going on?" he asked.

"How do you feel, Honey?" She studied him.

"I'm fine," he answered without looking at her.

"Well, good," she said, and a few seconds later answered his question. "After Rosalie laughed at my hair she went out to the garden. Lucille joined her and started reading to her. Ralph's out front wading around in bay."

"C'mon. This I've got to see." Dan said and grabbed her hand. Still, he didn't look at her.

"Which?"

"Lucille reading to Rosalie."

Joanna wondered if he really did feel better, but she led him to the canal end of the garden where Lucille and Rosalie sat at a round marble table opposite one another. Joanna stopped, leaned with Dan against the side of the house out of Lucille's line of vision. The sun hung low in the West, elongating shadows. The air was unusually still, neither warm nor cool. The brilliant colors of the sea, grass, and flowers grew muted in the fading light. Everything seemed to have the texture of velvet. She held Dan's hand.

"Listen Dan, she's reading from Job. She's reading Job here, of all places."

"God damn the day I was born and the night that forced me from the womb." Lucille's strong voice floated across the garden. "On that day let there be darkness; let it never have been created; let it sink back into the void. Let chaos overpower it; let black clouds overwhelm it; let the sun be plucked from its sky." Lucille held the book toward the setting sun as if its light would help her read. "Why couldn't I have died as they pulled me out of the dark?" She stopped, glanced at Rosalie's face.

Rosalie nodded.

"Why is there light for the wretched," Lucille read, "life for the bitter-hearted, who long for death, who seek it as if it were buried treasure, who smile when they reach the graveyard and laugh as their pit is dug. For God has hidden my way and put hedges across my path. I sit and gnaw on my grief; my groans pour out like water. My worst fears have happened; my nightmares have come to life. Silence and peace have abandoned me, and anguish camps in my heart."

The last rays of sunlight faded. The new moon, Frisbee-like, hung between Venus and Jupiter in the western sky, a sign, Joanna thought, that all was right in the world. She watched Rosalie stand, fluff out her dress as if Venus herself were watching, and place both hands on Lucille's shoulders.

"This is a magic place," Joanna whispered to Dan. His eyes were wet wounds.

Ralph came around the corner of the house wrapped in a beach towel. His feet were small, like his hands. Joanna wondered how they supported him. He looked older, spent. She realized he'd been avoiding them. She backed away to leave him alone with Dan, but Dan beckoned her to stay.

Ralph sat on the top step of the stairs leading to the raked beach. With his back to them, he spoke.

"I'm glad you came . . . A couple of months ago, just before your trial ended when I was flying home . . . the night of Rosalie's stroke, I relived in memory the hurricane at Pemaquid and the fight we had on that rock. You bit my hand. And we never mentioned it. Not once in all these years." He glanced back at Dan briefly. "I realized on that plane from Miami that our brief fight then was the genesis of our bond. I've been wanting to tell you, even though it doesn't matter." He turned and faced Dan. "Funny, isn't it? Now I feel your approbation—"

"No."

"Hear me, Dan. I know your values. You have to disapprove. My case, ours, was different." Looking like an oversized Roman in a toga, Ralph stood, moved toward them. "You had no hope with Bev," Ralph continued. "I had hope for Rosalie. That's why I had her stomach pumped when she took those pills. I still do, though she hates me." He rubbed his eyes. "Jesus, Dan, she was making progress. Consonant sounds were coming back. Sometimes I could understand what she said, and I encouraged her every way I knew." Closer in, he stopped, looked down at his bare feet and took a deep breath. "But she needed more than I could give her. She needed patience with herself, never her strong suit."

"Joanna and Lucille helped me to understand," Dan said and put his arm around Ralph's shoulders.

"Have to get some clothes on." Ralph gently removed Dan's arm and headed for the house. He stopped, looked back at Dan. "I don't need your approval, actually. I did what I had to do—just as you did." He smiled. "By the way, I'm damn glad to see you."

"Did you hear Lucille reading to Rosalie?" Dan asked him.

"Yes, from the water. She reads . . . beautifully." Ralph started laughing. Dan joined him. Both bent double, coughing and laughing. Joanna didn't know what struck them funny but was happy they were struck. Take two belly laughs, she thought, and call me in the morning.

She heard the ringing of a bell. Reminded her of sheep. No, cows. *That's a cowbell.* Then she heard the syncopated beat of a drum. Not a snare. No drumsticks either, just hands beating out a rhythm.

"That's Nigel," Ralph said. "Calling you for your private Junkanoo."

"Go get Lucille and Rosalie. Where'd they go?" Joanna said and threw her arms around Ralph.

"You got your hair cut," Ralph exclaimed. His smile filled the island.

*　　*　　*

Dan found Lucille in her room, loading film into a Polaroid camera, and Rosalie standing in the kitchen sucking on a piece of celery. He herded them onto the beach where he'd left Joanna looking expectant and even more gorgeous without that thick, mint-smelling, silky hair hiding her face. Ralph, dressed now in a plain sport shirt and trousers of varying shades of brown, sat beside her.

They formed an amphitheater on the beach and listened to the sound of the approaching cowbell. Annabel appeared first with

Nigel's drum, an oil barrel with a piece of cowhide stretched across the top. Soon the beast appeared. Nigel bounded forward wearing two three-foot pieces of cardboard painted in wavy stripes—the lion's mane careened back from a crushed Styrofoam mask that looked more like a goat than a lion. He rang the cowbell joyously then picked up his bell and beat an atavistic rhythm on the drum.

"That's Caliban if I ever saw him," Lucille said gleefully. She took a flash Polaroid of him.

"Caliban." Ralph blinked at the flash. "The earth critter, not the only one to worship a fool, eh?"

Dan nodded and watched Rosalie sitting outside the circle. She was looking at Ralph without venom, in fact, almost fondly. There's a time for hope, Dan thought, and a time for hopelessness. He looked at Joanna. She smiled at him and he wanted to take her to bed right then and make love to the beat of Nigel's drum.

Nigel roared forward and stomped his heels in the freshly raked sand, rang his cowbell, then danced by his drum for another round of pulsating beats. Dan wanted to keep his lust polished, but he began to feel seasick. *What did I eat?*

He heard Joanna clapping. Soon Ralph and Lucille joined in. Even Rosalie scooted closer.

As Lucille aimed the Polaroid at him, he stood to stretch his stomach muscles. A sharp blow struck him from behind as if someone had clubbed him between his scapulae. He bent over and felt a wrenching pain in his left arm. Suddenly he couldn't breathe. *Oh, shit, this is it. Don't panic! Heart, don't give up now.*

He curled into himself to keep from throwing up. *C'mon, heart, keep pumping.* From a distance came sounds of people screaming and running. The last thing he saw was Joanna's short fingers of hair framing a face contorted with pain. Why does she look like that? She can't be in labor yet. His thoughts were cut off by another blow to his back. The world faded away.

*   *   *

Joanna sat on a white wooden bench by a lattice covered window in the hall just outside Dan's hospital room. Through an open door she could see him. She listened to the sounds of carpentry coming from some project around the corner while she gazed at the intravenous tubes hanging from hooks near Dan's bed—beige rubber vines. No ivy. A tall, black orderly pushed a cart of bleach-scented laundry toward her. The cart's wheels rattled over the uneven tiles in the hallway. Sound of train wheels on metal tracks. The sound of a train is freedom itself, she thought, and mystery. Dan's in the lion's den bound by tubes.

She studied her blunt, unpainted fingernails, touched her tongue to the ribbed nail replacing the one Beaumont tore off in the hurricane, the tempest that freed her. The cloying scent of bleach dried out the silky air of the enchanted isle, stealing its colors. The black orderly delivered a stack of white sheets for the white walls. Hospital white. Sterile. Dead.

No! She lifted her head and listened. Hammering and sawing sounds are hope itself, she thought. Like train wheels. Building things, going places. Let there be an intervening God to keep him alive.

I'll take care of him. I'll learn to be the best nurse possible . . . and if he dies? No, he won't die. I'll shave him and trim his moustache and water his birds of paradise and bathe him with my tears and rub his skin with oil. Then when the baby comes I'll feed and clean and love both of them. My boundaries. Boundaries of a lifespan. My parentheses. I'll stand in the middle and hammer and saw and build a house for us, a mansion of hope and wonder. We'll explore the small things together . . . and if he dies? If he dies I will cling to him with my right hand and let him go with my left. He is part of me, yet separate, and I will feel as if my right arm had been ripped from its socket and I will weep in self pity over the painful loss of my arm but my soul will sustain me and our child. And if he lives through tomorrow and another tomorrow, I will know what to do. Each day I will hammer and saw and build a beautiful nest out of small moments, a nest so strong and supple it will thumb its nose at hurricanes and welcome lions in to play.

*   *   *

"Miss Lawrence? I'm Dr. Davidson."

Joanna awoke with a start.

"Come see your Dad." The doctor extended his hand. "He's an amazing survivor and we have plans to keep him that way."

"He's not my father. We're getting married!"

"Oh? Sorry," he said with a big grin. "Now I know what's keeping him alive. Come see him."

Joanna had already bolted into the room.

Dan opened his eyes and winked at her.

The End